THE DEAD VALLEY
AND OTHERS

THE DEAD VALLEY
AND OTHERS

H. P. LOVECRAFT'S FAVORITE STORIES
VOLUME II

Edited, with an Introduction
by

S. T. Joshi

DARK REGIONS PRESS
–2016–

TRADE PAPERBACK SECOND EDITION

The Dead Valley and others:
H.P. Lovecraft's Favorite Horror Stories, Volume 2
© 2014 Dark Renaissance Books

Introduction © 2012 by S. T. Joshi

Cover art © 2012 by Alex McVey

Previously Published by Joe Morey
Copy editor, Robert Mingee

Book design by Larry Roberts
Layout by F. J. Bergmann

ISBN: 978-1-62641-223-1

First published by Arcane Wisdom
in a 150 signed and numbered hardcover edition.

Dark Regions Press, LLC
P.O. Box 31022
Portland, OR 97231
United States of America
www.darkregions.com

Table of Contents

Introduction

H. P. Lovecraft wrote his long essay "Supernatural Horror in Literature" at almost the exact middle of his two-decade literary career: begun in November 1925, the essay was largely written in the early months of 1926, providing a welcome antidote to the general misery of Lovecraft's lonely life in the midst of the teeming millions of New York; but he continued to work on it bit by bit almost up to the time of its publication in the *Recluse* in the summer of 1927, even adding paragraphs to the proofs in the spring of that year. What is more, almost immediately Lovecraft began keeping, at the rear of his commonplace book, a list of "Books to mention in new edition of weird article." He finally got the chance to revise his essay in 1933, when the *Fantasy Fan* began serializing it; but by the time that fan magazine collapsed in February 1935, it had reprinted only eight of the ten chapters of the essay. Lovecraft continued to make additions and revisions, although these were not incorporated into the piece until it appeared posthumously in *The Outsider and Others* (1939).

What this means is that Lovecraft continued to read avidly in the weird literature both of the past and of his own day; in particular, he doggedly read every issue of *Weird Tales* as well as other pulps such as *Strange Tales* and even the first year of the science fiction magazine *Amazing Stories* (1926–27), in the (usually foiled) hope that he could come upon instances of genuine weirdness. By the 1930s, Lovecraft seems to have reached the limit of his patience with the shoddiness of pulp writing, noting with some exasperation to the prototypical pulp hack E. Hoffmann Price:

"Someone ought to go over the cheap magazines and pick out story-germs which have been ruined by popular treatment; then getting the authors' permission and *actually writing the stories*" (*SL* 4.163).

But if the pulp magazines were offering minimal aesthetic nourishment, the same could not be said for weird work in the actual literary world. What we find, in fact, is that Lovecraft was not only making continual discoveries of weird writers as the 1920s progressed (in some cases obtaining tips or actual volumes from friends and colleagues), but drawing upon what he had already read, sometimes a decade or more before, for the work he was himself writing during this period. As we know, Lovecraft's ecstatic return to his hometown of Providence, R.I., in April 1926 triggered a remarkable burst of fiction-writing such as he never experienced before or after: within a year of his return, he had written "The Call of Cthulhu," "The Silver Key," "Pickman's Model," *The Dream-Quest of Unknown Kadath*, *The Case of Charles Dexter Ward*, and "The Colour out of Space." A number of these tales feature elements from literary work he had read.

"The Call of Cthulhu" is a fascinating mosaic of influences while at the same time remaining emphatically original in its initial broaching of what would become Lovecraft's pseudomythology, labeled the "Cthulhu Mythos" by August Derleth. Guy de Maupassant's "The Horla" may be a central influence, but Lovecraft also found suggestive hints in A. Merritt's "The Moon Pool," which he had relished when it appeared in the *All-Story* in 1918. M. R. James's "Count Magnus," read in 1925, may have played its role in *The Case of Charles Dexter Ward*, especially the portrayal of the baleful Joseph Curwen. As for "The Colour out of Space"—a tale that reveals Lovecraft's fondness for and knowledge of chemistry, which probably led him to appreciate the chemical erudition found in Fitz-James O'Brien's "The Diamond Lens"— we can see the influence of Ambrose Bierce's "The Damned

Thing," with its provocative concluding line ("And, God help me! the Damned Thing is of such a color!"), a story that may also have played a role in "The Dunwich Horror" (1928), which similarly speaks of an invisible monster. Lovecraft also read John Metcalfe's "The Bad Lands"—another story of topographical horror—only a few months before writing his own tale, although I believe most readers will conclude that Lovecraft's is far and away the more powerful. The "bad place" topos has been so widely used in weird fiction that some "influences" on Lovecraft's story have proven to be imaginary: Lovecraft's description, in "Supernatural Horror in Literature," of Ralph Adams Cram's "The Dead Valley" (it "achieves a memorably potent degree of vague regional horror") would seem to make it a precursor to "The Colour out of Space," but Lovecraft read the Cram story years after writing his own.

"The Dunwich Horror" itself is a tissue of influences, and everything from Arthur Machen's "The Great God Pan" to Algernon Blackwood's "The Wendigo" to Harper Williams's obscure novel *The Thing in the Woods* (1924) has been brought forth to account for this or that detail of the novella; indeed, the number of influences on the story, including the central element of a "god" mating with a human (taken from Machen's tale), seems to point to a fundamental lack of originality that compels us to place "The Dunwich Horror" somewhat lower down in the corpus of Lovecraft's fiction. In this case, however, Lovecraft appears to have followed his own advice of using the core idea found in a pulp story and improving upon it: Anthony M. Rud's "Ooze," appearing in the first issue of *Weird Tales* (March 1923), clearly struck a chord with him. It is by no means an inferior work, but on the whole Lovecraft has improved upon the notion of an immense invisible monster that bursts out of a house where it has been confined.

Some features of the great novella "The Shadow over Innsmouth" (1931) has also been traced to earlier literary works, and three different stories in this volume are offered as evidence of that contention. The key element of a hybrid creature fusing human and fish physiology can be found in two noteworthy tales, Irvin S. Cobb's potent "Fishhead" (which Lovecraft read when it first appeared in the *Argosy* in 1911) and Robert W. Chambers's "The Harbor-Master" (1897), later a segment of the episodic novel *In Search of the Unknown* (1904). Lovecraft discovered Chambers in 1927, just as he was reading the proofs of "Supernatural Horror in Literature," and he quickly inserted a paragraph about Chambers's early weird work. These two stories, however, deal only with a *single case* of hybridism; to find an instance of *communal hybridism*, such as we find in "The Shadow over Innsmouth," one has to go to such a story as Algernon Blackwood's "Ancient Sorceries," perhaps the most powerful tale in the bestselling *John Silence—Physician Extraordinary* (1908).

Some cases of literary influence involve works too long for convenient reprinting in an anthology. For example, Lovecraft found some suggestive elements in James De Mille's *Strange Manuscript Found in a Copper Cylinder* (1888), and he clearly drew upon this novel for both "The Mound" (1929–30) and *At the Mountains of Madness* (1931). "The Thing on the Doorstep" (1933) deals with personality exchange, a much-used theme in supernatural fiction; in this case, Lovecraft explicitly found inspiration in two novel-length works, H. B. Drake's *The Shadowy Thing* (1928) and Barry Pain's *An Exchange of Souls* (1907). Both these novels have recently been reprinted by Hippocampus Press. As for "The Shadow out of Time" (1934–35), Lovecraft appears to have adapted some motifs from the obscure novel *Lazarus* (1925) by Henri Béraud (also reprinted by Hippocampus Press), as well as from the film *Berkeley Square* (1933). In his last original story, "The Haunter of the Dark" (1935), Lovecraft found several key points in Hanns Heinz Ewers's evocative story "The Spider." Mention has been made of Lovecraft's commonplace book—a set of jottings relating plot germs, fragments of imagery, and other details for possible use in his fiction. He of course frequently drew upon these jottings—begun in 1919 or 1920—for his own work, but on occasion he lent his commonplace book to friends and colleagues for their use. One entry is appended with the note "used by Dwyer" (referring to his friend Bernard Austin Dwyer), but this note was later crossed out, indicating that Dwyer did not in fact use the entry in question. Another entry was in fact used by Lovecraft's late colleague Henry S. Whitehead, who wrote the story "Cassius" (1931) around it. Lovecraft may well have related the entry *viva voce* to Whitehead when he visited him in Florida in 1931. Lovecraft later admitted that he himself would have written the story in a very different manner, but he nonetheless enjoyed what Whitehead had done with his conception.

It cannot be repeated often enough that, for all the borrowings of this or that detail from prior literary works, the overwhelming bulk of Lovecraft's fictional output remains emphatically original—original in philosophical orientation, in its intricate execution of the plot, and in its distinctive handling of landscape, character, and other elements. That his work has had such an immense influence on subsequent weird writing is itself a testimony of its fundamental originality of conception. Lovecraft spent a lifetime enjoying the weird literature of the previous two centuries, and he was not above acknowledging that some of his predecessors had devised elements of plot or imagery that he found suggestive; but the dynamism of his own imagination engendered a body of weird literature that revolutionized the genre so radically that it would never be the same. In this sense, Lovecraft is a watershed in the history of weird fiction, and a look at his literary influences can only emphasize that fact.

—S. T. Joshi

A Note on This Edition

This volume reprints fourteen stories that Lovecraft read and appreciated in the first decade or so of his literary career. I have supplied brief headnotes supplying background information on the author and work and suggestions as to the possible influence of the work on Lovecraft. The stories are arranged not by date of original writing or publication, but, so far as can be ascertained, by the date of Lovecraft's reading of them.

In the introduction and notes, the following abbreviations are used:

ES	*Essential Solitude: The Letters of H. P. Lovecraft and August Derleth* (New York: Hippocampus Press, 2008; 2 vols.)
MTS	*Mysteries of Time and Spirit: The Letters of H. P. Lovecraft and August Derleth* (San Francisco: Night Shade, 2002)
S	*The Annotated Supernatural Horror in Literature*, ed. S. T. Joshi (New York: Hippocampus Press, 2000)
SL	*Selected Letters* (Sauk City, WI: Arkham House, 1965–76; 5 vols.)

THE DIAMOND LENS

By Fitz-James O'Brien

In "Supernatural Horror in Literature" Lovecraft speaks in terms of high praise of Fitz-James O'Brien's "The Diamond Lens," "in which a young microscopist falls in love with a maiden of an infinitesimal world which he has discovered in a drop of water" (S 50). Clearly a major reason for Lovecraft's enjoyment of this tale was his own fascination with the natural sciences, particularly chemistry, which he discovered in 1898 and which led to the issuance of a hectographed paper that lasted more than a decade, the *Scientific Gazette* (1899–1909). O'Brien (1828–1862) is the author of several celebrated weird tales, notably "What Was It?" and "The Lost Room." His poetry is also of note, so that his death in the American Civil War "deprived us," as Lovecraft wrote, "of some masterful tales of strangeness and terror" (S 50).

1

I. THE BENDING OF THE TWIG

From a very early period of my life the entire bent of my inclinations had been towards microscopic investigations. When I was not more than ten years old, a distant relative of our family, hoping to astonish my inexperience, constructed a simple microscope for me, by drilling in a disk of copper a small hole, in which a drop of pure water was sustained by capillary attraction. This very primitive apparatus, magnifying some fifty diameters, presented, it is true, only indistinct and imperfect forms, but still sufficiently wonderful to work up my imagination to a preternatural state of excitement.

Seeing me so interested in this rude instrument, my cousin explained to me all that he knew about the principles of the microscope, related to me a few of the wonders which had been accomplished through its agency, and ended by promising to send me one regularly constructed, immediately on his return to the city. I counted the days, the hours, the minutes, that intervened between that promise and his departure.

Meantime I was not idle. Every transparent substance that bore the remotest resemblance to a lens I eagerly seized upon, and employed in vain attempts to realize that instrument, the theory of whose construction I as yet only vaguely comprehended. All panes of glass containing those oblate spheroidal knots familiarly known as "bull's eyes" were ruthlessly destroyed, in the hope of obtaining lenses of marvellous power. I even went so far as to extract the crystalline humor from the eyes of fishes and animals, and endeavored to press it into the microscopic service. I plead guilty to having stolen the glasses from my Aunt Agatha's spectacles, with a dim idea of grinding them into lenses of wondrous magnifying properties,—in which attempt it is scarcely necessary to say that I totally failed.

At last the promised instrument came. It was of that order known as Field's simple microscope, and had cost perhaps about fifteen dollars. As far as educational purposes went, a better apparatus could not have been selected. Accompanying it was a small treatise on the microscope,—its history, uses, and discoveries. I comprehended then for the first time the "Arabian Nights Entertainments." The dull veil of ordinary existence that hung across the world seemed suddenly to roll away, and to lay bare a land of enchantments. I felt towards my companions as the seer might feel towards the ordinary masses of men. I held conversations with nature in a tongue which they could not understand. I was in daily communication with living wonders, such as they never imagined in their wildest visions. I penetrated beyond the external portal of things, and roamed through the sanctuaries. Where they beheld only a drop of rain slowly rolling down the window-glass, I saw a universe of beings animated with all the passions common to physical life, and convulsing their minute sphere with struggles as fierce and protracted as those of men. In the common spots of mould, which my mother, good housekeeper that she was, fiercely scooped away from her jam pots, there abode for me, under the name of mildew, enchanted gardens, filled with dells and avenues of the densest foliage and most astonishing verdure, while from the fantastic boughs of these microscopic forests hung strange fruits glittering with green, and silver, and gold.

It was no scientific thirst that at this time filled my mind. It was the pure enjoyment of a poet to whom a world of wonders has been disclosed. I talked of my solitary pleasures to none. Alone with my microscope, I dimmed my sight, day after day and night after night, poring over the marvels which it unfolded to me. I was like one who, having discovered the ancient Eden still existing in all its primitive glory, should resolve to enjoy it in solitude, and never betray to mortal the secret of its locality. The rod of my life was bent at this moment. I destined myself to be a microscopist.

Of course, like every novice, I fancied myself a discoverer. I was ignorant at the time of the thousands of acute intellects engaged in the same pursuit as myself, and with the advantage of instruments a thousand times more powerful than mine. The names of Leeuwenhoek, Williamson, Spencer, Ehrenberg, Schultz, Dujardin, Schact, and Schleiden were then entirely unknown to me, or if known, I was ignorant of their patient and wonderful researches. In every fresh specimen of cryptogamia which I placed beneath my instrument I believed that I discovered wonders of which the world was as yet ignorant. I remember well the thrill of delight and admiration that shot through me the first time that I discovered the common wheel animalcule (*Rotifera vulgaris*) expanding and contracting its flexible spokes, and seemingly rotating through the water. Alas! as I grew older, and obtained some works treating of my favorite study, I found that I was only on the threshold of a science to the investigation of which some of the greatest men of the age were devoting their lives and intellects.

As I grew up, my parents, who saw but little likelihood of anything practical resulting from the examination of bits of moss and drops of water through a brass tube and a piece of glass, were anxious that I should choose a profession. It was their desire that I should enter the counting-house of my uncle, Ethan Blake, a prosperous merchant, who carried on business in New York. This suggestion I decisively combated. I had no taste for trade; I should only make a failure; in short, I refused to become a merchant.

But it was necessary for me to select some pursuit. My parents were staid New England people, who insisted on the necessity of labor; and therefore, although, thanks to the bequest of my poor Aunt Agatha, I should, on coming of age, inherit a small fortune sufficient to place me above want, it was decided that, instead of waiting for this, I should act the nobler part, and employ the intervening years in rendering myself independent.

After much cogitation I complied with the wishes of my family, and selected a profession. I determined to study medicine at the New York Academy. This disposition of my future suited me. A removal from my relatives would enable me to dispose of my time as I pleased without fear of detection. As long as I paid my Academy fees, I might shirk attending the lectures if I chose; and, as I never had the remotest intention of standing an examination, there was no danger of my being "plucked." Besides, a metropolis was the place for me. There I could obtain excellent instruments, the newest publications, intimacy with men of pursuits kindred with my own,—in short, all things necessary to insure a profitable devotion of my life to my beloved science. I had an abundance of money, few desires that were not bounded by my illuminating mirror on one side and my object-glass on the other; what, therefore, was to prevent my becoming an illustrious investigator of the veiled worlds? It was with the most buoyant hope that I left my New England home and established myself in New York.

II. THE LONGING OF A MAN OF SCIENCE

My first step, of course, was to find suitable apartments. These I obtained, after a couple of days' search, in Fourth Avenue; a very pretty second-floor unfurnished, containing sitting-room, bedroom, and a smaller apartment which I intended to fit up as a laboratory. I furnished my lodgings simply, but rather elegantly, and then devoted all my energies to the adornment of the temple of my worship. I visited Pike, the celebrated optician, and passed in review his splendid collection of microscopes,—Field's Compound, Hingham's, Spencer's, Nachet's Binocular (that founded on the principles of the stereoscope), and at length fixed upon that form known as Spencer's Trunnion Microscope, as combining the greatest number of improvements with an almost perfect freedom from tremor. Along with this I purchased every possible accessory,—draw-tubes, micrometers, a *camera-lucida*, lever-stage, achromatic condensers, white cloud illuminators, prisms, parabolic condensers, polarizing apparatus, forceps, aquatic boxes, fishing-tubes, with a host of other articles, all of which would have been useful in the hands of an experienced microscopist, but, as I afterwards discovered, were not of the slightest present value to me. It takes years of practice to know how to use a complicated microscope. The optician looked suspiciously at me as I made these wholesale purchases. He evidently was uncertain whether to set me down as some scientific celebrity or a madman. I think he inclined to the latter belief. I suppose I was mad. Every great genius is mad upon the subject in which he is greatest. The unsuccessful madman is disgraced and called a lunatic.

Mad or not, I set myself to work with a zeal which few scientific students have ever equalled. I had everything to learn relative to the delicate study upon which I had embarked,—a study involving the most earnest patience, the most rigid analytic powers, the steadiest hand, the most untiring eye, the most refined and subtle manipulation.

For a long time half my apparatus lay inactively on the shelves of my laboratory, which was now most amply furnished with every possible contrivance for facilitating my investigations. The fact was that I did not know how to use some of my scientific implements,—never having been taught microscopics,—and those whose use I understood theoretically were of little avail, until by practice I could attain the necessary delicacy of handling. Still, such was the fury of my ambition, such the untiring perseverance of my experiments, that, difficult of credit as it may be, in the course of one year I became theoretically and practically an accomplished microscopist.

During this period of my labors, in which I submitted specimens of every substance that came under my observation to the action of my lenses, I became a discoverer,—in a small way, it is true, for I was very young, but still a discoverer. It was I who destroyed Ehrenberg's theory that the *Volvox globator* was an animal, and proved that his "monads" with stomachs and eyes were merely phases of the formation of a vegetable cell, and were, when they reached their mature state, incapable of the act of conjugation, or any true generative act, without which no organism rising to any stage of life higher than vegetable can be said to be complete. It was I who resolved the singular problem of rotation in the cells and hairs of plants into ciliary attraction, in spite of the assertions of Mr. Wenharn and others, that my explanation was the result of an optical illusion.

But notwithstanding these discoveries, laboriously and painfully made as they were, I felt horribly dissatisfied. At every step I found myself stopped by the imperfections of my instruments. Like all active microscopists, I gave my imagination full play. Indeed, it is a common complaint against many such, that they supply the defects of their instruments with the creations of their brains. I imagined depths beyond depths in nature which the limited power of my lenses prohibited me from exploring. I lay awake at night constructing imaginary microscopes of immeasurable power, with which I seemed to pierce through all the envelopes of matter down to its original atom. How I cursed

7

those imperfect mediums which necessity through ignorance compelled me to use! How I longed to discover the secret of some perfect lens, whose magnifying power should be limited only by the resolvability of the object, and which at the same time should be free from spherical and chromatic aberrations, in short from all the obstacles over which the poor microscopist finds himself, continually stumbling! I felt convinced that the simple microscope, composed of a single lens of such vast yet perfect power was possible of construction. To attempt to bring the compound microscope up to such a pitch would have been commencing at the wrong end; this latter being simply a partially successful endeavor to remedy those very defects of the simple instrument, which, if conquered, would leave nothing to be desired.

It was in this mood of mind that I became a constructive microscopist. After another year passed in this new pursuit, experimenting on every imaginable substance,—glass, gems, flints, crystals, artificial crystals formed of the alloy of various vitreous materials,—in short, having constructed as many varieties of lenses as Argus had eyes, I found myself precisely where I started, with nothing gained save an extensive knowledge of glass-making. I was almost dead with despair. My parents were surprised at my apparent want of progress in my medical studies, (I had not attended one lecture since my arrival in the city,) and the expenses of my mad pursuit had been so great as to embarrass me very seriously.

I was in this frame of mind one day, experimenting in my laboratory on a small diamond,—that stone, from its great refracting power, having always occupied my attention more than any other, when a young Frenchman, who lived on the floor above me, and who was in the habit of occasionally visiting me, entered the room.

I think that Jules Simon was a Jew. He had many traits of

the Hebrew character: a love of jewelry, of dress, and of good living. There was something mysterious about him. He always had something to sell, and yet went into excellent society. When I say sell, I should perhaps have said peddle; for his operations were generally confined to the disposal of single articles,—a picture, for instance, or a rare carving in ivory, or a pair of duelling-pistols, or the dress of a Mexican *caballero*. When I was first furnishing my rooms, he paid me a visit, which ended in my purchasing an antique silver lamp, which he assured me was a Cellini,—it was handsome enough even for that,—and some other knickknacks for my sitting-room. Why Simon should pursue this petty trade I never could imagine. He apparently had plenty of money, and had the *entrée* of the best houses in the city,—taking care, however, I suppose, to drive no bargains within the enchanted circle of the Upper Ten. I came at length to the conclusion that this peddling was but a mask to cover some greater object, and even went so far as to believe my young acquaintance to be implicated in the slave-trade. That, however, was none of my affair.

On the present occasion, Simon entered my room in a state of considerable excitement.

"*Ah! mon ami!*" he cried, before I could even offer him the ordinary salutation, "it has occurred to me to be the witness of the most astonishing things in the world. I promenade myself to the house of Madame _____. How does the little animal—*le renard*—name himself in the Latin?"

"Vulpes," I answered.

"Ah! yes,—Vulpes. I promenade myself to the house of Madame Vulpes."

"The spirit medium?"

"Yes, the great medium. Great heavens! what a woman! I write on a slip of paper many of questions concerning affairs the most secret,—affairs that conceal themselves in the abysses of my heart the most profound; and behold! by example! what occurs? This

9

devil of a woman makes me replies the most truthful to all of them. She talks to me of things that I do not love to talk of to myself. What am I to think? I am fixed to the earth!"

"Am I to understand you, M. Simon, that this Mrs. Vulpes replied to questions secretly written by you, which questions related to events known only to yourself?"

"Ah! more than that, more than that," he answered, with an air of some alarm. "She related to me things— But," he added, after a pause, and suddenly changing his manner, "why occupy ourselves with these follies? It was all the biology, without doubt. It goes without saying that it has not my credence.—But why are we here, *mon ami*? It has occurred to me to discover the most beautiful thing as you can imagine,—a vase with green lizards on it, composed by the great Bernard Palissy. It is in my apartment; let us mount. I go to show it to you."

I followed Simon mechanically; but my thoughts were far from Palissy and his enamelled ware, although I, like him, was seeking in the dark a great discovery. This casual mention of the spiritualist, Madame Vulpes, set me on a new track. What if this spiritualism should be really a great fact? What if, through communication with more subtile organisms than my own, I could reach at a single bound the goal, which perhaps a life of agonizing mental toil would never enable me to attain?

While purchasing the Palissy vase from my friend Simon, I was mentally arranging a visit to Madame Vulpes.

III. The Spirit of Leeuwenhoek

Two evenings after this, thanks to an arrangement by letter and the promise of an ample fee, I found Madame Vulpes awaiting me at her residence alone. She was a coarse-featured woman, with keen and rather cruel dark eyes, and an exceedingly sensual expression about her mouth and under jaw. She received me in perfect silence, in an apartment on the ground floor, very sparely furnished. In the centre of the room, close to where Mrs. Vulpes sat, there was a common round mahogany table. If I had come for the purpose of sweeping her chimney, the woman could not have looked more indifferent to my appearance. There was no attempt to inspire the visitor with awe. Everything bore a simple and practical aspect. This intercourse with the spiritual world was evidently as familiar an occupation with Mrs. Vulpes as eating her dinner or riding in an omnibus.

"You come for a communication, Mr. Linley?" said the medium, in a dry, business-like tone of voice.

"By appointment,—yes."

"What sort of communication do you want?—a written one?"

"Yes,—I wish for a written one." "From any particular spirit?" "Yes." "Have you ever known this spirit on this earth?" "Never. He died long before I was born. I wish merely to obtain from him some information which he ought to be able to give better than any other."

"Will you seat yourself at the table, Mr. Linley," said the medium, "and place your hands upon it?"

I obeyed,—Mrs. Vulpes being seated opposite to me, with her hands also on the table. We remained thus for about a minute and a half, when a violent succession of raps came on the table, on the back of my chair, on the floor immediately under my feet, and even on the windowpanes. Mrs. Vulpes smiled composedly.

"They are very strong to-night," she remarked. "You are fortunate." She then continued, "Will the spirits communicate with this gentleman?"

Vigorous affirmative.

"Will the particular spirit he desires to speak with communicate?"

A very confused rapping followed this question.

"I know what they mean," said Mrs. Vulpes, addressing herself to me; "they wish you to write down the name of the particular spirit that you desire to converse with. Is that so?" she added, speaking to her invisible guests. That it was so was evident from the numerous affirmatory responses. While this was going on, I tore a slip from my pocket-book, and scribbled a name, under the table. "Will this spirit communicate in writing with this gentleman?" asked the medium once more. After a moment's pause, her hand seemed to be seized with a violent tremor, shaking so forcibly that the table vibrated. She said that a spirit had seized her hand and would write. I handed her some sheets of paper that were on the table, and a pencil. The latter she held loosely in her hand, which presently began to move over the paper with a singular and seemingly involuntary motion. After a few moments had elapsed, she handed me the paper, on which I found written, in a large, uncultivated hand, the words, "He is not here, but has been sent for." A pause of a minute or so now ensued, during which Mrs. Vulpes remained perfectly silent, but the raps continued at regular intervals. When the short period I mention had elapsed, the hand of the medium was again seized with its convulsive tremor, and she wrote, under this strange influence, a few words on the paper, which she handed to me. They were as follows:—

"I am here. Question me.
"Leeuwenhoek."

I was astounded. The name was identical with that I had written beneath the table, and carefully kept concealed. Neither was it at all probable that an uncultivated woman like Mrs. Vulpes should know even the name of the great father of microscopics. It may have been biology; but this theory was soon doomed to be destroyed. I wrote on my slip—still concealing it from Mrs. Vulpes—a series of questions, which, to avoid tediousness, I shall place with the responses, in the order in which they occurred:—

I.—Can the microscope be brought to perfection?

Spirit.—Yes.

I.—Am I destined to accomplish this great task?

Spirit.—You are.

I.—I wish to know how to proceed to attain this end. For the love which you bear to science, help me!

Spirit.—A diamond of one hundred and forty carats, submitted to electro-magnetic currents for a long period, will experience a rearrangement of its atoms inter se, and from that stone you will form the universal lens.

I.—Will great discoveries result from the use of such a lens?

Spirit.—So great that all that has gone before is as nothing.

I.—But the refractive power of the diamond is so immense, that the image will be formed within the lens. How is that difficulty to be surmounted?

Spirit.—Pierce the lens through its axis, and the difficulty is obviated. The image will be formed in the pierced space, which will itself serve as a tube to look through. Now I am called. Good night.

I cannot at all describe the effect that these extraordinary communications had upon me. I felt completely bewildered. No biological theory could account for the discovery of the lens. The medium might, by means of biological *rapport* with my mind, have gone so far as to read my questions, and reply to them coherently. But biology could not enable her to discover that magnetic currents would so alter the crystals of the diamond as to remedy its previous defects, and admit of its being polished into a perfect lens. Some such theory may have passed through my head, it is true; but if so, I had forgotten it. In my excited condition of mind there was no course left but to become a convert, and it was in a state of the most painful nervous exaltation that I left the medium's house that evening. She accompanied me to the door, hoping that I was satisfied. The raps followed us as we went through the hall, sounding on the balusters, the flooring, and even the lintels of the door. I hastily expressed my satisfaction, and escaped hurriedly into the cool night air. I walked home with but one thought possessing me,—how to obtain a diamond of the immense size required. My entire means multiplied a hundred times over would have been inadequate to its purchase. Besides, such stones are rare, and become historical. I could find such only in the regalia of Eastern or European monarchs.

IV. THE EYE OF MORNING

There was a light in Simon's room as I entered my house. A vague impulse urged me to visit him. As I opened the door of his sitting-room unannounced, he was bending, with his back toward me, over a carcel lamp, apparently engaged in minutely examining some object which he held in his hands. As I entered, he started suddenly, thrust his hand into his breast pocket, and turned to me with a face crimson with confusion.

"What!" I cried, "poring over the miniature of some fair lady? Well, don't blush so much; I won't ask to see it."

Simon laughed awkwardly enough, but made none of the negative protestations usual on such occasions. He asked me to take a seat.

"Simon," said I, "I have just come from Madame Vulpes."

This time Simon turned as white as a sheet, and seemed stupefied, as if a sudden electric shock had smitten him. He babbled some incoherent words, and went hastily to a small closet where he usually kept his liquors. Although astonished at his emotion, I was too preoccupied with my own idea to pay much attention to anything else.

"You say truly when you call Madame Vulpes a devil of a

woman," I continued. "Simon, she told me wonderful things to-night, or rather was the means of telling me wonderful things. Ah! if I could only get a diamond that weighed one hundred and forty carats!"

Scarcely had the sigh with which I uttered this desire died upon my lips, when Simon, with the aspect of a wild beast, glared at me savagely, and, rushing to the mantelpiece, where some foreign weapons hung on the wall, caught up a Malay *creese*, and brandished it furiously before him.

"No!" he cried in French, into which he always broke when excited. "No! you shall not have it! You are perfidious! You have consulted with that demon, and desire my treasure! But I shall die first! Me! I am brave! You cannot make me fear!"

All this, uttered in a loud voice trembling with excitement, astounded me. I saw at a glance that I had accidentally trodden upon the edges of Simon's secret, whatever it was. It was necessary to reassure him.

"My dear Simon," I said, "I am entirely at a loss to know what you mean. I went to Madame Vulpes to consult her on a scientific problem, to the solution of which I discovered that a diamond of the size I just mentioned was necessary. You were never alluded to during the evening, nor, so far as I was concerned, even thought of. What can be the meaning of this outburst? If you happen to have a set of valuable diamonds in your possession, you need fear nothing from me. The diamond which I require you could not possess; or, if you did possess it, you would not be living here."

Something in my tone must have completely reassured him; for his expression immediately changed to a sort of constrained merriment, combined, however, with a certain suspicious attention to my movements. He laughed, and said that I must bear with him; that he was at certain moments subject to a species of vertigo, which betrayed itself in incoherent speeches, and that the attacks passed off as rapidly as they came. He put his weapon aside while making this explanation, and endeavored, with some success, to assume a more cheerful air.

All this did not impose on me in the least. I was too much accustomed to analytical labors to be baffled by so flimsy a veil. I determined to probe the mystery to the bottom. "Simon," I said, gayly, "let us forget all this over a bottle of Burgundy. I have a case of Lausseure's *Clos Vougeot* down-stairs, fragrant with the odors and ruddy with the sunlight of the Côte d'Or. Let us have up a couple of bottles. What say you?"

"With all my heart," answered Simon, smilingly.

I produced the wine and we seated ourselves to drink. It was of a famous vintage, that of 1848, a year when war and wine throve together,—and its pure but powerful juice seemed to impart renewed vitality to the system. By the time we had half finished the second bottle, Simon's head, which I knew was a weak one, had begun to yield, while I remained calm as ever, only that every draught seemed to send a flush of vigor through my limbs. Simon's utterance became more and more indistinct. He took to singing French chansons of a not very moral tendency. I rose suddenly from the table just at the conclusion of one of those incoherent verses, and, fixing my eyes on him with a quiet smile, said: "Simon, I have deceived you. I learned your secret this evening. You may as well be frank with me. Mrs. Vulpes, or rather one of her spirits, told me all."

He started with horror. His intoxication seemed for the moment to fade away, and he made a movement towards the weapon that he had a short time before laid down. I stopped him with my hand.

"Monster!" he cried, passionately, "I am ruined! What shall I do? You shall never have it! I swear by my mother!"

"I don't want it," I said; "rest secure, but be frank with me. Tell me all about it."

The drunkenness began to return. He protested with maudlin

16

earnestness that I was entirely mistaken,—that I was intoxicated; then asked me to swear eternal secrecy, and promised to disclose the mystery to me. I pledged myself, of course, to all. With an uneasy look in his eyes, and hands unsteady with drink and nervousness, he drew a small case from his breast and opened it.

Heavens! How the mild lamp-light was shivered into a thousand prismatic arrows, as it fell upon a vast rose-diamond that glittered in the case! I was no judge of diamonds, but I saw at a glance that this was a gem of rare size and purity. I looked at Simon with wonder, and—must I confess it?—with envy. How could he have obtained this treasure?

In reply to my questions, I could just gather from his drunken statements (of which, I fancy, half the incoherence was affected) that he had been superintending a gang of slaves engaged in diamond-washing in Brazil; that he had seen one of them secrete a diamond, but, instead of informing his employers, had quietly watched the negro until he saw him bury his treasure; that he had dug it up and fled with it, but that as yet he was afraid to attempt to dispose of it publicly,—so valuable a gem being almost certain to attract too much attention to its owner's antecedents,—and he had not been able to discover any of those obscure channels by which such matters are conveyed away safely. He added, that, in accordance with the oriental practice, he had named his diamond with the fanciful title of "The Eye of Morning."

While Simon was relating this to me, I regarded the great diamond attentively. Never had I beheld anything so beautiful. All the glories of light, ever imagined or described, seemed to pulsate in its crystalline chambers. Its weight, as I learned from Simon, was exactly one hundred and forty carats. Here was an amazing coincidence. The hand of destiny seemed in it. On the very evening when the spirit of Leeuwenhoek communicates to me the great secret of the microscope, the priceless means which he directs me to employ start up within my easy reach! I determined, with the most perfect deliberation, to possess myself of Simon's diamond.

I sat opposite to him while he nodded over his glass, and calmly revolved the whole affair. I did not for an instant contemplate so foolish an act as a common theft, which would of course be discovered, or at least necessitate flight and concealment, all of which must interfere with my scientific plans. There was but one step to be taken,—to kill Simon. After all, what was the life of a little peddling Jew, in comparison with the interests of science? Human beings are taken every day from the condemned prisons to be experimented on by surgeons. This man, Simon, was by his own confession a criminal, a robber, and I believed on my soul a murderer. He deserved death quite as much as any felon condemned by the laws: why should I not, like government, contrive that his punishment should contribute to the progress of human knowledge? The means for accomplishing everything I desired lay within my reach. There stood upon the mantelpiece a bottle half full of French laudanum. Simon was so occupied with his diamond, which I had just restored to him, that it was an affair of no difficulty to drug his glass. In a quarter of an hour he was in a profound sleep.

I now opened his waistcoat, took the diamond from the inner pocket in which he had placed it, and removed him to the bed, on which I laid him so that his feet hung down over the edge. I had possessed myself of the Malay *creese*, which I held in my right hand, while with the other I discovered as accurately as I could by pulsation the exact locality of the heart. It was essential that all the aspects of his death should lead to the surmise of self-murder. I calculated the exact angle at which it was probable that the weapon, if levelled by Simon's own hand, would enter his breast; then with one powerful blow I thrust it up to the hilt in the very spot which I desired to penetrate. A convulsive thrill ran through Simon's limbs. I heard a smothered sound issue from his throat, precisely like the bursting of a large air-bubble, sent up by a diver, when it reaches the surface of the water; he turned half round on his side, and, as if to assist my plans more effectually, his right hand, moved by some mere spasmodic impulse, clasped the handle of the creese, which it remained holding with extraordinary muscular tenacity. Beyond this there was no apparent struggle. The laudanum, I presume, paralyzed the usual nervous action. He must have died instantly.

There was yet something to be done. To make it certain that all suspicion of the act should be diverted from any inhabitant of the house to Simon himself, it was necessary that the door should be found in the morning locked on the inside. How to do this, and afterwards escape myself? Not by the window; that was a physical impossibility. Besides, I was determined that the windows also should be found bolted. The solution was simple enough. I descended softly to my own room for a peculiar instrument which I had used for holding small slippery substances, such as minute spheres of glass, etc. This instrument was nothing more than a long slender hand-vice, with a very powerful grip, and a considerable leverage, which last was accidentally owing to the shape of the handle. Nothing was simpler than, when the key was in the lock, to seize the end of its stem in this vice, through the keyhole, from the outside, and so lock the door. Previously, however, to doing this, I burned a number of papers on Simon's hearth. Suicides almost always burn papers before they destroy themselves. I also emptied some more laudanum into Simon's glass,—having first removed from it all traces of wine,—cleaned the other wine-glass, and brought the bottles away with me. If traces of two persons drinking had been found in the room, the question naturally would have arisen, Who was the second? Besides, the wine-bottles might have been identified as belonging to me. The laudanum I poured out to account for its presence in his stomach, in case of a *postmortem* examination. The theory naturally would be, that he first intended to poison himself, but, after swallowing a little of the drug, was either disgusted with its taste, or changed his mind from other motives, and chose the dagger. These arrangements made, I walked out, leaving the gas burning, locked the door with my vice, and went to bed.

Simon's death was not discovered until nearly three in the afternoon. The servant, astonished at seeing the gas burning,—the light streaming on the dark landing from under the door,—peeped through the keyhole and saw Simon on the bed. She gave the alarm. The door was burst open, and the neighborhood was in a fever of excitement.

Every one in the house was arrested, myself included. There was an inquest; but no clew to his death beyond that of suicide could be obtained. Curiously enough, he had made several speeches to his friends the preceding week, that seemed to point to self-destruction. One gentleman swore that Simon had said in his presence that "he was tired of life." His landlord affirmed that Simon, when paying him his last month's rent, remarked that "he should not pay him rent much longer." All the other evidence corresponded,—the door locked inside, the position of the corpse, the burnt papers. As I anticipated, no one knew of the possession of the diamond by Simon, so that no motive was suggested for his murder. The jury, after a prolonged examination, brought in the usual verdict, and the neighborhood once more settled down into its accustomed quiet.

V. ANIMULA

The three months succeeding Simon's catastrophe I devoted night and day to my diamond lens. I had constructed a vast galvanic battery, composed of nearly two thousand pairs of plates,—a higher power I dared not use, lest the diamond should be calcined. By means of this enormous engine I was enabled to send a powerful current of electricity continually through my great diamond, which it seemed to me gained in lustre every day. At the expiration of a month I commenced the grinding and polishing of the lens, a work of intense toil and exquisite delicacy. The great density of the stone, and the care required to be taken with the curvatures of the surfaces of the lens, rendered the labor the severest and most harassing that I had yet undergone. At last the eventful moment came; the lens was completed. I stood trembling on the threshold of new worlds. I had the realization of Alexander's famous wish before me. The lens lay on the table, ready to be placed upon its platform. My hand fairly shook as I enveloped a drop of water with a thin coating of oil of turpentine, preparatory to its examination,—a process necessary in order to prevent the rapid evaporation of the water. I now placed the drop on a thin slip of glass under the lens, and throwing upon it, by the combined aid of a prism and a mirror, a powerful stream of light, I approached my eye to the minute hole drilled through the axis of the lens. For an instant I saw nothing save what seemed to be an illuminated chaos, a vast luminous abyss. A pure white light, cloudless and serene, and seemingly limitless as space itself, was my first impression. Gently, and with the greatest care, I depressed the lens a few hair's-breadths. The wondrous illumination still continued, but as the lens approached the object a scene of indescribable beauty was unfolded to my view. I seemed to gaze upon a vast space, the limits of which extended far beyond my vision. An atmosphere of magical luminousness permeated the entire field of view. I was amazed to see no trace of animalculous life. Not a living thing, apparently, inhabited that dazzling expanse. I comprehended instantly that, by the wondrous power of my lens, I had penetrated beyond the grosser particles of aqueous matter, beyond the realms of infusoria and protozoa, down to the original gaseous globule, into whose luminous

21

interior I was gazing, as, into all almost boundless dome filled with a supernatural radiance.

It was, however, no brilliant void into which I looked. On every side I beheld beautiful inorganic forms, of unknown texture, and colored with the most enchanting hues. These forms presented the appearance of what might be called, for want of a more specific definition, foliated clouds of the highest rarity; that is, they undulated and broke into vegetable formations, and were tinged with splendors compared with which the gilding of our autumn woodlands is as dross compared with gold. Far away into the illimitable distance stretched long avenues of these gaseous forests, dimly transparent, and painted with prismatic hues of unimaginable brilliancy. The pendent branches waved along the fluid glades until every vista seemed to break through half-lucent ranks of many-colored drooping silken pennons. What seemed to be either fruits or flowers, pied with a thousand hues, lustrous and ever varying, bubbled from tile crowns, of this fairy foliage. No hills, no lakes, no rivers, no forms animate or inanimate, were to be seen, save those vast auroral copses that floated serenely in the luminous stillness, with leaves and fruits and flowers gleaming with unknown fires, unrealizable by mere imagination.

How strange, I thought, that this sphere should be thus condemned to solitude! I had hoped, at least, to discover some new form of animal life,—perhaps of a lower class than any with which we are at present acquainted, but still, some living organism. I found my newly discovered world, if I may so speak, a beautiful chromatic desert.

While I was speculating on the singular arrangements of the internal economy of Nature, with which she so frequently splinters into atoms our most compact theories, I thought I beheld a form moving slowly through the glades of one of the prismatic forests. I looked more attentively, and found that I was not mistaken. Words cannot depict the anxiety with which I awaited the nearer approach of this mysterious object. Was it merely some inanimate substance, held in suspense in the attenuated atmosphere of the globule? or was it an animal endowed with vitality and motion? It approached, flitting behind the gauzy, colored veils of cloud-foliage, for seconds dimly revealed, then vanishing. At last the violet pennons that trailed nearest to me vibrated; they were gently pushed aside, and the form floated out into the broad light.

It was a female human shape. When I say human, I mean it possessed the outlines of humanity,—but there the analogy ends. Its adorable beauty lifted it illimitable heights beyond the loveliest daughter of Adam.

I cannot, I dare not, attempt to inventory the charms of this divine revelation of perfect beauty. Those eyes of mystic violet, dewy and serene, evade my words. Her long, lustrous hair following her glorious head in a golden wake, like the track sown in heaven by a falling star, seems to quench my most burning phrases with its splendors. If all the bees of Hybla nestled upon my lips, they would still sing but hoarsely the wondrous harmonies of outline that enclosed her form.

She swept out from between the rainbow-curtains of the cloud-trees into the broad sea of light that lay beyond. Her motions were those of some graceful naiad, cleaving, by a mere effort of her will, the clear, unruffled waters that fill the chambers of the sea. She floated forth with the serene grace of a frail bubble ascending through the still atmosphere of a June day. The perfect roundness of her limbs formed suave and enchanting curves. It was like listening to the most spiritual symphony of Beethoven the divine, to watch the harmonious flow of lines. This, indeed, was a pleasure cheaply purchased at any price. What cared I, if I had waded to the portal of this wonder through another's blood? I would have given my own to enjoy one such moment of intoxication and delight. Breathless with gazing on this lovely wonder, and forgetful for an instant of everything save her presence, I withdrew my eye from the microscope eagerly,—alas! As my gaze fell on the thin slide that lay beneath my instrument, the bright light from mirror and from prism sparkled on a colorless drop of water! There, in that tiny bead of dew, this beautiful being was forever imprisoned. The planet Neptune was not more distant from me than she. I hastened once more to apply my eye to the microscope.

Animula (let me now call her by that dear name which I subsequently bestowed on her) had changed her position. She had again approached the wondrous forest, and was gazing earnestly upwards. Presently one of the trees—as I must call them—unfolded a long ciliary process, with which it seized one of the gleaming fruits that glittered on its summit, and, sweeping slowly down, held it within reach of Animula. The sylph took it in her delicate hand and began to eat. My attention was so entirely absorbed by her, that I could not apply myself to the task of determining whether this singular plant was or was not instinct with volition.

I watched her, as she made her repast, with the most profound attention. The suppleness of her motions sent a thrill of delight through my frame; my heart beat madly as she turned her beautiful eyes in the direction of the spot in which I stood. What would I not have given to have had the power to precipitate myself into that luminous ocean, and float with her through those groves of purple and gold! While I was thus breathlessly following her every movement, she suddenly started, seemed to listen for a moment, and then cleaving the brilliant ether in which she was floating, like a flash of light, pierced through the opaline forest, and disappeared.

Instantly a series of the most singular sensations attacked me. It seemed as if I had suddenly gone blind. The luminous sphere was still before me, but my daylight had vanished. What caused this sudden disappearance? Had she a lover or a husband? Yes, that was the solution! Some signal from a happy fellow-being had vibrated through the avenues of the forest, and she had obeyed the summons.

The agony of my sensations, as I arrived at this conclusion, startled me. I tried to reject the conviction that my reason forced upon me. I battled against the fatal conclusion,—but in vain. It was so. I had no escape from it. I loved an animalcule!

It is true that, thanks to the marvellous power of my microscope, she appeared of human proportions. Instead of presenting the revolting aspect of the coarser creatures, that live and struggle and die, in the more easily resolvable portions of the water-drop, she was fair and delicate and of surpassing beauty. But of what account was all that? Every time that my eye was withdrawn from the instrument, it fell on a miserable drop of water, within which, I must be content to know, dwelt all that could make my life lovely.

Could she but see me once! Could I for one moment pierce the mystical walls that so inexorably rose to separate us, and whisper all that filled my soul, I might consent to be satisfied for the rest of my life with the knowledge of her remote sympathy. It would be something to have established even the faintest personal link to bind us together,—to know that at times, when roaming through those enchanted glades, she might think of the wonderful stranger, who had broken the monotony of her life with his presence, and left a gentle memory in her heart!

But it could not be. No invention of which human intellect was capable could break down the barriers that nature had erected. I might feast my soul upon her wondrous beauty, yet she must always remain ignorant of the adoring eyes that day and night gazed upon her, and, even when closed, beheld her in dreams. With a bitter cry of anguish I fled from the room, and, flinging myself on my bed, sobbed myself to sleep like a child.

VI. THE SPILLING OF THE CUP

I arose the next morning almost at daybreak, and rushed to my microscope. I trembled as I sought the luminous world in miniature that contained my all. Animula was there. I had left the gas-lamp, surrounded by its moderators, burning, when I went to bed the night before. I found the sylph bathing, as it were, with an expression of pleasure animating her features, in the brilliant light which surrounded her. She tossed her lustrous golden hair over her shoulders with innocent coquetry. She lay at full length in the transparent medium, in which she supported herself with ease, and gambolled with the enchanting grace that the nymph Salmacis might have exhibited when she sought to conquer the modest Hermaphroditus. I tried an experiment to satisfy myself if her powers of reflection were developed. I lessened the lamp-light considerably. By the dim light that remained, I could see an expression of pain flit across her face. She looked upward suddenly, and her brows contracted. I flooded the stage of the microscope again with a full stream of light, and her whole expression changed. She sprang forward like some substance deprived of all weight. Her eyes sparkled and her lips moved. Ah! if science had only the means of conducting and reduplicating sounds, as it does the rays of light, what carols of happiness would then have entranced my ears! what jubilant hymns to Adonis would have thrilled the illumined air!

I now comprehended how it was that the Count de Gabalis peopled his mystic world with sylphs,—beautiful beings whose breath of life was lambent fire, and who sported forever in regions of purest ether and purest light. The Rosicrucian had anticipated the wonder that I had practically realized.

How long this worship of my strange divinity went on thus

I scarcely know. I lost all note of time. All day from early dawn, and far into the night, I was to be found peering through that wonderful lens. I saw no one, went nowhere, and scarce allowed myself sufficient time for my meals. My whole life was absorbed in contemplation as rapt as that of any of the Romish saints. Every hour that I gazed upon the divine form strengthened my passion,—a passion that was always overshadowed by the maddening conviction, that, although I could gaze on her at will, she never, never could behold me!

At length, I grew so pale and emaciated, from want of rest, and continual brooding over my insane love and its cruel conditions, that I determined to make some effort to wean myself from it. "Come," I said, "this is at best but a fantasy. Your imagination has bestowed on Animula charms which in reality she does not possess. Seclusion from female society has produced this morbid condition of mind. Compare her with the beautiful women of your own world, and this false enchantment will vanish." I looked over the newspapers by chance. There I beheld the advertisement of a celebrated *danseuse* who appeared nightly at Niblo's. The Signorina Caradolce had the reputation of being the most beautiful as well as the most graceful woman in the world. I instantly dressed and went to the theatre.

The curtain drew up. The usual semicircle of fairies in white muslin were standing on the right toe around the enamelled flower-bank, of green canvas, on which the belated prince was sleeping. Suddenly a flute is heard. The fairies start. The trees open, the fairies all stand on the left toe, and the queen enters. It was the Signorina. She bounded forward amid thunders of applause, and, lighting on one foot, remained poised in air.

Heavens! was this the great enchantress that had drawn monarchs at her chariotwheels? Those heavy muscular limbs, those thick ankles, those cavernous eyes, that stereotyped smile, those crudely painted cheeks! Where were the vermeil blooms, the liquid expressive eyes, the harmonious limbs of Animula?

The Signorina danced. What gross, discordant movements! The play of her limbs was all false and artificial. Her bounds were painful athletic efforts; her poses were angular and distressed the eye. I could bear it no longer; with an exclamation of disgust that drew every eye upon me, I rose from my seat in the very middle of the Signorina's *pas-de-fascination*, and abruptly quitted the house.

I hastened home to feast my eyes once more on the lovely form of my sylph. I felt that henceforth to combat this passion would be impossible. I applied my eye to the lens. Animula was there,—but what could have happened? Some terrible change seemed to have taken place during my absence. Some secret grief seemed to cloud the lovely features of her I gazed upon. Her face had grown thin and haggard; her limbs trailed heavily; the wondrous lustre of her golden hair had faded. She was ill!—ill, and I could not assist her! I believe at that moment I would have gladly forfeited all claims to my human birthright, if I could only have been dwarfed to the size of an animalcule, and permitted to console her from whom fate had forever divided me. I racked my brain for the solution of this mystery. What was it that afflicted the sylph? She seemed to suffer intense pain. Her features contracted, and she even writhed, as if with some internal agony. The wondrous forests appeared also to have lost half their beauty. Their hues were dim and in some places faded away altogether. I watched Animula for hours with a breaking heart, and she seemed absolutely to wither away under my very eye. Suddenly I remembered that I had not looked at the water-drop for several days. In fact, I hated to see it; for it reminded me of the natural barrier between Animula and myself. I hurriedly looked down on the stage of the microscope. The slide was still there,—but, great heavens! the water-drop had vanished! The awful truth burst upon me; it had evaporated, until it had become so minute as to be invisible to the naked eye; I had been gazing on its last atom, the one that contained

Animula,—and she was dying! I rushed again to the front of the lens, and looked through. Alas! the last agony had seized her. The rainbow-hued forests had all melted away, and Animula lay struggling feebly in what seemed to be a spot of dim light. Ah! the sight was horrible: the limbs once so round and lovely shrivelling up into nothings; the eyes—those eyes that shone like heaven—being quenched into black dust; the lustrous golden hair now lank and discolored. The last throe came. I beheld that final struggle of the blackening form—and I fainted.

When I awoke out of a trance of many hours, I found myself lying amid the wreck of my instrument, myself as shattered in mind and body as it. I crawled feebly to my bed, from which I did not rise for months.

They say now that I am mad; but they are mistaken. I am poor, for I have neither the heart nor the will to work; all my money is spent, and I live on charity. Young men's associations that love a joke invite me to lecture on Optics before them, for which they pay me, and laugh at me while I lecture. "Linley, the mad microscopist," is the name I go by. I suppose that I talk incoherently while I lecture. Who could talk sense when his brain is haunted by such ghastly memories, while ever and anon among the shapes of death I behold the radiant form of my lost Animula!

THE HORLA

By Guy de Maupassant

Of Guy de Maupassant's "The Horla" Lovecraft writes in "Supernatural Horror in Literature": "Relating the advent to France of an invisible being who lives on water and milk, sways the minds of others, and seems to be the vanguard of a horde of extra-terrestrial organisms arrived on earth to subjugate and overwhelm mankind, this tense narrative is perhaps without a peer in its particular department" (*S* 40). This plot description makes the story sound like a remarkable anticipation of Lovecraft's own "The Call of Cthulhu" (1926). Lovecraft first read the story in Joseph Lewis French's anthology *Masterpieces of Mystery* (1920), which he had obtained in New York in 1922; it is from this anonymous translation that the following text is taken.

French novelist and short story writer Guy de Maupassant (1850–1893) attained celebrity by dozens of short stories and several novels, but much of his fame today rests upon the score or more of pscyhological and supernatural horror tales he wrote toward the end of his life, when he was suffering psychological problems as a result of syphilis. "The Horla" ("Le Horla") was first published in a short version (*Gil Blas*, 26 October 1886), then in a long version (Ollendorff, 1887); the latter is the better known.

31

ay 8th. What a lovely day! I have spent all the morning lying in the grass in front of my house, under the enormous plantain tree which covers it, and shades and shelters the whole of it. I like this part of the country and I am fond of living here because I am attached to it by deep roots, profound and delicate roots which attach a man to the soil on which his ancestors were born and died, which attach him to what people think and what they eat, to the usages as well as to the food, local expressions, the peculiar language of the peasants, to the smell of the soil, of the villages and of the atmosphere itself. I love my house in which I grew up. From my windows I can see the Seine which flows by the side of my garden, on the other side of the road, almost through my grounds, the great and wide Seine, which goes to Rouen and Havre, and which is covered with boats passing to and fro. On the left, down yonder, lies Rouen, that large town with its blue roofs, under its pointed Gothic towers. They are innumerable, delicate or broad, dominated by the spire of the cathedral, and full of bells which sound through the blue air on fine mornings, sending their sweet and distant iron clang to me; their metallic sound which the breeze wafts in my direction, now stronger and now weaker, according as the wind is stronger or lighter.

What a delicious morning it was!

About eleven o'clock, a long line of boats drawn by a steam tug, as big as a fly, and which scarcely puffed while emitting its thick smoke, passed my gate.

After two English schooners, whose red flag fluttered toward the sky, there came a magnificent Brazilian threemaster; it was perfectly white and wonderfully clean and shining. I saluted it, I hardly know why, except that the sight of the vessel gave me great pleasure.

May 12th. I have had a slight feverish attack for the last few days, and I feel ill, or rather I feel low-spirited.

Whence do these mysterious influences come, which change our happiness into discouragement, and our self-confidence into diffidence? One might almost say that the air, the invisible air is full of unknowable Forces, whose mysterious presence we have to endure. I wake up in the best spirits, with an inclination to sing in my throat. Why? I go down by the side of the water, and suddenly, after walking a short distance, I return home wretched, as if some misfortune were awaiting me there. Why? Is it a cold shiver which, passing over my skin, has upset my nerves and given me low spirits? Is it the form of the clouds, or the color of the sky, or the color of the surrounding objects which is so changeable, which have troubled my thoughts as they passed before my eyes? Who can tell? Everything that surrounds us, everything that we see without looking at it, everything that we touch without knowing it, everything that we handle without feeling it, all that we meet without clearly distinguishing it, has a rapid, surprising and inexplicable effect upon us and upon our organs, and through them on our ideas and on our heart itself.

How profound that mystery of the Invisible is! We cannot fathom it with our miserable senses, with our eyes which are unable to perceive what is either too small or too great, too near to, or too far from us; neither the inhabitants of a star nor of a drop of water … with our ears that deceive us, for they transmit to us the vibrations of the air in sonorous notes. They are fairies who work the miracle of changing that movement into noise, and by that metamorphosis give birth to music, which makes the mute agitation of nature musical … with our sense of smell which is smaller than that of a dog … with our sense of taste which can scarcely distinguish the age of a wine!

Oh! If we only had other organs which would work other miracles in our favor, what a number of fresh things we might discover around us!

May 16th. I am ill, decidedly! I was so well last month! I am feverish, horribly feverish, or rather I am in a state of feverish enervation, which makes my mind suffer as much as my body. I have without ceasing that horrible sensation of some danger threatening me, that apprehension of some coming misfortune or of approaching death, that presentiment which is, no doubt, an attack of some illness which is still unknown, which germinates in the flesh and in the blood.

May 18th. I have just come from consulting my medical man, for I could no longer get any sleep. He found that my pulse was high, my eyes dilated, my nerves highly strung, but no alarming symptoms. I must have a course of shower-baths and of bromide of potassium.

May 25th. No change! My state is really very peculiar. As the evening comes on, an incomprehensible feeling of disquietude seizes me, just as if night concealed some terrible menace toward me. I dine quickly, and then try to read, but I do not understand the words, and can scarcely distinguish the letters. Then I walk up and down my drawing-room, oppressed by a feeling of confused and irresistible fear, the fear of sleep and fear of my bed.

About ten o'clock I go up to my room. As soon as I have got in I double lock, and bolt it: I am frightened—of what? Up till the present time I have been frightened of nothing—I open my cupboards, and look under my bed; I listen—I listen—to what? How strange it is that a simple feeling of discomfort, impeded or heightened circulation, perhaps the irritation of a nervous thread, a slight congestion, a small disturbance in the imperfect and delicate functions of our living machinery, can turn the most lighthearted of men into a melancholy one, and make a coward of the bravest! Then, I go to bed, and I wait for sleep as a man might wait for the executioner. I wait for its coming with dread, and my heart beats and my legs tremble, while my whole body shivers beneath the warmth of the bedclothes, until the moment when I suddenly fall asleep, as one would throw oneself into a pool of stagnant water in order to drown oneself. I do not feel coming over me, as I used to do formerly, this perfidious sleep which is close to me and watching me, which is going to seize me by the head, to close my eyes and annihilate me.

I sleep—a long time—two or three hours perhaps—then a dream—no—a nightmare lays hold on me. I feel that I am in bed and asleep—I feel it and I know it—and I feel also that somebody is coming close to me, is looking at me, touching me, is getting on to my bed, is kneeling on my chest, is taking my neck between his hands and squeezing it—squeezing it with all his might in order to strangle me.

I struggle, bound by that terrible powerlessness which paralyzes us in our dreams; I try to cry out—but I cannot; I want to move—I cannot; I try, with the most violent efforts and out of breath, to turn over and throw off this being which is crushing and suffocating me—I cannot! And then, suddenly, I wake up, shaken and bathed in perspiration; I light a candle and find that I am alone, and after that crisis, which occurs every night, I at length fall asleep and slumber tranquilly till morning.

June 2d. My state has grown worse. What is the matter with me? The bromide does me no good, and the showerbaths have no effect whatever. Sometimes, in order to tire myself out, though I am fatigued enough already, I go for a walk in the forest of Roumare. I used to think at first that the fresh light and soft air, impregnated with the odor of herbs and leaves, would instill new blood into my veins and impart fresh energy to my heart. I turned into a broad ride in the wood, and then I turned toward La Bouille, through a narrow path, between two rows of exceedingly tall trees, which placed a thick, green, almost black roof between the sky and me.

A sudden shiver ran through me, not a cold shiver, but a shiver of agony, and so I hastened my steps, uneasy at being alone in the wood, frightened stupidly and without reason, at the profound solitude. Suddenly it seemed to me as if I were being followed, that somebody was walking at my heels, close, quite close to me, near enough to touch me.

I turned round suddenly, but I was alone. I saw nothing behind me except the straight, broad ride, empty and bordered by high trees, horribly empty; on the other side it also extended until it was lost in the distance, and looked just the same, terrible.

I closed my eyes. Why? And then I began to turn round on one heel very quickly, just like a top. I nearly fell down, and opened my eyes; the trees were dancing round me and the earth heaved; I was obliged to sit down. Then, ah! I no longer remembered how I had come! What a strange idea! What a strange, strange idea! I did not the least know. I started off to the right, and got back into the avenue which had led me into the middle of the forest.

June 3d. I have had a terrible night. I shall go away for a few weeks, for no doubt a journey will set me up again.

July 2d. I have come back, quite cured, and have had a most delightful trip into the bargain. I have been to Mont Saint-Michel, which I had not seen before.

What a sight, when one arrives as I did, at Avranches toward the end of the day! The town stands on a hill, and I was taken into the public garden at the extremity of the town. I uttered a cry of astonishment. An extraordinarily large bay lay extended before me, as far as my eyes could reach, between two hills which were lost to sight in the mist; and in the middle of this immense yellow bay, under a clear, golden sky, a peculiar hill rose up, somber and pointed in the midst of the sand. The sun had just disappeared, and under the still flaming sky the outline of that fantastic rock stood out, which bears on its summit a fantastic monument.

At daybreak I went to it. The tide was low as it had been the night before, and I saw that wonderful abbey rise up before me as I approached it. After several hours' walking, I reached the enormous mass of rocks which supports the little town, dominated by the great church. Having climbed the steep and narrow street, I entered the most wonderful Gothic building that has ever been built to God on earth, as large as a town, full of low rooms which seem buried beneath vaulted roofs, and lofty galleries supported by delicate columns.

I entered this gigantic granite jewel which is as light as a bit of lace, covered with towers, with slender belfries to which spiral staircases ascend, and which raise their strange heads that bristle with chimeras, with devils, with fantastic animals, with monstrous flowers, and which are joined together by finely carved arches, to the blue sky by day, and to the black sky by night.

When I had reached the summit, I said to the monk who accompanied me: "Father, how happy you must be here!" And he replied: "It is very windy, Monsieur;" and so we began to talk while watching the rising tide, which ran over the sand and covered it with a steel cuirass.

And then the monk told me stories, all the old stories belonging to the place, legends, nothing but legends.

One of them struck me forcibly. The country people, those belonging to the Mornet, declare that at night one can hear talking going on in the sand, and then that one hears two goats bleat, one with a strong, the other with a weak voice. Incredulous people declare that it is nothing but the cry of the sea birds, which occasionally resembles bleatings, and occasionally human lamentations; but belated fishermen swear that they have met an old shepherd, whose head, which is covered by his cloak, they can never see, wandering on the downs, between two tides, round the little town placed so far out of the world, and who is guiding and walking before them, a he-goat with a man's face, and a she-goat with a woman's face, and both of them with white hair; and talking incessantly, quarreling in a strange language, and then suddenly ceasing to talk in order to bleat with all their might.

"Do you believe it?" I asked the monk. "I scarcely know," he replied, and I continued: "If there are other beings besides ourselves on this earth, how comes it that we have not known it for so long a time, or why have you not seen them? How is it that I have not seen them?" He replied: "Do we see the hundred thousandth part of what exists? Look here; there is the wind, which is the strongest force in nature, which knocks down men, and blows down buildings, uproots trees, raises the sea into mountains of water, destroys cliffs and casts great ships onto the breakers; the wind which kills, which whistles, which sighs, which roars—have you ever seen it, and can you see it? It exists for all that, however."

I was silent before this simple reasoning. That man was a philosopher, or perhaps a fool; I could not say which exactly, so I held my tongue. What he had said, had often been in my own thoughts.

July 3d. I have slept badly; certainly there is some feverish influence here, for my coachman is suffering in the same way as I am. When I went back home yesterday, I noticed his singular paleness, and I asked him: "What is the matter with you, Jean?"

"The matter is that I never get any rest, and my nights devour my days. Since your departure, monsieur, there has been a spell over me."

However, the other servants are all well, but I am very frightened of having another attack, myself.

July 4th. I am decidedly taken again; for my old nightmares have returned. Last night I felt somebody leaning on me who was sucking my life from between my lips with his mouth. Yes, he was sucking it out of my neck, like a leech would have done. Then he got up, satiated, and I woke up, so beaten, crushed and annihilated that I could not move. If this continues for a few days, I shall certainly go away again.

July 5th. Have I lost my reason? What has happened, what I saw last night, is so strange, that my head wanders when I think of it!

As I do now every evening, I had locked my door, and then, being thirsty, I drank half a glass of water, and I accidentally noticed that the water bottle was full up to the cut-glass stopper.

Then I went to bed and fell into one of my terrible sleeps, from which I was aroused in about two hours by a still more terrible shock.

Picture to yourself a sleeping man who is being murdered and who wakes up with a knife in his chest, and who is rattling in his throat, covered with blood, and who can no longer breathe, and is going to die, and does not understand anything at all about it—there it is.

Having recovered my senses, I was thirsty again, so I lit a candle and went to the table on which my water bottle was. I lifted it up and tilted it over my glass, but nothing came out. It was empty! It was completely empty! At first I could not understand it at all, and then suddenly I was seized by such a terrible feeling that I had to sit down, or rather I fell into a chair! Then I sprang up with a bound to look about me, and then I sat down again, overcome by astonishment and fear, in front of the transparent crystal bottle! I looked at it with fixed eyes, trying to conjecture, and my hands trembled! Somebody had drunk the water, but who? I? I without any doubt. It could surely only be I? In that case I was a somnambulist, I lived, without knowing it, that double mysterious life which makes us doubt whether there are not two beings in us, or whether a strange, unknowable and invisible being does not at such moments, when our soul is in a state of torpor, animate our captive body which obeys this other being, as it does us ourselves, and more than it does ourselves.

Oh! Who will understand my horrible agony? Who will understand the emotion of a man who is sound in mind, wide awake, full of sound sense, and who looks in horror at the remains of a little water that has disappeared while he was asleep, through the glass of a water bottle? And I remained there until it was daylight, without venturing to go to bed again.

July 6th. I am going mad. Again all the contents of my water bottle have been drunk during the night—or rather, I have drunk it! But is it I? Is it I? Who could it be? Who? Oh! God! Am I going mad? Who will save me?

July 10th. I have just been through some surprising ordeals. Decidedly I am mad! And yet!—

On July 6th, before going to bed, I put some wine, milk, water, bread and strawberries on my table. Somebody drank—I drank—all the water and a little of the milk, but neither the wine, bread nor the strawberries were touched.

On the seventh of July I renewed the same experiment, with the same results, and on July 8th, I left out the water and the milk and nothing was touched.

Lastly, on July 9th I put only water and milk on my table, taking care to wrap up the bottles in white muslin and to tie down the stoppers. Then I rubbed my lips, my beard and my hands with pencil lead, and went to bed.

Irresistible sleep seized me, which was soon followed by a terrible awakening. I had not moved, and my sheets were not marked. I rushed to the table. The muslin round the bottles remained intact; I undid the string, trembling with fear. All the water had been drunk, and so had the milk! Ah! Great God!—

I must start for Paris immediately.

July 12th. Paris. I must have lost my head during the last few days! I must be the plaything of my enervated imagination, unless I am really a somnambulist, or that I have been brought under the power of one of those influences which have been proved to exist, but which have hitherto been inexplicable, which are called suggestions. In any case, my mental state bordered on madness, and twenty-four hours of Paris sufficed to restore me to my equilibrium.

Yesterday after doing some business and paying some visits which instilled fresh and invigorating mental air into me, I wound up my evening at the *Théâtre Français*. A play by Alexandre Dumas the Younger was being acted, and his active and powerful mind completed my cure. Certainly solitude is dangerous for active minds. We require men who can think and can talk, around us. When we are alone for a long time we people space with phantoms.

I returned along the boulevards to my hotel in excellent spirits. Amid the jostling of the crowd I thought, not without irony, of my terrors and surmises of the previous week, because I believed, yes, I believed, that an invisible being lived beneath my roof. How weak our head is, and how quickly it is terrified and goes astray, as soon as we are struck by a small, incomprehensible fact.

Instead of concluding with these simple words: "I do not understand because the cause escapes me," we immediately imagine terrible mysteries and supernatural powers.

July 14th. Fête of the Republic. I walked through the streets, and the crackers and flags amused me like a child. Still it is very foolish to be merry on a fixed date, by a Government decree. The populace is an imbecile flock of sheep, now steadily patient, and now in ferocious revolt. Say to it: "Amuse yourself," and it amuses itself. Say to it: "Go and fight with your neighbor," and it goes and fights. Say to it: "Vote for the Emperor," and it votes for the Emperor, and then say to it: "Vote for the Republic," and it votes for the Republic.

Those who direct it are also stupid; but instead of obeying men they obey principles, which can only be stupid, sterile, and false, for the very reason that they are principles, that is to say, ideas which are considered as certain and unchangeable, in this world where one is certain of nothing, since light is an illusion and noise is an illusion.

July 16th. I saw some things yesterday that troubled me very much.

I was dining at my cousin's Madame Sablé, whose husband is colonel of the 76th Chasseurs at Limoges. There were two young women there, one of whom had married a medical man, Dr. Parent, who devotes himself a great deal to nervous diseases and the extraordinary manifestations to which at this moment experiments in hypnotism and suggestion give rise.

He related to us at some length, the enormous results obtained by English scientists and the doctors of the medical school at Nancy, and the facts which he adduced appeared to me so strange, that I declared that I was altogether incredulous.

"We are," he declared, "on the point of discovering one of the most important secrets of nature, I mean to say, one of its most important secrets on this earth, for there are certainly some which are of a different kind of importance up in the stars, yonder. Ever since man has thought, since he has been able to express and write down his thoughts, he has felt himself close to a mystery which is impenetrable to his coarse and imperfect senses, and he endeavors to supplement the want of power of his organs by the efforts of his intellect. As long as that intellect still remained in its elementary stage, this intercourse with invisible spirits assumed forms whch were commonplace though terrifying. Thence sprang the popular belief in the supernatural, the legends of wandering spirits, of fairies, of gnomes, ghosts, I might even say the legend of God, for our conceptions of the workman-creator, from whatever religion they may have come down to us, are certainly the most mediocre, the stupidest and the most unacceptable inventions that ever sprang from the frightened brain of any human creatures. Nothing is truer than what Voltaire says: 'God made man in His own image, but man has certainly paid Him back again.'

"But for rather more than a century, men seem to have had a presentiment of something new. Mesmer and some others have put us on an unexpected track, and especially within the last two or three years, we have arrived at really surprising results."

My cousin, who is also very incredulous, smiled, and Dr. Parent said to her: "Would you like me to try and send you to sleep, Madame?"

"Yes, certainly."

She sat down in an easy-chair, and he began to look at her fixedly, so as to fascinate her. I suddenly felt myself somewhat uncomfortable, with a beating heart and a choking feeling in my throat. I saw that Madame Sablé's eyes were growing heavy, her mouth twitched and her bosom heaved, and at the end of ten minutes she was asleep.

"Stand behind her," the doctor said to me, and so I took a seat behind her. He put a visiting card into her hands, and said to her: "This is a looking-glass; what do you see in it?" And she replied: "I see my cousin." "What is he doing?" "He is twisting his mustache." "And now?" "He is taking a photograph out of his pocket." "Whose photograph is it?" "His own."

That was true, and that photograph had been given me that same evening at the hotel.

"What is his attitude in this portrait?" "He is standing up with his hat in his hand."

So she saw on that card, on that piece of white paste-board, as if she had seen it in a looking-glass. The young women were frightened, and exclaimed:

"That is quite enough! Quite, quite enough!"

But the doctor said to her authoritatively: "You will get up at eight o'clock to-morrow morning; then you will go and call on your cousin at his hotel and ask him to lend you five thousand francs which your husband demands of you, and which he will ask for when he sets out on his coming journey."

Then he woke her up.

On returning to my hotel, I thought over this curious *séance* and I was assailed by doubts, not as to my cousin's absolute and undoubted good faith, for I had known her as well as if she had been my own sister ever since she was a child, but as to a possible trick on the doctor's part. Had not he, perhaps, kept a glass hidden in his hand, which he showed to the young woman in her sleep, at the same time as he did the card? Professional conjurers do things which are just as singular.

So I went home and to bed, and this morning, at about half-past eight, I was awakened by my footman, who said to me: "Madame Sablé has asked to see you immediately, Monsieur," so I dressed hastily and went to her.

She sat down in some agitation, with her eyes on the floor, and without raising her veil she said to me: "My dear cousin, I am going to ask a great favor of you." "What is it, cousin?" "I do not like to tell you, and yet I must. I am in absolute want of five thousand francs." "What, you?" "Yes, I, or rather my husband, who has asked me to procure them for him."

I was so stupefied that I stammered out my answers. I asked myself whether she had not really been making fun of me with Doctor Parent, if it were not merely a very well-acted farce which had been got up beforehand. On looking at her attentively, however, my doubts disappeared. She was trembling with grief, so painful was this step to her, and I was sure that her throat was full of sobs.

I knew that she was very rich and so I continued: "What! Has not your husband five thousand francs at his disposal! Come, think. Are you sure that he commissioned you to ask me for them?"

She hesitated for a few seconds, as if she were making a great effort to search her memory, and then she replied: "Yes ... yes, I am quite sure of it."

"He has written to you?"

She hesitated again and reflected, and I guessed the torture of her thoughts. She did not know. She only knew that she was to borrow five thousand francs of me for her husband. So she told a lie. "Yes, he has written to me." "When, pray? You did not mention it to me yesterday." "I received his letter this morning." "Can you show it me?" "No; no ... no ... it contained private matters ... things too personal to ourselves.... I burnt it." "So your husband runs into debt?"

She hesitated again, and then murmured: "I do not know."

Thereupon I said bluntly: "I have not five thousand francs at my disposal at this moment, my dear cousin."

She uttered a kind of cry as if she were in pain and said: "Oh! oh! I beseech you, I beseech you to get them for me ..."

She got excited and clasped her hands as if she were praying to me! I heard her voice change its tone; she wept and stammered, harassed and dominated by the irresistible order that she had received.

"Oh! oh! I beg you to ... if you knew what I am suffering ... I want them to-day."

I had pity on her: "You shall have them by and by, I swear to you." "Oh! thank you! thank you! How kind you are!" I continued: "Do you remember what took place at your house last night?" "Yes." "Do you remember that Doctor Parent sent you to sleep?" "Yes." "Oh! Very well then; he ordered you to come to me this morning to borrow five thousand francs, and at this moment you are obeying that suggestion."

She considered for a few moments, and then replied: "But as it is my husband who wants them ..."

For a whole hour I tried to convince her, but could not

succeed, and when she had gone I went to the doctor. He was just going out, and he listened to me with a smile, and said: "Do you believe now?" "Yes, I cannot help it." "Let us go to your cousin's."

She was already dozing on a couch, overcome with fatigue. The doctor felt her pulse, looked at her for some time with one hand raised toward her eyes which she closed by degrees under the irresistible power of this magnetic influence, and when she was asleep, he said:

"Your husband does not require the five thousand francs any longer! You must, therefore, forget that you asked your cousin to tend them to you, and, if he speaks to you about it, you will not understand him."

Then he woke her up, and I took out a pocketbook and said: "Here is what you asked me for this morning, my dear cousin." But she was so surprised that I did not venture to persist; nevertheless, I tried to recall the circumstance to her, but she denied it vigorously, thought that I was making fun of her, and in the end very nearly lost her temper.

☙

There! I have just come back, and I have not been able to eat any lunch, for this experiment has altogether upset me.

July 19th. Many people to whom I have told the adventure have laughed at me. I no longer know what to think. The wise man says: Perhaps?

July 21st. I dined at Bougival, and then I spent the evening at a boatmen's ball. Decidedly everything depends on place and surroundings. It would be the height of folly to believe in the supernatural on the île de la Grenouillière[1] ... but on the top of Mont Saint-Michel? and in India? We are terribly under the influence of our surroundings. I shall return home next week.

---

1. Frog-island.

July 30th. I came back to my own house yesterday. Everything is going on well.

August 2d. Nothing fresh; it is splendid weather, and I spend my days in watching the Seine flow past.

August 4th. Quarrels among my servants. They declare that the glasses are broken in the cupboards at night. The footman accuses the cook, who accuses the needlewoman, who accuses the other two. Who is the culprit? A clever person, to be able to tell.

August 6th. This time I am not mad. I have seen ... I have seen ... I have seen...! I can doubt no longer I have seen it...!

I was walking at two o'clock among my rose trees, in the full sunlight ... in the walk bordered by autumn roses which are beginning to fall. As I stopped to look at a *Géant de Bataille*, which had three splendid blooms, I distinctly saw the stalk of one of the roses bend, close to me, as if an invisible hand had bent it, and then break, as if that hand had picked it! Then the flower raised itself, following the curve which a hand would have described in carrying it toward a mouth, and it remained suspended in the transparent air, all alone and motionless, a terrible red spot, three yards from my eyes. In desperation I rushed at it to take it! I found nothing; it had disappeared. Then I was seized with furious rage against myself, for it is not allowable for a reasonable and serious man to have such hallucinations.

But was it a hallucination? I turned round to look for the stalk, and I found it immediately under the bush, freshly broken, between two other roses which remained on the branch, and I returned home then, with a much disturbed mind; for I am certain now, as certain as I am of the alternation of day and night, that there exists close to me an invisible being that lives on milk and on water, which can touch objects, take them and change their places; which is, consequently, endowed with a material nature, although it is imperceptible to our senses, and which lives as I do, under my roof....

47

August 7th. I slept tranquilly. He drank the water out of my decanter, but did not disturb my sleep.

I ask myself whether I am mad. As I was walking just now in the sun by the riverside, doubts as to my own sanity arose in me; not vague doubts such as I have had hitherto, but precise and absolute doubts. I have seen mad people, and I have known some who have been quite intelligent, lucid, even clear-sighted in every concern of life, except on one point. They spoke clearly, readily, profoundly on everything, when suddenly their thoughts struck upon the breakers of their madness and broke to pieces there, and were dispersed and foundered in that furious and terrible sea, full of bounding waves, fogs and squalls, which is called *madness*.

I certainly should think that I was mad, absolutely mad, if I were not conscious, did not perfectly know my state, if I did fathom it by analyzing it with the most complete lucidity. I should, in fact, be a reasonable man who was laboring under a hallucination. Some unknown disturbance must have been excited in my brain, one of those disturbances which physiologists of the present day try to note and to fix precisely, and that disturbance must have caused a profound gulf in my mind and in the order and logic of my ideas. Similar phenomena occur in the dreams which lead us through the most unlikely phantasmagoria, without causing us any surprise, because our verifying apparatus and our sense of control has gone to sleep, while our imaginative faculty wakes and works. Is it not possible that one of the imperceptible keys of the cerebral finger-board has been paralyzed in me? Some men lose the recollection of proper names, or of verbs or of numbers or merely of dates, in consequence of an accident. The localization of all the particles of thought has been proved nowadays; what then would there be surprising in the fact that my faculty of controlling the unreality of certain hallucinations should be destroyed for the time being!

I thought of all this as I walked by the side of the water. The sun was shining brightly on the river and made earth delightful, while it filled my looks with love for life, for the swallows, whose agility is always, delightful in my eyes, for the plants by the riverside, whose rustling is a pleasure to my ears.

By degrees, however, an inexplicable feeling of discomfort seized me. It seemed to me as if some unknown force were numbing and stopping me, were preventing me from going farther and were calling me back. I felt that painful wish to return which oppresses you when you have left a beloved invalid at home, and when you are seized by a presentiment that he is worse. I, therefore, returned in spite of myself, feeling certain that I should find some bad news awaiting me, a letter or a telegram. There was nothing, however, and I was more surprised and uneasy than if I had had another fantastic vision.

August 8th. I spent a terrible evening yesterday. He does not show himself any more, but I feel that he is near me, watching me, looking at me, penetrating me, dominating me and more redoubtable when he hides himself thus, than if he were to manifest his constant and invisible presence by supernatural phenomena. However, I slept.

August 9th. Nothing, but I am afraid.

August 10th. Nothing; what will happen to-morrow?

August 11th. Still nothing ; I cannot stop at home with this fear hanging over me and these thoughts in my mind; I shall go away.

August 12th. Ten o'clock at night. All day long I have been trying to get away, and have not been able. I wished to accomplish this simple and easy act of liberty—go out—get into my carriage in order to go to Rouen—and I have not been able to do it. What is the reason?

August 13th. When one is attacked by certain maladies, all the springs of our physical being appear to be broken, all our energies destroyed, all our muscles relaxed, our bones to have become as soft as our flesh, and our blood as liquid as water. I am experiencing that in my moral being in a strange and distressing manner. I have no longer any strength, any courage, any self-control, nor even any power to set my own will in motion. I have no power left to will anything, but some one does it for me and I obey.

August 14th. I am lost! Somebody possesses my soul and governs it! Somebody orders all my acts, all my movements, all my thoughts. I am no longer anything in myself, nothing except an enslaved and terrified spectator of all the things which I do. I wish to go out; I cannot. He does not wish to, and so I remain, trembling and distracted in the armchair in which he keeps me sitting. I merely wish to get up and to rouse myself, so as to think that I am still master of myself: I cannot! I am riveted to my chair, and my chair adheres to the ground in such a manner that no force could move us.

Then suddenly, I must, I must go to the bottom of my garden to pick some strawberries and eat them, and I go there. I pick the strawberries and I eat them! Oh! my God! my God! Is there a God? If there be one, deliver me! save me! succor me! Pardon! Pity! Mercy! Save me! Oh! what sufferings! what torture! what horror!

August 15th. Certainly this is the way in which my poor cousin was possessed and swayed, when she came to borrow five thousand francs of me. She was under the power of a strange will which had entered into her, like another soul, like another parasitic and ruling soul. Is the world coming to an end?

But who is he, this invisible being that rules me? This unknowable being, this rover of a supernatural race?

Invisible beings exist, then! How is it then that since the beginning of the world they have never manifested themselves in such a manner precisely as they do to me? I have never read anything which resembles what goes on in my house. Oh! If I could only leave it, if I could only go away and flee, so as never to return, I should be saved; but I cannot.

August 16th. I managed to escape to-day for two hours, like a prisoner who finds the door of his dungeon accidentally open. I suddenly felt that I was free and that he was far away, and so I gave orders to put the horses in as quickly as possible, and I drove to Rouen. Oh! How delightful to be able to say to a man who obeyed you: "Go to Rouen!"

I made him pull up before the library, and I begged them to lend me Dr. Herrmann Herestauss's treatise on the unknown inhabitants of the ancient and modern world.

Then, as I was getting into my carriage, I intended to say: "To the railway station!" but instead of this I shouted—I did not say, but I shouted—in such a loud voice that all the passers-by turned round: "Home!" and I fell back onto the cushion of my carriage, overcome by mental agony. He had found me out and regained possession of me.

August 17th. Oh! What a night! what a night! And yet it seems to me that I ought to rejoice. I read until one o'clock in the morning! Herestauss, Doctor of Philosophy and Theogony, wrote the history and the manifestation of all those invisible beings which hover around man, or of whom he dreams. He describes their origin, their domains, their power; but none of them resembles the one which haunts me. One might say that man, ever since he has thought, has had a foreboding of, and feared a new being, stronger than himself, his successor in this world, and that, feeling him near, and not being able to foretell the nature of that master, he has, in his terror, created the whole race of hidden beings, of vague phantoms born of fear.

Having, therefore, read until one o'clock in the morning, I went and sat down at the open window, in order to cool my forehead and my thoughts, in the calm night air. It was very pleasant and warm! How I should have enjoyed such a night formerly!

There was no moon, but the stars darted out their rays in the dark heavens. Who inhabits those worlds? What forms, what living beings, what animals are there yonder? What do those who are thinkers in those distant worlds know more than we do? What can they do more than we can? What do they see which we do not know? Will not one of them, some day or other, traversing space, appear on our earth to conquer it, just as the Norsemen formerly crossed the sea in order to subjugate nations more feeble than themselves?

We are so weak, so unarmed, so ignorant, so small, we who live on this particle of mud which turns round in a drop of water.

I fell asleep, dreaming thus in the cool night air, and then, having slept for about three quarters of an hour, I opened my eyes without moving, awakened by I know not what confused and strange sensation. At first I saw nothing, and then suddenly it appeared to me as if a page of a book which had remained open on my table, turned over of its own accord. Not a breath of air had come in at my window, and I was surprised and waited. In about four minutes, I saw, I saw, yes I saw with my own eyes another page lift itself up and fall down on the others, as if a finger had turned it over. My armchair was empty, appeared empty, but I knew that he was there, he, and sitting in my place, and that he was reading.

With a furious bound, the bound of an enraged wild beast that wishes to disembowel its tamer, I crossed my room to seize him, to strangle him, to kill him…! But before I could reach it, my chair fell over as if somebody had run away from me …my table rocked, my lamp fell and went out, and my window closed as if some thief had been surprised and had fled out into the night, shutting it behind him.

So he had run away: he had been afraid; he, afraid of me!

So … so … to-morrow … or later some day or other … I should be able to hold him in my clutches and crush him against the ground! Do not dogs occasionally bite and strangle their masters?

August 18th. I have been thinking the whole day long. Oh! yes, I will obey him, follow his impulses, fulfill all his wishes, show myself humble, submissive, a coward. He is the stronger; but an hour will come …

August 19th. I know … I know … I know all. I have just read the following in the *Revue du Monde Scientifique*: "A curious piece of news comes to us from Rio de Janeiro. Madness, an epidemic of madness, which may be compared to that contagious madness which attacked the people of Europe in the Middle Ages, is at this moment raging in the Province of San-Paulo. The frightened inhabitants are leaving their houses, deserting their villages, abandoning their land, saying that they are pursued, possessed, governed like human cattle by invisible, though tangible beings, a species of vampire, which feed on their life while they are asleep, and who, besides, drink water and milk without appearing to touch any other nourishment.

"Professor Dom Pedro Henriques, accompanied by several medical savants, has gone to the Province of San-Paulo, in order to study the origin and the manifestations of this surprising madness on the spot, and to propose such measures to the Emperor as may appear to him to be most fitted to restore the mad population to reason."

Ah! Ah! I remember now that fine Brazilian three-master which passed in front of my windows as it was going up the Seine, on the 8th of last May! I thought it looked so pretty, so white and bright! That Being was on board of her, coming from there, where its race sprang from. And it saw me! It saw my house which was also white, and it sprang from the ship onto the land. Oh! Good heavens!

Now I know, I can divine. The reign of man is over, and he has come. He whom disquieted priests exorcised, whom sorcerers evoked on dark nights, without yet seeing him appear, to whom the presentiments of the transient masters of the world lent all the monstrous or graceful forms of gnomes, spirits, genii, fairies, and familiar spirits. After the coarse conceptions of primitive fear, more clearsighted men foresaw it more clearly. Mesmer divined him, and ten years ago physicians accurately discovered the nature of his power, even before he exercised it himself. They played with that weapon of their new Lord, the sway of a mysterious will over the human soul, which had become enslaved. They called it magnetism, hypnotism, suggestion ... what do I know? I have seen them amusing themselves like impudent children with this horrible power! Woe to us! Woe to man! He has come, the ... the ... what does he call himself ... the ... I fancy that he is shouting out his name to me and I do not hear him ... the ... yes ... he is shouting it out ... I am listening ... I cannot ... repeat ... it ... Horla ... I have heard ... the Horla ... it is he ... the Horla ... he has come...!

Ah! the vulture has eaten the pigeon, the wolf has eaten the lamb; the lion has devoured the buffalo with sharp horns; man has killed the lion with an arrow, with a sword, with gunpowder; but the Horla will make of man what we have made of the horse and of the ox: his chattel, his slave and his food, by the mere power of his will. Woe to us!

But, nevertheless, the animal sometimes revolts and kills the man who has subjugated it,... I should also like ... I shall be able to ... but I must know him, touch him, see him! Learned men say that beasts' eyes, as they differ from ours, do not distinguish like ours do ... And my eye cannot distinguish this newcomer who is oppressing me.

Why? Oh! Now I remember the words of the monk at Mont Saint-Michel: "Can we see the hundred-thousandth part of what exists? Look here; there is the wind which is the strongest force in nature, which knocks men, and blows down buildings, uproots

54

trees, raises the sea into mountains of water, destroys cliffs and casts great ships onto the breakers; the wind which kills, which whistles, which sighs, which roars—have you ever seen it, and can you see it? It exists for all that, however!"

And I went on thinking: my eyes are so weak, so imperfect, that they do not even distinguish hard bodies, if they are as transparent as glass…! If a glass without tinfoil behind it were to bar my way, I should run into it, just as a bird which has flown into a room breaks its head against the window panes. A thousand things, moreover, deceive him and lead him astray. How should it then be surprising that he cannot perceive a fresh body which is traversed by the light?

A new being! Why not? It was assuredly bound to come! Why should we be the last? We do not distinguish it, like all the others created before us. The reason is, that its nature is more perfect, its body finer and more finished than ours, that ours is so weak, so awkwardly conceived, encumbered with organs that are always tired, always on the strain like locks that are too complicated, which lives like a plant and like a beast, nourishing itself with difficulty on air, herbs and flesh, an animal machine which is a prey to maladies, to malformations, to decay; broken-winded, badly regulated, simple and eccentric, ingeniously badly made, a coarse and a delicate work, the outline of a being which might become intelligent and grand.

We are only a few, so few in this world, from the oyster up to man. Why should there not be one more, when once that period is accomplished which separates the successive apparitions from all the different species?

Why not one more? Why not, also, other trees with immense, splendid flowers, perfuming whole regions? Why not other elements besides fire, air, earth and water? There are four, only four, those nursing fathers of various beings! What a pity! Why are they not forty, four hundred, four thousand! How poor everything

THE HORLA

is, how mean and wretched! grudgingly given, dryly invented, clumsily made! Ah! the elephant and the hippopotamus, what grace! And the camel, what elegance!

But, the butterfly you will say, a flying flower! I dream of one that should be as large as a hundred worlds, with wings whose shape, beauty, colors, and motion I cannot even express. But I see it … it flutters from star to star, refreshing them and perfuming them with the light and harmonious breath of its flight…! And the people up there look at it as it passes in an ecstasy of delight…!

৩

What is the matter with me? It is he, the Horla who haunts me, and who makes me think of these foolish things! He is within me, he is becoming my soul; I shall kill him!

August 19th. I shall kill him. I have seen him! Yesterday I sat down at my table and pretended to write very assiduously. I knew quite well that he would come prowling round me, quite close to me, so close that I might perhaps be able to touch him, to seize him. And then! … then I should have the strength of desperation; I should have my hands, my knees, my chest, my forehead, my teeth to strangle him, to crush him, to bite him, to tear him to pieces. And I watched for him with all my overexcited organs.

I had lighted my two lamps and the eight wax candles on my mantelpiece, as if by this light I could have discovered him.

My bed, my old oak bed with its columns, was opposite to me; on my right was the fireplace; on my left the door which was carefully closed, after I had left it open for some time, in order to attract him; behind me was a very high wardrobe with a looking-glass in it, which served me to make my toilet every day, and in which I was in the habit of looking at myself from head to foot every time I passed it.

So I pretended to be writing in order to deceive him, for he

56

also was watching me, and suddenly I felt, I was certain that he was reading over my shoulder, that he was there, almost touching my ear.

I got up so quickly, with my hands extended, that I almost fell. Eh! well...? It was as bright as at midday, but I did not see myself in the glass! ... It was empty, clear, profound, full of light! But my figure was not reflected in it ... and I, I was opposite to it! I saw the large, clear glass from top to bottom, and I looked at it with unsteady eyes; and I did not dare to advance; I did not venture to make a movement, nevertheless, feeling perfectly that he was there, but that he would escape me again, he whose imperceptible body had absorbed my reflection.

How frightened I was! And then suddenly I began to see myself through a mist in the depths of the looking-glass, in a mist as it were through a sheet of water; and it seemed to me as if this water were flowing slowly from left to right, and making my figure clearer every moment. It was like the end of an eclipse. Whatever it was that hid me, did not appear to possess any clearly defined outlines, but a sort of opaque transparency, which gradually grew clearer.

At last I was able to distinguish myself completely, as I do every day when I look at myself. I had seen it! And the horror of it remained with me and makes me shudder even now.

August 20th. How could I kill it, as I could not get hold of it? Poison? But it would see me mix it with the water; and then, would our poisons have any effect on its impalpable body? No ... no ... no doubt about the matter ... Then? ... then...?

August 21st. I sent for a blacksmith from Rouen, and ordered iron shutters of him for my room, such as some private hotels in Paris have on the ground floor, for fear of thieves, and he is going to make me a similar door as well. I have made myself out as a coward, but I do not care about that!

September 10th. Rouen, Hotel Continental. It is done...; it is done … but is he dead? My mind is thoroughly upset by what I have seen.

Well, then, yesterday the locksmith having put on the iron shutters and door I left everything open until midnight, although it was getting cold.

Suddenly I felt that he was there, and joy, mad joy, took possession of me. I got up softly, and I walked to the right and left for some time, so that he might not guess anything; then I took off my boots and put on my slippers carelessly; then I fastened the iron shutters and going back to the door quickly I double-locked it with a padlock, putting the key into my pocket.

Suddenly I noticed that he was moving restlessly round me, that in his turn he was frightened and was ordering me to let him out. I nearly yielded, though I did not yet, but putting my back to the door I half opened it, just enough to allow me to go out backward, and as I am very tall, my head touched the lintel. I was sure that he had not been able to escape, and I shut him up quite alone, quite alone. What happiness! I had him fast. Then I ran downstairs; in the drawing-room, which was under my bedroom, I took the two lamps and I poured all the oil onto the carpet, the furniture, everywhere; then I set fire to it and made my escape, after having carefully double-locked the door.

I went and hid myself at the bottom of the garden in a clump of laurel bushes. How long it was! how long it was! Everything was dark, silent, motionless, not a breath of air and not a star, but heavy banks of clouds which one could not see, but which weighed, oh! so heavily on my soul.

I looked at my house and waited. How long it was! I already began to think that the fire had gone out of its own accord, or that he had extinguished it, when one of the lower windows gave way under the violence of the flames, and a long, soft, caressing sheet of red flame mounted up the white wall and kissed it as high as the roof. The light fell onto the trees, the branches, and the leaves, and a shiver of fear pervaded them also! The birds awoke; a dog began to howl, and it seemed to me as if the day were breaking! Almost immediately two other windows flew into fragments, and I saw that the whole of the lower part of my house was nothing but a terrible furnace. But a cry, a horrible, shrill, heartrending cry, a woman's cry, sounded through the night, and two garret windows were opened! I had forgotten the servants! I saw the terrorstruck faces, and their frantically waving arms…!

Then, overwhelmed with horror, I set off to run to the village, shouting: "Help! help! fire! fire!" I met some people who were already coming onto the scene, and I went back with them to see!

By this time the house was nothing but a horrible and magnificent funeral pile, a monstrous funeral pile which lit up the whole country, a funeral pile where men were burning, and where he was burning also, He, He, my prisoner, that new Being, the new master, the Horla!

Suddenly the whole roof fell in between the walls, and a volcano of flames darted up to the sky. Through all the windows which opened onto that furnace I saw the flames darting, and I thought that he was there, in that kiln, dead.

Dead? perhaps? … His body? Was not his body, which was transparent, indestructible by such means as would kill ours? If he was not dead? … Perhaps time alone has power over that Invisible and Redoubtable Being. Why this transparent, unrecognizable body, this body belonging to a spirit, if it also had to fear ills, infirmities and premature destruction?

Premature destruction? All human terror springs from that! After man, the Horla. After him who can die every day, at any hour, at any moment, by any accident, he came who was only to die at his own proper hour and minute, because he had touched the limits of his existence!

No … no … without any doubt … he is not dead. Then … then … I suppose I must kill myself!

THE MOON POOL

By A. Merritt

Lovecraft did not mention A. Merritt's "The Moon Pool" in "Supernatural Horror in Literature," since he excluded works of "popular" weird fiction from that treatise; but he did list the story among his "Favorite Weird Stories." This is a sufficient indication of Lovecraft's high regard for the work, as is the fact that he preserved the issue of the *All-Story Weekly* (June 22, 1918) in which the tale originally appeared. Merritt later revised the story as the first section of the novel *The Moon Pool* (1919); of this version Lovecraft stated in a letter to August Derleth: "I read that in the *All-Story* nearly a decade ago, & admired the first part (originally a separate complete novel) more than any other popular weird tale (i.e., of cheap magazine grade) I have ever read. It has the real thing in the way of atmosphere." (April 8, 1927; *ES* 81–82). The story could well have influenced "The Call of Cthulhu," especially in its citation of a "moon door" that seems similar to the large door that opens when sunken R'lyeh rises from the depths of the Pacific and causes Cthulhu to emerge momentarily.

Merritt (1882–1943) was a celebrated writer of fantasy, science fiction, and weird fiction for the Munsey pulps, but Lovecraft believed that Merritt had commercialized his work to gain popular renown. He had dinner with Merritt in New York on January 8, 1934.

1. The Throckmartin Mystery

I am breaking a long silence to clear the name of Dr. David Throckmartin and to lift the shadow of scandal from that of his wife and of Dr. Charles Stanton, his assistant. That I have not found the courage to do so before, all men who are jealous of their scientific reputations will understand when they have read the facts entrusted to me alone.

I shall first recapitulate what has actually been known of the Throckmartin expedition to the island of Ponape in the Carolines—the Throckmartin Mystery, as it is called.

Dr. Throckmartin set forth, you will recall, to make some observations of Nan-Matal, that extraordinary group of island ruins, remains of a high and prehistoric civilization, that are clustered along the vast shore of Ponape. With him went his wife to whom he had been wedded less than half a year. The daughter of Professor Frazier-Smith, she was as deeply interested and almost as well informed as he upon these relics of a vanished race that titanically strew certain islands of the Pacific and form the basis for the theory of a submerged Pacific continent.

Mrs. Throckmartin, it will be recalled, was much younger, fifteen years at least, than her husband. Dr. Charles Stanton, who accompanied them as Dr. Throckmartin's assistant, was about her age. These three and a Swedish woman, Thora Helversen, who had been Edith Throckmartin's nurse in babyhood and who was entirely devoted to her, made up the expedition.

Dr. Throckmartin planned to spend a year among the ruins, not only of Ponape, but of Lele—the twin centers of that colossal riddle of humanity whose answer has its roots in immeasurable antiquity; a weird flower of man-made civilization that blossomed ages before the seeds of Egypt were sown; of whose arts we know little and of whose science and secret knowledge of nature nothing.

He carried with him complete equipment for his work and gathered at Ponape a dozen or so natives for laborers. They went straight to Metalanim harbor and set up their camp on the island called Uschen-Tau in the group known as the Nan-Matal. You will remember that these islands are entirely uninhabited and are shunned by the people on the main island.

Three months later Dr. Throckmartin appeared at Port Mooresby, Papua. He came on a schooner manned by Solomon Islanders and commanded by a Chinese halfbreed captain. He reported that he was on his way to Melbourne for additional scientific equipment and whites to help him in his excavations, saying that the superstition of the natives made their aid negligible. He went immediately on board the steamer *Southern Queen* which was sailing that same morning. Three nights later he disappeared from the *Southern Queen* and it was officially reported that he had met death either by being swept overboard or by casting himself into the sea.

A relief-boat sent with the news to Ponape found the Throckmartin camp on the island Uschen-Tau and a smaller camp on the island called Nan-Tanach. All the equipment, clothing, supplies were intact. But of Mrs. Throckmartin, of Dr. Stanton, or of Thora Helversen they could find not a single trace!

The natives who had been employed by the archeologist were questioned. They said that the ruins were the abode of great spirits—*ani*—who were particularly powerful when the moon was at the full. On these nights all the islanders were doubly careful to give the ruins wide berth. Upon being employed, they had demanded leave from the day before full moon until it was on the wane and this had been granted them by Dr. Throckmartin. Thrice they had left the expedition alone on these nights. On their third return they had found the four white people gone and they "knew that the *ani* had eaten them." They were afraid and had fled.

That was all.

The Chinese half-caste was found and reluctantly testified at last that he had picked Dr. Throckmartin up from a small boat about fifty miles off Ponape. The scientist had seemed half mad, but he had given the seaman a large sum of money to bring him to Port Moresby and to say, if questioned, that he had boarded the boat at Ponape harbor.

That is all that has been known to anyone of the fate of the Throckmartin expedition.

Why, you will ask, do I break silence now; and how came I in possession of the facts I am about to set forth?

To the first I answer: I was at the Geographical Club recently and I overheard two members talking. They mentioned the name of Throckmartin and I became an eavesdropper. One said:

"Of course what probably happened was that Throckmartin killed them all. It's a dangerous thing for a man to marry a woman so much younger than himself and then throw her into the necessarily close company of exploration with a man as young and as agreeable as Stanton was. The inevitable happened, no doubt. Throckmartin discovered; avenged himself. Then followed remorse and suicide."

"Throckmartin didn't seem to be that kind," said the other thoughtfully.

"No, he didn't," agreed the first.

"Isn't there another story?" went on the second speaker. "Something about Mrs. Throckmartin running away with Stanton and taking the woman, Thora, with her? Somebody told me they had been recognized in Singapore recently."

"You can take your pick of the two stories," replied the other man. "It's one or the other, I suppose."

It was neither one nor the other of them. I know—and I will answer now the second question—because I was with Throckmartin when he—vanished. I know what he told me and I know what my own eyes saw. Incredible, abnormal, against all the known facts of our science as it was, I testify to it. And it is my intention, after this is published, to sail to Ponape, to go to the Nan-Matal and to the islet beneath whose frowning walls dwells the mystery that Throckmartin sought and found—and that at the last sought and found Throckmartin!

I will leave behind me a copy of the map of the islands that he gave me. Also his sketch of the great courtyard of Nan-Tanach, the location of the moon door, his indication of the probable location of the moon pool and the passage to it and his approximation of the position of the shining globes. If I do not return and there are any with enough belief, scientific curiosity and courage to follow, these will furnish a plain trail. I will now proceed straightforwardly with my narrative.

For six months I had been on the d'Entrecasteaux Islands gathering data for the concluding chapters of my book upon "Flora of the Volcanic Islands of the South Pacific." The day before, I had reached Port Moresby and had seen my specimens safely stored on board the *Southern Queen*. As I sat on the upper deck that morning I thought, with homesick mind, of the long leagues between me and Melbourne and the longer ones between Melbourne and New York.

It was one of Papua's yellow mornings, when she shows herself in her most somber, most baleful mood. The sky was a smoldering ocher. Over the island brooded a spirit sullen, implacable and alien; filled with the threat of latent, malefic forces waiting to be unleashed. It seemed an emanation from the untamed, sinister heart of Papua herself—sinister even when she smiles. And now and then, on the wind, came a breath from unexplored jungles, filled with unfamiliar odors, mysterious, and menacing.

It is on such mornings that Papua speaks to you of her immemorial ancientness and of her power. I am not unduly imaginative but it is a mood that makes me shrink—I mention it because it bears directly upon Dr. Throckmartin's fate. Nor is the mood Papua's alone. I have felt it in New Guinea, in Australia, in the Solomons and in the Carolines. But it is in Papua that it seems most articulate. It is as though she said: "I am the ancient of days; I have seen the earth in the throes of its shaping; I am the primeval; I have seen races born and die and, lo, in my breast are secrets that would blast you by the telling, you pale babes of a puling age. You and I ought not be in the same world; yet I am and I shall be! Never will you fathom me and you I hate though I tolerate! I tolerate—but how long?"

And then I seem to see a giant paw that reaches from Papua toward the outer world, stretching and sheathing monstrous claws.

All feel this mood of hers. Her own people have it woven in them, part of their web and woof; flashing into light unexpectedly like a soul from another universe; masking itself as swiftly.

I fought against Papua as every white man must on one of her yellow mornings. And as I fought I saw a tall figure come striding down the pier. Behind him came a KapaKapa boy swinging a new valise. There was something familiar about the tall man. As he reached the gangplank he looked up straight into my eyes, stared at me for a moment and waved his hand. It was Dr. Throckmartin!

Coincident with my recognition of him there came a shock of surprise that was definitely—unpleasant. It was Throckmartin—but there was something disturbingly different about him and the man I had known so well and had bidden farewell less than a year before. He was then, as you know, just turned forty, lithe, erect, muscular; the face of a student and of a seeker. His controlling expression was one of enthusiasm, of intellectual keenness, of—what shall I say—expectant search. His ever eagerly questioning brain had stamped itself upon his face.

I sought in my mind for an explanation of that which I had felt on the flash of his greeting. Hurrying down to the lower deck I found him with the purser. As I spoke he turned and held out to me an eager hand—and then I saw what the change was that had come over him!

He knew, of course, by my face the uncontrollable shock that my closer look had given me. His eyes filled and he turned briskly to the purser; then hurried off to his stateroom, leaving me standing, half dazed.

At the stair he half turned. "Oh, Goodwin," he said. "I'd like to see you later. Just now—there's something I must write before we start—" He went up swiftly.

"'E looks rather queer—eh?" said the purser. "Know 'im well, sir? Seems to 'ave given you quite a start, sir."

I made some reply and went slowly to my chair. I tried to analyze what it was that had disturbed me so; what profound change in Throckmartin that had so shaken me. Now it came to me. It was as though the man had suffered some terrific soul searing shock of rapture and horror combined; some soul cataclysm that in its climax had remolded his face deep from within, setting on it the seal of wedded joy and fear. As though indeed ecstasy supernal and terror infernal had once come to him hand in hand, taken possession of him, looked out of his eyes and, departing, left behind upon him ineradicably their shadow.

Alternately I looked out over the port and paced about the deck, striving to read the riddle; to banish it from my mind. And all the time still over Papua brooded its baleful spirit of ancient evil, unfathomable, not to be understood; nor had it lifted when the *Southern Queen* lifted anchor and steamed out into the gulf.

2. Down the Moon Path

I watched with relief the shores sink down behind us; welcomed the touch of the free sea wind. We seemed to be drawing away from something malefic; something that lurked within the island spell I have described, and the thought crept into my mind, spoke— whispered rather—from Throckmartin's face. I had hoped—and within the hope was an inexplicable shrinking, an unexpressed dread—that I would meet Throckmartin at lunch. He did not come down and I was sensible of a distinct relief within my disappointment. All that afternoon I lounged about uneasily but still he kept to his cabin. Nor did he appear at dinner.

Dusk and night fell swiftly. I was warm and went back to my deck-chair. The *Southern Queen* was rolling to a disquieting swell and I had the place to myself.

Over the heavens was a canopy of cloud, glowing faintly and testifying to the moon riding behind it. There was much phosphorescence. Now and then, before the ship and at the sides, arose those strange little swirls of mist that steam up from the Southern Ocean like the breath of sea monsters, whirl for a moment and disappear. I lighted a cigarette and tried once more to banish Throckmartin's face from my mind.

Suddenly the deck door opened and through it came Throckmartin himself. He paused uncertainly, looked up at the sky with a curiously eager, intent gaze, hesitated, then closed the door behind him.

"Throckmartin," I called. "Come sit with me. It's Goodwin."

Immediately he made his way to me, sitting beside me with a gasp of relief that I noted curiously. His hand touched mine and gripped it with tenseness that hurt. His hand was icelike. I puffed up my cigarette and by its glow scanned him closely. He was watching a large swirl of the mist that was passing before the ship. The phosphorescence beneath it illumined it with a fitful opalescence. I saw fear in his eyes. The swirl passed; he sighed; his grip relaxed and he sank back.

"Throckmartin," I said, wasting no time in preliminaries. "What's wrong? Can I help you?"

He was silent.

"Is your wife all right and what are you doing here when I heard you had gone to the Carolines for a year?" I went on.

I felt his body grow tense again. He did not speak for a moment and then:

"I'm going to Melbourne, Goodwin," he said. "I need a few things—need them urgently. And more men—white men." His voice was low; preoccupied. It was as though the brain that dictated the words did so perfunctorily, half impatiently; aloof, watching, strained to catch the first hint of approach of something dreaded.

"You are making progress then?" I asked. It was a banal question, put forth in a blind effort to claim his attention.

"Progress?" he repeated. "Progress—"

He stopped abruptly; rose from his chair, gazed intently toward the north. I followed his gaze. Far, far away the moon had broken through the clouds. Almost on the horizon, you could see the faint luminescence of it upon the quiet sea. The distant patch of light quivered and shook. The clouds thickened again and it was gone. The ship raced southward, swiftly.

Throckmartin dropped into his chair. He lighted a cigarette with a hand that trembled. The flash of the match fell on his face and I noted with a queer thrill of apprehension that its unfamiliar expression had deepened; become curiously intensified as though a faint acid had passed over it, etching its lines faintly deeper.

"It's the full moon tonight, isn't it?" he asked, palpably with studied inconsequence.

"The first night of full moon," I answered. He was silent again.

69

I sat silent too, waiting for him to make up his mind to speak. He turned to me as though he had made a sudden resolution.

"Goodwin," he said. "I do need help. If ever man needed it, I do. Goodwin—can you imagine yourself in another world, alien, unfamiliar, a world of terror, whose unknown joy is its greatest terror of all; you all alone there; a stranger! As such a man would need help, so I need—"

He paused abruptly and arose to his feet stiffly; the cigarette dropped from his fingers. I saw that the moon had again broken through the clouds, and this time much nearer. Not a mile away was the patch of light that it threw upon the waves. Back of it, to the rim of the sea was a lane of moonlight; it was a gleaming gigantic serpent racing over the rim of the world straight and surely toward the ship.

Throckmartin gazed at it as though turned to stone. He stiffened to it as a pointer does to a hidden covey. To me from him pulsed a thrill of terror—but terror tinged with an unfamiliar, an infernal joy. It came to me and passed away—leaving me trembling with its shock of bitter sweet.

He bent forward, all his soul in his eyes. The moon path swept closer, closer still. It was now less than half a mile away. From it the ship fled; almost it came to me, as though pursued. Down upon it, swift and straight, a radiant torrent cleaving the waves, raced the moon stream. And then— "Good God!" breathed Throckmartin, and if ever the words were a prayer and an invocation they were.

And then, for the first time—I saw—*it!*

The moon path, as I have said, stretched to the horizon and was bordered by darkness. It was as though the clouds above had been parted to form a lane—drawn aside like curtains or as the waters of the Red Sea were held back to let the hosts of Israel through. On each side of the stream was the black shadow cast by the folds of the high canopies. And straight as a road between the opaque walls gleamed, shimmered and danced the shining, racing, rapids of moonlight.

Far, it seemed immeasurably far, along this stream of silver fire I sensed, rather than saw, something coming. It drew into sight as a deeper glow within the light. On and on it sped toward us—an opalescent mistiness that swept on with the suggestion of some winged creature in darting flight. Dimly there crept into my mind memory of the Dyak legend of the winged messenger of Buddha—the Akla bird whose feathers are woven of the moon rays, whose heart is a living opal, whose wings in flight echo the crystal clear music of the white stars—but whose beak is of frozen flame and shreds the souls of the unbelievers. Still it sped on, and now there came to me sweet, insistent tinklings—like a pizzicati on violins of glass, crystalline, as purest, clearest glass transformed to sound. And again the myth of the Akla bird came to me.

But now it was close to the end of the white path; close up to the barrier of darkness still between the ship and the sparkling head of the moon stream. And now it beat up against that barrier as a bird against the bars of its cage. And I knew that this was no mist born of sea and air. It whirled with shimmering plumes, with swirls of lacy light, with spirals of living vapor. It held within it odd, unfamiliar gleams as of shifting mother-of-pearl. Coruscations and glittering atoms drifted through it as though it drew them from the rays that bathed it.

Nearer and nearer it came, borne on the sparkling waves, and less and less grew the protecting wall of shadow between it and us. The crystalline sounds were louder—rhythmic as music from another planet.

Now I saw that within the mistiness was a core, a nucleus of intenser light-veined, opaline, effulgent, intensely alive. And above it, tangled in the plumes and spirals that throbbed and whirled were seven glowing lights.

Through all the incessant but strangely ordered movement of the—*thing*—these lights held firm and steady. They were seven—

like seven little moons. One was of a pearly pink, one of delicate nacreous blue, one of lambent saffron, one of the emerald you see in the shallow waters of tropic isles; a deathly white; a ghostly amethyst; and one of the silver that is seen only when the flying fish leap beneath the moon. There they shone—these seven little varicolored orbs within the opaline mistiness of whatever it was that, poised and expectant, waited to be drawn to us on the light filled waves.

The tinkling music was louder still. It pierced the ears with a shower of tiny lances; it made the heart beat jubilantly—and checked it dolorously. It closed your throat with a throb of rapture and gripped it tight like the hand of infinite sorrow!

Came to me now a murmuring cry, stilling the crystal clear notes, it was articulate—but as though from something utterly foreign to this world. The ear took the cry and translated with conscious labor into the sounds of earth. And even as it compassed, the brain shrank from it irresistibly and simultaneously it seemed, reached toward it with irresistible eagerness.

"Av-o-lo-ha! Av-o-lo-ha!" So the cry seemed to throb.

The grip of Throckmartin's hand relaxed. He walked stiffly toward the front of the deck, straight toward the vision, now but a few yards away from the bow. I ran toward him and gripped him—and fell back. For now his face had lost all human semblance. Utter agony and utter ecstasy—there they were side by side, not resisting each other; unholy inhuman companions blending into a look that none of God's creatures should wear—and deep, deep as his soul! A devil and a god dwelling harmoniously side by side! So must Satan, newly fallen, still divine, seeing heaven and contemplating hell, have looked.

And then—swiftly the moon path faded! The clouds swept over the sky as though a hand had drawn them together. Up from the south came a roaring squall. As the moon vanished what I had seen vanished with it—blotted out as an image on a magic lantern; the tinkling ceased abruptly-leaving a silence like that which follows an abrupt and stupendous thunder clap. There was nothing about us but silence and blackness!

Through me there passed a great trembling as one who had stood on the very verge of the gulf wherein the men of the Louisades say lurks the fisher of the souls of men, and has been plucked back by sheerest chance.

Throckmartin passed an arm around me.

"It is as I thought," he said. In his voice was a new note; of the calm certainty that has swept aside a waiting terror of the unknown. "Now I know! Come with me to my cabin, old friend. For now that you too have seen I can tell you"—he hesitated—"what it was you saw," he ended.

As we passed through the door we came face to face with the ship's first officer. Throckmartin turned quickly, but not soon enough for the mate not to see and stare with amazement. His eyes turned questioningly to me.

With a strong effort of will Throckmartin composed his face into at least a semblance of normality.

"Are we going to have much of a storm?" he asked.

"Yes," said the mate. Then the seaman, getting the better of his curiosity, added, profanely: "We'll probably have it all the way to Melbourne."

Throckmartin straightened as though with a new thought. He gripped the officer's sleeve eagerly.

"You mean at least cloudy weather—for"—he hesitated—"for the next three nights, say?"

"And for three more," replied the mate.

"Thank God!" cried Throckmartin, and I think I never heard such relief and hope as was in his voice.

The sailor stood amazed. "Thank God?" he repeated. "Thank— what d'ye mean?"

But Throckmartin was moving onward to his cabin. I started

to follow. The first officer stopped me.

"Your friend," he said, "is he ill?"

"The sea!" I answered hurriedly. "He's not used to it. I am going to look after him."

I saw doubt and disbelief in the seaman's eyes but I hurried on. For I knew now that Throckmartin was ill indeed—but that it was a sickness neither the ship's doctor nor any other could heal.

3. "Dead! All Dead!"

Throckmartin was sitting on the side of his berth as I entered. He had taken off his coat. He was leaning over, face in hands.

"Lock the door," he said quietly, not raising his head. "Close the portholes and draw the curtains—and—have you an electric flash in your pocket—a good, strong one?"

He glanced at the small pocket flash I handed him and clicked it on. "Not big enough I'm afraid," he said. "And after all"—he hesitated—"it's only a theory."

"What's only a theory?" I asked in astonishment.

"Thinking of it as a weapon against—what you saw," he said, with a wry smile.

"Throckmartin," I cried. "What was it? Did I really see—that thing—there in the moon path? Did I really hear—"

"This, for instance," he interrupted.

Softly he whispered: "Av-o-lo-ha!" With the murmur I seemed to hear again the crystalline unearthly music; an echo of it, faint, sinister, mocking, jubilant.

"Throckmartin," I said. "What was it? What are you flying from, man? Where is your wife—and Stanton?"

"Dead!" he said monotonously. "Dead! All dead!" Then as I recoiled in horror—"All dead. Edith, Stanton, Thora—dead—or worse. And Edith in the moon pool—with them—drawn by

74

what you saw on the moon path—and that wants me—and that has put its brand upon me—and pursues me."

With a vicious movement he ripped open his shirt.

"Look at this," he said. I gazed. Around his chest, an inch above his heart, the skin was white as pearl. The whiteness was sharply defined against the healthy tint of the body. He turned and I saw it ran around his back. It circled him. The band made a perfect cincture about two inches wide.

"Burn it!" he said, and offered me his cigarette. I drew back. He gestured—peremptorily. I pressed the glowing end of the cigarette into the ribbon of white flesh. He did not flinch nor was there odor of burning nor, as I drew the little cylinder away, any mark upon the whiteness.

"Feel it!" he commanded again. I placed my fingers upon the band. It was cold—like frozen marble.

He handed me a small penknife.

"Cut!" he ordered. This time, my scientific interest fully aroused, I did so without reluctance. The blade cut into flesh. I waited for the blood to come. None appeared. I drew out the knife and thrust it in again, fully a quarter of an inch deep. I might have been cutting paper so far as any evidence followed that what I was piercing was human skin and muscle.

Another thought came to me and I drew back, revolted.

"Throckmartin," I whispered. "Not leprosy!"

"Nothing so easy," he said. "Look again and find the places you cut."

I looked, as he bade me, and in the white ring there was not a single mark. Where I had pressed the blade there was no trace. It was as though the skin had parted to make way for the blade and closed.

Throckmartin arose and drew his shirt about him.

"Two things you have seen," he said. "*It*—and its mark—the seal it placed on me that gives it, I think, the power to follow me.

Seeing, you must believe my story. Goodwin, I tell you again that my wife is dead—or worse—I do not know; the prey of—what you saw; so, too, is Stanton; so Thora. How—" He stopped for a moment. Then continued:

"And I am going to Melbourne for the things to empty its den and its shrine; for dynamite to destroy it and its lair—if anything made on earth will destroy it; and for white men with courage to use them. Perhaps—perhaps after you have heard, you will be one of these men?" He looked at me a bit wistfully. "And now—do not interrupt me, I beg of you, till I am through—for"—he smiled wanly—"the mate may be wrong. And if he is"—he arose and paced twice about the room—"if he is, I may not have time to tell you."

"Throckmartin," I answered, "I have no closed mind. Tell me—and if I can I will help."

He took my hand and pressed it.

"Goodwin," he began, "if I have seemed to take the death of my wife lightly—or rather"—his face contorted—"or rather—if I have seemed to pass it by as something not of first importance to me—believe me it is not so. If the rope is long enough—if what the mate says is so—if there is cloudy weather until the moon begins to wane—I can conquer—that I know. But if it does not—if the dweller in the moon pool gets me—then must you or some one avenge my wife—and me—and Stanton. Yet I cannot believe that God would let a thing like that conquer! But why did He then let it take my Edith? And why does He allow it to exist? Are there things stronger than God, do you think, Goodwin?"

He turned to me feverishly. I hesitated.

"I do not know just how you define God," I said. "If you mean the will to know, working through science—"

He waved me aside impatiently.

"Science," he said. "What is our science against—that? Or against the science of whatever cursed, vanished race that made it—or made the way for it to enter this world of ours?"

With an effort he regained control of himself.

"Goodwin," he said, "do you know at all of the ruins on the Carolines; the cyclopean, megolithic cities and harbors of Ponape and Lele, of Kusaie, of Ruk and Hogolu, and a score of other islets there? Particularly, do you know of the Nan-Matal and Metalanim?"

"Of the Metalanim I have heard and seen photographs," I said. "They call it, don't they, the Lost Venice of the Pacific?"

"Look at this map," said Throckmartin. He handed me the map. "That," he went on, "is Christian's map of Metalanim harbor and the Nan-Matal. Do you see the rectangles marked Nan-Tanach?"

"Yes," I said.

"There," he said, "under those walls is the moon pool and the seven gleaming lights that raise the dweller in the pool and the altar and shrine of the dweller. And there in the moon pool with it lie Edith and Stanton and Thora."

"The dweller in the moon pool?" I repeated half-incredulously.

"The thing you saw," said Throckmartin solemnly.

A solid sheet of rain swept the ports, and the *Southern Queen* began to roll on the rising swells. Throckmartin drew another deep breath of relief, and drawing aside a curtain peered out into the night. Its blackness seemed to reassure him. At any rate, when he sat again he was calm.

"There are no more wonderful ruins in the world than those of the island Venice of Metalanim on the east shore of Ponape," he said almost casually. "They take in some fifty islets and cover with their intersecting canals and lagoons about twelve square miles. Who built them? None knows! When were they built? Ages before the memory of present man, that is sure. Ten thousand, twenty thousand, a hundred thousand years ago—the last more likely.

"All these islets, Goodwin, are squared, and their shores are frowning sea-walls of gigantic basalt blocks hewn and put in place by the hands of ancient man. Each inner water-front is faced with a terrace of those basalt blocks which stand out six feet above the shallow canals that meander between them. On the islets behind these walls are cyclopean and time-shattered fortresses, palaces, terraces, pyramids; immense courtyards, strewn with ruins—and all so old that they seem to wither the eyes of those who look on them.

"There has been a great subsidence. You can stand out of Metalanim harbor for three miles and look down upon the tops of similar monolithic structures and walls twenty feet below you in the water.

"And all about, strung on their canals, are the bulwarked islets with their enigmatic giant walls peering through the dense growths of mangroves—dead, deserted for incalculable ages; shunned by those who live near.

"You as a botanist are familiar with the evidence that a vast shadowy continent existed in the Pacific—a continent that was not rent asunder by volcanic forces as was that legendary one of Atlantis in the Eastern Ocean. My work in Java, in Papua, and in the Ladrones had set my mind upon this Pacific lost land. Just as the Azores are believed to be the last high peaks of Atlantis, so evidence came to me steadily that Ponape and Lele and their basalt bulwarked islets were the last points of the slowly sunken western land clinging still to the sunlight, and had been the last refuge and sacred places of the rulers of that race which had lost their immemorial home under the rising waters of the Pacific.

"I believed that under these ruins I might find the evidence of what I sought. Time and again I had encountered legends of subterranean networks beneath the Nan-Matal, of passages running back into the main island itself; basalt corridors that followed the lines of the shallow canals and ran under them to islet after islet, linking them in mysterious chains.

"My—my wife and I had talked before we were married of making this our great work. After the honeymoon we prepared for the expedition. It was to be my monument. Stanton was as enthusiastic as ourselves. We sailed, as you know, last May in fulfilment of our dreams.

"At Ponape we selected, not without difficulty, workmen to help us—diggers. I had to make extraordinary inducements before I could get together my force. Their beliefs are gloomy, these Ponapeans. They people their swamps, their forests, their mountains and shores with malignant spirits—*ani* they call them. And they are afraid—bitterly afraid of the isles of ruins and what they think the ruins bide. I do not wonder—now! For their fear has come down to them, through the ages, from the people 'before their fathers,' as they call them, who, they say, made these mighty spirits their slaves and messengers.

"When they were told where they were to go, and how long we expected to stay, they murmured. Those who, at last, were tempted made what I thought then merely a superstitious proviso that they were to be allowed to go away on the three nights of the full moon. If only I had heeded them and gone, too!"

He stopped and again over his face the lines etched deep. "We passed," he went on, "into Metalanim harbor. Off to our left—a mile away arose a massive quadrangle. Its walls were all of forty feet high and hundreds of feet on each side. As we passed it our natives grew very silent; watched it furtively, fearfully. I knew it for the ruins that are called Nan-Tanach, the 'place of frowning walls.' And at the silence of my men I recalled what Christian had written of this place; of how he had come upon its ancient platforms and tetragonal enclosures of stonework; its wonder of tortuous alleyways and labyrinth of shallow canals; grim masses of stonework peering out from behind verdant screens; cyclopean barricades. And now, when we had turned into its ghostly shadows, straightaway the merriment of our guides was hushed and conversation died down to whispers. For we were close to Nan-Tanach—the place of lofty walls, the most remarkable of all the Metalanim ruins." He arose and stood over me.

"Nan-Tanach, Goodwin," he said solemnly—"a place where merriment is hushed indeed and words are stifled; Nan-Tanach—where the moon pool lies hidden—lies hidden behind the moon rock, but sends its diabolic soul out—even through the prisoning stone." He raised clenched hands. "Oh, Heaven," he breathed, "grant me that I may blast it from earth!"

He was silent for a little time.

"Of course I wanted to pitch our camp there," he began again quietly, "but I soon gave up that idea. The natives were panic-stricken—threatened to turn back. 'No,' they said, 'too great *ani* there. We go to any other place—but not there.' Although, even then, I felt that the secret of the place was in Nan-Tanach, I found it necessary to give in. The laborers were essential to the success of the expedition, and I told myself that after a little time had passed and I had persuaded them that there was nothing anywhere that could molest them, we would move our tents to it. We finally picked for our base the islet called Uschen-Tau—you see it here—" He pointed to the map. "It was close to the isle of desire, but far enough away from it to satisfy our men. There was an excellent camping-place there and a spring of fresh water. It offered, besides, an excellent field for preliminary work before attacking the larger ruins. We pitched our tents, and in a couple of days the work was in full swing."

4. THE MOON ROCK

"I do not intend to tell you now," Throckmartin continued, "the results of the next two weeks, Goodwin, nor of what we found.

Later—if I am allowed I will lay all that before you. It is sufficient to say that at the end of those two weeks I had found confirmation of many of my theories, and we were well under way to solve a mystery of humanity's youth—so we thought. But enough. I must hurry on to the first stirrings of the inexplicable thing that was in store for us.

"The place, for all its decay and desolation, had not infected us with any touch of morbidity—that is, not Edith, Stanton or myself. My wife was happy—never had she been happier. Stanton and she, while engrossed in the work as much as I, were of the same age, and they frankly enjoyed the companionship that only youth can give youth. I was glad—never jealous.

"But Thora was very unhappy. She was a Swede, as you know, and in her blood ran the beliefs and superstitions of the Northland—some of them so strangely akin to those of this far southern land; beliefs of spirits of mountain and forest and water—werewolves and beings malign. From the first she showed a curious sensitivity to what, I suppose, may be called the 'influences' of the place. She said it 'smelled' of ghosts and warlocks.

"I laughed at her then—but now I believe that this sensitivity of what we call primitive people is perhaps only a clearer perception of the unknown which we, who deny the unknown, have lost.

"A prey to these fears, Thora always followed my wife about like a shadow; carried with her always a little sharp hand-ax, and although we twitted her about the futility of chopping fantoms with such a weapon she would not relinquish it.

"Two weeks slipped by, and at their end the spokesman for our natives came to us. The next night was the full of the moon, he said. He reminded me of my promise. They would go back to their village next morning; they would return after the third night, as at that time the power of the *ani* would begin to wane with the moon. They left us sundry charms for our 'protection,' and solemnly cautioned us to keep as far away as possible from Nan-Tanach during their absence—although their leader politely informed us that, no doubt, we were stronger than the spirits. Half-exasperated, half-amused I watched them go.

"No work could be done without them, of course, so we decided to spend the days of their absence junketing about the southern islets of the group. Under the moon the ruins were inexpressibly weird and beautiful. We marked down several spots for subsequent exploration, and on the morning of the third day set forth along the east face of the breakwater for our camp on Uschen-Tau, planning to have everything in readiness for the return of our men the next day.

"We landed just before dusk, tired and ready for our cots. It was only a little after ten o'clock when Edith awakened me.

"'Listen!' she said. 'Lean over with your ear close to the ground!' I did so, and seemed to hear, far, far below, as though coming up from great distances, a faint chanting. It gathered strength, died down, ended; began, gathered volume, faded away into silence.

"'It's the waves rolling on rocks somewhere,' I said. 'We're probably over some ledge of rock that carries the sound.'

"'It's the first time I've heard it,' replied my wife doubtfully.

We listened again. Then through the dim rhythms, deep beneath us, another sound came. It drifted across the lagoon that lay between us and Nan-Tanach in little tinkling waves. It was music—of a sort; I won't describe the strange effect it had upon me. You've felt it—"

"You mean on the deck?" I asked.

Throckmartin nodded. "I went to the flap of the tent," he continued, "and peered out. As I did so Stanton lifted his flap and walked out into the moonlight, looking over to the other islet and listening. I called to him.

"'That's the queerest sound!' he said. He listened again.

82

'Crystalline! Like little notes of translucent glass. Like the bells of crystal on the sistrums of Isis at Dendarah Temple,' he added half-dreamily. We gazed intently at the island. Suddenly, on the gigantic sea-wall, moving slowly, rhythmically, we saw a little group of lights. Stanton laughed.

"'The beggars!' he exclaimed. 'That's why they wanted to get away, is it? Don't you see, Dave, it's some sort of a festival—rites of some kind that they hold during the full moon! That's why they were so eager to have us *keep* away, too.'

"I felt a curious sense of relief, although I had not been sensible of any oppression. The explanation seemed good. It explained the tinkling music and also the chanting—worshipers, no doubt, in the ruins—their voices carried along passages I now knew honeycombed the whole Nan-Matal.

"'Let's slip over,' suggested Stanton—but I would not.

"'They're a difficult lot as it is,' I said. 'If we break into one of their religious ceremonies they'll probably never forgive us. Let's keep out of any family party where we haven't been invited.'

"'That's so,' agreed Stanton.

"The strange tinkling music, if music it can be called, rose and fell, rose and fell—now laden with sorrow, now filled with joy.

"'There's something—something very unsettling about it,' said Edith at last soberly. 'I wonder what they make those sounds with. They frighten me half to death, and, at the same time, they make me feel as though some enormous rapture was just around the corner.'

"I had noted this effect, too, although I had said nothing of it. And at the same time there came to me a clear perception that the chanting which had preceded it had seemed to come from a vast multitude—thousands more than the place we were contemplating could possibly have held. Of course, I thought, this might be due to some acoustic property of the basalt; an amplification of sound by some gigantic sounding-board of rock; still—

"'It's devilish uncanny!' broke in Stanton, answering my thought.

"And as he spoke the flap of Thora's tent was raised and out into the moonlight strode the old Swede. She was the great Norse type—tall, deep-breasted, molded on the old Viking lines. Her sixty years had slipped from her. She looked like some ancient priestess of Odin."

He hesitated. "She knew," he said slowly, "something more far-seeing than my science had given her sight. She warned me—she warned me! Fools and mad that we are to pass such things by without heed!" He brushed a hand over his eyes.

"She stood there," he went on. "Her eyes were wide, brilliant, staring. She thrust her head forward toward Nan Tanach, regarding the moving lights; she listened. Suddenly she raised her arms and made a curious gesture to the moon. It was—an archaic—movement; she seemed to drag it from remote antiquity—yet in it was a strange suggestion of power. Twice she repeated this gesture and—the tinkling died away! She turned to us.

"'Go!' she said, and her voice seemed to come from far distances. 'Go from here—and quickly! Go while you may. They have called—' She pointed to the islet. 'They know you are here. They wait.' Her eyes widened further. 'It is there,' she wailed. 'It beckons—the—the—'

"She fell at Edith's feet, and as she fell over the lagoon came again the tinklings, now with a quicker note of jubilance—almost of triumph.

"We ran to Thora, Stanton and I, and picked her up. Her head rolled and her face, eyes closed, turned as though drawn full into the moonlight. I felt in my heart a throb of unfamiliar fear—for her face had changed again. Stamped upon it was a look of mingled transport and horror—alien, terrifying, strangely revolting. It was"—he thrust his face close to my eyes—"what you see in mine!"

For a dozen heart-beats I stared at him, fascinated; then he sank back again into the half-shadow of the berth. "I managed to hide her face from Edith," he went on.

"I thought she had suffered some sort of a nervous seizure. We carried her into her tent. Once within the unholy mask dropped from her, and she was again only the kindly, rugged old woman. I watched her throughout the night. The sounds from Nan-Tanach continued until about an hour before moonset. In the morning Thora awoke, none the worse, apparently. She had had bad dreams, she said. She could not remember what they were—except that they had warned her of danger. She was oddly sullen, and I noted that throughout the morning her gaze returned again half-fascinatedly, half-wonderingly to the neighboring isles.

"That afternoon the natives returned. They were so exuberant in their apparent relief to find us well and intact that Stanton's suspicions of them were confirmed. He slyly told their leader that 'from the noise they had made on Nan-Tanach the night before they must have thoroughly enjoyed themselves.'

"I think I never saw such stark terror as the Ponapean manifested at the remark! Stanton himself was so plainly startled that he tried to pass it over as a jest. He met poor success! The men seemed panic-stricken, and for a time I thought they were about to abandon us—but they did not. They pitched their camp at the western side of the island—out of sight of Nan-Tanach. I noticed that they built large fires, and whenever I awoke that night I heard their voices in slow, minor chant—one of their song 'charms,' I thought drowsily, against evil *ani*. I heard nothing else; the place of frowning walls was wrapped in silence—no lights showed. The next morning the men were quiet, a little depressed, but as the hours wore on they regained their spirits, and soon life at the camp was going on just as it had before.

"You will understand, Goodwin, how the occurrences I have related would excite the scientific curiosity. We rejected immediately, of course, any explanation admitting the supernatural. Why not? Except the curiously disquieting effects of the tinkling music and Thora's behavior there was nothing to warrant any such fantastic theories—even if our minds had been the kind to harbor them.

"We came to the conclusion that there must be a passageway between Ponape and Nan-Tanach, known to the natives—and used by them during their rites. Ceremonies were probably held in great vaults or caverns beneath the ruins.

"We decided at last that on the next departure of our laborers we would set forth immediately to Nan-Tanach. We would investigate during the day, and at evening my wife and Thora would go back to camp, leaving Stanton and me to spend the night on the island, observing from some safe hiding-place what might occur.

"The moon waned; appeared crescent in the west; waxed slowly toward the full. Before the men left us they literally prayed us to accompany them. Their importunities only made us more eager to see what it was that, we were now convinced, they wanted to conceal from us. At least that was true of Stanton and myself. It was not true of Edith. She was thoughtful, abstracted—reluctant. Thora, on the other hand, showed an unusual restlessness, almost an eagerness to go. Goodwin"—he paused—"Goodwin, I know now that the poison was working in Thora—and that women have perceptions that we men lack—forebodings, sensings. I wish to Heaven I had known it then—Edith!" he cried suddenly. "Edith—come back to me! Forgive me!"

I stretched the decanter out to him. He drank deeply. Soon he had regained control of himself.

"When the men were out of sight around the turn of the harbor," he went on, "we took our boat and made straight for Nan-Tanach. Soon its mighty sea-wall towered above us. We passed through the water-gate with its gigantic hewn prisms of basalt and landed beside a half-submerged pier. In front of us stretched a series of giant steps leading into a vast court strewn with fragments of fallen pillars. In the center of the court, beyond the shattered pillars, rose another terrace of basalt blocks, concealing, I knew, still another enclosure.

"And now, Goodwin, for the better understanding of what follows and to guide you, should I—not be able—to accompany you when you go there, listen carefully to my description of this place: Nan-Tanach is literally three rectangles. The first rectangle is the sea-wall, built up of monoliths. Gigantic steps lead up from the landing of the sea-gate through the entrance to the courtyard.

"This courtyard is surrounded by another, inner basalt wall.

"Within the courtyard is the second enclosure. Its terrace, of the same basalt as the outer walls, is about twenty feet high. Entrance is gained to it by many breaches which time has made in its stonework. This is the inner court, the heart of Nan-Tanach! There lies the great central vault with which is associated the one name of living being that has come to us out of the mists of the past. The natives say it was the treasure-house of Chau-te-leur, a mighty king who reigned long 'before their fathers.' As Chau is the ancient Ponapean word both for sun and king, the name means 'place of the sun king.'

"And opposite this place of the sun king is the moon rock that hides the moon pool.

"It was Stanton who first found what I call the moon rock. We had been inspecting the inner courtyard; Edith and Thora were getting together our lunch. I forgot to say that we had previously gone all over the islet and had found not a trace of living thing. I came out of the vault of Chaute-leur to find Stanton before a part of the terrace studying it wonderingly.

"'What do you make of this?' he asked me as I came up. He pointed to the wall. I followed his finger and saw a slab of stone about fifteen feet high and ten wide. At first all I noticed was the

87

exquisite nicety with which its edges joined the blocks about it. Then I realized that its color was subtly different—tinged with gray and of a smooth, peculiar—deadness.

"'Looks more like calcite than basalt,' I said. I touched it and withdrew my hand quickly, for at the contact every nerve in my arm tingled as though a shock of frozen electricity had passed through it. It was not cold as we know cold that I felt. It was a chill force—the phrase I have used—frozen electricity—describes it better than anything else. Stanton looked at me oddly.

"'So you felt it, too,' he said. 'I was wondering whether I was developing hallucinations like Thora. Notice, by the way, that the blocks beside it are quite warm beneath the sun.'

"I felt them and touched the grayish stone again. The same faint shock ran through my hand—a tingling chill that had in it a suggestion of substance, of force. We examined the slab more closely. Its edges were cut as though by an engraver of jewels. They fitted against the neighboring blocks in almost a hair-line. Its base, we saw, was slightly curved, and fitted as closely as top and sides upon the huge stones on which it rested. And then we noted that these stones had been hollowed to follow the line of the gray stone's foot. There was a semicircular depression running from one side of the slab to the other. It was as though the gray rock stood in the center of a shallow cup—revealing half, covering half. Something about this hollow attracted me. I reached down and felt it. Goodwin, although the balance of the stones that formed it, like all the stones of the courtyard, were rough and age-worn—this was as smooth, as even surfaced as though it just left the hands of the polisher.

"'It's a door!' exclaimed Stanton. 'It swings around in that little cup. That's what makes the hollow so smooth.'

"'Maybe you're right,' I replied. 'But how the devil can we open it?'

"We went over the slab again—pressing upon its edges,

thrusting against its sides. During one of those efforts I happened to look up—and cried out. For a foot above and on each side of the corner of the gray rock's lintel I had seen a slight convexity, visible only from the angle at which my gaze struck it. These bosses on the basalt were circular, eighteen inches in diameter, as we learned later, and at the center extended two inches only beyond the face of the terrace. Unless one looked directly up at them while leaning against the moon rock—for this slab, Goodwin, is the moon rock—they were invisible. And none would dare stand there!

"We carried with us a small scaling-ladder, and up this I went. The bosses were apparently nothing more than chiseled curvatures in the stone. I laid my hand on the one I was examining, and drew it back so sharply I almost threw myself from the ladder. In my palm, at the base of my thumb, I had felt the same shock that I had in touching the slab below. I put my hand back. The impression came from a spot not more than an inch wide. I went carefully over the entire convexity, and six times more the chill ran through my arm. There were, Goodwin, seven circles an inch wide in the curved place, each of which communicated the precise sensation I have described. The convexity on the opposite side of the slab gave precisely the same results. But no amount of touching or of pressing these spots singly or in any combination gave the slightest promise of motion to the slab itself.

"'And yet—they're what open it,' said Stanton positively.

"'Why do you say that?' I asked.

"'I—don't know,' he answered hesitatingly. 'But something tells me so. Throck,' he went on half earnestly, half laughingly, 'the purely scientific part of me is fighting the purely human part of me. The scientific part is urging me to find some way to get that slab either down or open. The human part is just as strongly urging me to do nothing of the sort and get away while I can!'

"He laughed again—shamefacedly.

"'Which will it be?' he asked—and I thought that in his tone the human side of him was ascendant.

"'It will probably stay as it is—unless we blow it to bits,' I said.

"'I thought of that,' he answered, 'and—I wouldn't dare,' he added somberly enough. And even as I had spoken there came to me the same feeling that he had expressed. It was as though something passed out of the gray rock that struck my heart as a hand strikes an impious lip. We turned away—uneasily, and faced Thora coming through a breach in the terrace.

"'Miss Edith wants you quick,' she began—and stopped. I saw her eyes go past me and widen. She was looking at the gray rock. Her body grew suddenly rigid; she took a few stiff steps forward and ran straight to it. We saw her cast herself upon its breast, hands and face pressed against it; heard her scream as though her very soul was being drawn from her—and watched her fall at its foot. As we picked her up I saw steal from her face the look I had observed when I first heard the crystal music of Nan-Tanach— that unhuman mingling of opposites!"

5. Av-o-lo-ha

"We carried Thora back, down to where Edith was waiting. We told her what had happened and what we had found. She listened gravely, and as we finished Thora sighed and opened her eyes.

"'I would like to see the stone,' she said. 'Charles, you stay here with Thora.' We passed through the outer court silently— and stood before the rock. She touched it, drew back her hand as I had; thrust it forward again resolutely and held it there. She seemed to be listening. Then she turned to me.

"'David,' said my wife, and the wistfulness in her voice hurt me—'David, would you be very, very disappointed if we went from here—without trying to find out any more about it—would you?'

"Goodwin, I never wanted anything so much in my life as I wanted to learn what that rock concealed. You will understand—the cumulative curiosity that all the happenings had caused; the certainty that before me was an entrance to a place that, while known to the natives—for I still clung to that theory—was utterly unknown to any man of my race; that within, ready for my finding, was the answer to the stupendous riddle of these islands and a lost chapter in the history of humanity. There before me—and was I asked to turn away, leaving it unread!

"Nevertheless, I tried to master my desire, and I answered—'Edith, not a bit if you want us to do it.'

"She read my struggle in my eyes. She looked at me searchingly for a moment and then turned back toward the gray rock. I saw a shiver pass through her. I felt a tinge of remorse and pity!

"'Edith,' I exclaimed, 'we'll go!'

"She looked at me hard. 'Science is a jealous mistress,' she quoted. 'No, after all it may be just fancy. At any rate, you can't run away. No! But, Dave, I'm going to stay too!'

"'You are not!' I exclaimed. 'You're going back to the camp with Thora. Stanton and I will be all right.'

"'I'm going to stay,' she repeated. And there was no changing her decision. As we neared the others she laid a hand on my arm. 'Dave,' she said, 'If there should be something—well—inexplicable tonight—something that seems—too dangerous—will you promise to go back to our own islet tomorrow, or, while we can, and wait until the natives return?'

"I promised eagerly—for the desire to stay and see what came with the night was like a fire within me.

"And would to Heaven I had not waited another moment, Goodwin; would to Heaven I had gathered them all together then and sailed back on the instant through the mangroves to Uschen-Tau!

"We found Thora on her feet again and singularly composed.

She claimed to have no more recollection of what had happened after she had spoken to Stanton and to me in front of the gray rock than she had after the seizure on Uschen-Tau. She grew sullen under our questioning, precisely as she had before. But to my astonishment, when she heard of our arrangements for the night, she betrayed a febrile excitement that had in it something of exultance.

"We had picked a place about five hundred feet away from the steps leading into the outer court.

"We settled down just before dusk to wait for whatever might come. I was nearest the giant steps; next to me Edith; then Thora, and last Stanton. Each of us had with us automatic pistols, and all, except Thora, had rifles.

"Night fell. After a time the eastern sky began to lighten, and we knew that the moon was rising; grew lighter still, and the orb peeped over the sea; swam suddenly into full sight. Edith gripped my hand, for, as though the full emergence into the heavens had been a signal, we heard begin beneath us the deep chanting. It came from illimitable depths.

"The moon poured her rays down upon us, and I saw Stanton start. On the instant I caught the sound that had roused him. It came from the inner enclosure. It was like a long, soft sighing. It was not human; seemed in some way—mechanical. I glanced at Edith and then at Thora. My wife was intently listening. Thora sat, as she had since we had placed ourselves, elbows on knees, her hands covering her face.

"And then suddenly from the moonlight flooding us there came to me a great drowsiness. Sleep seemed to drip from the rays and fall upon my eyes, closing them—closing them inexorably. I felt Edith's hand relax in mine, and under my own heavy lids saw her nodding. I saw Stanton's head fall upon his breast and his body sway drunkenly. I tried to rise—to fight against the profound desire for slumber that pressed in on me.

"And as I fought I saw Thora raise her head as though listening; saw her rise and turn her face toward the gateway. For a moment she gazed, and my drugged eyes seemed to perceive within it a deeper, stronger radiance. Thora looked at us. There was infinite despair in her face—and expectancy. I tried again to rise—and a surge of sleep rushed over me. Dimly, as I sank within it, I heard a crystalline chiming; raised my lids once more with a supreme effort, saw Thora, bathed in light, standing at the top of the stairs, and then—sleep took me for its very own—swept me into the very heart of oblivion!

"Dawn was breaking when I wakened. Recollection rushed back on me and I thrust a panic-stricken hand out toward Edith; touched her and felt my heart give a great leap of thankfulness. She stirred, sat up, rubbing dazed eyes. I glanced toward Stanton. He lay on his side, back toward us, head in arms.

"Edith looked at me laughingly. 'Heavens! What sleep!' she said. Memory came to her. Her face paled. 'What happened?' she whispered. 'What made us sleep like that?' She looked over to Stanton, sprang to her feet, ran to him, shook him. He turned over with a mighty yawn, and I saw relief lighten her face as it had lightened my heart.

"Stanton raised himself stiffly. He looked at us. 'What's the matter?' he exclaimed. 'You look as though you've seen ghosts!'

"Edith caught my hands. 'Where's Thora?' she cried. Before I could answer she ran out into the open calling: 'Thora! Thora!'

"Stanton stared at me. 'Taken!' was all I could say. Together we went to my wife, now standing beside the great stone steps, looking up fearfully at the gateway into the terraces. There I told them what I had seen before sleep had drowned me. And together then we ran up the stairs, through the court and up to the gray rock.

"The gray rock was closed as it had been the day before, nor was there trace of its having opened. No trace! Even as I thought

93

this Edith dropped to her knees before it and reached toward something lying at its foot. It was a little piece of gray silk. I knew it for part of the kerchief Thora wore about her hair. Edith took the fragment; hesitated. I saw then that it had been cut from the kerchief as though by a razor-edge; I saw, too, that a few threads ran from it—down toward the base of the slab; ran to the base of the gray rock and—under it! The gray rock was a door! And it had opened and Thora had passed through it!

"I think, Goodwin, that for the next few minutes we all were a little insane. We beat upon that diabolic entrance with our hands, with stones and clubs. At last reason came back to us. Stanton set forth for the camp to bring back blasting powder and tools. While he was gone Edith and I searched the whole islet for any other clue. We found not a trace of Thora nor any indication of any living being save ourselves. We went back to the gateway to find Stanton returned.

"Goodwin, during the next two hours we tried every way in our power to force entrance through the slab. The rock within effective blasting radius of the cursed door resisted our drills. We tried explosions at the base of the slab with charges covered by rock. They made not the slightest impression on the surface beneath, expending their force, of course, upon the slighter resistance of their coverings.

"Afternoon found us hopeless, so far as breaking through the rock was concerned. Night was coming on and before it came we would have to decide our course of action. I wanted to go to Ponape for help. But Edith objected that this would take hours and after we had reached there it would be impossible to persuade our men to return with us that night, if at all. What then was left? Clearly only one of two choices: to go back to our camp and wait for our men to return and on their return try to persuade them to go with us to Nan-Tanach. But this would mean the abandonment of Thora for at least two days. We could not do it;

94

it would have been too cowardly.

"The other choice was to wait where we were for night to come; to wait for the rock to open as it had the night before, and to make a sortie through it for Thora before it could close again. With the sun had come confidence; at least a shattering of the mephitic mists of superstition with which the strangeness of the things that had befallen us had clouded for a time our minds. In that brilliant light there seemed no place for fantoms.

"The evidence that the slab had opened was unmistakable, but might not Thora simply have *found* it open through some mechanism, still working after ages, and dependent for its action upon laws of physics unknown to us upon the full light of the moon? The assertion of the natives that the *ani* had greatest power at this time might be a far-flung reflection of knowledge which had found ways to use forces contained in moonlight, as we have found ways to utilize the forces in the sun's rays. If so, Thora was probably behind the slab, sending out prayers to us for help.

"But how explain the sleep that had descended upon us? Might it not have been some emanation from plants or gaseous emanations from the island itself? Such things were far from uncommon, we agreed. In some way, the period of their greatest activity might coincide with the period of the moon, but if this were so why had not Thora also slept?

"As dusk fell we looked over our weapons. Edith was an excellent shot with both rifle and pistol. With the idea that the impulse toward sleep was the result either of emanations such as I have described or man made, we constructed rough-and-ready but effective neutralizers, which we placed over our mouths and nostrils. We had decided that my wife was to remain in the hollow spot. Stanton would take up a station on the far side of the stairway and I would place myself opposite him on the side near Edith. The place I picked out was less than five hundred feet from her, and I could reassure myself now as to her safety, as I looked down upon the hollow wherein she crouched. As the phenomena had previously synchronized with the rising of the moon, we had no reason to think they would occur any earlier this night.

"A faint glow in the sky heralded the moon. I kissed Edith, and Stanton and I took our places. The moon dawn increased rapidly; the disk swam up, and in a moment it seemed was shining in full radiance upon ruins and sea.

"As it rose there came as on the night before the curious little sighing sound from the inner terrace. I saw Stanton straighten up and stare intently through the gateway, rifle ready. Even at the distance he was from me, I discerned amazement in his eyes. The moonlight within the gateway thickened, grew stronger. I watched his amazement grow into sheer wonder.

"I arose.

"'Stanton, what do you see?' I called cautiously. He waved a silencing hand. I turned my head to look at Edith. A shock ran through me. She lay upon her side. Her face was turned full toward the moon. She was in deepest sleep!

"As I turned again to call to Stanton, my eyes swept the head of the steps and stopped, fascinated. For the moonlight had thickened more. It seemed to be—curdled—there; and through it ran little gleams and veins of shimmering white fire. A languor passed through me. It was not the ineffable drowsiness of the preceding night. It was a sapping of all will to move. I tore my eyes away and forced them upon Stanton. I tried to call out to him. I had not the will to make my lips move. I had struggled against this paralysis and as I did so I felt through me a sharp shock. It was like a blow. And with it came utter inability to make a single motion. Goodwin, I could not even move my eyes!

"I saw Stanton leap upon the steps and move toward the gateway. As he did so the light in the courtyard grew dazzlingly brilliant. Through it rained tiny tinklings that set the heart to racing with pure joy and stilled it with terror.

"And now for the first time I heard that cry '*Av-o-lo-ha! Av-o-lo-ha!*' the cry you heard on deck. It murmured with the strange effect of a sound only partly in our own space—as though it were part of a fuller phrase passing through from another dimension and losing much as it came; infinitely caressing, infinitely cruel!

"On Stanton's face I saw come the look I dreaded—and yet knew would appear; that mingled expression of delight and fear. The two lay side by side as they had on Thora, but were intensified. He walked on up the stairs; disappeared beyond the range of my fixed gaze. Again I heard the murmur—'*Av-o-1o-ha!*' There was triumph in it now and triumph in the storm of tinklings that swept over it.

"For another heart-beat there was silence. Then a louder burst of sound and ringing through it Stanton's voice from the courtyard—a great cry—a scream—filled with ecstasy insupportable and horror unimaginable! And again there was silence. I strove to burst the invisible bonds that held me. I could not. Even my eyelids were fixed. Within them my eyes, dry and aching, burned.

"Then, Goodwin—I first saw the inexplicable! The crystalline music swelled. Where I sat I could take in the gateway and its basalt portals, rough and broken, rising to the top of the wall forty feet above, shattered, ruined portals—unclimbable. From this gateway an intenser light began to flow. It grew, it gushed, and into it, into my sight, walked Stanton.

"Stanton! But—Goodwin! What a vision!" He ceased. I waited—waited.

6. INTO THE MOON POOL

"Goodwin," Throckmartin said at last, "I can describe him only as a thing of living light. He radiated light; was filled with light;

97

overflowed with it. Around him was a shining cloud that whirled through and around him in radiant swirls, shimmering tentacles, luminescent, coruscating spirals.

"I saw his face. It shone with a rapture too great to be borne by living men, and was shadowed with insuperable misery. It was as though his face had been remolded by the hand of God and the hand of Satan, working together and in harmony. You have seen it on my face. But you have never seen it in the degree that Stanton bore it. The eyes were wide open and fixed, as though upon some inward vision of hell and heaven! He walked like the corpse of a man damned who carried within him an angel of light.

"The music swelled again. I heard again the murmuring—'Av-o-lo-ha!' Stanton turned, facing the ragged side of the portal. And then I saw that the light that filled and surrounded him had a nucleus, a core—something shiftingly human shaped—that dissolved and changed, gathered itself, whirled through and beyond him and back again. And as this shining nucleus passed through him Stanton's whole body pulsed with light. As the luminescence moved, there moved with it, still and serene always, seven tiny globes of light like seven little moons.

"So much I saw and then swiftly Stanton seemed to be lifted—levitated—up the unscalable wall and to its top. The glow faded from the moonlight, the tinkling music grew fainter. I tried again to move. The spell still held me fast. The tears were running down now from my rigid lids and brought relief to my tortured eyes.

"I have said my gaze was fixed. It was. But from the side, peripherally, it took in a part of the far wall of the outer enclosure. Ages seemed to pass and I saw a radiance stealing along it. Soon there came into sight the figure that was Stanton. Far away he was—on the gigantic wall. But still I could see the shining spirals whirling jubilantly around and through him; felt rather than saw his tranced face beneath the seven lights. A swirl of crystal notes, and he had passed. And all the time, as though from some opened well of light, the courtyard gleamed and sent out silver fires that dimmed the moon-rays, yet seemed strangely to be a part of them.

"Ten times he passed before me so. The luminescence came with the music; swam for a while along the man-made cliff of basalt and passed away. Between times eternities rolled and still I crouched there, a helpless thing of stone with eyes that would not close!

"At last the moon neared the horizon. There came a louder burst of sound; the second, and last, cry of Stanton, like an echo of the first! Again the soft sigh from the inner terrace. Then— utter silence. The light faded; the moon was setting and with a rush life and power to move returned to me, I made a leap for the steps, rushed up them, through the gateway and straight to the gray rock. It was closed—as I knew it would be. But did I dream it or did I hear, echoing through it as though from vast distances a triumphant shouting—'*Av-o-lo-ha! Av-o-lo-ha!*'?

"I remembered Edith. I ran back to her. At my touch she wakened; looked at me wonderingly; raised herself on a hand.

"'Dave!' she said, 'I slept—after all.' She saw the despair on my face and leaped to her feet. 'Dave!' she cried. 'What is it? Where's Charles?'

"I lighted a fire before I spoke. Then I told her. And for the balance of that night we sat before the flames, arms around each other—like two frightened children."

Suddenly Throckmartin held his hands out to me appealingly. "Goodwin, old friend!" he cried. "Don't look at me as though I were mad. It's truth, absolute truth. Wait—"

I comforted him as well as I could. After a little time he took up his story.

"Never," he said, "did man welcome the sun as we did that morning. As soon as it was light we went back to the courtyard. The basalt walls whereon I had seen Stanton were black and silent. The terraces were as they had been. The gray slab was in its place. In the shallow hollow at its base was—nothing. Nothing—nothing was there anywhere on the islet of Stanton—not a trace, not a sign on Nan-Tanach to show that he had ever lived.

"What were we to do? Precisely the same arguments that had kept us there the night before held good now—and doubly good. We could not abandon these two; could not go as long as there was the faintest hope of finding them—and yet for love of each other how could we remain? I loved my wife, Goodwin—how much I never knew until that day; and she loved me as deeply.

"'It takes only one each night,' she said. 'Beloved, let it take me.'

"I wept, Goodwin. We both wept.

"'We will meet it together,' she said. And it was thus at last that we arranged it."

"That took great courage indeed, Throckmartin," I interrupted. He looked at me eagerly.

"You do believe then?" he exclaimed.

"I believe," I said. He pressed my hand with a grip that nearly crushed it.

"Now," he told me, "I do not fear. If I—fail, you will prepare and carry on the work."

I promised. And—Heaven forgive me—that was three years ago.

"It did take courage," he went on, again quietly. "More than courage. For we knew it was renunciation. Each of us in our hearts felt that one of us would not be there to see the sun rise. And each of us prayed that the death, if death it was, would not come first to the other.

"We talked it all over carefully, bringing to bear all our power of analysis and habit of calm, scientific thought. We considered minutely the time element in the phenomena. Although the deep chanting began at the very moment of moonrise, fully five minutes had passed between its full lifting and the strange sighing sound from the inner terrace. I went back in memory over the happenings of the night before. At least fifteen minutes had intervened between the first heralding sigh and the intensification of the moonlight in the courtyard. And this glow grew for at least ten minutes more before the first burst of the crystal notes.

"The sighing sound—of what had it reminded me? Of course—of a door revolving and swishing softly along its base.

"'Edith!' I cried. 'I think I have it! The gray rock opens five minutes after upon the moonrise. But whoever or whatever it is that comes through it must wait until the moon has risen higher, or else it must come from a distance. The thing to do is not to wait for it, but to surprise it before it passes out the door. We will go into the inner court early. You will take your rifle and pistol and hide yourself where you can command the opening—if the slab does open. The instant it moves I will enter. It's our best chance, Edith. I think it's our only one.'

"My wife demurred strongly. She wanted to go with me. But I convinced her that it was better for her to stand guard without, prepared to help me if I were forced from what lay behind the rock again into the open.

"The day passed too swiftly. In the face of what we feared our love seemed stronger than ever. Was it the flare of the spark before extinguishment? I wondered. We prepared and ate a good dinner. We tried to keep our minds from anything but scientific aspect of the phenomena. We agreed that whatever it was its cause must be human, and that we must keep that fact in mind every second. But what kind of men could create such prodigies? We thrilled at the thought of finding perhaps the remnants of a vanished race, living perhaps in cities over whose rocky skies the Pacific rolled; exercising there the lost wisdom of the half-gods of earth's youth.

"At the half-hour before moonrise we two went into the inner courtyard. I took my place at the side of the gray rock. Edith crouched behind a broken pillar twenty feet away, slipped her rifle-barrel over it so that it would cover the opening.

"The minutes crept by. The courtyard was very quiet. The darkness lessened and through the breaches of the terrace I watched the far sky softly lighten. With the first pale flush the stillness became intensified. It deepened—became unbearably—expectant. The moon rose, showed the quarter, the half, then swam up into full sight like a great bubble.

"Its rays fell upon the wall before me and suddenly upon the convexities I have described seven little circles of light sprang out. They gleamed, glimmered, grew brighter—shone. The gigantic slab before me turned as though on a pivot, sighing softly as it moved.

"For a moment I gasped in amazement. It was like a conjurer's trick. And the moving slab I noticed was also glowing, becoming opalescent like the little shining circles above.

"Only for a second I gazed and then with a word to Edith flung myself through the opening which the slab had uncovered. Before me was a platform and from the platform steps led downward into a smooth corridor. This passage was not dark, it glowed with the same faint silvery radiance as the door. Down it I raced. As I ran, plainer than ever before, I heard the chanting. The passage turned abruptly, passed parallel to the walls of the outer courtyard and then once more led abruptly downward. Still I ran, and as I ran I looked at the watch on my wrist. Less than three minutes had elapsed.

"The passage ended. Before me was a high vaulted arch. For a moment I paused. It seemed to open into space; a space filled with lambent, coruscating, many-colored mist whose brightness grew even as I watched. I passed through the arch and stopped in sheer awe!

"In front of me was a pool. It was circular, perhaps twenty feet wide. Around it ran a low, softly curved lip of glimmering silvery stone. Its water was palest blue. The pool with its silvery rim was like a great blue eye staring upward.

"Upon it streamed seven shafts of radiance. They poured down upon the blue eye like cylindrical torrents; they were like shining pillars of light rising from a sapphire floor.

"One was the tender pink of the pearl; one of the aurora's green; a third a deathly white; the fourth the blue in mother-of-pearl; a shimmering column of pale amber; a beam of amethyst; a shaft of molten silver. Such are the colors of the seven lights that stream upon the moon pool. I drew closer, awestricken. The shafts did not illumine the depths. They played upon the surface and seemed there to diffuse, to melt into it. The pool drank them!

"Through the water tiny gleams of phosphorescence began to dart, sparkles and coruscations of pale incandescence. And far, far below I sensed a movement, a shifting glow as of something slowly rising.

"I looked upward, following the radiant pillars to their source. Far above were seven shining globes, and it was from these that the rays poured. Even as I watched their brightness grew. They were like seven moons set high in some caverned heaven. Slowly their splendor increased, and with it the splendor of the seven beams streaming from them. It came to me that they were crystals of some unknown kind set in the roof of the moon pool's vault and that their light was drawn from the moon shining high above them. They were wonderful, those lights—and what must have been the knowledge of those who set them there!

"Brighter and brighter they grew as the moon climbed higher, sending its full radiance down through them. I tore my gaze away and stared at the pool. It had grown milky, opalescent. The rays gushing into it seemed to be filling it; it was alive with sparklings, scintillations, glimmerings. And the luminescence I had seen rising from its depths was larger, nearer!

"A swirl of mist floated up from its surface. It drifted within the embrace of the rosy beam and hung there for a moment. The beam seemed to embrace it, sending through it little shining corpuscles, tiny rosy spiralings. The mist absorbed the rays, was strengthened by it, gained substance. Another swirl sprang into the amber shaft, clung and fed there, moved swiftly toward the first and mingled with it. And now other swirls arose, here and there, too fast to be counted, hung poised in the embrace of the light streams; flashed and pulsed into each other.

"Thicker and thicker still they arose until the surface of the pool was a pulsating pillar of opalescent mist; steadily growing stronger; drawing within it life from the seven beams falling upon it; drawing to it from below the darting, red atoms of the pool. Into its center was passing the luminescence I had sensed rising from the far depths. And the center glowed, throbbed—began to send out questing swirls and tendrils.

"There forming before me was that which had walked with Stanton, which had taken Thora—the thing I had come to find!

"With the shock of realization my brain sprang into action. My hand fell to my pistol and I fired shot after shot into its radiance. The place rang with the explosions and there came to me a sense of unforgivable profanation. Devilish as I knew it to be, that chamber of the moon pool seemed also—in some way— holy. As though a god and a demon dwelt there, inextricably commingled.

"As I shot the pillar wavered; the water grew more disturbed. The mist swayed and shook; gathered itself again. I slipped a second clip into the automatic and, another idea coming to me, took careful aim at one of the globes in the roof. From thence I knew came the force that shaped the dweller in the pool. From the pouring rays came its strength. If I could destroy them I could check its forming. I fired again and again. If I hit the globes I did no damage. The little motes in their beams danced with the motes in the mist, troubled. That was all.

"Up from the pool like little bells, like bubbles of crystal notes rose the tinklings. Their notes were higher, had lost their sweetness, were angry, as it were, with themselves.

"And then out from the inexplicable, hovering over the pool, swept a shining swirl. It caught me above the heart; wrapped itself around me. I felt an icy coldness and then there rushed over me a mingled ecstasy and horror. Every atom of me quivered with delight and at the same time shrank with despair. There was nothing loathsome in it. But it was as though the icy soul of evil and the fiery soul of good had stepped together within me. The pistol dropped from my hand.

"So I stood while the pool gleamed and sparkled; the streams of light grew more intense and the mist glowed and strengthened. I saw that its shining core had shape—but a shape that my eyes and brain could not define. It was as though a being of another sphere should assume what it might of human semblance, but was not able to conceal that what human eyes saw was but a part of it. It was neither man nor woman; it was unearthly and androgynous. Even as I found its human semblance it changed. And still the mingled rapture and terror held me. Only in a little corner of my brain dwelt something untouched; something that held itself apart and watched. Was it the soul? I have never believed—and yet—

"Over the head of the misty body there sprang suddenly out seven little lights. Each was the color of the beam beneath which it rested. I knew now that the dweller was—complete!

"And then—behind me I heard a scream. It was Edith's voice. It came to me that she had heard the shots and followed me. I felt every faculty concentrate into a mighty effort. I wrenched myself free from the gripping tentacle and it swept back. I turned to catch Edith, and as I did so slipped—fell. As I dropped I saw the radiant shape above the pool leap swiftly for me!

"There was the rush past me and as the dweller paused, straight into it raced Edith, arms outstretched to shield me from it!"

He trembled.

"She threw herself squarely within its diabolic splendor," he whispered. "She stopped and reeled as though she had encountered solidity. And as she faltered it wrapped its shining self around her. The crystal tinklings burst forth jubilantly. The light filled her, ran through and around her as it had with Stanton, and I saw drop upon her face—the look. From the pillar came the murmur— '*Av-o-lo-ha!*' The vault echoed it.

"'Edith!' I cried. 'Edith!' I was in agony. She must have heard me, even through the—thing. I saw her try to free herself. Her rush had taken her to the very verge of the moon pool. She tottered; and in an instant—she fell—with the radiance still holding her, still swirling and winding around and through her—into the moon pool! She sank, Goodwin, and with her went—the dweller!

"I dragged myself to the brink. Far down I saw a shining, many-colored nebulous cloud descending; caught a glimpse of Edith's face, disappearing; her eyes stared up to me filled with supernal ecstasy and horror. And—vanished!

"I looked about me stupidly. The seven globes still poured their radiance upon the pool. It was pale-blue again. Its sparklings and coruscations were gone. From far below there came a muffled outburst of triumphant chanting!

"'Edith!' I cried again. 'Edith, come back to me!' And then a darkness fell upon me. I remember running back through the shimmering corridors and out into the courtyard. Reason had left me. When it returned I was far out at sea in our boat wholly estranged from civilization. A day later I was picked up by the schooner in which I came to Port Moresby.

"I have formed a plan; you must hear it, Goodwin—" He fell upon his berth. I bent over him. Exhaustion and the relief of telling his story had been too much for him. He slept like the dead.

7. The Dweller Comes

All that night I watched over him. When dawn broke I went to my room to get a little sleep myself. But my slumber was haunted.

The next day the storm was unabated. Throckmartin came to me at lunch. He looked better. His strange expression had waned. He had regained much of his old alertness.

"Come to my cabin," he said. There, he stripped his shirt from him. "Something is happening," he said. "The mark is smaller." It was as he said.

"I'm escaping," he whispered jubilantly. "Just let me get to Melbourne safely, and then we'll see who'll win! For, Goodwin, I'm not at all sure that Edith is dead—as we know death—nor that the others are. There was something outside experience there—some great mystery."

And all that day he talked to me of his plans.

"There's a natural explanation, of course," he said. "My theory is that the moon rock is of some composition sensitive to the action of moon rays; somewhat as the metal selenium is to sun rays. There is a powerful quality in moonlight, as both science and legends can attest. We know of its effect upon the mentality, the nervous system, even upon certain diseases.

"The moon slab is of some material that reacts to moonlight. The circles over the top are, without doubt, its operating agency. When the light strikes them they release the mechanism that opens the slab, just as you can open doors with sunlight by an ingenious arrangement of selenium-cells. Apparently it takes the strength of the full moon to do this. We will first try a concentration of the rays of the nearly full moon upon these circles to see whether that will open the rock. If it does we will be able to investigate the pool without interruption from—from—what emanates.

"Look, here on the chart are their locations. I have made this in duplicate for you in the event of something happening to me."

He worked upon the chart a little more.

"Here," he said, "is where I believe the seven great globes to be. They are probably hidden somewhere in the ruins of the islet called Tau, where they can catch the first moon rays. I have calculated that when I entered I went so far this way—here is the turn; so far this way, took this other turn and ran down this long, curving corridor to the hall of the moon pool. That ought to make lights, at least approximately, here." He pointed.

"They are certainly cleverly concealed, but they must be open to the air to get the light. They should not be too hard to find. They must be found." He hesitated again. "I suppose it would be safer to destroy them, for it is clearly through them that the phenomenon of the pool is manifested; and yet, to destroy so wonderful a thing! Perhaps the better way would be to have some men up by them, and if it were necessary, to protect those below, to destroy them on signal. Or they might simply be covered. That would neutralize them. To destroy them—" He hesitated again. "No, the phenomenon is too important to be destroyed without fullest investigation." His face clouded again. "But it is *not* human; it can't be," he muttered. He turned to me and laughed. "The old conflict between science and too frail human credulity!" he said.

Again—"We need half a dozen diving-suits. The pool must be entered and searched to its depths. That will indeed take courage, yet in the time of the new moon it should be safe, or perhaps better after the dweller is destroyed or made safe."

We went over plans, accepted them, rejected them, and still the storm raged—and all that day and all that night.

I hurry to the end. That afternoon there came a steady lightening of the clouds which Throckmartin watched with deep uneasiness. Toward dusk they broke away suddenly and soon the sky was clear. The stars came twinkling out.

"It will be tonight," Throckmartin said to me. "Goodwin, friend, stand by me. Tonight it will come, and I must fight."

I could say nothing. About an hour before moonrise we went to his cabin. We fastened the port-holes tightly and turned on the lights. Throckmartin had some queer theory that the electric rays would be a bar to his pursuer. I don't know why. A little later he complained of increasing sleepiness.

"But it's just weariness," he said. "Not at all like that other drowsiness. It's an hour till moonrise still," he yawned at last. "Wake me up a good fifteen minutes before."

He lay upon the berth. I sat thinking. I came to myself with a start. What time was it? I looked at my watch and jumped to the port-hole. It was full moonlight; the orb had been up for fully half an hour. I strode over to Throckmartin and shook him by the shoulder.

"Up, quick, man!" I cried. He rose sleepily. His shirt fell open at the neck and I looked, in amazement, at the white band around his chest. Even under the electric light it shone softly, as though little flecks of light were in it.

Throckmartin seemed only half-awake. He looked down at his breast, saw the glowing cincture, and smiled.

"Oh, yes," he said drowsily, "it's coming—to take me back to Edith! Well, I'm glad."

"Throckmartin!" I cried. "Wake up! Fight."

"Fight!" he said. "No use; keep the maps; come after us."

He went to the port and drowsily drew aside the curtain. The moon traced a broad path of light straight to the ship. Under its rays the band around his chest gleamed brighter and brighter; shot forth little rays; seemed to move.

He peered out intently and, suddenly, before I could stop him, threw open the port. I saw a glimmering presence moving swiftly along the moon path toward us, skimming over the waters.

And with it raced little crystal tinklings and far off I heard a long-drawn murmuring cry.

On the instant the lights went out in the cabin, evidently throughout the ship, for I heard shouting above. I sprang back into a corner and crouched there. At the porthole was a radiance; swirls and spirals of living white cold fire. It poured into the cabin and it was filled with dancing motes of light, and over the radiant core of it shone seven little lights like tiny moons. It gathered Throckmartin to it.

Light pulsed through and from him. I saw his skin turn to a translucent, shimmering whiteness like illumined porcelain. His face became unrecognizable, inhuman with the monstrous twin expressions. So he stood for a moment. The pillar of light seemed to hesitate and the seven lights to contemplate me. I shrank further down into the corner. I saw Throckmartin drawn to the port. The room filled with murmuring. I fainted.

When I awakened the lights were burning again.

But of Throckmartin there was no trace!

There are some things that we are bound to regret all our lives. I suppose I was unbalanced by what I had seen. I could not think clearly. But there came to me the sheer impossibility of telling the ship's officers what I had seen; what Throckmartin had told me. They would accuse me, I felt, of his murder. At neither appearance of the phenomenon had any save our two selves witnessed it. I was certain of this because they would surely have discussed it. Why none had seen it I do not know.

The next morning when Throckmartin's absence was noted, I merely said that I had left him early in the evening. It occurred to no one to doubt me, or to question me further. His strangeness had caused much comment; all had thought him half-mad. And so it was officially reported that he had fallen or jumped from the ship during the failure of the lights the cause of which was another mystery of that night.

Afterward, the same inhibition held me back from making his and my story known to my fellow scientists.

But this inhibition is suddenly dead, and I am not sure that its death is not a summons from Throckmartin.

And now I am going to Nan-Tanach to make amends for my cowardice by seeking out the dweller. So sure am I that all I have written here is absolutely true.

COUNT MAGNUS

By M. R. James

In "Supernatural Horror in Literature" Lovecraft devotes nearly three pages to a description of M. R. James's "Count Magnus," which Lovecraft felt typified many aspects of the Jamesian ghost story. The tale can be regarded as exemplary in many ways—in its complexity of structure, subtlety of detail, and air of realism gained through inclusion of authentic scholarship. Lovecraft may well have been thinking of this tale when he recommended, in "Notes on Writing Weird Fiction" (1933), that a writer should make two synopses for a story, one recording the events in order of chronological occurrence, the other in order of narration in the tale. The scholar Richard Ward has made a convincing claim that "Count Magnus" had a significant influence on the portrayal of Joseph Curwen in *The Case of Charles Dexter Ward* (1927).

M. R. James (1862–1936) was an authority on medieval manuscripts and cathedral history as well as Provost of Eton College. He eventually produced four collections of ghost stories between 1904 and 1925, all of which Lovecraft owned; the stories were gathered as The *Collected Ghost Stories* of M. R. James (1931).

By what means the papers out of which I have made a connected story came into my hands is the last point which the reader will learn from these pages. But it is necessary to prefix to my extracts from them a statement of the form in which I possess them.

They consist, then, partly of a series of collections for a book of travels, such a volume as was a common product of the forties and fifties. Horace Marryat's *Journal of a Residence in Jutland and the Danish Isles* is a fair specimen of the class to which I allude. These books usually treated of some unfamiliar district on the Continent. They were illustrated with woodcuts or steel plates. They gave details of hotel accommodation, and of means of communication, such as we now expect to find in any well-regulated guidebook, and they dealt largely in reported conversations with intelligent foreigners, racy innkeepers and garrulous peasants. In a word, they were chatty.

Begun with the idea of furnishing material for such a book, my papers as they progressed assumed the character of a record of one single personal experience, and this record was continued up to the very eve, almost, of its termination.

The writer was a Mr. Wraxall. For my knowledge of him I have to depend entirely on the evidence his writings afford, and from these I deduce that he was a man past middle age, possessed of some private means, and very much alone in the world. He had, it seems, no settled abode in England, but was a denizen of hotels and boarding-houses. It is probable that he entertained the idea of settling down at some future time which never came; and I think it also likely that the Pantechnicon fire in the early seventies must have destroyed a great deal that would have thrown light on his antecedents, for he refers once or twice to property of his that was warehoused at that establishment.

It is further apparent that Mr. Wraxall had published a book, and that it treated of a holiday he had once taken in Brittany. More than this I cannot say about his work, because a diligent search in bibliographical works has convinced me that it must have appeared either anonymously or under a pseudonym.

As to his character, it is not difficult to form some superficial opinion. He must have been an intelligent and cultivated man. It seems that he was near being a Fellow of his college at Oxford—Brasenose, as I judge from the Calendar. His besetting fault was pretty clearly that of overinquisitiveness, possibly a good fault in a traveller, certainly a fault for which this traveller paid dearly enough in the end.

On what proved to be his last expedition, he was plotting another book. Scandinavia, a region not widely known to Englishmen forty years ago, had struck him as an interesting field. He must have lighted on some old books of Swedish history or memoirs, and the idea had struck him that there was room for a book descriptive of travel in Sweden, interspersed with episodes from the history of some of the great Swedish families. He procured letters of introduction, therefore, to some persons of quality in Sweden, and set out thither in the early summer of 1863.

Of his travels in the North there is no need to speak, nor of his residence of some weeks in Stockholm. I need only mention that some *savant* resident there put him on the track of an important collection of family papers belonging to the proprietors of an ancient manor-house in Vestergothland, and obtained for him permission to examine them. The manor-house, or *herrgård*, in question is to be called Råbäck (pronounced something like Roebeck), though that is not its name. It is one of the best buildings of its kind in all the country, and the picture of it in Dahlenberg's *Suecia antiqua et moderna*, engraved in 1694, shows it very much as the tourist may see it to-day. It was built soon after 1600, and is, roughly speaking, very much like an English house of that period in respect of material—red-brick with stone facings—and style. The man who built it was a scion of the great house of De la Gardie, and his descendants possess it still. De la Gardie is the name by which I will designate them when mention of them becomes necessary.

They received Mr. Wraxall with great kindness and courtesy, and pressed him to stay in the house as long as his researches lasted. But, preferring to be independent, and mistrusting his powers of conversing in Swedish, he settled himself at the village inn, which turned out quite sufficiently comfortable, at any rate during the summer months. This arrangement would entail a short walk daily to and from the manor-house of something under a mile. The house itself stood in a park, and was protected—we should say grown up—with large old timber. Near it you found the walled garden, and then entered a close wood fringing one of the small lakes with which the whole country is pitted. Then came the wall of the demesne, and you climbed a steep knoll—a knob of rock lightly covered with soil—and on the top of this stood the church, fenced in with tall dark trees. It was a curious building to English eyes. The nave and aisles were low, and filled with pews and galleries. In the western gallery stood the handsome old organ, gaily painted, and with silver pipes. The ceiling was flat, and had been adorned by a seventeenth-century artist with a strange and hideous "Last Judgment," full of lurid flames, falling cities, burning ships, crying souls, and brown and smiling demons. Handsome brass coronæ hung from the roof; the pulpit was like a doll's-house, covered with little painted wooden cherubs and saints; a stand with three hour-glasses was hinged to the preacher's desk. Such sights as these may be seen in many a church in Sweden now, but what distinguished this one was an addition to the original building. At the eastern end of the north aisle the builder of the manor-house had erected a mausoleum for himself and his family. It was a largish eight-sided building, lighted by a series of oval windows, and it had a domed roof, topped by a kind of pumpkin-shaped object rising into a spire, a form in which Swedish architects greatly delighted. The roof was of copper externally, and was painted black, while the walls, in common with those of the church, were staringly white. To this mausoleum there was no access from the church. It had a portal and steps of its own on the northern side.

Past the churchyard the path to the village goes, and not more than three or four minutes bring you to the inn door.

On the first day of his stay at Råbäck Mr. Wraxall found the church door open, and made those notes of the interior which I have epitomized. Into the mausoleum, however, he could not make his way. He could by looking through the keyhole just descry that there were fine marble effigies and sarcophagi of copper, and a wealth of armorial ornament, which made him very anxious to spend some time in investigation.

The papers he had come to examine at the manorhouse proved to be of just the kind he wanted for his book. There were family correspondence, journals, and accountbooks of the earliest owners of the estate, very carefully kept and clearly written, full of amusing and picturesque detail. The first De la Gardie appeared in them as a strong and capable man. Shortly after the building of the mansion there had been a period of distress in the district, and the peasants had risen and attacked several châteaux and done some damage. The owner of Råbäck took a leading part in suppressing the trouble, and there was reference to executions of ringleaders and severe punishments inflicted with no sparing hand.

The portrait of this Magnus de la Gardie was one of the best in the house, and Mr. Wraxall studied it with no little interest after his day's work. He gives no detailed description of it, but I gather that the face impressed him rather by its power than by its beauty or goodness; in fact, he writes that Count Magnus was an almost phenomenally ugly man.

On this day Mr. Wraxall took his supper with the family, and walked back in the late but still bright evening.

"I must remember," he writes, "to ask the sexton if he can let me into the mausoleum at the church. He evidently has access to it himself, for I saw him to-night standing on the steps, and, as I thought, locking or unlocking the door."

I find that early on the following day Mr. Wraxall had some conversation with his landlord. His setting it down at such length as he does surprised me at first; but I soon realized that the papers I was reading were, at least in their beginning, the materials for the book he was meditating, and that it was to have been one of those quasi-journalistic productions which admit of the introduction of an admixture of conversational matter.

His object, he says, was to find out whether any traditions of Count Magnus de la Gardie lingered on in the scenes of that gentleman's activity, and whether the popular estimate of him were favourable or not. He found that the Count was decidedly not a favourite. If his tenants came late to their work on the days which they owed to him as Lord of the Manor, they were set on the wooden horse, or flogged and branded in the manor-house yard. One or two cases there were of men who had occupied lands which encroached on the lord's domain, and whose houses had been mysteriously burnt on a winter's night, with the whole family inside. But what seemed to dwell on the innkeeper's mind most—for he returned to the subject more than once—was that the Count had been on the Black Pilgrimage, and had brought something or someone back with him.

You will naturally inquire, as Mr. Wraxall did, what the Black Pilgrimage may have been. But your curiosity on the point must remain unsatisfied for the time being, just as his did. The landlord was evidently unwilling to give a full answer, or indeed any answer, on the point, and, being called out for a moment, trotted off with obvious alacrity, only putting his head in at the door a few minutes afterwards to say that he was called away to Skara, and should not be back till evening.

So Mr. Wraxall had to go unsatisfied to his day's work at the manor-house. The papers on which he was just then engaged soon put his thoughts into another channel, for he had to occupy himself with glancing over the correspondence between Sophia Albertina in Stockholm and her married cousin Ulrica Leonora at Råbäck in the years 1705–1710. The letters were of exceptional interest from the light they threw upon the culture of that period in Sweden, as anyone can testify who has read the full edition of them in the publications of the Swedish Historical Manuscripts Commission.

In the afternoon he had done with these, and after returning the boxes in which they were kept to their places on the shelf, he proceeded, very naturally, to take down some of the volumes nearest to them, in order to determine which of them had best be his principal subject of investigation next day. The shelf he had hit upon was occupied mostly by a collection of account-books in the writing of the first Count Magnus. But one among them was not an account-book, but a book of alchemical and other tracts in another sixteenth-century hand. Not being very familiar with alchemical literature, Mr. Wraxall spends much space which he might have spared in setting out the names and beginnings of the various treatises: The book of the Phœnix, book of the Thirty Words, book of the Toad, book of Miriam, Turba

119

philosophorum, and so forth; and then he announces with a good deal of circumstance his delight at finding, on a leaf originally left blank near the middle of the book, some writing of Count Magnus himself headed "Liber nigræ peregrinationis." It is true that only a few lines were written, but there was quite enough to show that the landlord had that morning been referring to a belief at least as old as the time of Count Magnus, and probably shared by him. This is the English of what was written:

"If any man desires to obtain a long life, if he would obtain a faithful messenger and see the blood of his enemies, it is necessary that he should first go into the city of Chorazin, and there salute the prince ..." Here there was an erasure of one word, not very thoroughly done, so that Mr. Wraxall felt pretty sure that he was right in reading it as *aëris* ("of the air"). But there was no more of the text copied, only a line in Latin: "*Quære reliqua hujus materiei inter secretiora*" (See the rest of this matter among the more private things).

It could not be denied that this threw a rather lurid light upon the tastes and beliefs of the Count; but to Mr. Wraxall, separated from him by nearly three centuries, the thought that he might have added to his general forcefulness alchemy, and to alchemy something like magic, only made him a more picturesque figure; and when, after a rather prolonged contemplation of his picture in the hall, Mr. Wraxall set out on his homeward way, his mind was full of the thought of Count Magnus. He had no eyes for his surroundings, no perception of the evening scents of the woods or the evening light on the lake; and when all of a sudden he pulled up short, he was astonished to find himself already at the gate of the churchyard, and within a few minutes of his dinner. His eyes fell on the mausoleum.

"Ah," he said, "Count Magnus, there you are. I should dearly like to see you."

"Like many solitary men," he writes, "I have a habit of talking to myself aloud; and, unlike some of the Greek and Latin particles, I do not expect an answer. Certainly, and perhaps fortunately in this case, there was neither voice nor any that regarded: only the woman who, I suppose, was cleaning up the church, dropped some metallic object on the floor, whose clang startled me. Count Magnus, I think, sleeps sound enough."

That same evening the landlord of the inn, who had heard Mr. Wraxall say that he wished to see the clerk or deacon (as he would be called in Sweden) of the parish, introduced him to that official in the inn parlour. A visit to the De la Gardie tomb-house was soon arranged for the next day, and a little general conversation ensued.

Mr. Wraxall, remembering that one function of Scandinavian deacons is to teach candidates for Confirmation, thought he would refresh his own memory on a Biblical point.

"Can you tell me," he said, "anything about Chorazin?"

The deacon seemed startled, but readily reminded him how that village had once been denounced.

"To be sure," said Mr. Wraxall; "it is, I suppose, quite a ruin now?"

"So I expect," replied the deacon. "I have heard some of our old priests say that Antichrist is to be born there; and there are tales—"

"Ah! what tales are those?" Mr. Wraxall put in.

"Tales, I was going to say, which I have forgotten," said the deacon; and soon after that he said good night.

The landlord was now alone, and at Mr. Wraxall's mercy; and that inquirer was not inclined to spare him.

"Herr Nielsen," he said, "I have found out something about the Black Pilgrimage. You may as well tell me what you know. What did the Count bring back with him?"

Swedes are habitually slow, perhaps, in answering, or perhaps the landlord was an exception. I am not sure; but Mr. Wraxall notes that the landlord spent at least one minute in looking at him before he said anything at all. Then he came close up to his guest, and with a good deal of effort he spoke:

"Mr. Wraxall, I can tell you this one little tale, and no more—not any more. You must not ask anything when I have done. In my grandfather's time—that is, ninety-two years ago—there were two men who said: 'The Count is dead; we do not care for him. We will go to-night and have a free hunt in his wood'—the long wood on the hill that you have seen behind Råbäck. Well, those that heard them say this, they said: 'No, do not go; we are sure you will meet with persons walking who should not be walking. They should be resting, not walking.' These men laughed. There were no forest-men to keep the wood, because no one wished to hunt there. The family were not here at the house. These men could do what they wished.

"Very well, they go to the wood that night. My grandfather was sitting here in this room. It was the summer, and a light night. With the window open, he could see out to the wood, and hear.

"So he sat there, and two or three men with him, and they listened. At first they hear nothing at all; then they hear someone—you know how far away it is—they hear someone scream, just as if the most inside part of his soul was twisted out of him. All of them in the room caught hold of each other, and they sat so for three-quarters of an hour. Then they hear someone else, only about three hundred ells off. They hear him laugh out loud : it was not one of those two men that laughed, and, indeed, they have all of them said that it was not any man at all. After that they hear a great door shut.

"Then, when it was just light with the sun, they all went to the priest. They said to him:

"'Father, put on your gown and your ruff, and come to bury these men, Anders Bjornsen and Hans Thorbjorn.'

"You understand that they were sure these men were dead.

So they went to the wood—my grandfather never forgot this. He said they were all like so many dead men themselves. The priest, too, he was in a white fear. He said when they came to him:

"'I heard one cry in the night, and I heard one laugh afterwards. If I cannot forget that, I shall not be able to sleep again.'

"So they went to the wood, and they found these men on the edge of the wood. Hans Thorbjorn was standing with his back against a tree, and all the time he was pushing with his hands—pushing something away from him which was not there. So he was not dead. And they led him away, and took him to the house at Nykjoping, and he died before the winter; but he went on pushing with his hands. Also Anders Bjornsen was there; but he was dead. And I tell you this about Anders Bjornsen, that he was once a beautiful man, but now his face was not there, because the flesh of it was sucked away off the bones. You understand that? My grandfather did not forget that. And they laid him on the bier which they brought, and they put a cloth over his head, and the priest walked before; and they began to sing the psalm for the dead as well as they could. So, as they were singing the end of the first verse, one fell down, who was carrying the head of the bier, and the others looked back, and they saw that the cloth had fallen off, and the eyes of Anders Bjornsen were looking up, because there was nothing to close over them. And this they could not bear. Therefore the priest laid the cloth upon him, and sent for a spade, and they buried him in that place."

The next day Mr. Wraxall records that the deacon called for him soon after his breakfast, and took him to the church and mausoleum. He noticed that the key of the latter was hung on a nail just by the pulpit, and it occurred to him that, as the church door seemed to be left unlocked as a rule, it would not be difficult for him to pay a second and more private visit to the monuments if there proved to be more of interest among them than could be digested at first. The building, when he entered it, he found not unimposing. The monuments, mostly large erections of the seventeenth and eighteenth centuries, were dignified if luxuriant, and the epitaphs and heraldry were copious. The central space of the domed room was occupied by three copper sarcophagi, covered with finely-engraved ornament. Two of them had, as is commonly the case in Denmark and Sweden, a large metal crucifix on the lid. The third, that of Count Magnus, as it appeared, had, instead of that, a full-length effigy engraved upon it, and round the edge were several bands of similar ornament representing various scenes. One was a battle, with cannon belching out smoke, and walled towns, and troops of pikemen. Another showed an execution. In a third, among trees, was a man running at full speed, with flying hair and outstretched hands. After him followed a strange form; it would be hard to say whether the artist had intended it for a man, and was unable to give the requisite similitude, or whether it was intentionally made as monstrous as it looked. In view of the skill with which the rest of the drawing was done, Mr. Wraxall felt inclined to adopt the latter idea. The figure was unduly short, and was for the most part muffled in a hooded garment which swept the ground. The only part of the form which projected from that shelter was not shaped like any hand or arm. Mr. Wraxall compares it to the tentacle of a devil-fish, and continues: "On seeing this, I said to myself, 'This, then, which is evidently an allegorical representation of some kind—a fiend pursuing a hunted soul—may be the origin of the story of Count Magnus and his mysterious companion. Let us see how the huntsman is pictured: doubtless it will be a demon blowing his horn.'" But, as it turned out, there was no such sensational figure, only the semblance of a cloaked man on a hillock, who stood leaning on a stick, and watching the hunt with an interest which the engraver had tried to express in his attitude.

Mr. Wraxall noted the finely-worked and massive steel padlocks—three in number—which secured the sarcophagus.

One of them, he saw, was detached, and lay on the pavement. And then, unwilling to delay the deacon longer or to waste his own working-time, he made his way onward to the manor-house.

"It is curious," he notes, "how on retracing a familiar path one's thoughts engross one to the absolute exclusion of surrounding objects. To-night, for the second time, I had entirely failed to notice where I was going (I had planned a private visit to the tomb-house to copy the epitaphs), when I suddenly, as it were, awoke to consciousness, and found myself (as before) turning in at the churchyard gate, and, I believe, singing or chanting some such words as, 'Are you awake, Count Magnus? Are you asleep, Count Magnus?' and then something more which I have failed to recollect. It seemed to me that I must have been behaving in this nonsensical way for some time."

He found the key of the mausoleum where he had expected to find it, and copied the greater part of what he wanted; in fact, he stayed until the light began to fail him.

"I must have been wrong," he writes, "in saying that one of the padlocks of my Count's sarcophagus was unfastened; I see to-night that two are loose. I picked both up, and laid them carefully on the window-ledge, after trying unsuccessfully to close them. The remaining one is still firm, and, though I take it to be a spring lock, I cannot guess how it is opened. Had I succeeded in undoing it, I am almost afraid I should have taken the liberty of opening the sarcophagus. It is strange, the interest I feel in the personality of this, I fear, somewhat ferocious and grim old noble."

The day following was, as it turned out, the last of Mr. Wraxall's stay at Råbäck. He received letters connected with certain investments which made it desirable that he should return to England; his work among the papers was practically done, and travelling was slow. He decided, therefore, to make his farewells, put some finishing touches to his notes, and be off.

These finishing touches and farewells, as it turned out, took more time than he had expected. The hospitable family insisted on his staying to dine with them—they dined at three—and it was verging on half-past six before he was outside the iron gates of Råbäck. He dwelt on every step of his walk by the lake, determined to saturate himself, now that he trod it for the last time, in the sentiment of the place and hour. And when he reached the summit of the churchyard knoll, he lingered for many minutes, gazing at the limitless prospect of woods near and distant, all dark beneath a sky of liquid green. When at last he turned to go, the thought struck him that surely he must bid farewell to Count Magnus as well as the rest of the De la Gardies. The church was but twenty yards away, and he knew where the key of the mausoleum hung. It was not long before he was standing over the great copper coffin, and, as usual, talking to himself aloud. "You may have been a bit of a rascal in your time, Magnus," he was saying," but for all that I should like to see you, or, rather—"

"Just at that instant," he says, "I felt a blow on my foot. Hastily enough I drew it back, and something fell on the pavement with a clash. It was the third, the last of the three padlocks which had fastened the sarcophagus. I stooped to pick it up, and—Heaven is my witness that I am writing only the bare truth—before I had raised myself there was a sound of metal hinges creaking, and I distinctly saw the lid shifting upwards. I may have behaved like a coward, but I could not for my life stay for one moment. I was outside that dreadful building in less time than I can write—almost as quickly as I could have said—the words; and what frightens me yet more, I could not turn the key in the lock. As I sit here in my room noting these facts, I ask myself (it was not twenty minutes ago) whether that noise of creaking metal continued, and I cannot tell whether it did or not. I only know that there was something more than I have written that alarmed me, but whether it was sound or sight I am not able to remember. What is this that I have done?"

Poor Mr. Wraxall! He set out on his journey to England on the next day, as he had planned, and he reached England in safety; and yet, as I gather from his changed hand and inconsequent jottings, a broken man. One of several small notebooks that have come to me with his papers gives, not a key to, but a kind of inkling of, his experiences. Much of his journey was made by canal-boat, and I find not less than six painful attempts to enumerate and describe his fellow-passengers. The entries are of this kind:

"24. Pastor of village in Skåne. Usual black coat and soft black hat.
"25. Commercial traveller from Stockholm going to Troll-hättan. Black cloak, brown hat.
"26. Man in long black cloak, broad-leafed hat, very old-fashioned."

This entry is lined out, and a note added: "Perhaps identical with No. 13. Have not yet seen his face." On referring to No. 13, I find that he is a Roman priest in a cassock.

The net result of the reckoning is always the same. Twenty-eight people appear in the enumeration, one being always a man in a long black cloak and broad hat, and the other a "short figure in dark cloak and hood." On the other hand, it is always noted that only twenty-six passengers appear at meals, and that the man in the cloak is perhaps absent, and the short figure is certainly absent.

On reaching England, it appears that Mr. Wraxall landed at Harwich, and that he resolved at once to put himself out of the reach of some person or persons whom he never specifies, but whom he had evidently come to regard as his pursuers. Accordingly he took a vehicle—it was a closed fly—not trusting the railway, and drove across country to the village of Belchamp St. Paul. It was about nine o'clock on a moonlight August night when he neared the place. He was sitting forward, and looking out of the window at the fields and thickets—there was little else to be seen—racing past him. Suddenly he came to a cross-road. At the corner two figures were standing motionless; both were in dark cloaks; the taller one wore a hat, the shorter a hood. He had no time to see their faces, nor did they make any motion that he could discern. Yet the horse shied violently and broke into a gallop, and Mr. Wraxall sank back into his seat in something like desperation. He had seen them before.

Arrived at Belchamp St. Paul, he was fortunate enough to find a decent furnished lodging, and for the next twenty-four hours he lived, comparatively speaking, in peace. His last notes were written on this day. They are too disjointed and ejaculatory to be given here in full, but the substance of them is clear enough. He is expecting a visit from his pursuers—how or when he knows not—and his constant cry is "What has he done?" and "Is there no hope?" Doctors, he knows, would call him mad, policemen would laugh at him. The parson is away. What can he do but lock his door and cry to God?

People still remembered last year at Belchamp St. Paul how a strange gentleman came one evening in August, years back; and how the next morning but one he was found dead, and there was an inquest; and the jury that viewed the body fainted, seven of 'em did, and none of 'em wouldn't speak to what they see, and the verdict was visitation of God; and how the people as kep' the 'ouse moved out that same week, and went away from that part. But they do not, I think, know that any glimmer of light has ever been thrown, or could be thrown, on the mystery. It so happened that last year the little house came into my hands as part of a legacy. It had stood empty since 1863, and there seemed no prospect of letting it; so I had it pulled down, and the papers of which I have given you an abstract were found in a forgotten cupboard under the window in the best bedroom.

THE DAMNED THING

By Ambrose Bierce

Ambrose Bierce's "The Damned Thing," in Lovecraft's words, "chronicles the hideous devastations of an invisible entity that waddles and flounders on the hills and in the wheatfields by night and day" (*S* 51). The final line of the story—"I am not mad; there are colors that we cannot see. And, God help me! the Damned Thing is of such a color!"—at once brings to mind the mysterious entity (or entities) in "The Colour out of Space," which have come to earth in a meteorite: "The colour ... was almost impossible to describe; and it was only by analogy that they called it colour at all." Bierce himself may have gained some tips on the handling of the "invisible monster" theme from FitzJames O'Brien's "What Was It?" (1859) (although he himself protested that that story was not an influence on his own) and from Maupassant's "The Horla"; but Bierce's execution of the tale is very much his own.

Ambrose Bierce (1842–1924?) was better known in his day as a fearless and satirical journalist, chiefly for the Hearst newspapers in San Francisco and Washington, D.C. He published two celebrated story collections, *Tales of Soldiers and Civilians* (1891; later titled *In the Midst of Life*) and *Can Such Things Be?* (1893), containing some of the finest stories ever written about the Civil War and also containing a substantial array of psychological and supernatural horror fiction. Bierce also wrote poetry, fables, and the celebrated *Devil's Dictionary* (1906).

I. One does not always eat what is on the table

By the light of a tallow candle which had been placed on one end of a rough table a man was reading something written in a book. It was an old account book, greatly worn; and the writing was not, apparently, very legible, for the man sometimes held the page close to the flame of the candle to get a stronger light on it. The shadow of the book would then throw into obscurity a half of the room, darkening a number of faces and figures; for besides the reader, eight other men were present. Seven of them sat against the rough log walls, silent, motionless, and the room being small, not very far from the table. By extending an arm any one of them could have touched the eighth man, who lay on the table, face upward, partly covered by a sheet, his arms at his sides. He was dead.

The man with the book was not reading aloud, and no one spoke; all seemed to be waiting for something to occur; the dead man only was without expectation. From the blank darkness outside came in, through the aperture that served for a window, all the ever unfamiliar noises of night in the wilderness—the long nameless note of a distant coyote; the stilly pulsing thrill of tireless insects in trees; strange cries of night birds, so different from those of the birds of day; the drone of great blundering beetles, and all that mysterious chorus of small sounds that seem always to have been but half heard when they have suddenly ceased, as if conscious of an indiscretion. But nothing of all this was noted in that company; its members were not overmuch addicted to idle interest in matters of no practical importance; that was obvious in every line of their rugged faces—obvious even in the dim light of the single candle. They were evidently men of the vicinity—farmers and woodsmen.

The person reading was a trifle different; one would have said of him that he was of the world, worldly, albeit there was that in his attire which attested a certain fellowship with the organisms of his environment. His coat would hardly have passed muster in San Francisco; his foot-gear was not of urban origin, and the hat that lay by him on the floor (he was the only one uncovered) was such that if one had considered it as an article of mere personal adornment he would have missed its meaning. In countenance the man was rather prepossessing, with just a hint of sternness; though that he may have assumed or cultivated, as appropriate to one in authority. For he was a coroner. It was by virtue of his office that he had possession of the book in which he was reading; it had been found among the dead man's effects—in his cabin where the inquest was now taking place.

When the coroner had finished reading he put the book into his breast pocket. At that moment the door was pushed open and a young man entered. He, clearly, was not of mountain birth and breeding: he was clad as those who dwell in cities. His clothing was dusty, however, as from travel. He had, in fact, been riding hard to attend the inquest.

The coroner nodded; no one else greeted him.

"We have waited for you," said the coroner. "It is necessary to have done with this business to-night."

The young man smiled. "I am sorry to have kept you," he said. "I went away, not to evade your summons, but to post to my newspaper an account of what I suppose I am called back to relate."

The coroner smiled.

"The account that you posted to your newspaper," he said, "differs, probably, from that which you will give here under oath."

"That," replied the other, rather hotly and with a visible flush, "is as you please. I used manifold paper and have a copy of what I sent. It was not written as news, for it is incredible, but as fiction. It may go as a part of my testimony under oath."

"But you say it is incredible."

"That is nothing to you, sir, if I also swear that it is true."

The coroner was silent for a time, his eyes upon the floor. The men about the sides of the cabin talked in whispers, but seldom withdrew their gaze from the face of the corpse. Presently the coroner lifted his eyes and said: "We will resume the inquest."

The men removed their hats. The witness was sworn.

"What is your name?" the coroner asked.

"William Harker."

"Age?"

"Twenty-seven."

"You knew the deceased, Hugh Morgan?"

"Yes."

"You were with him when he died?"

"Near him."

"How did that happen—your presence, I mean?"

"I was visiting him at this place to shoot and fish. A part of my purpose, however, was to study him and his odd, solitary way of life. He seemed a good model for a character in fiction. I sometimes write stories."

"I sometimes read them."

"Thank you."

"Stories in general—not yours."

Some of the jurors laughed. Against a sombre background humor shows high lights. Soldiers in the intervals of battle laugh easily, and a jest in the death chamber conquers by surprise.

"Relate the circumstances of this man's death," said the coroner. "You may use any notes or memoranda that you please."

The witness understood. Pulling a manuscript from his breast pocket he held it near the candle and turning the leaves until he found the passage that he wanted began to read.

II. What may happen in a field of wild oats

"… The sun had hardly risen when we left the house. We were looking for quail, each with a shotgun, but we had only one dog. Morgan said that our best ground was beyond a certain ridge that he pointed out, and we crossed it by a trail through the *chaparral*. On the other side was comparatively level ground, thickly covered with wild oats. As we emerged from the *chaparral* Morgan was but a few yards in advance. Suddenly we heard, at a little distance to our right and partly in front, a noise as of some animal thrashing about in the bushes, which we could see were violently agitated.

"'We've started a deer,' I said. 'I wish we had brought a rifle.'

"Morgan, who had stopped and was intently watching the agitated *chaparral*, said nothing, but had cocked both barrels of his gun and was holding it in readiness to aim. I thought him a trifle excited, which surprised me, for he had a reputation for exceptional coolness, even in moments of sudden and imminent peril.

"'O, come,' I said. 'You are not going to fill up a deer with quail-shot, are you?'

"Still he did not reply; but catching a sight of his face as he turned it slightly toward me I was struck by the intensity of his look. Then I understood that we had serious business in hand and my first conjecture was that we had 'jumped' a grizzly. I advanced to Morgan's side, cocking my piece as I moved.

"The bushes were now quiet and the sounds had ceased, but Morgan was as attentive to the place as before.

"'What is it? What the devil is it?' I asked.

"'That Damned Thing!' he replied, without turning his head. His voice was husky and unnatural. He trembled visibly.

"I was about to speak further, when I observed the wild oats near the place of the disturbance moving in the most inexplicable way. I can hardly describe it. It seemed as if stirred by a streak of wind, which not only bent it, but pressed it down—crushed it so that it did not rise; and this movement was slowly prolonging itself directly toward us.

"Nothing that I had ever seen had affected me so strangely as this unfamiliar and unaccountable phenomenon, yet I am unable to recall any sense of fear. I remember—and tell it here because, singularly enough, I recollected it then—that once in looking carelessly out of an open window I momentarily mistook a small tree close at hand for one of a group of larger trees at a little distance away. It looked the same size as the others, but being more distinctly and sharply defined in mass and detail seemed out of harmony with them. It was a mere falsification of the law of aërial perspective, but it startled, almost terrified me. We so rely upon the orderly operation of familiar natural laws that any seeming suspension of them is noted as a menace to our safety, a warning of unthinkable calamity. So now the apparently causeless movement of the herbage and the slow, undeviating approach of the line of disturbance were distinctly disquieting. My companion appeared actually frightened, and I could hardly credit my senses when I saw him suddenly throw his gun to his shoulder and fire both barrels at the agitated grain! Before the smoke of the discharge had cleared away I heard a loud savage cry—a scream like that of a wild animal—and flinging his gun upon the ground Morgan sprang away and ran swiftly from the spot. At the same instant I was thrown violently to the ground by the impact of something unseen in the smoke—some soft, heavy substance that seemed thrown against me with great force.

"Before I could get upon my feet and recover my gun, which seemed to have been struck from my hands, I heard Morgan crying out as if in mortal agony, and mingling with his cries were such hoarse, savage sounds as one hears from fighting dogs. Inexpressibly terrified, I struggled to my feet and looked in the direction of Morgan's retreat; and may Heaven in mercy spare me from another sight like that! At a distance of less than thirty yards was my friend, down upon one knee, his head thrown back at a frightful angle, hatless, his long hair in disorder and his whole body in violent movement from side to side, backward and forward. His right arm was lifted and seemed to lack the hand—at least, I could see none. The other arm was invisible. At times, as my memory now reports this extraordinary scene, I could discern but a part of his body; it was as if he had been partly blotted out—I cannot otherwise express it—then a shifting of his position would bring it all into view again.

"All this must have occurred within a few seconds, yet in that time Morgan assumed all the postures of a determined wrestler vanquished by superior weight and strength. I saw nothing but him, and him not always distinctly. During the entire incident his shouts and curses were heard, as if through an enveloping uproar of such sounds of rage and fury as I had never heard from the throat of man or brute!

"For a moment only I stood irresolute, then throwing down my gun I ran forward to my friend's assistance. I had a vague belief that he was suffering from a fit, or some form of convulsion. Before I could reach his side he was down and quiet. All sounds had ceased, but with a feeling of such terror as even these awful events had not inspired I now saw again the mysterious movement of the wild oats, prolonging itself from the trampled area about the prostrate man toward the edge of a wood. It was only when it had reached the wood that I was able to withdraw my eyes and look at my companion. He was dead."

III. A MAN THOUGH NAKED MAY BE IN RAGS

The coroner rose from his seat and stood beside the dead man. Lifting an edge of the sheet he pulled it away, exposing the entire body, altogether naked and showing in the candle-light a claylike yellow. It had, however, broad maculations of bluish black, obviously caused by extravasated blood from contusions. The chest and sides looked as if they had been beaten with a bludgeon. There were dreadful lacerations; the skin was torn in strips and shreds.

The coroner moved round to the end of the table and undid a silk handkerchief which had been passed under the chin and knotted on the top of the head. When the handkerchief was drawn away it exposed what had been the throat. Some of the jurors who had risen to get a better view repented their curiosity and turned away their faces. Witness Harker went to the open window and leaned out across the sill, faint and sick. Dropping the handkerchief upon the dead man's neck the coroner stepped to an angle of the room and from a pile of clothing produced one garment after another, each of which he held up a moment for inspection. All were torn, and stiff with blood. The jurors did not make a closer inspection. They seemed rather uninterested. They had, in truth, seen all this before; the only thing that was new to them being Harker's testimony.

"Gentlemen," the coroner said, "we have no more evidence, I think. Your duty has been already explained to you; if there is nothing you wish to ask you may go outside and consider your verdict."

The foreman rose—a tall, bearded man of sixty, coarsely clad.

"I should like to ask one question, Mr. Coroner," he said. "What asylum did this yer last witness escape from?"

"Mr. Harker," said the coroner, gravely and tranquilly, "from what asylum did you last escape?"

Harker flushed crimson again, but said nothing, and the seven jurors rose and solemnly filed out of the cabin.

"If you have done insulting me, sir," said Harker, as soon as he and the officer were left alone with the dead man, "I suppose I am at liberty to go?"

"Yes."

Harker started to leave, but paused, with his hand on the door latch. The habit of his profession was strong in him—stronger than his sense of personal dignity. He turned about and said:

"The book that you have there—I recognize it as Morgan's diary. You seemed greatly interested in it; you read in it while I was testifying. May I see it? The public would like—"

"The book will cut no figure in this matter," replied the official, slipping it into his coat pocket; "all the entries in it were made before the writer's death."

As Harker passed out of the house the jury reëntered and stood about the table, on which the now covered corpse showed under the sheet with sharp definition. The foreman seated himself near the candle, produced from his breast pocket a pencil and scrap of paper and wrote rather laboriously the following verdict, which with various degrees of effort all signed:

"We, the jury, do find that the remains come to their death at the hands of a mountain lion, but some of us thinks, all the same, they had fits."

IV. An explanation from the tomb

In the diary of the late Hugh Morgan are certain interesting entries having, possibly, a scientific value as suggestions. At the inquest upon his body the book was not put in evidence; possibly the coroner thought it not worth while to confuse the jury. The date of the first of the entries mentioned cannot be ascertained; the upper part of the leaf is torn away; the part of the entry remaining follows:

"... would run in a half-circle, keeping his head turned always toward the centre, and again he would stand still, barking furiously. At last he ran away into the brush as fast as he could go. I thought at first that he had gone mad, but on returning to the house found no other alteration in his manner than what was obviously due to fear of punishment.

"Can a dog see with his nose? Do odors impress some cerebral centre with images of the thing that emittedthem?...

"*Sept. 2.*—Looking at the stars last night as they rose above the crest of the ridge east of the house, I observed them successively disappear—from left to right. Each was eclipsed but an instant, and only a few at the same time, but along the entire length of the ridge all that were within a degree or two of the crest were blotted out. It was as if something had passed along between me and them; but I could not see it, and the stars were not thick enough to define its outline. Ugh I don't like this."

Several weeks' entries are missing, three leaves being torn from the book.

"*Sept. 27.*—It has been about here again—I find evidences of its presence every day. I watched again all last night in the same cover, gun in hand, double-charged with buckshot. In the morning the fresh footprints were there, as before. Yet I would have sworn that I did not sleep—indeed, I hardly sleep at all. It is terrible, insupportable! If these amazing experiences are real I shall go mad; if they are fanciful I am mad already.

"*Oct. 3.*—I shall not go—it shall not drive me away. No, this is *my* house, *my* land. God hates a coward....

"*Oct. 5.*—I can stand it no longer; I have invited Harker to pass a few weeks with me—he has a level head. I can judge from his manner if he thinks me mad.

"*Oct. 7.*—I have the solution of the mystery; it came to me last night—suddenly, as by revelation. How simple—how terribly simple!

"There are sounds that we cannot hear. At either end of the scale are notes that stir no chord of that imperfect instrument, the human ear. They are too high or too grave. I have observed a flock of blackbirds occupying an entire tree-top—the tops of several trees—and all in full song. Suddenly—in a moment—at absolutely the same instant—all spring into the air and fly away. How? They could not all see one another—whole tree-tops intervened. At no point could a leader have been visible to all. There must have been a signal of warning or command, high and shrill above the din, but by me unheard. I have observed, too, the same simultaneous flight when all were silent, among not only blackbirds, but other birds—quail, for example, widely separated by bushes—even on opposite sides of a hill.

"It is known to seamen that a school of whales basking or sporting on the surface of the ocean, miles apart, with the convexity of the earth between, will sometimes dive at the same instant—all gone out of sight in a moment. The signal has been sounded—too grave for the ear of the sailor at the masthead and his comrades on the deck—who nevertheless feel its vibrations in the ship as the stones of a cathedral are stirred by the bass of the organ.

"As with sounds, so with colors. At each end of the solar spectrum the chemist can detect the presence of what are known as 'actinic' rays. They represent colors—integral colors in the composition of light—which we are unable to discern. The human eye is an imperfect instrument; its range is but a few octaves of the real 'chromatic scale.' I am not mad; there are colors that we cannot see.

"And, God help me! the Damned Thing is of such a color!"

THE DEAD VALLEY

By Ralph Adams Cram

"The Dead Valley" by Ralph Adams Cram (1863–1942) was mentioned only in the revised version of "Supernatural Horror in Literature," Lovecraft noting that the tale "achieves a memorably potent degree of vague regional horror through subtleties of atmosphere and description" (*S* 53). In his letters Lovecraft refers frequently to Cram's distinguished career as an architect and medievalist. Lovecraft never encountered Cram's extremely rare collection of ghost stories, *Black Spirits and White* (1895), where "The Dead Valley" was first published; instead, he read the story in Joseph Lewis French's anthology *Ghosts, Grim and Gentle* (1926), in September 1928 (see MTS 229). The tale has curious affinities with "The Colour out of Space" (1927), especially in its landscape descriptions; but Lovecraft read the story more than a year after writing his own.

I have a friend, Olof Ehrensvärd, a Swede by birth, who yet, by reason of a strange and melancholy mischance of his early boyhood, has thrown his lot with that of the New World. It is a curious story of a headstrong boy and a proud and relentless family: the details do not matter here, but they are sufficient to weave a web of romance around the tall yellow-bearded man with the sad eyes and the voice that gives itself perfectly to plaintive little Swedish songs remembered out of childhood. In the winter evenings we play chess together, he and I, and after some close, fierce battle has been fought to a finish—usually with my defeat— we fill our pipes again, and Ehrensärd tells me stories of the far, half-remembered days in the fatherland, before he went to sea: stories that grow very strange and incredible as the night deepens and the fire falls together, but stories that, nevertheless, I fully believe.

One of them made a strong impression on me, so I set it down here, only regretting that I cannot reproduce the curiously perfect English and the delicate accent which to me increased the fascination of the tale. Yet, as best I can remember it, here it is.

"I never told you how Nils and I went over the hills to Hallsberg, and how we found the Dead Valley, did I? Well, this is the way it happened. I must have been about twelve years old, and Nils Sjöberg, whose father's estate joined ours, was a few months younger. We were inseparable just at that time, and whatever we did, we did together.

"Once a week it was market day in Engelholm, and Nils and I went always there to see the strange sights that the market gathered from all the surrounding country. One day we quite lost our hearts, for an old man from across the Elfborg had brought a little dog to sell, that seemed to us the most beautiful dog in all the world. He was a round, woolly puppy, so funny that Nils and I sat down on the ground and laughed at him, until he came and played with us in so jolly a way that we felt that there was only one really desirable thing in life, and that was the little dog of the old man from across the hills. But alas! we had not half money enough wherewith to buy him, so we were forced to beg the old man not to sell him before the next market day, promising that we would bring the money for him then. He gave us his word, and we ran home very fast and implored our mothers to give us money for the little dog.

"We got the money, but we could not wait for the next market day. Suppose the puppy should be sold! The thought frightened us so that we begged and implored that we might be allowed to go over the hills to Hallsberg where the old man lived, and get the little dog ourselves, and at last they told us we might go. By starting early in the morning we should reach Hallsberg by three o'clock, and it was arranged that we should stay there that night with Nils's aunt, and, leaving by noon the next day, be home again by sunset.

"Soon after sunrise we were on our way, after having received minute instructions as to just what we should do in all possible and impossible circumstances, and finally a repeated injunction that we should start for home at the same hour the next day, so that we might get safely back before nightfall.

"For us, it was magnificent sport, and we started off with our rifles, full of the sense of our very great importance: yet the journey was simple enough, along a good road, across the big hills we knew so well, for Nils and I had shot over half the territory this side of the dividing ridge of the Elfborg. Back of Engelholm lay a long valley, from which rose the low mountains, and we had to cross this, and then follow the road along the side of the hills for three or four miles, before a narrow path branched off to the left, leading up through the pass.

"Nothing occurred of interest on the way over, and we reached Hallsberg in due season, found to our inexpressible joy that the little dog was not sold, secured him, and so went to the house of Nils's aunt to spend the night.

"Why we did not leave early on the following day, I can't quite remember; at all events, I know we stopped at a shooting range just outside of the town, where most attractive pasteboard pigs were sliding slowly through painted foliage, serving so as beautiful marks. The result was that we did not get fairly started for home until afternoon, and as we found ourselves at last pushing up the side of the mountain with the sun dangerously near their summits, I think we were a little scared at the prospect of the examination and possible punishment that awaited us when we got home at midnight.

"Therefore we hurried as fast as possible up the mountain side, while the blue dusk closed in about us, and the light died in the purple sky. At first we had talked hilariously, and the little dog had leaped ahead of us with the utmost joy. Latterly, however, a curious oppression came on us; we did not speak or even whistle, while the dog fell behind, following us with hesitation in every muscle.

"We had passed through the foothills and the low spurs of the mountains, and were almost at the top of the main range, when life seemed to go out of everything, leaving the world dead, so suddenly silent the forest became, so stagnant the air. Instinctively we halted to listen.

"Perfect silence,—the crushing silence of deep forests at night; and more, for always, even in the most impenetrable fastnesses of the wooded mountains, is the multitudinous murmur of little lives, awakened by the darkness, exaggerated and intensified by the stillness of the air and the great dark: but here and now the silence seemed unbroken even by the turn of a leaf, the movement of a twig, the note of night bird or insect. I could hear the blood beat through my veins; and the crushing of the grass under our feet as we advanced with hesitating steps sounded like the falling of trees.

"And the air was stagnant,—dead. The atmosphere seemed to lie upon the body like the weight of sea on a diver who has ventured too far into its awful depths. What we usually call silence seems so only in relation to the din of ordinary experience. This was silence in the absolute, and it crushed the mind while it intensified the senses, bringing down the awful weight of inextinguishable fear.

"I know that Nils and I stared towards each other in abject terror, listening to our quick, heavy breathing, that sounded to our acute senses like the fitful rush of waters. And the poor little dog we were leading justified our terror. The black oppression seemed to crush him even as it did us. He lay close on the ground, moaning feebly, and dragging himself painfully and slowly closer to Nils's feet. I think this exhibition of utter animal fear was the last touch, and must inevitably have blasted our reason—mine anyway; but just then, as we stood quaking on the bounds of madness, came a sound, so awful, so ghastly, so horrible, that it seemed to rouse us from the dead spell that was on us.

"In the depth of the silence came a cry, beginning as a low, sorrowful moan, rising to a tremulous shriek, culminating in a yell that seemed to tear the night in sunder and rend the world as by a cataclysm. So fearful was it that I could not believe it had actual existence: it passed previous experience, the powers of belief, and for a moment I thought it the result of my own animal terror, an hallucination born of tottering reason.

"A glance at Nils dispelled this thought in a flash. In the pale light of the high stars he was the embodiment of all possible human fear, quaking with an ague, his jaw fallen, his tongue out, his eyes protruding like those of a hanged man. Without a word we fled, the panic of fear giving us strength, and together, the little dog caught close in Nils's arms, we sped down the side of the cursed mountains,—anywhere, goal was of no account: we had but one impulse—to get away from that place.

"So under the black trees and the far white stars that flashed through the still leaves overhead, we leaped down the mountain side, regardless of path or landmark, straight through the tangled underbrush, across mountain streams, through fens and copses, anywhere, so only that our course was downward.

"How long we ran thus, I have no idea, but by and by the forest fell behind, and we found ourselves among the foothills, and fell exhausted on the dry short grass, panting like tired dogs.

"It was lighter here in the open, and presently we looked around to see where we were, and how we were to strike out in order to find the path that would lead us home. We looked in vain for a familiar sign. Behind us rose the great wall of black forest on the flank of the mountain: before us lay the undulating mounds of low foothills, unbroken by trees or rocks, and beyond, only the fall of black sky bright with multitudinous stars that turned its velvet depth to a luminous gray.

"As I remember, we did not speak to each other once: the terror was too heavy on us for that, but by and by we rose simultaneously and started out across the hills.

"Still the same silence, the same dead, motionless air—air that was at once sultry and chilling: a heavy heat struck through with an icy chill that felt almost like the burning of frozen steel. Still carrying the helpless dog, Nils pressed on through the hills, and I followed close behind. At last, in front of us, rose a slope of moor touching the white stars. We climbed it wearily, reached the top, and found ourselves gazing down into a great, smooth valley, filled halfway to the brim with—what?

"As far as the eye could see stretched a level plain of ashy white, faintly phosphorescent, a sea of velvet fog that lay like motionless water, or rather like a floor of alabaster, so dense did it appear, so seemingly capable of sustaining weight. If it were possible, I think that sea of dead white mist struck even greater terror into my soul than the heavy silence or the deadly cry—so ominous was it, so utterly unreal, so phantasmal, so impossible, as it lay there like a dead ocean under the steady stars. Yet through that mist we must go! there seemed no other way home, and, shattered with abject fear, mad with the one desire to get back, we started down the slope to where the sea of milky mist ceased, sharp and distinct around the stems of the rough grass.

"I put one foot into the ghostly fog. A chill as of death struck through me, stopping my heart, and I threw myself backward on the slope. At that instant came again the shriek, close, close, right in our ears, in ourselves, and far out across that damnable sea I saw the cold fog lift like a water-spout and toss itself high in writhing convolutions towards the sky. The stars began to grow dim as thick vapor swept across them, and in the growing dark I saw a great, watery moon lift itself slowly above the palpitating sea, vast and vague in the gathering mist.

"This was enough: we turned and fled along the margin of the white sea that throbbed now with fitful motion below us, rising, rising, slowly and steadily, driving us higher and higher up the side of the foothills.

"It was a race for life; that we knew. How we kept it up I cannot understand, but we did, and at last we saw the white sea fall behind us as we staggered up the end of the valley, and then down into a region that we knew, and so into the old path. The last thing I remember was hearing a strange voice, that of Nils, but horribly changed, stammer brokenly, 'The dog is dead!' and then the whole world turned around twice, slowly and resistlessly, and consciousness went out with a crash.

"It was some three weeks later, as I remember, that I awoke in my own room, and found my mother sitting beside the bed. I could not think very well at first, but as I slowly grew strong again, vague flashes of recollection began to come to me, and little by little the whole sequence of events of that awful night in the Dead Valley came back. All that I could gain from what was told me was that three weeks before I had been found in my own bed, raging sick, and that my illness grew fast into brain fever. I tried to speak of the dread things that had happened to me, but I saw at once that no one looked on them save as the hauntings of a dying frenzy, and so I closed my mouth and kept my own counsel.

"I must see Nils, however, and so I asked for him. My mother told me that he also had been ill with a strange fever, but that he was now quite well again. Presently they brought him in, and when we were alone I began to speak to him of the night on the mountain. I shall never forget the shock that struck me down on my pillow when the boy denied everything: denied having gone with me, ever having heard the cry, having seen the valley, or feeling the deadly chill of the ghostly fog. Nothing would shake his determined ignorance, and in spite of myself I was forced to admit that his denials came from no policy of concealment, but from blank oblivion.

"My weakened brain was in a turmoil. Was it all but the floating phantasm of delirium? Or had the horror of the real thing blotted Nils's mind into blankness so far as the events of the night in the Dead Valley were concerned? The latter explanation seemed the only one, else how explain the sudden illness which in a night had struck us both down? I said nothing more, either to Nils or to my own people, but waited, with a growing determination that, once well again, I would find that valley if it really existed.

"It was some weeks before I was really well enough to go, but finally, late in September, I chose a bright, warm, still day, the last smile of the dying summer, and started early in the morning along the path that led to Hallsberg. I was sure I knew where the trail struck off to the right, down which we had come from the valley of dead water, for a great tree grew by the Hallsberg path at the point where, with a sense of salvation, we had found the home road. Presently I saw it to the right, a little distance ahead.

"I think the bright sunlight and the clear air had worked as a tonic to me, for by the time I came to the foot of the great pine, I had quite lost faith in the verity of the vision that haunted me, believing at last that it was indeed but the nightmare of madness. Nevertheless, I turned sharply to the right, at the base of the tree, into a narrow path that led through a dense thicket. As I did so I tripped over something. A swarm of flies sung into the air around me, and looking down I saw the matted fleece, with the poor little bones thrusting through, of the dog we had bought in Hallsberg.

"Then my courage went out with a puff, and I knew that it all was true, and that now I was frightened. Pride and the desire for adventure urged me on, however, and I pressed into the close thicket that barred my way. The path was hardly visible: merely the worn road of some small beasts, for, though it showed in the crisp grass, the bushes above grew thick and hardly penetrable. The land rose slowly, and rising grew clearer, until at last I came out on a great slope of hill, unbroken by trees or shrubs, very like my memory of that rise of land we had topped in order that we might find the dead valley and the icy fog. I looked at the sun; it was bright and clear, and all around insects were humming in the autumn air, and birds were darting to and fro. Surely there was no danger, not until nightfall at least; so I began to whistle, and with a rush mounted the last crest of brown hill.

"There lay the Dead Valley! A great oval basin, almost as smooth and regular as though made by man. On all sides the grass crept over the brink of the encircling hills, dusty green on the crests, then fading into ashy brown, and so to a deadly white, this last color forming a thin ring, running in a long line around the slope. And then? Nothing. Bare, brown, hard earth, glittering with grains of alkali, but otherwise dead and barren. Not a tuft of grass, not a stick of brushwood, not even a stone, but only the vast expanse of beaten clay.

"In the midst of the basin, perhaps a mile and a half away, the level expanse was broken by a great dead tree, rising leafless and gaunt into the air. Without a moment's hesitation I started down into the valley and made for this goal. Every particle of fear seemed to have left me, and even the valley itself did not look so very terrifying. At all events, I was driven by an overwhelming curiosity, and there seemed to be but one thing in the world to do,—to get to that Tree! As I trudged along over the hard earth, I noticed that the multitudinous voices of birds and insects had died away. No bee or butterfly hovered through the air, no insects leaped or crept over the dull earth. The very air itself was stagnant.

"As I drew near the skeleton tree, I noticed the glint of sunlight on a kind of white mound around its roots, and I wondered curiously. It was not until I had come close that I saw its nature.

"All around the roots and barkless trunk was heaped a wilderness of little bones. Tiny skulls of rodents and of birds, thousands of them, rising about the dead tree and streaming off for several yards in all directions, until the dreadful pile ended in isolated skulls and scattered skeletons. Here and there a larger bone appeared,—the thigh of a sheep, the hoofs of a horse, and to one side, grinning slowly, a human skull.

"I stood quite still, staring with all my eyes, when suddenly the dense silence was broken by a faint, forlorn cry high over my head. I looked up and saw a great falcon turning and sailing downward just over the tree. In a moment more she fell motionless on the bleaching bones.

"Horror struck me, and I rushed for home, my brain whirling, a strange numbness growing in me. I ran steadily, on and on. At last I glanced up. Where was the rise of hill? I looked around wildly. Close before me was the dead tree with its pile of bones. I had circled it round and round, and the valley wall was still a mile and a half away.

"I stood dazed and frozen. The sun was sinking, red and dull, towards the line of hills. In the east the dark was growing fast. Was there still time? *Time!* It was not *that* I wanted, it was *will!* My feet seemed clogged as in a nightmare. I could hardly drag them over the barren earth. And then I felt the slow chill creeping through me. I looked down. Out of the earth a thin mist was rising, collecting in little pools that grew ever larger until they joined here and there, their currents swirling slowly like thin blue smoke. The western hills halved the copper sun. When it was dark I should hear that shriek again, and then I should die. I knew that, and with every remaining atom of will I staggered towards the red west through the writhing mist that crept clammily around my ankles, retarding my steps.

"And as I fought my way off from the Tree, the horror grew, until at last I thought I was going to die. The silence pursued me like dumb ghosts, the still air held my breath, the hellish fog caught at my feet like cold hands.

"But I won! though not a moment too soon. As I crawled on my hands and knees up the brown slope, I heard, far away and high in the air, the cry that already had almost bereft me of reason. It was faint and vague, but unmistakable in its horrible intensity. I glanced behind. The fog was dense and pallid, heaving undulously up the brown slope. The sky was gold under the setting sun, but below was the ashy gray of death. I stood for a moment on the brink of this sea of hell, and then leaped down the slope. The sunset opened before me, the night closed behind, and as I crawled home weak and tired, darkness shut down on the Dead Valley."

151

THE BAD LANDS

By John Metcalfe

Lovecraft discussed John Metcalfe's "The Bad Lands" in the revised version of "Supernatural Horror in Literature," stating that it "contain[s] gradations of horror that strongly savour of genius" (*S* 58). Lovecraft read the story—which was included in Metcalfe's celebrated collection *The Smoking Leg and Other Stories* (1925)—in April 1926. He wrote to his aunt Lillian D. Clark: "Sonny [Frank Belknap Long] produc'd a new horror book from the library—a short-story collection by John Metcalfe entitled 'The Smoking Leg'— in which I had time to read three stories. One of the tales—'The Bad Lands'—is full of such genuine cosmic horror that I am almost resolved to mention it in my article" (April 15, 1926). The story may have had its influence on "The Colour out of Space" (written March 1927), especially in its portrayal of an anomalously dead landscape.

British writer John Metcalfe (1891–1965) wrote a substantial amount of weird and science fiction, especially in *The Smoking Leg* and its successor, *Judas and Other Stories* (1931). He also wrote a short novel of vampirism, *The Feasting Dead* (1954), published by Arkham House.

It is now perhaps fifteen years ago that Brent Ormerod, seeking the rest and change of scene that should help him to slay the demon neurosis, arrived in Todd towards the close of a mid-October day. A decrepit fly bore him to the one hotel, where his rooms were duly engaged, and it is this vision of himself sitting in the appalling vehicle that makes him think it was October or thereabouts, for he distinctly remembers the determined settling down of the dusk that forced him to drive when he would have preferred to follow his luggage on foot.

He decided immediately that five o'clock was an unsuitable time to arrive in Todd. The atmosphere, as it were, was not receptive. There was a certain repellent quality about the frore autumn air, and something peculiarly shocking in the way in which desultory little winds would spring up in darkening streets to send the fallen leaves scurrying about in hateful, furtive whirlpools.

Dinner, too, at the hotel hardly brought the consolation he had counted on. The meal itself was unexceptionable, and the room cheerful and sufficiently well filled for that time of year, yet one trivial circumstance was enough to send him upstairs with his temper ruffled and his nerves on edge. They had put him to a table with a one-eyed man, and that night the blank eye haunted all his dreams.

But for the first eight or nine days at Todd things went fairly well with him. He took frequent cold baths and regular exercise and made a point of coming back to the hotel so physically tired that to get into bed was usually to drop immediately into sleep. He wrote back to his sister, Joan, at Kensington that his nerves were already much improved and that only another fortnight seemed needed to complete the cure. "Altogether a highly satisfactory week."

Those who have been to Todd remember it as a quiet, secretive watering-place, couched watchfully in a fold of a long range of low hills along the Norfolk coast. It has been pronounced "restful" by those in high authority, for time there has a way of passing dreamily as if the days, too, were being blown past like the lazy clouds on the wings of wandering breezes. At the back, the look of the land is somehow strangely forbidding, and it is wiser to keep to the shore and the more neighbouring villages. Salterton, for instance, has been found quite safe and normal.

There are long stretches of sand dunes to the west, and by their side a nine-hole golf-course. Here, at the time of Brent's visit, stood an old and crumbling tower, an enigmatic structure which he found interesting from its sheer futility. Behind it an inexplicable road seemed to lead with great decision most uncomfortably to nowhere…. Todd, he thought, was in many ways a nice spot, but he detected in it a tendency to grow on one unpleasantly.

He came to this conclusion at the end of the ninth day, for it was then that he became aware of a peculiar uneasiness, an indescribable *malaise*.

This feeling of disquiet he at first found himself quite unable to explain or analyse. His nerves he had thought greatly improved since he had left Kensington, and his general health was good. He decided, however, that perhaps yet more exercise was necessary, and so he walked along the links and the sand dunes to the queer tower and the inexplicable road that lay behind it three times a day instead of twice.

His discomfort rapidly increased. He would become conscious, as he set out for his walk, of a strange sinking at his heart and of a peculiar moral disturbance which was very difficult to describe. These sensations attained their maximum when he had reached his goal upon the dunes, and he suffered then what something seemed to tell him was very near the pangs of spiritual dissolution.

It was on the eleventh day that some faint hint of the meaning of these peculiar symptoms crossed his mind. For the first time he asked himself why it was that of all the many rambles he had taken in Todd since his arrival each one seemed inevitably to bring him to the same place—the yellow sand dunes with the mysterious-looking tower in the background. Something in the bland foolishness of the structure seemed to have magnetised him, and in the unaccountable excitement which the sight of it invariably produced, he had found himself endowing it with almost human characteristics.

With its white nightcap dome and its sides of pale yellow stucco it might seem at one moment to be something extravagantly ridiculous, a figure of fun at which one should laugh and point. Then, as likely as not, its character would change a little, and it would take on the abashed and crestfallen look of a jester whose best joke has fallen deadly flat, while finally, perhaps, it would develop with startling rapidity into a jovial old gentleman laughing madly at Ormerod from the middle distance out of infinite funds of merriment.

Now Brent was well aware of the dangers of an obsession such as this, and he immediately resolved to rob the tower of its unwholesome fascination by simply walking straight up to it, past it, and onwards along the road that stretched behind it.

It was on the morning of one of the last October days that he set out from the hotel with this intention in his mind. He reached the dunes at about ten, and plodded with some difficulty across them in the direction of the tower. As he neared it his accustomed sensations became painfully apparent, and presently increased to such a pitch that it was all he could do to continue on his way.

He remembered being struck again with the peculiar character of the winding road that stretched before him into a hazy distance where everything seemed to melt and swim in shadowy vagueness. On his left the gate stood open, to his right the grotesque form of the tower threatened....

Now he had reached it, and its shadow fell straight across his path. He did not halt to examine it, but strode forward through the open gate and entered upon the winding road. At the same moment he was astonished to notice that the painful clutch at his heart was immediately lifted, and that with it, too, all the indescribable uneasiness which he had characterised to himself as "moral" had utterly disappeared.

He had walked on for some little distance before another rather remarkable fact struck his attention. The country was no longer vague; rather, it was peculiarly distinct, and he was able to see for long distances over what seemed considerable stretches of park-like land, grey, indeed, in tone and somehow sad with a most poignant melancholy, yet superficially, at least, well cultivated and in some parts richly timbered. He looked behind him to catch a glimpse of Todd and of the sea, but was surprised to find that in that direction the whole landscape was become astonishingly indistinct and shadowy.

It was not long before the mournful aspect of the country about him began so to depress him and work upon his nerves that he debated with himself the advisability of returning at once to the hotel. He found that the ordinary, insignificant things about him were becoming charged with sinister suggestion and that the scenery on all sides was rapidly developing an unpleasant tendency to the *macabre*. Moreover, his watch told him that it was now half-past eleven—and lunch was at one. Almost hastily he turned about and began to descend the winding road.

It was about an hour later that he again reached the tower and saw the familiar dunes stretching once more before him. For some reason or other he seemed to have found the way back much longer and more difficult than the outward journey, and it was with a feeling of distinct relief that he actually passed through the gate and set his face towards Todd.

He did not go out again that afternoon, but sat smoking and thinking in the hotel. In the lounge he spoke to a man who sat in a chair beside him.

"What a queer place that is all at the back there behind the dunes!"

His companion's only comment was a somewhat drowsy grunt.

"Behind the tower," pursued Ormerod, "the funny tower at the other end of the links. The most Godforsaken, dismal place you can imagine. And simply miles of it!"

The other, roused to coherence much against his will, turned slowly round.

"Don't know it," he said. "There's a large farm where you say, and the other side of that is a river, and then you come to Harkaby or somewhere."

He closed his eyes and Ormerod was left to ponder the many difficulties of his remarks.

At dinner he found a more sympathetic listener. Mr. Stanton-Boyle had been in Todd a week when Brent arrived, and his sensitive, young-old face with the eager eyes and the quick, nervous contraction of the brows had caught the newcomer's attention from the first. Up to now, indeed, they had only exchanged commonplaces, but to-night each seemed more disposed towards intimacy. Ormerod began.

"I suppose you've walked around the country at the back here a good deal?" he said.

"No," replied the other. "I never go there now. I went there once or twice and that was enough."

"Why?"

"Oh, it gets on my nerves, that's all. Do you get any golf here?"

The conversation passed to other subjects, and it was not until both were smoking together over liqueur brandies in the lounge that it returned to the same theme. And then they came to a remarkable conclusion.

"The country at the back of this place," said Brent's companion, "is somehow abominable. It ought to be blown up or something. I don't say it was always like that. Last year, for instance, I don't remember noticing it at all. I fancy it may have been depressing enough, but it was not—not abominable. It's gone abominable since then, particularly to the southwest!"

They said good-night after agreeing to compare notes on Todd, S.W., and Ormerod had a most desolating dream wherein he walked up and up into a strange dim country, full of sighs and whisperings and crowding, sombre trees, where hollow breezes blew fitfully, and a queer house set with lofty pine shone out white against a lurid sky....

On the next day he walked again past the tower and through the gate and along the winding road. As he left Todd behind him and began the slow ascent among the hills he became conscious of some strange influence that hung over the country like a brooding spirit. The clearness of the preceding day was absent; instead all seemed nebulous and indistinct, and the sad landscape dropped behind and below him in the numb, unreal recession of a dream.

It was about four o'clock, and as he slowly ascended into the mournful tracts the greyness of the late autumn day was deepening into dusk. All the morning, clouds had been gathering in the west, and now the dull ache of the damp sky gave the uneasy sense of impending rain. Here a fitful wind blew the gold flame of a sear leaf athwart the November gloom, and out along the horizon great leaden masses were marching out to sea.

A terrible sense of loneliness fell upon the solitary walker trudging up into the sighing country, and even the sight of scattered habitations, visible here and there among the shadows, seemed only to intensify his feeling of dream and unreality. Everywhere the uplands strained in the moist wind, and the lines of gaunt firs that marched against the horizon gloom pointed ever out to sea. The wan crowding on of the weeping heavens, the settled pack of those leaning firs, and the fitful scurry of the leaves in the chill blast down the lane smote upon his spirit as something unutterably sad and terrible. On his right a skinny blackthorn shot up hard and wiry towards the dull grey sky; there ahead trees in a wood fluttered ragged yellow flags against the dimness.

A human figure appeared before him, and presently he saw that it was a man, apparently a labourer. He carried tools upon his shoulders, and his head was bent so that it was only when Ormerod addressed him that he looked up and showed a withered countenance. "What is the name of all this place?" said Brent, with a wide sweep of his arm.

"This," said the labourer, in a voice so thin and tired that it seemed almost like the cold breath of the wind that drove beside them, "is Hayes-in-the-Up. Of course, though, it'll be a mile farther on for you before you get to Fennington." He pointed in the direction from which he had just come, turned his sunken eyes again for a moment upon Ormerod, and then quickly faded down the descending path.

Brent looked after him wondering, but as he swept his gaze about him much of his wonder vanished. All around, the wan country seemed to rock giddily beneath those lowering skies, so heavy with the rain that never fell; all around, the sailing uplands seemed to heave and yearn under the sad tooting of the damp November wind. Oh, he could well imagine that the men of this weary, twilight region would be worn and old before their time, with its sinister stare in their eyes and its haggard gloom abroad in their pinched faces!

Thinking thus, he walked on steadily, and it was not long before certain words of the man he had met rose with uneasy suggestion to the surface of his mind. What, he asked himself, was Fennington? Somehow he did not think that the name stood for another village; rather, the word seemed to connect itself ominously with the dream he had had some little time ago. He shuddered, and had not walked many paces farther before he found that his instinct was correct.

Opposite him, across a shallow valley, stood that white house, dimly set in giant pine. Here the winds seemed almost visible as they strove in those lofty trees, and the constant rush by of the weeping sky behind made all the view seem to tear giddily through some unreal, watery medium. A striking resemblance of the pines to palm-trees and a queer effect of light which brought the white façade shaking bright against the sailing cloud-banks gave the whole a strangely exotic look.

Gazing at it across the little valley, Ormerod felt somehow that this, indeed, was the centre and hub of the wicked country, the very kernel and essence of this sad, unwholesome land that he saw flung wide in weariness about him. This abomination was it that magnetised him, that attracted him from afar with fatal fascination, and threatened him with untold disaster. Almost sobbing, he descended his side of the valley and then rose again to meet the house.

Park-like land surrounded the building, and from the smooth turf arose the pines and some clusters of shrubs. Amongst these Ormerod walked carefully till he was suddenly so near that he could look into a small room through its open window whilst he sheltered in a large yew whose dusky skirts swept the ground.

The room seemed strangely bare and deserted. A small table was pushed to one side, and dust lay thick upon it. Nearer

Ormerod a chair or two appeared, and, opposite, a great, black mantelpiece glowered in much gloom. In the centre of the floor was set the object that seemed to dominate the whole.

This was a large and cumbrous spinning-wheel of forbidding mien. It glistened foully in the dim light, and its many moulded points pricked the air in very awful fashion. Waiting there in the close stillness, the watcher fancied he could see the treadle stir. Quickly, with beating heart, beset by sudden dread, he turned away, retraced his steps among the sheltering shrubs, and descended to the valley bottom.

He climbed up the other side, and was glad to walk rapidly away down the winding path till, on turning his head, it was no longer possible to see the evil house he had just left.

It must have been near six o'clock when, on approaching the gate and tower, weary from his walk and anxious to reach the familiar and reassuring atmosphere of the hotel, he came suddenly upon a man walking through the darkness in the same direction as himself. It was Stanton-Boyle.

Ormerod quickly overtook him and spoke. "You have no idea," he said, "how glad I am to see you. We can walk back together now."

As they strolled to the hotel Brent described his walk, and he saw the other trembling. Presently Stanton-Boyle looked at him earnestly and spoke. "I've been there too," he said, "and I feel just as you do about it. I feel that that place Fennington is the centre of the rottenness. I looked through the window, too, and saw the spinningwheel and—" He stopped suddenly. "No," he went on quietly a moment later, "I won't tell you what else I saw!"

"It ought to be destroyed!" shouted Ormerod. A curious excitement tingled in his blood. His voice was loud, so that people passing them in the street turned and gazed after them. His eyes were very bright. He went on, pulling Stanton-Boyle's arm impressively. "I shall destroy it!" he said. "I shall burn it and I shall most assuredly smash that old spinning-wheel and break off its horrid spiky points!" He had a vague sense of saying curious and unusual things, but this increased rather than moderated his unaccountable elation.

Stanton-Boyle seemed somewhat abnormal too. He seemed to be gliding along the pavement with altogether unexampled smoothness and nobility as he turned his glowing eyes on Brent. "Destroy it!" he said. "Burn it! Before it is too late and it destroys you. Do this and you will be an unutterably brave man!"

When they reached the hotel Ormerod found a telegram awaiting him from Joan. He had not written to her for some time and she had grown anxious and was coming down herself on the following day. He must act quickly, before she came, for her mind in this matter would be unsympathetic. That night as he parted from Stanton-Boyle his eyes blazed in a high resolve. "To-morrow," he said, as he shook the other's hand, "I shall attempt it."

The following morning found the neurotic as good as his word. He carried matches and a tin of oil. His usually pale cheeks were flushed and his eyes sparkled strangely. Those who saw him leave the hotel remembered afterwards how his limbs had trembled and his speech halted. Stanton-Boyle, who was to see him off at the tower, reflected these symptoms in a less degree. Both men were observed to set out arm-in-arm engaged in earnest conversation.

At about noon Stanton-Boyle returned. He had walked with Ormerod to the sand dunes, and there left him to continue on his strange mission alone. He had seen him pass the tower, strike the fatal gate in the slanting morning sun, and then dwindle up the winding path till he was no more than an intense, pathetic dot along that way of mystery.

As he returned he was aware of companionship along the street. He looked round and noticed a policeman strolling in much abstraction some fifty yards behind him. Again at the hotel-entrance he turned about. The same figure in blue uniform was visible, admiring the houses opposite from the shade of an adjacent lamp-post. Stanton-Boyle frowned and withdrew to lunch.

At half-past two Joan arrived. She inquired nervously for Ormerod, and was at once addressed by Stanton-Boyle, who had waited for her in the entrance hall as desired by Brent. "Mr. Ormerod," he told her, "is out. He is very sorry. Will you allow me the impropriety of introducing myself? My name is Stanton-Boyle...."

Joan tore open the note which had been left for her by Ormerod. She seemed to find the contents unsatisfactory, for she proceeded to catechise Stanton-Boyle upon her brother's health and general habit of life at Todd. Following this she left the hotel hastily after ascertaining the direction from which Ormerod might be expected to return.

Stanton-Boyle waited. The moments passed, heavy, anxious, weighted with the sense of coming trouble. He sat and smoked. Discreet and muffled noises from within the hotel seemed full somehow of uneasy suggestion and foreboding. Outside, the street looked very gloomy in the November darkness. Something, assuredly, would happen directly.

It came, suddenly. A sound of tramping feet and excited cries that grew rapidly in volume and woke strange echoes in the reserved autumnal roads. Presently the tumult lessened abruptly, and only broken, fitful shouts and staccato ejaculations stabbed the silence. Stanton-Boyle jumped to his feet and walked hurriedly to the entrance hall.

Here there were cries and hustlings and presently strong odours and much suppressed excitement. He saw Joan talking very quickly to the manager of the hotel. She seemed to be developing a Point of View, and it was evident that it was not the manager's. For some time the press of people prevented him from discovering the cause of the commotion, but here and there he could make out detached sentences: "Tried to set old Hackney's farm on fire—" "But they'd seen him before and another man too, so—" "Asleep in the barn several times."

Before long all but the hotel residents had dispersed, and in the centre of the considerable confusion which still remained, it was now possible to see Ormerod supported by two policemen. A third hovered in the background with a large notebook. As Stanton-Boyle gazed, Brent lifted his bowed head so that their eyes met. "I have done it," he said. "I smashed it up. I brought back one of its points in my pocket.... Overcoat, left hand ... as a proof." Having pronounced which words Mr. Ormerod fainted very quietly.

For some time there was much disturbance. The necessary arrangements for the temporary pacification of the Law and of the Hotel had to be carried through, and after that Ormerod had to be got to bed. It was only after the initial excitement had in large measure abated that Stanton-Boyle ventured to discuss the matter over the after-dinner coffee. He had recognised one of the three policemen as the man whom he had noticed in the morning, and had found it well to retire from observation until he and his companions had left the hotel. Now, however, he felt at liberty to explain his theories of the situation to such as chose to listen.

He held forth with peculiar vehemence and with appropriate gestures. He spoke of a new kind of terre mauvaise, of strange regions, connected, indeed, with definite geographical limits upon the earth, yet somehow apart from them and beyond them. "The relation," he said, "is rather one of parallelism and correspondence than of actual connection. I honestly believe that these regions do exist, and are quite as 'real' in their way as the ordinary world we know. We might say they consist in a special and separated set of stimuli to which only certain minds in certain conditions are able to respond. Such a district seems to be superimposed upon the country to the southwest of this place."

A laugh arose. "You won't get the magistrate to believe that," said someone. "Why, all where you speak of past that gate by the dunes is just old Hackney's farm and nothing else."

"Of course," said another. "It was one of old Hackney's barns he was setting alight, I understand. I was speaking to one of the policemen about it. He said that fellow Ormerod had always been fossicking around there, and had gone to sleep in the barn twice. I expect it's all bad dreams."

A third spoke derisively. "Surely," he said, "you don't really expect us to believe in your Bad Lands. It's like Jack and the Beanstalk."

"All right!" said Stanton-Boyle. "Have it your own way! I know my use of the term 'Bad Lands' may be called incorrect, because it usually means that bit in the States, you know—but that's a detail. I tell you I've run up against things like this before. There was the case of Dolly Wishart, but no, I won't say anything about that—you wouldn't believe it."

The group around looked at him oddly. Suddenly there was a stir, and a man appeared in the doorway. He carried Ormerod's overcoat.

"This may settle the matter," he said. "I heard him say he'd put something in the pocket. He said—"

Stanton-Boyle interrupted him excitedly. "Why, yes," he said. "I'd forgotten that. What I was telling you about—the spinning-wheel. It will be interesting to see if—" He stopped and fumbled in the pockets. In another moment he brought out something which he held in his extended hand for all to see.

It was part of the handle of a patent separator—an object familiar enough to any who held even meagre acquaintance with the life of farms, and upon it could still be discerned the branded letters G. P. H.

"George Philip Hackney," interpreted the unbelievers with many smiles.

OOZE

By Anthony M. Rud

Lovecraft refers to Anthony M. Rud's "Ooze," which appeared in the first issue (March 1923) of *Weird Tales*, only glancingly in a letter to the editor published in the March 1924 issue; but that the story struck him is evidenced by his apparent appropriation of one important element from it—the bursting out of an invisible monster from its confinement in a house—in his own story "The Dunwich Horror" (1928). It is possible that Lovecraft regarded "Ooze" as failing to develop the promise of its plot to its fullest advantage, so that he felt inclined to see if he could do better.

Anthony M. Rud (1893–1942) published several stories in *Weird Tales* (some under the pseudonym "R. Anthony") in random issues from 1923 to 1934, but contributed voluminously to other pulps, including *Argosy, Detective Fiction Weekly*, and *Short Stories*. Most of his work was in the detective or crime genre rather than that of weird fiction.

In the heart of a second-growth piney-woods jungle of southern Alabama, a region sparsely settled save by backwoods blacks and Cajans—that queer, half-wild people descended from Acadian exiles of the middle eighteenth century—stands a strange, enormous ruin.

Interminable trailers of Cherokee rose, white-laden during a single month of spring, have climbed the heights of its three remaining walls. Palmetto fans rise knee high above the base. A dozen scattered live oaks, now belying their nomenclature because of choking tufts of gray, Spanish moss and two-foot circlets of mistletoe parasite which have stripped bare of foliage the gnarled, knotted limbs, lean fantastic beards against the crumbling brick.

Immediately beyond, where the ground becomes soggier and lower—dropping away hopelessly into the tangle of dogwood, holly, poison sumac and pitcher plants that is Moccasin Swamp—undergrowth of ti-ti and annis has formed a protecting wall impenetrable to all save the furtive ones. Some few outcasts utilize the stinking depths of that sinister swamp, distilling "shinny" or "pure cawn" liquor for illicit trade.

Tradition states that this is the case, at least—a tradition which antedates that of the premature ruin by many decades. I believe it, for during evenings intervening between investigations of the awesome spot I often was approached as a possible customer by wood-billies who could not fathom how anyone dared venture near without plenteous fortification of liquid courage.

I knew "shinny," therefore I did not purchase it for personal consumption. A dozen times I bought a quart or two, merely to establish credit among the Cajans, pouring away the vile stuff immediately into the sodden ground. It seemed then that only through filtration and condensation of their dozens of weird tales regarding "Daid House" could I arrive at understanding of the mystery and weight of horror hanging about the place.

Certain it is that out of all the superstitious cautioning, head-wagging and whispered nonsensities I obtained only two indisputable facts. The first was that no money, and no supporting battery of ten-gauge shotguns loaded with chilled shot, could induce either Cajan or darky of the region to approach within five hundred yards of that flowering wall! The second fact I shall dwell upon later.

Perhaps it would be as well, as I am only a mouthpiece in this chronicle, to relate in brief why I came to Alabama on this mission.

I am a scribbler of general fact articles, no fiction writer as was Lee Cranmer—though doubtless the confession is superfluous. Lee was my roommate during college days. I knew his family well, admiring John Corliss Cranmer even more than I admired the son and friend—and almost as much as Peggy Breede whom Lee married. Peggy liked me, but that was all. I cherish sanctified memory of her for just that much, as no other woman before or since has granted this gangling dyspeptic even a hint of joyous and sorrowful intimacy.

Work kept me to the city. Lee, on the other hand, coming of wealthy family—and, from the first, earning from his short-stories and novel royalties more than I wrested from editorial coffers—needed no anchorage. He and Peggy honeymooned a four-month trip to Alaska, visited Honolulu next winter, fished for salmon on

Cain's River, New Brunswick, and generally enjoyed the outdoors at all seasons.

They kept an apartment in Wilmette, near Chicago, yet, during the few spring and fall seasons they were "home," both preferred to rent a suite at one of the country clubs to which Lee belonged. I suppose they spent thrice or five times the amount Lee actually earned, yet for my part I only honored that the two should find such great happiness in life and still accomplish artistic triumph.

They were honest, zestful young Americans, the type—and pretty nearly the only type—two million dollars cannot spoil. John Corliss Cranmer, father of Lee, though as different from his boy as a microscope is different from a painting by Remington, was even further from being dollar conscious. He lived in a world bounded only by the widening horizon of biological science—and his love for the two who would carry on that Cranmer name.

Many a time I used to wonder how it could be that as gentle, clean-souled and lovable a gentleman as John Corliss Cranmer could have ventured so far into scientific research without attaining small-caliber atheism. Few do. He believed both in God and human kind. To accuse him of murdering his boy and the girl wife who had come to be loved as the mother of baby Elsie—as well as blood and flesh of his own family—was a gruesome, terrible absurdity! Yes, even when John Corliss Cranmer was declared unmistakably insane!

Lacking a relative in the world, baby Elsie was given to me—and the middle-aged couple who had accompanied the three as servants about half of the known world. Elsie would be Peggy over again. I worshiped her, knowing that if my stewardship of her interests could make of her a woman of Peggy's loveliness and worth I should not have lived in vain. And at four Elsie stretched out her arms to me after a vain attempt to jerk out the bobbed tail of Lord Dick, my tolerant old Airedale—and called me "papa."

I felt a deep-down choking … yes, those strangely long black lashes some day might droop in fun or coquetry, but now baby Elsie held a wistful, trusting seriousness in depths of ultramarine eyes—that same seriousness which only Lee had brought to Peggy.

Responsibility in one instant became double. That she might come to love me as more than foster parent was my dearest wish. Still, through selfishness I could not rob her of rightful heritage; she must know in after years. And the tale that I would tell her must not be the horrible suspicion which had been bandied about in common talk!

I went to Alabama, leaving Elsie in the competent hands of Mrs. Daniels and her husband, who had helped care for her since birth.

In my possession, prior to the trip, were the scant facts known to authorities at the time of John Corliss Cranmer's escape and disappearance. They were incredible enough.

For conducting biological research upon forms of protozon life, John Corliss Cranmer had hit upon this region of Alabama. Near a great swamp teeming with microscopic organisms, and situated in a semi-tropical belt where freezing weather rarely intruded to harden the bogs, the spot seemed ideal for his purpose.

Through Mobile he could secure supplies daily by truck. The isolation suited. With only an octoroon man to act as chef, houseman and valet for the times he entertained no visitors, he brought down scientific apparatus, occupying temporary quarters in the village of Burdett's Corners while his woods house was in process of construction.

By all accounts the Lodge, as he termed it, was a substantial affair of eight or nine rooms, built of logs and planed lumber bought at Oak Grove. Lee and Peggy were expected to spend a portion of each year with him; quail, wild turkey and deer abounded, which fact made such a vacation certain to please the pair. At other times all save four rooms was closed.

This was in 1907, the year of Lee's marriage. Six years later when I came down, no sign of a house remained except certain mangled and rotting timbers projecting from viscid soil—or what seemed like soil. And a twelve-foot wall of brick had been built to enclose the house completely! One portion of this had fallen *inward!*

II

I wasted weeks of time at first, interviewing officials of the police department at Mobile, the town marshals and county sheriffs of Washington and Mobile counties, and officials of the psychopathic hospital from which Cranmer made his escape.

In substance the story was one of baseless homicidal mania. Cranmer the elder had been away until late fall, attending two scientific conferences in the North, and then going abroad to compare certain of his findings with those of a Dr. Gemmler of Prague University. Unfortunately, Gemmler was assassinated by a religious fanatic shortly afterward. The fanatic voiced virulent objection to all Mendelian research as blasphemous. This was his only defense. He was hanged.

Search of Gemmler's notes and effects revealed nothing save an immense amount of laboratory data on karyokinesis—the process of chromosome arrangement occurring in first growing cells of higher animal embryos. Apparently Cranmer had hoped to develop some similarities, or point out differences between hereditary factors occurring in lower forms of life and those half demonstrated in the cat and monkey. The authorities had found nothing that helped me. Cranmer had gone crazy; was that not sufficient explanation?

Perhaps it was for them, but not for me—and Elsie.

But to the slim basis of fact I was able to unearth:

No one wondered when a fortnight passed without appearance of any person from the Lodge. Why should anyone worry? A provision salesman in Mobile called up twice, but failed to complete a connection. He merely shrugged. The Cranmers had gone away somewhere on a trip. In a week, a month, a year they would be back. Meanwhile he lost commissions, but what of it? He had no responsibility for these queer nuts up there in the piney-woods. Crazy? Of course! Why should any guy with millions to spend shut himself up among the Cajans and draw microscope-enlarged notebook pictures of—what the salesman called—"germs"?

A stir was aroused at the end of the fortnight, but the commotion confined itself to building circles. Twenty carloads of building brick, fifty bricklayers, and a quarter-acre of fine-meshed wire—the sort used for screening off pens of rodents and small marsupials in a zoological garden—were ordered, *damn expense, hurry!* by an unshaved, tattered man who identified himself with difficulty as John Corliss Cranmer.

He looked strange, even then. A certified check for the total amount, given in advance, and another check of absurd size slung toward a labor entrepreneur, silenced objection, however. These millionaires were apt to be flighty. When they wanted something they wanted it at tap of the bell. Well, why not drag down the big profits? A poorer man would have been jacked up in a day. Cranmer's fluid gold bathed him in immunity to criticism.

The encircling wall was built, and roofed with wire netting which drooped about the squat-pitch of the Lodge. Curious inquiries of workmen went unanswered until the final day.

Then Cranmer, a strange, intense apparition who showed himself more shabby than a quay derelict, assembled every man jack of the workmen. In one hand he grasped a wad of blue slips—fifty-six of them. In the other he held a Luger automatic.

"I offer each man a thousand dollars for *silence!*" he announced.

"As an alternative—*death!* You know little. Will all of you consent to swear upon your honor that nothing which has occurred here will be mentioned elsewhere? By this I mean *absolute* silence! You will not come back here to investigate anything. You will not tell your wives. You will not open your mouths even upon the witness stand in case you are called! My price is one thousand apiece.

"In case one of you betrays me *I give you my word that this man shall die!* I am rich. I can hire men to do murder. Well, what do you say?"

The men glanced apprehensively about. The threatening Luger decided them. To a man they accepted the blue slips—and, save for one witness who lost all sense of fear and morality in drink, none of the fifty-six has broken his pledge, as far as I know. That one bricklayer died later in delirium tremens.

It might have been different had not John Corliss Cranmer escaped.

III

They found him the first time, mouthing meaningless phrases concerning an amoeba—one of the tiny forms of protoplasmic life he was known to have studied. Also he leaped into a hysteria of self-accusation. He had murdered two innocent people! The tragedy was his crime. He had drowned them in ooze! Ah, God!

Unfortunately for all concerned, Cranmer, dazed and indubitably stark insane, chose to perform a strange travesty on fishing four miles to the west of his lodge—on the further border of Moccasin Swamp. His clothing had been torn to shreds, his hat was gone, and he was coated from head to foot with gluey mire. It was far from strange that the good folk of Shanksville, who never had glimpsed the eccentric millionaire, failed to associate him with Cranmer.

They took him in, searched his pockets—finding no sign save an inordinate sum of money—and then put him under medical care. Two precious weeks elapsed before Dr. Quirk reluctantly acknowledged that he could do nothing more for this patient, and notified the proper authorities.

Then much more time was wasted. Hot April and half of still hotter May passed by before the loose ends were connected. Then it did little good to know that this raving unfortunate was Cranmer, or that the two persons of whom he shouted in disconnected delirium actually had disappeared. Alienists absolved him of responsibility. He was confined in a cell reserved for the violent.

Meanwhile, strange things occurred back at the Lodge—which now, for good and sufficient reason, was becoming known to dwellers of the woods as Dead House. Until one of the walls fell in, however, there had been no chance to see—unless one possessed the temerity to climb either one of the tall live oaks, or mount the barrier itself. No doors or opening of any sort had been placed in that hastily-constructed wall!

By the time the western side of the wall fell, not a native for miles around but feared the spot far more than even the bottomless, snake-infested bogs which lay to west and north.

The single statement was all John Corliss Cranmer ever gave to the world. It proved sufficient. An immediate search was instituted. It showed that less than three weeks before the day of initial reckoning, his son and Peggy had come to visit him for the second time that winter—leaving Elsie behind in company of the Daniels pair. They had rented a pair of Gordons for quail hunting, and had gone out. That was the last anyone had seen of them.

The backwoods Negro who glimpsed them stalking a covey behind their two pointing dogs had known no more—even when sweated through twelve hours of third degree. Certain suspicious circumstances (having to do only with his regular pursuit of "shinny" transportation) had caused him to fall under suspicion at first. He was dropped.

Two days later the scientist himself was apprehended—a gibbering idiot who sloughed his pole—holding on to the baited hook—into a marsh where nothing save moccasins, an errant alligator, or amphibian life could have been snared.

His mind was three-quarters dead. Cranmer then was in the state of the dope fiend who rouses to a sitting position to ask seriously how many Bolshevists were killed by Julius Caesar before he was stabbed by Brutus, or why it was that Roller canaries sang only on Wednesday evenings. He knew that tragedy of the most sinister sort had stalked through his life—but little more, at first. Later the police obtained that one statement that he had murdered two human beings, but never could means or motive be established. Official guess as to the means was no more than wild conjecture; it mentioned enticing the victims to the noisome depths of Moccasin Swamp, there to let them flounder and sink.

The two were his son and daughter-in-law, Lee and Peggy!

IV

By feigning coma—then awakening with suddenness to assault three attendants with incredible ferocity and strength—John Corliss Cranmer escaped from Elizabeth Ritter Hospital.

How he hid, how he managed to traverse sixty-odd intervening miles and still balk detection, remains a minor mystery to be explained only by the assumption that maniacal cunning sufficed to outwit saner intellects.

Traverse these miles he did, though until I was fortunate enough to uncover evidence to this effect, it was supposed generally that he had made his escape as stowaway on one of the banana boats, or had buried himself in some portion of the nearer woods where he was unknown. The truth ought to be welcome to householders of Shanksville, Burdett's Corners and vicinage—those excusably prudent ones who to this day keep loaded shotguns handy and barricade their doors at nightfall.

The first ten days of my investigation may be touched upon in brief. I made headquarters in Burdett's Corners, and drove out each morning, carrying lunch and returning for my grits and piney-woods pork or mutton before nightfall. My first plan had been to camp out at the edge of the swamp, for opportunity to enjoy the outdoors comes rarely in my direction. Yet after one cursory examination of the premises I abandoned the idea. I did not want to camp alone there. And I am less superstitious than a real estate agent.

It was, perhaps, psychic warning; more probably the queer, faint, salty odor as of fish left to decay, which hung about the ruin, made too unpleasant an impression upon my olfactory sense. I experienced a distinct chill every time the lengthening shadows caught me near Dead House.

The smell impressed me. In newspaper reports of the case one ingenious explanation had been worked out. To the rear of the spot where Dead House had stood—inside the wall—was a swampy hollow circular in shape. Only a little real mud lay in the bottom of the bowlike depression now, but one reporter on the staff of *The Mobile Register* guessed that during the tenancy of the lodge it had been a fishpool. Drying up of the water had killed the fish, who now permeated the remnant of mud with this foul odor.

The possibility that Cranmer had needed to keep fresh fish at hand for some of his experiments silenced the natural objection that in a country where every stream holds gar, pike, bass, catfish and many other edible varieties, no one would dream of stocking a stagnant puddle.

After tramping about the enclosure, testing the queerly brittle, desiccated top stratum of earth within and speculating concerning the possible purpose of the wall, I cut off a long limb of chinaberry and probed the mud. One fragment of fish spine would confirm the guess of that imaginative reporter.

I found nothing resembling a piscal skeleton, but established several facts. First, this mud crater had definite bottom only three or four feet below the surface of remaining ooze. Second, the fishy stench became stronger as I stirred. Third, at one time the mud, water, or whatever had comprised the balance of content, had reached the rim of the bowl. The last showed by certain marks plain enough when the crusty, two-inch stratum of upper coating was broken away. It was puzzling.

The nature of that thin, desiccated effluvium which seemed to cover everything even to the lower foot or two of brick, came in for next inspection. It was strange stuff, unlike any earth I ever had seen, though undoubtedly some form of scum drained in from the swamp at the time of river floods or cloudbursts (which in this section are common enough in spring and fall). It crumbled beneath the fingers. When I walked over it, the stuff crunched hollowly. In fainter degree it possessed the fishy odor also.

I took some samples where it lay thickest upon the ground, and also a few where there seemed to be no more than a depth of a sheet of paper. Later I would have a laboratory analysis made.

Apart from any possible bearing the stuff might have upon the disappearance of my three friends, I felt the tug of article interest—that wonder over anything strange or seemingly inexplicable which lends the hunt for fact a certain glamor and romance all its own. To myself I was going to have to explain sooner or later just why this layer covered the entire space within the walls and was not perceptible anywhere outside! The enigma could wait, however—or so I decided.

Far more interesting were the traces of violence apparent on wall and what once had been a house. The latter seemed to have been ripped from its foundations by a giant hand, crushed out of semblance to a dwelling, and then cast in fragments about the base of wall—mainly on the south side, where heaps of twisted, broken timbers lay in profusion. On the opposite side there had been such heaps once, but now only charred sticks, coated with that grayblack, omipresent coat of desiccation, remained. These piles of charcoal had been sifted and examined most carefully by the authorities, as one theory had been advanced that Cranmer had burned the bodies of his victims. Yet no sign whatever of human remains was discovered.

The fire, however, pointed out one odd fact which controverted the reconstructions made by detectives months before. The latter, suggesting the dried scum to have drained in from the swamp, believed that the house timbers had floated out to the sides of the wall—there to arrange themselves in a series of piles! The absurdity of such a theory showed even more plainly in the fact that if the scum had filtered through in such a flood, the timbers most certainly had been dragged into piles *previously!* Some had burned—*and the scum coated their charred surfaces!*

What had been the force which had torn the lodge to bits as if in spiteful fury? Why had the parts of the wreckage been burned, the rest to escape?

Right here I felt was the keynote to the mystery, yet I could imagine no explanation. That John Corliss Cranmer himself— physically sound, yet a man who for decades had led a sedentary life—could have accomplished such destruction, unaided, was difficult to believe.

V

I turned my attention to the wall, hoping for evidence which might suggest another theory.

That wall had been an example of the worst snide construction. Though little more than a year old, the parts left standing showed evidence that they had begun to decay the day the last brick was laid. The mortar had fallen from the interstices. Here and there a brick had cracked and dropped out. Fibrils of the climbing vines had penetrated crevices, working for early destruction.

And one side already had fallen.

It was here that the first glimmering suspicion of the terrible truth was forced upon me. The scattered bricks, even those which had rolled inward toward the gaping foundation lodge, *had not been coated with scum!* This was curious, yet it could be explained by surmise that the flood itself had undermined this weakest portion of the wall. I cleared away a mass of brick from the spot on which the structure had stood; to my surprise I found it exceptionally firm! Hard red clay lay beneath! The flood conception was faulty; only some great force, exerted from inside or outside, could have wreaked such destruction.

When careful measurement, analysis and deduction convinced me—mainly from the fact that the lowermost layers of brick all had fallen *outward*, while the upper portions toppled in—I began to link up this mysterious and horrific force with the one which had rent the Lodge asunder. It looked as though a typhoon or gigantic centrifuge had needed elbow room in ripping down the wooden structure.

But I got nowhere with the theory, though in ordinary affairs I am called a man of too great imaginative tendencies. No less than three editors have cautioned me on this point. Perhaps it was the narrowing influence of great personal sympathy—yes, and love. I make no excuses, though beyond a dim understanding that some terrific, implacable force must have made this spot his playground, I ended my ninth day of note-taking and investigation almost as much in the dark as I had been while a thousand miles away in Chicago.

Then I started among the darkies and Cajans. A whole day I listened to yarns of the days which preceded Cranmer's escape from Elizabeth Ritter Hospital—days in which furtive men sniffed poisoned air for miles around Dead House, finding the odor intolerable. Days in which it seemed none possessed nerve enough to approach close. Days when the most fanciful tales of mediaeval superstitions were spun. These tales I shall not give; the truth is incredible enough.

At noon upon the eleventh day I chanced upon Rori Pailleron, a Cajan—and one of the least prepossessing of all with whom I had come in contact. "Chanced" perhaps is a bad word. I had listed every dweller of the woods within a five mile radius. Ron was sixteenth on my list. I went to him only after interviewing all four of the Crabiers and two whole families of Pichons. And Rori regarded me with the utmost suspicion until I made him a present of the two quarts of "shinny" purchased of the Pichons.

Because long practice has perfected me in the technique of seeming to drink another man's awful liquor—no, I'm not in absolute prohibitionist; fine wine or twelve-yearin-cask Bourbon whiskey arouses my definite interest—I fooled Pailleron from the start. I shall omit preliminaries, and leap to the first admission from him that he knew more concerning Dead House and its former inmates than any of the other darkies or Cajans roundabout.

"... But I ain't talkin'. *Sacre!* If I should open my gab, what might fly out? It is for keeping silent, y'r damn right...!"

I agreed. He was a wise man—educated to some extent in the queer schools and churches maintained exclusively by Cajans in the depths of the woods, yet naive withal. We drank. And I never had to ask another leading question. The liquor made him want to interest me; and the only extraordinary topic in this whole neck of the woods was the Dead House.

Three-quarters of a pint of acrid, nauseous fluid, and he hinted darkly. A pint, and he told me something I scarcely could believe. Another half-pint ... But I shall give his confession in condensed form.

He had known Joe Sibley, the octoroon chef, houseman and valet who served Cranmer. Through Joe, Rori had furnished certain indispensables in way of food to the Cranmer household. At first, these salable articles had been exclusively vegetable—white and yellow turnip, sweet potatoes, corn and beans—but later, *meat!*

Yes, meat especially—whole lambs, slaughtered and quartered, the coarsest variety of piney-woods pork and beef, all in immense quantity!

VI

In December of the fatal winter Lee and his wife stopped down at the Lodge for ten days or thereabouts.

They were enroute to Cuba at the time, intending to be away five or six weeks. Their original plan had been only to wait over a day or so in the piney-woods, but something caused an amendment to the scheme.

The two dallied. Lee seemed to have become vastly absorbed in something—so much absorbed that it was only when Peggy insisted upon continuing their trip, that he could tear himself away.

It was during those ten days that he began buying meat. Meager bits of it at first—a rabbit, a pair of squirrels, or perhaps a few quail beyond the number he and Peggy shot. Rori furnished the game, thinking nothing of it except that Lee paid double prices—and insisted upon keeping the purchases secret from other members of the household.

"I'm putting it across on the Governor, Rori!" he said once with a wink. "Going to give him the shock of his life. So you mustn't let on, even to Joe about what I want you to do. Maybe it won't work out, but if it does…! Dad'll have the scientific world at his feet! He doesn't blow his own horn anywhere near enough, you know."

Rori didn't know. Hadn't a suspicion what Lee was talking about. Still, if this rich, young idiot wanted to pay him a half dollar in good silver coin for a quail that anyone—himself included—could knock down with a fivecent shell, Rori was well satisfied to keep his mouth shut. Each evening he brought some of the small game. And each day Lee Cranmer seemed to have use for an additional quail or so.…

When he was ready to leave for Cuba, Lee came forward with the strangest of propositions. He fairly whispered his vehemence and desire for secrecy! He would tell Rori, and would pay the Cajan five hundred dollars—half in advance, and half at the end of five weeks when Lee himself would return from Cuba—provided Rori agreed to adhere absolutely to a certain secret program! The money was more than a fortune to Rori; it was undreamt-of affluence. The Cajan acceded.

"He wuz tellin' me then how the ol' man had raised some kind of pet," Rori confided, "an' wanted to get shet of it. So he give it to Lee, tellin' him to kill it, but Lee was sot on foolin' him. W'at I ask yer is, w'at kind of a pet is it w'at lives down in a mud sink an' *eats a couple hawgs every night?*"

I couldn't imagine, so I pressed him for further details. Here at last was something which sounded like a clue!

He really knew too little. The agreement with Lee provided that if Rori carried out the provisions exactly, he should be paid extra and at his exorbitant scale of all additional outlay, when Lee returned.

The young man gave him a daily schedule which Rori showed. Each evening he was to procure, slaughter and cut up a definite—and growing—amount of meat. Every item was checked, and I saw that they ran from five pounds up to forty!

"What in heaven's name did you do with it?" I demanded, excited now and pouring him an additional drink for fear caution might return to him.

"Took it through the bushes in back an' slung it in the mud sink there! An' suthin' come up an' drug it down!"

"A 'gator?"

"*Diable!* How should I know? It was dark. I wouldn't go close." He shuddered, and the fingers which lifted his glass shook as with sudden chill. "Mebbe you'd of done it, huh? Not *me*, though! The young fellah tole me to sling it in, an' I slung it.

"A couple times I come around in the light, but there wasn't nuthin' there you could see. Jes' mud, an' some water. Mebbe the thing didn't come out in daytimes...."

"Perhaps not," I agreed, straining every mental resource to imagine what Lee's sinister pet could have been. "But you said something about *two hogs a day?* What did you mean by that? This paper, proof enough that you're telling the truth so far, states that on the thirty-fifth day you were to throw forty pounds of meat—any kind—into the sink. Two hogs, even the piney-woods variety, weigh a lot more than forty pounds!"

"Them was after—after he come back!"

From this point onward, Rori's tale became more and more enmeshed in the vagaries induced by bad liquor. His tongue thickened. I shall give his story without attempt to reproduce further verbal barbarities, or the occasional prodding I had to give in order to keep him from maundering into foolish jargon.

Lee had paid munificently. His only objection to the manner in which Rori had carried out his orders was that the orders themselves had been deficient. The pet, he said, had grown enormously. It was hungry, ravenous. Lee himself had supplemented the fare with huge pails of scraps from the kitchen.

From that day Lee purchased from Rori whole sheep and hogs!

The Cajan continued to bring the carcasses at nightfall, but no longer did Lee permit him to approach the pool. The young man appeared chronically excited now. He had a tremendous secret— one the extent of which even his father did not guess, and one which would astonish the world! Only a week or two more and he would spring it. First he would have to arrange certain data.

Then came the day when everyone disappeared from Dead House. Rori came around several times, but concluded that all of the occupants had folded tents and departed—doubtless taking their mysterious "pet" along. Only when he saw from a distance Joe, the octoroon servant, returning along the road on foot toward the Lodge, did his slow mental processes begin to ferment. That afternoon Rori visited the strange place for the next to last time.

He did not go to the Lodge itself—and there were reasons. While still some hundreds of yards away from the place a terrible, sustained screaming reached his ears! It was faint, yet unmistakably the voice of Joe! Throwing a pair of number two shells into the breach of his shotgun, Rori hurried on, taking his usual path through the brush at the back.

He saw—and as he told me even "shinny" drunkenness fled his chattering tones—Joe, the octoroon. Aye, he stood in the yard, far from the pool into which Rori had thrown the carcasses—*and Joe could not move!*

Rori failed to explain in full, but *something*, a slimy, amorphous something, which glistened in the sunlight, already had engulfed the man to his shoulders! Breath was cut off. Joe's contorted face writhed with horror and beginning suffocation. One hand—all that was free of the rest of him!—beat feebly upon the rubbery, translucent thing that was engulfing his body!

Then Joe sank from sight....

VII

Five days of liquored indulgence passed before Rori, alone in his shaky cabin, convinced himself that he had seen a phantasy born of alcohol. He came back the last time—to find a high wall of brick surrounding the Lodge, and including the pool of mud into which he had thrown the meat!

While he hesitated, circling the place without discovering an opening—which he would not have dared to use, even had he found it—a crashing, tearing of timbers, and persistent sound of awesome destruction came from within. He swung himself into one of the oaks near the wall. And he was just in time to see the last supporting stanchions of the Lodge give way *outward!*

The whole structure came apart. The roof fell in—yet seemed to move after it had fallen! Logs of wall deserted retaining grasp of their spikes like layers of plywood in the grasp of the shearing machine!

That was all. Soddenly intoxicated now, Rori mumbled more phrases, giving me the idea that on another day when he became sober once more, he might add to his statements, but I—numbed to the soul—scarcely cared. If that which he related was true, what nightmare of madness must have been consummated here!

I could vision some things now which concerned Lee and Peggy, horrible things. Only remembrance of Elsie kept me faced forward in the search—for now it seemed almost that the handiwork of a madman must be preferred to what Rori claimed to have seen! What had been that sinister, translucent thing? That glistening thing which jumped upward about a man, smothering, engulfing?

Queerly enough, though such a theory as came most easily to mind now would have outraged reason in me if suggested concerning total strangers, I asked myself only what details of Rori's revelation had been exaggerated by fright and fumes of liquor. And as I sat on the creaking bench in his cabin, staring unseeing as he lurched down to the floor, fumbling with a lock box of green tin which lay under his cot, and muttering, the answer to all my questions lay within reach!

It was not until next day, however, that I made the discovery. Heavy of heart I had reexamined the spot where the Lodge had stood, then made my way to the Cajan's cabin again, seeking sober confirmation of what he had told me during intoxication.

In imagining that such a spree for Rori would be ended by a single night, however, I was mistaken. He lay sprawled almost as I had left him. Only two factors were changed. No "shinny" was left—and lying open, with its miscellaneous contents strewed about, was the tin box. Rori somehow had managed to open it with the tiny key still clutched in his hand.

Concern for his safety alone was what made me notice the box. It was a receptacle for small fishing tackle of the sort carried here and there by any sportsman. Tangles of Dowagiac minnows, spoon hooks ranging in size to silver-backed number eights; three reels still carrying line of different weights, spinners, casting plugs, wobblers, floating baits, were spilled out upon the rough plank flooring where they might snag Rori badly if he rolled. I gathered them, intending to save him an accident.

With the miscellaneous assortment in my hands, however, I stopped dead. Something had caught my eye—something lying flush with the bottom of the lock box! I stared, and then swiftly tossed the hooks and other impedimenta upon the table. What I had glimpsed there in the box was a loose-leaf notebook of the sort used for recording laboratory data! And Rori scarcely could read, let alone write!

Feverishly, a riot of recognition, surmise, hope and fear bubbling in my brain, I grabbed the book and threw it open. At once I knew that this was the end. The pages were scribbled in pencil, but the handwriting was that precise chirography I knew as belonging to John Corliss Cranmer, the scientist!

"… Could he not have obeyed my instructions! Oh, God! This …"

These were the words at top of the first page which met my eye.

Because knowledge of the circumstances, the relation of which I pried out of the reluctant Rori only some days later when I had him in Mobile as a police witness for the sake of my friend's vindication, is necessary to understanding, I shall interpolate.

Rori had not told me everything, On his late visit to the vicinage of Dead House he saw more. A crouching figure, seated Turk fashion on top of the wall, appeared to be writing industriously. Rori recognized the man as Cranmer, yet did not hail him. He had no opportunity.

Just as the Cajan came near, Cranmer rose, thrust the notebook, which had rested across his knees, into the box. Then he turned, tossed outside the wall both the locked box and a ribbon to which was attached the key.

Then his arms raised toward heaven, For five seconds he seemed to invoke the mercy of Power beyond all of man's scientific prying. And finally he leaped, *inside…!*

Rori did not climb to investigate. He knew that directly below this portion of wall lay the mud sink into which he had thrown the chunks of meat!

VIII

This is a true transcription of the statement I inscribed, telling the sequence of actual events at Dead House. The original of the statement now lies in the archives of the detective department.

Cranmer's notebook, though written in a precise hand, yet betrayed the man's insanity by incoherence and frequent repetitions. My statement has been accepted now, both by alienists and by detectives who had entertained different theories in respect to the case. It quashes the noisome hints and suspicions regarding three of the finest Americans who ever lived—and also one queer supposition dealing with supposed criminal tendencies in poor Joe, the octoroon.

John Corliss Cranmer *went* insane for sufficient cause!

As readers of popular fiction know well, Lee Cranmer's *forte* was the writing of what is called—among fellows in the craft—the pseudo-scientific story. In plain words, this means a yarn, based upon solid fact in the field of astronomy, chemistry, anthropology or whatnot, which carries to logical conclusion unproved theories of men who devote their lives to searching out further nadirs of fact.

In certain fashion these men are allies of science. Often they visualize something which has not been imagined even by the best of men from whom they secure data, thus opening new horizons of possibility. In a large way Jules Verne was one of these men in his day; Lee Cranmer bade fair to carry on the work in worthy fashion—work taken up for a period by an Englishman named Wells, but abandoned for stories of a different—and, in my humble opinion, less absorbing—type.

Lee wrote three novels, all published, which dealt with such subjects—two of the three secured from his own father's labors, and the other speculating upon the discovery and possible uses of inter-atomic energy. Upon John Corliss Cranmer's return from Prague that fatal winter, the father informed Lee that a greater subject than any with which the young man had dealt, now could be tapped.

Cranmer, senior, had devised a way in which the limiting

factors in protozoic life and *growth*, could be nullified; in time, and with cooperation of biologists who specialized upon *karyokinesis* and embryology of higher forms, he hoped—to put the theory in pragmatic terms—to be able to grow swine the size of elephants, quail or woodcock with breasts from which a hundredweight of white meat could be cut away, and steers whose dehorned heads might butt at the third story of a skyscraper!

Such result would revolutionize the methods of food supply, of course. It also would hold out hope for all undersized specimens of humanity—provided only that if factors inhibiting growth could be deleted, some method of stopping gianthood also could be developed.

Cranmer the elder, through use of an undescribed (in the notebook) growth medium of which one constituent was *agar-agar*, and the use of radium emanations, had succeeded in bringing about apparently unrestricted growth in the paramœcium protozoan, certain of the vegetable growths (among which were bacteria), and in the amorphous cell of protoplasm known as the amœba—the last a single cell containing only neucleolus, neucleus, and a space known as the contractile vacuole which somehow aided in throwing off particles impossible to assimilate directly. This point may be remembered in respect to the piles of lumber left near the outside walls surrounding Dead House!

When Lee Cranmer and his wife came south to visit, John Corliss Cranmer showed his son an amœba—normally an organism visible under low-power microscope—which he had absolved from natural growth inhibitions. This amœba, a rubbery, amorphous mass of protoplasm, was of the size then of a large beef liver. It could have been held in two cupped hands, placed side by side.

"How large could it grow?" asked Lee, wide-eyed and interested.

"So far as I know," answered the father, "there is no limit—

now! It might, if it got food enough, grow to be as big as the Masonic Temple!

"But take it out and kill it. Destroy the organism utterly—burning the fragments—else there is no telling what might happen. The amœba, as I have explained, reproduces by simple division. Any fragment remaining might be dangerous."

Lee took the rubbery, translucent giant cell—but he did not obey orders. Instead of destroying it as his father had directed, Lee thought out a plan. Suppose he should grow this organism to tremendous size? Suppose, when the tale of his father's accomplishment were spread, an amœba of many tons weight could be shown in evidence? Lee, of somewhat sensational cast of mind, determined instantly to keep secret the fact that he was not destroying the organism, but encouraging its further growth. Thought of possible peril never crossed his mind.

He arranged to have the thing fed—allowing for normal increase of size in an abnormal thing. It fooled him only in growing much more rapidly. When he came back from Cuba the amœba practically filled the whole of the mud sink hollow. He had to give it much greater supplies....

The giant cell came to absorb as much as two hogs in a single day. During daylight, while hunger still was appeased, it never emerged, however. That remained for the time that it could secure no more food near at hand to satisfy its ravenous and increasing appetite.

Only instinct for the sensational kept Lee from telling Peggy, his wife, all about the matter. Lee hoped to spring a *coup* which would immortalize his father, and surprise his wife terrifically. Therefore, he kept his own counsel—and made bargains with the Cajan, Rori, who supplied food daily for the shapeless monster of the pool.

The tragedy itself came suddenly and unexpectedly. Peggy, feeding the two Gordon setters that Lee and she used for quail hunting, was in the Lodge yard before sunset. She romped alone, as Lee himself was dressing.

Of a sudden her screams cut the still air! Without her knowledge, ten-foot *pseudopods*—those flowing tentacles of protoplasm sent forth by the sinister occupant of the pool—slid out and around her putteed ankles.

For a moment she did not understand. Then, at first suspicion of the horrid truth, her cries rent the air. Lee, at that time struggling to lace a pair of high shoes, straightened, paled, and grabbed a revolver as he dashed out.

In another room a scientist, absorbed in his notetaking, glanced up, frowned, and then—recognizing the voice—shed his white gown and came out. He was too late to do aught but gasp with horror.

In the yard Peggy was half engulfed in a squamous, rubbery something which at first he could not analyze.

Lee, his boy, was fighting with the sticky folds, and slowly, surely, losing his own grip upon the earth!

IX

John Corliss Cranmer was by no means a coward; he stared, cried aloud, then ran indoors, seizing the first two weapons which came to hand—a shotgun and hunting knife which lay in sheath in a cartridged belt across hook of the hall-tree. The knife was ten inches in length and razor keen.

Cranmer rushed out again. He saw an indecent fluid something—which as yet he had not had time to classify—lumping itself into a six-foot-high center before his very eyes!

It looked like one of the micro-organisms he had studied! One grown to frightful dimensions. An amœba!

There, some minutes suffocated in the rubbery folds—yet still apparent beneath the glistening ooze of this monster—were two bodies.

They were dead. He knew it. Nevertheless he attacked the flowing, senseless monster with his knife. Shot would do no good. And he found that even the deep, terrific slashes made by his knife closed together in a moment and healed. The monster was invulnerable to ordinary attack!

A pair of pseudopods sought out his ankles, attempting to bring him low. Both of these he severed—and escaped. Why did he try? He did not know. The two whom he had sought to rescue were dead, buried under folds of this horrid thing he knew to be his own discovery and fabrication. him. Then it was that revulsion and insanity came upon

There ended the story of John Corliss Cranmer, save for one hastily scribbled paragraph—evidently written at the time Rori had seen him atop the wall.

May we not supply with assurance the intervening steps?

Cranmer was known to have purchased a whole pen of hogs a day or two following the tragedy. These animals never were seen again. During the time the wall was being constructed is it not reasonable to assume that he fed the giant organism within—to keep it quiet? His scientist brain must have visualized clearly the havoc horror which could be wrought by the loathsome thing if it ever were driven by hunger to flow away from the Lodge and prey upon the countryside!

With the wall once in place, he evidently figured that starvation or some other means which he could supply would kill the thing. One of the means had been made by setting fire to several piles of the disgorged timbers; probably this had no effect whatever.

The amœba was to accomplish still more destruction. In the throes of hunger it threw its gigantic, formless strength against the house walls *from the inside*; then every edible morsel within was assimilated, the logs, rafters and other fragments being worked out through the contractile *vacuole*.

During some of its last struggles, undoubtedly, the side wall of brick was weakened—not to collapse, however, until the giant amœba could take advantage of the breach.

In final death lassitude, the amœba stretched itself out in a thin layer over the ground. There it succumbed, though there is no means of estimating how long a time intervened.

The last paragraph in Cranmer's notebook, scrawled so badly that it is possible some words I have not deciphered correctly, read as follows:

> "In my work I have found the means of creating a monster. The unnatural thing, in turn, has destroyed my work and those whom I held dear. It is in vain that I assure myself of innocence of spirit. Mine is the crime of presumption. Now, as expiation—worthless though that may be—I give myself ..."

It is better not to think of that last leap, and the struggle of an insane man in the grip of the dying monster.

FISHHEAD

By Irvin S. Cobb

When Irvin S. Cobb's "Fishhead" appeared in the *Argosy* on January 11, 1913, among those who expressed enthusiasm for the tale was twenty-two-year-old H. P. Lovecraft, in one of his earliest published letters: "It is the belief of the writer that very few short stories of equal merit have been published anywhere during recent years" (*Argosy*, February 8, 1913). Lovecraft cites the tale again in "Supernatural Horror in Literature," calling it "banefully effective in its portrayal of unnatural affinities between a hybrid idiot and the strange fish of an isolated lake, which at the last avenge their biped kinsman's murder" (*S* 53–54)—a description that immediately brings to mind similar unnatural affinities between the inhabitants of Innsmouth and the ichthyic denizens of the deep described in "The Shadow over Innsmouth."

Cobb (1876–1944) was not primarily a fantaisiste, but rather a humorist. Among his more celebrated writings are a series of "guyed books" to selected American states and an autobiography, *Exit Laughing* (1941).

It goes past the powers of my pen to try to describe Reelfoot Lake for you so that you, reading this, will get the picture of it in your mind as I have it in mine. For Reelfoot Lake is like no other lake that I know anything about. It is an afterthought of Creation.

The rest of this continent was made and had dried in the sun for thousands of years—for millions of years for all I know—before Reelfoot came to be. It's the newest big thing in nature on this hemisphere probably, for it was formed by the great earthquake of 1811, just a little more than a hundred years ago. That earthquake of 1811 surely altered the face of the earth on the then far frontier of this country. It changed the course of rivers, it converted hills into what are now the sunk lands of three states, and it turned the solid ground to jelly and made it roll in waves like the sea. And in the midst of the retching of the land and the vomiting of the waters it depressed to varying depths a section of the earth crust sixty miles long, taking it down—trees, hills, hollows and all; and a crack broke through to the Mississippi River so that for three days the river ran up stream, filling the hole.

The result was the largest lake south of the Ohio, lying mostly in Tennessee, but extending up across what is now the Kentucky line, and taking its name from a fancied resemblance in its outline to the splay, reeled foot of a cornfield negro. Niggerwool Swamp, not so far away, may have got its name from the same man who christened Reelfoot; at least so it sounds.

Reelfoot is, and has always been, a lake of mystery. In places it is bottomless. Other places the skeletons of the cypress trees that went down when the earth sank still stand upright, so that if the sun shines from the right quarter and the water is less muddy than common, a man peering face downward into its depths sees, or thinks he sees, down below him the bare top-limbs upstretching like drowned men's fingers, all coated with the mud of years and bandaged with pennons of the green lake slime. In still other places the lake is shallow for long stretches, no deeper than breast deep to a man, but dangerous because of the weed growths and the sunken drifts which entangle a swimmer's limbs. Its banks are mainly mud, its waters are muddied too, being a rich coffee color in the spring and a copperish yellow in the summer, and the trees along its shore are mud colored clear up to their lower limbs after the spring floods, when the dried sediment covers their trunks with a thick, scrofulous-looking coat.

There are stretches of unbroken woodland around it and slashes where the cypress knees rise countlessly like headstones and footstones for the dead snags that rot in the soft ooze. There are deadenings with the lowland corn growing high and rank below and the bleached, fire-blackened girdled trees rising above, barren of leaf and limb. There are long, dismal flats where in the spring the clotted frog-spawn clings like patches of white mucus among the weed stalks and at night the turtles crawl out to lay clutches of perfectly round, white eggs with tough, rubbery shells in the sand. There are bayous leading off to nowhere and sloughs that wind aimlessly, like great, blind worms, to finally join the big river that rolls its semi-liquid torrents a few miles to the westward.

So Reelfoot lies there, flat in the bottoms, freezing lightly in the winter, steaming torridly in the summer, swollen in the spring when the woods have turned a vivid green and the buffalo gnats by the million and the billion fill the flooded hollows with their pestilential buzzing, and in the fall ringed about gloriously with

197

all the colors which the first frost brings—gold of hickory, yellow-russet of sycamore, red of dogwood and ash and purple-black of sweet-gum.

But the Reelfoot country has its uses. It is the best game and fish country, natural or artificial, that is left in the South today. In their appointed seasons the duck and the geese flock in, and even semi-tropical birds, like the brown pelican and the Florida snakebird, have been known to come there to nest. Pigs, gone back to wildness, range the ridges, each razor-backed drove captained by a gaunt, savage, slab-sided old boar. By night the bull frogs, inconceivably big and tremendously vocal, bellow under the banks.

It is a wonderful place for fish—bass and crappie and perch and the snouted buffalo fish. How these edible sorts live to spawn and how their spawn in turn live to spawn again is a marvel, seeing how many of the big fish-eating cannibal fish there are in Reelfoot. Here, bigger than anywhere else, you find the garfish, all bones and appetite and horny plates, with a snout like an alligator, the nearest link, naturalists say, between the animal life of today and the animal life of the Reptilian Period. The shovel-nose cat, really a deformed kind of freshwater sturgeon, with a great fanshaped membranous plate jutting out from his nose like a bowsprit, jumps all day in the quiet places with mighty splashing sounds, as though a horse had fallen into the water. On every stranded log the huge snapping turtles lie on sunny days in groups of four and six, baking their shells black in the sun, with their little snaky heads raised watchfully, ready to slip noiselessly off at the first sound of oars grating in the row-locks.

But the biggest of them all are the catfish. These are monstrous creatures, these catfish of Reelfoot—scaleless, slick things, with corpsy, dead eyes and poisonous fins like javelins and long whiskers dangling from the sides of their cavernous heads. Six and seven feet long they grow to be and to weigh two hundred pounds or more, and they have mouths wide enough to take in a man's foot or a man's fist and strong enough to break any hook save the strongest and greedy enough to eat anything, living or dead or putrid, that the horny jaws can master. Oh, but they are wicked things, and they tell wicked tales of them down there. They call them man-eaters and compare them, in certain of their habits, to sharks.

Fishhead was of a piece with this setting. He fitted into it as an acorn fits its cup. All his life he had lived on Reelfoot, always in the one place, at the mouth of a certain slough. He had been born there, of a negro father and a half-breed Indian mother, both of them now dead, and the story was that before his birth his mother was frightened by one of the big fish, so that the child came into the world most hideously marked. Anyhow, Fishhead was a human monstrosity, the veritable embodiment of nightmare. He had the body of a man—a short, stocky, sinewy body—but his face was as near to being the face of a great fish as any face could be and yet retain some trace of human aspect. His skull sloped back so abruptly that he could hardly be said to have a forehead at all; his chin slanted off right into nothing. His eyes were small and round with shallow, glazed, pale-yellow pupils, and they were set wide apart in his head and they were unwinking and staring, like a fish's eyes. His nose was no more than a pair of tiny slits in the middle of the yellow mask. His mouth was the worst of all. It was the awful mouth of a catfish, lipless and almost inconceivably wide, stretching from side to side. Also when Fishhead became a man grown his likeness to a fish increased, for the hair upon his face grew out into two tightly kinked, slender pendants that drooped down either side of the mouth like the beards of a fish.

If he had any other name than Fishhead, none excepting he knew it. As Fishhead he was known and as Fishhead he answered. Because he knew the waters and the woods of Reelfoot better than any other man there, he was valued as a guide by the city men who came every year to hunt or fish; but there were few such jobs that Fishhead would take. Mainly he kept to himself, tending his corn patch, netting the lake, trapping a little and in season pot hunting for the city markets. His neighbors, ague-bitten whites and malaria-proof negroes alike, left him to himself. Indeed for the most part they had a superstitious fear of him. So he lived alone, with no kith nor kin, nor even a friend, shunning his kind and shunned by them.

His cabin stood just below the state line, where Mud Slough runs into the lake. It was a shack of logs, the only human habitation for four miles up or down. Behind it the thick timber came shouldering right up to the edge of Fishhead's small truck patch, enclosing it in thick shade except when the sun stood just overhead. He cooked his food in a primitive fashion, outdoors, over a hole in the soggy earth or upon the rusted red ruin of an old cook stove, and he drank the saffron water of the lake out of a dipper made of a gourd, faring and fending for himself, a master hand at skiff and net, competent with duck gun and fish spear, yet a creature of affliction and loneliness, part savage, almost amphibious, set apart from his fellows, silent and suspicious.

In front of his cabin jutted out a long fallen cottonwood trunk, lying half in and half out of the water, its top side burnt by the sun and worn by the friction of Fishhead's bare feet until it showed countless patterns of tiny scrolled lines, its under side black and rotted and lapped at unceasingly by little waves like tiny licking tongues. Its farther end reached deep water. And it was a part of Fishhead, for no matter how far his fishing and trapping might take him in the daytime, sunset would find him back there, his boat drawn up on the bank and he on the outer end of this log. From a distance men had seen him there many times, sometimes squatted, motionless as the big turtles that would crawl upon its dipping tip in his absence, sometimes erect and vigilant like a creek crane, his misshapen yellow form outlined against the yellow sun, the yellow water, the yellow banks—all of them yellow together.

If the Reelfooters shunned Fishhead by day they feared him by night and avoided him as a plague, dreading even the chance of a casual meeting. For there were ugly stories about Fishhead—stories which all the negroes and some of the whites believed. They said that a cry which had been heard just before dusk and just after, skittering across the darkened waters, was his calling cry to the big cats, and at his bidding they came trooping in, and that in their company he swam in the lake on moonlight nights, sporting with them, diving with them, even feeding with them on what manner of unclean things they fed. The cry had been heard many times, that much was certain, and it was certain also that the big fish were noticeably thick at the mouth of Fishhead's slough. No native Reelfooter, white or black, would willingly wet a leg or an arm there.

Here Fishhead had lived and here he was going to die. The Baxters were going to kill him, and this day in midsummer was to be the time of the killing. The two Baxters—Jake and Joel—were coming in their dugout to do it. This murder had been a long time in the making. The Baxters had to brew their hate over a slow fire for months before it reached the pitch of action. They were poor whites, poor in everything—repute and worldly goods and standing—a pair of fever-ridden squatters who lived on whisky and tobacco when they could get it, and on fish and cornbread when they couldn't.

The feud itself was of months' standing. Meeting Fishhead one day in the spring on the spindly scaffolding of the skiff landing at Walnut Log, and being themselves far overtaken in liquor and vainglorious with a bogus alcoholic substitute for courage, the brothers had accused him, wantonly and without proof, of running their trotline and stripping it of the hooked catch—an unforgivable sin among the water dwellers and the shanty boaters of the South. Seeing that he bore this accusation in silence, only eyeing them steadfastly, they had been emboldened then to slap his face, whereupon he turned and gave them both the beating of their lives—bloodying their noses and bruising their lips with hard blows against their front teeth, and finally leaving them, mauled and prone, in the dirt. Moreover, in the onlookers a sense of the everlasting fitness of things had triumphed over race prejudice and allowed them—two freeborn, sovereign whites—to be licked by a nigger.

Therefore, they were going to get the nigger. The whole thing had been planned out amply. They were going to kill him on his log at sundown. There would be no witnesses to see it, no retribution to follow after it. The very ease of the undertaking made them forget even their inborn fear of the place of Fishhead's habitation.

For more than an hour now they had been coming from their shack across a deeply indented arm of the lake. Their dugout, fashioned by fire and adz and draw-knife from the bole of a gum tree, moved through the water as noiselessly as a swimming mallard, leaving behind it a long, wavy trail on the stilled waters. Jake, the better oarsman sat flat in the stern of the round-bottomed craft, paddling with quick, splashless strokes. Joel, the better shot, was squatted forward. There was a heavy, rusted duck gun between his knees.

Though their spying upon the victim had made them certain sure he would not be about the shore for hours, a doubled sense of caution led them to hug closely the weedy banks. They slid along the shore like shadows, moving so swiftly and in such silence that the watchful mud turtles barely turned their snaky heads as they passed. So, a full hour before the time, they came slipping around the mouth of the slough and made for a natural ambuscade which the mixed breed had left within a stone's jerk of his cabin to his own undoing.

Where the slough's flow joined deeper water a partly uprooted tree was stretched, prone from shore, at the top still thick and green with leaves that drew nourishment from the earth in which the half-uncovered roots yet held, and twined about with an exuberance of trumpet vines and wild fox-grapes. All about was a huddle of drift—last year's cornstalks, shreddy strips of bark, chunks of rotted weed, all the riffle and dunnage of a quiet eddy. Straight into this green clump glided the dugout and swung, broadside on, against the protecting trunk of the tree, hidden from the inner side by the intervening curtains of rank growth, just as the Baxters had intended it should be hidden, when days before in their scouting they marked this masked place of waiting and included it, then and there, in the scope of their plans.

There had been no hitch or mishap. No one had been abroad in the late afternoon to mark their movements—and in a little while Fishhead ought to be due. Jake's woodman's eye followed the downward swing of the sun speculatively. The shadows, thrown shoreward, lengthened and slithered on the small ripples. The small noises of the day died out; the small noises of the coming night began to multiply. The green-bodied flies went away and big mosquitoes, with speckled gray legs, came to take the places of the flies. The sleepy lake sucked at the mud banks with small mouthing sounds as though it found the taste of the raw mud agreeable. A monster crawfish, big as a chicken lobster, crawled out of the top of his dried mud chimney and perched himself there, an armored sentinel on the watchtower. Bull bats began to flitter back and forth above the tops of the trees. A pudgy muskrat, swimming with head up, was moved to sidle off briskly as he met a cottonmouth moccasin snake, so fat and swollen with summer poison that it looked almost like a legless lizard as it moved along the surface of the water in a series of slow torpid S's. Directly above the head of either of the waiting assassins a compact little swarm of midges hung, holding to a sort of kite-shaped formation.

A little more time passed and Fishhead came out of the woods at the back, walking swiftly, with a sack over his shoulder. For a few seconds his deformities showed in the clearing, then the black inside of the cabin swallowed him up. By now the sun was almost down. Only the red nub of it showed above the timber line across the lake, and the shadows lay inland a long way. Out beyond, the big cats were stirring, and the great smacking sounds as their twisting bodies leaped clear and fell back in the water came shoreward in a chorus.

But the two brothers in their green covert gave heed to nothing except the one thing upon which their hearts were set and their nerves tensed. Joel gently shoved his gunbarrels across the log, cuddling the stock to his shoulder and slipping two fingers caressingly back and forth upon the triggers. Jake held the narrow dugout steady by a grip upon a fox-grape tendril.

A little wait and then the finish came. Fishhead emerged from the cabin door and came down the narrow footpath to the water and out upon the water on his log. He was barefooted and bareheaded, his cotton shirt open down the front to show his yellow neck and breast, his dungaree trousers held about his waist by a twisted tow string. His broad splay feet, with the prehensile toes outspread, gripped the polished curve of the log as he moved along its swaying, dipping surface until he came to its outer end and stood there erect, his chest filling, his chinless face lifted up and something of mastership and dominion in his poise. And then—his eye caught what another's eyes might have missed— the round, twin ends of the gun barrels, the fixed gleams of Joel's eyes, aimed at him through the green tracery.

In that swift passage of time, too swift almost to be measured by seconds, realization flashed all through him, and he threw his head still higher and opened wide his shapeless trap of a mouth, and out across the lake he sent skittering and rolling his cry. And in his cry was the laugh of a loon, and the croaking bellow of a frog, and the bay of a hound, all the compounded night noises of the lake. And in it, too, was a farewell and a defiance and an appeal. The heavy roar of the duck gun came.

At twenty yards the double charge tore the throat out of him. He came down, face forward, upon the log and clung there, his trunk twisting distortedly, his legs twitching and kicking like the legs of a speared frog, his shoulders hunching and lifting spasmodically as the life ran out of him all in one swift coursing flow. His head canted up between the heaving shoulders, his eyes looked full on the staring face of his murderer, and then the blood came out of his mouth and Fishhead, in death still as much fish as man, slid flopping, head first, off the end of the log and sank, face downward, slowly, his limbs all extended out. One after another a string of big bubbles came up to burst in the middle of a widening reddish stain on the coffee-colored water.

The brothers watched this, held by the horror of the thing they had done, and the cranky dugout, tipped far over by the recoil of the gun, took water steadily across its gunwale; and now there was a sudden stroke from below upon its careening bottom and it went over and they were in the lake. But shore was only twenty feet away, the trunk of the uprooted tree only five. Joel, still holding fast to his hot gun, made for the log, gaining it with one stroke. He threw his free arm over it and clung there, treading water, as he shook his eyes free. Something gripped him—some great, sinewy, unseen thing gripped him fast by the thigh, crushing down on his flesh.

He uttered no cry, but his eyes popped out and his mouth set in a square shape of agony, and his fingers gripped into the bark of the tree like grapples. He was pulled down and down, by steady jerks, not rapidly but steadily, so steadily, and as he went his fingernails tore four little white strips in the tree bark. His mouth went under, next his popping eyes, then his erect hair, and finally his clawing, clutching hand, and that was the end of him.

Jake's fate was harder still, for he lived longer—long enough to see Joel's finish. He saw it through the water that ran down his face, and with a great surge of his whole body he literally flung himself across the log and jerked his legs up high into the air to save them. He flung himself too far, though, for his face and chest hit the water on the far side. And out of this water rose the head of a great fish, with the lake slime of years on its flat, black head, its whiskers bristling, its corpsy eyes alight. Its horny jaws closed and clamped in the front of Jake's flannel shirt. His hand struck out wildly and was speared on a poisoned fin, and unlike Joel, he went from sight with a great yell and a whirling and a churning of the water that made the cornstalks circle on the edges of a small whirlpool.

But the whirlpool soon thinned away into widening rings of ripples and the cornstalks quit circling and became still again, and only the multiplying night noises sounded about the mouth of the slough.

$$\mathcal{C} \mathcal{S}$$

The bodies of all three came ashore on the same day near the same place. Except for the gaping gunshot wound where the neck met the chest, Fishhead's body was unmarked. But the bodies of the two Baxters were so marred and mauled that the Reelfooters buried them together on the bank without ever knowing which might be Jake's and which might be Joel's.

THE HARBOR-MASTER

By Robert W. Chambers

In 1927 Lovecraft discovered the early work of Robert W. Chambers (1865–1933), who showed tremendous promise as a fantaisiste in such volumes as *The King in Yellow* (1895), *The Maker of Moons* (1896), *The Mystery of Choice* (1897), and *In Search of the Unknown* (1904), only to descend to hackneyed romances that are now universally and deservedly forgotten. While being most fond of *The King in Yellow* (to the point of mentioning it in his joke essay "History of the *Necronomicon*" [1927] and citing such of Chambers's creations as the Yellow Sign in his own fiction), Lovecraft recorded that "'The Harbor-Master' gave me quite a wallop in 1926 [*sic*]" (*SL* 4.144)—no surprise, since the figure of the harbor-master bears similarities to the batrachian inhabitants of Innsmouth described in "The Shadow over Innsmouth" (1931). "The Harbor-Master" was first published in *Ainslee's Magazine* (August 1899) and slightly revised to become the first five chapters of the episodic novel *In Search of the Unknown*. Lovecraft added that he "did not care for the rest of the volume," probably because of the increasing romantic element that we find infiltrating "The Harbor-Master" itself.

I

Because it all seems so improbable—so horribly impossible to me now, sitting here safe and sane in my own library—I hesitate to record an episode which already appears to me less horrible than grotesque. Yet, unless this story is written now, I know I shall never have the courage to tell the truth about the matter—not from fear of ridicule, but because I myself shall soon cease to credit what I now know to be true. Yet scarcely a month has elapsed since I heard the stealthy purring of what I believed to be the shoaling undertow—scarcely a month ago, with my own eyes, I saw that which, even now, I am beginning to believe never existed. As for the harbor-master—and the blow I am now striking at the old order of things—But of that I shall not speak now, or later; I shall try to tell the story simply and truthfully, and let my friends testify as to my probity and the publishers of this book corroborate them.

On the 29th of February I resigned my position under the government and left Washington to accept an offer from Professor Farrago—whose name he kindly permits me to use—and on the first day of April I entered upon my new and congenial duties as general superintendent of the water-fowl department connected with the Zoological Gardens then in course of erection at Bronx Park, New York.

For a week I followed the routine, examining the new

foundations, studying the architect's plans, following the surveyors through the Bronx thickets, suggesting arrangements for water-courses and pools destined to be included in the enclosures for swans, geese, pelicans, herons, and such of the waders and swimmers as we might expect to acclimate in Bronx Park.

It was at that time the policy of the trustees and officers of the Zoological Gardens neither to employ collectors nor to send out expeditions in search of specimens. The society decided to depend upon voluntary contributions, and I was always busy, part of the day, in dictating answers to correspondents who wrote offering their services as hunters of big game, collectors of all sorts of fauna, trappers, snarers, and also to those who offered specimens for sale, usually at exorbitant rates.

To the proprietors of five-legged kittens, mangy lynxes, moth-eaten coyotes, and dancing bears I returned courteous but uncompromising refusals—of course, first submitting all such letters, together with my replies, to Professor Farrago.

One day toward the end of May, however, just as I was leaving Bronx Park to return to town, Professor Lesard, of the reptilian department, called out to me that Professor Farrago wanted to see me a moment; so I put my pipe into my pocket again and retraced my steps to the temporary, wooden building occupied by Professor Farrago, general superintendent of the Zoological Gardens. The professor, who was sitting at his desk before a pile of letters and replies submitted for approval by me, pushed his glasses down and looked over them at me with a whimsical smile that suggested amusement, impatience, annoyance, and perhaps a faint trace of apology.

"Now, here's a letter," he said, with a deliberate gesture towards a sheet of paper impaled on a file—"a letter that I suppose you remember." He disengaged the sheet of paper and handed it to me.

"Oh yes," I replied, with a shrug; "of course the man is mistaken—or—"

"Or what?" demanded Professor Farrago, tranquilly, wiping his glasses.

"—Or a liar," I replied.

After a silence he leaned back in his chair and bade me read the letter to him again, and I did so with a contemptuous tolerance for the writer, who must have been either a very innocent victim or a very stupid swindler. I said as much to Professor Farrago, but, to my surprise, he appeared to waver.

"I suppose," he said, with his near-sighted, embarrassed smile, "that nine hundred and ninety-nine men in a thousand would throw that letter aside and condemn the writer as a liar or a fool?"

"In my opinion," said I, "he's one or the other."

"He isn't—in mine," said the professor, placidly.

"What!" I exclaimed. "Here is a man living all alone on a strip of rock and sand between the wilderness and the sea, who wants you to send somebody to take charge of a bird that doesn't exist!"

"How do you know," asked Professor Farrago, "that the bird in question does not exist?"

"It is generally accepted," I replied, sarcastically, "that the great auk has been extinct for years. Therefore I may be pardoned for doubting that our correspondent possesses a pair of them alive."

"Oh, you young fellows," said the professor, smiling wearily, "you embark on a theory for destinations that don't exist."

He leaned back in his chair, his amused eyes searching space for the imagery that made him smile.

"Like swimming squirrels, you navigate with the help of Heaven and a stiff breeze, but you never land where you hope to—do you?"

Rather red in the face, I said: "Don't you believe the great auk to be extinct?"

"Audubon saw the great auk."

"Who has seen a single specimen since?"

"Nobody—except our correspondent here," he replied,

laughing. I laughed, too, considering the interview at an end, but the professor went on, coolly:

"Whatever it is that our correspondent has—and I am daring to believe that it is the great auk itself—I want you to secure it for the society."

When my astonishment subsided my first conscious sentiment was one of pity. Clearly, Professor Farrago was on the verge of dotage—ah, what a loss to the world!

I believe now that Professor Farrago perfectly interpreted my thoughts, but he betrayed neither resentment nor impatience. I drew a chair up beside his desk—there was nothing to do but to obey, and this fool's errand was none of my conceiving.

Together we made out a list of articles necessary for me and itemized the expenses I might incur, and I set a date for my return, allowing no margin for a successful termination to the expedition.

"Never mind that," said the professor. "What I want you to do is to get those birds here safely. Now, how many men will you take?"

"None," I replied, bluntly; "it's a useless expense, unless there is something to bring back. If there is I'll wire you, you may be sure."

"Very well," said Professor Farrago, good-humoredly, "you shall have all the assistance you may require. Can you leave to-night?"

The old gentleman was certainly prompt. I nodded, half-sulkily, aware of his amusement.

"So," I said, picking up my hat, "I am to start north to find a place called Black Harbor, where there is a man named Halyard who possesses, among other household utensils, two extinct great auks—"

We were both laughing by this time. I asked him why on earth he credited the assertion of a man he had never before heard of.

"I suppose," he replied, with the same half-apologetic, half-humorous smile, "it is instinct. I feel, somehow, that this man Halyard has got an auk—perhaps two. I can't get away from the idea that we are on the eve of acquiring the rarest of living creatures. It's odd for a scientist to talk as I do; doubtless you're shocked—admit it, now!"

But I was not shocked; on the contrary, I was conscious that the same strange hope that Professor Farrago cherished was beginning, in spite of me, to stir my pulses, too.

"If he has—" I began, then stopped.

The professor and I looked hard at each other in silence.

"Go on," he said, encouragingly.

But I had nothing more to say, for the prospect of beholding with my own eyes a living specimen of the great auk produced a series of conflicting emotions within me which rendered speech profanely superfluous.

As I took my leave Professor Farrago came to the door of the temporary, wooden office and handed me the letter written by the man Halyard. I folded it and put it into my pocket, as Halyard might require it for my own identification.

"How much does he want for the pair?" I asked.

"Ten thousand dollars. Don't demur—if the birds are really—"

"I know," I said, hastily, not daring to hope too much.

"One thing more," said Professor Farrago, gravely; "you know, in that last paragraph of his letter, Halyard speaks of something else in the way of specimens—an undiscovered species of amphibious biped—just read that paragraph again, will you?"

I drew the letter from my pocket and read as he directed:

"When you have seen the two living specimens of the great auk, and have satisfied yourself that I tell the truth, you may be wise enough to listen without prejudice to a statement I shall make concerning the existence of the strangest creature ever fashioned. I will merely say, at

212

this time, that the creature referred to is an amphibious biped and inhabits the ocean near this coast. More I cannot say, for I personally have not seen the animal, but I have a witness who has, and there are many who affirm that they have seen the creature. You will naturally say that my statement amounts to nothing; but when your representative arrives, if he be free from prejudice, I expect his reports to you concerning this sea-biped will confirm the solemn statements of a witness I know to be unimpeachable.

"Yours truly,

"Burton Halyard.
"Black Harbor."

"Well," I said, after a moment's thought, "here goes for the wild-goose chase."

"Wild auk, you mean," said Professor Farrago, shaking hands with me. "You will start to-night, won't you?"

"Yes, but Heaven knows how I'm ever going to land in this man Halyard's door-yard. Good-bye!"

"About that sea-biped—" began Professor Farrago, shyly.

"Oh, don't!" I said; "I can swallow the auks, feathers and claws, but if this fellow Halyard is hinting he's seen an amphibious creature resembling a man—"

"—Or a woman," said the professor, cautiously.

I retired, disgusted, my faith shaken in the mental vigor of Professor Farrago.

II

The three days' voyage by boat and rail was irksome. I bought my kit at Sainte Croix, on the Central Pacific Railroad, and on June 1st I began the last stage of my journey via the Sainte Isole broad-gauge, arriving in the wilderness by daylight. A tedious forced march by blazed trail, freshly spotted on the wrong side, of course, brought me to the northern terminus of the rusty, narrow-gauge lumber railway which runs from the heart of the hushed pine wilderness to the sea.

Already a long train of battered flat-cars, piled with sluice-props and roughly hewn sleepers, was moving slowly off into the brooding forest gloom, when I came in sight of the track; but I developed a gratifying and unexpected burst of speed, shouting all the while. The train stopped; I swung myself aboard the last car, where a pleasant young fellow was sitting on the rear brake, chewing spruce and reading a letter.

"Come aboard, sir," he said, looking up with a smile; "I guess you're the man in a hurry."

"I'm looking for a man named Halyard," I said, dropping rifle and knapsack on the fresh-cut, fragrant pile of pine. "Are you Halyard?"

"No, I'm Francis Lee, bossing the mica pit at Port-of-Waves," he replied, "but this letter is from Halyard, asking me to look out for a man in a hurry from Bronx Park, New York."

"I'm that man," said I, filling my pipe and offering him a share of the weed of peace, and we sat side by side smoking very amiably, until a signal from the locomotive sent him forward and I was left alone, lounging at ease, head pillowed on both arms, watching the blue sky flying through the branches overhead.

Long before we came in sight of the ocean I smelled it; the

fresh, salt aroma stole into my senses, drowsy with the heated odor of pine and hemlock, and I sat up, peering ahead into the dusky sea of pines.

Fresher and fresher came the wind from the sea, in puffs, in mild, sweet breezes, in steady, freshening currents, blowing the feathery crowns of the pines, setting the balsam's blue tufts rocking.

Lee wandered back over the long line of flats, balancing himself nonchalantly as the cars swung around a sharp curve, where water dripped from a newly propped sluice that suddenly emerged from the depths of the forest to run parallel to the railroad track.

"Built it this spring," he said, surveying his handiwork, which seemed to undulate as the cars swept past. "It runs to the cove—or ought to—" He stopped abruptly with a thoughtful glance at me.

"So you're going over to Halyard's?" he continued, as though answering a question asked by himself.

I nodded.

"You've never been there—of course?"

"No," I said, "and I'm not likely to go again."

I would have told him why I was going if I had not already begun to feel ashamed of my idiotic errand.

"I guess you're going to look at those birds of his," continued Lee, placidly.

"I guess I am," I said, sulkily, glancing askance to see whether he was smiling.

But he only asked me, quite seriously, whether a great auk was really a very rare bird; and I told him that the last one ever seen had been found dead off Labrador in January, 1870. Then I asked him whether these birds of Halyard's were really great auks, and he replied, somewhat indifferently, that he supposed they were—at least, nobody had ever before seen such birds near Port-of-Waves.

"There's something else," he said, running a pinesliver through his pipe-stem—"something that interests us all here more than auks, big or little. I suppose I might as well speak of it, as you are bound to hear about it sooner or later."

He hesitated, and I could see that he was embarrassed, searching for the exact words to convey his meaning.

"If," said I, "you have anything in this region more important to science than the great auk, I should be very glad to know about it."

Perhaps there was the faintest tinge of sarcasm in my voice, for he shot a sharp glance at me and then turned slightly. After a moment, however, he put his pipe into his pocket, laid hold of the brake with both hands, vaulted to his perch aloft, and glanced down at me.

"Did you ever hear of the harbor-master?" he asked, maliciously.

"Which harbor-master?" I inquired.

"You'll know before long," he observed, with a satisfied glance into perspective.

This rather extraordinary observation puzzled me. I waited for him to resume, and, as he did not, I asked him what he meant.

"If I knew," he said, "I'd tell you. But, come to think of it, I'd be a fool to go into details with a scientific man. You'll hear about the harbor-master—perhaps you will see the harbor-master. In that event I should be glad to converse with you on the subject."

I could not help laughing at his prim and precise manner, and, after a moment, he also laughed, saying:

"It hurts a man's vanity to know he knows a thing that somebody else knows he doesn't know. I'm damned if I say another word about the harbor-master until you've been to Halyard's!"

"A harbor-master," I persisted, "is an official who superintends the mooring of ships—isn't he?"

But he refused to be tempted into conversation, and we

lounged silently on the lumber until a long, thin whistle from the locomotive and a rush of stinging salt-wind brought us to our feet. Through the trees I could see the bluish-black ocean, stretching out beyond black headlands to meet the clouds; a great wind was roaring among the trees as the train slowly came to a stand-still on the edge of the primeval forest.

Lee jumped to the ground and aided me with my rifle and pack, and then the train began to back away along a curved side-track which, Lee said, led to the mica-pit and company stores.

"Now what will you do?" he asked, pleasantly. "I can give you a good dinner and a decent bed to-night if you like—and I'm sure Mrs. Lee would be very glad to have you stop with us as long as you choose."

I thanked him, but said that I was anxious to reach Halyard's before dark, and he very kindly led me along the cliffs and pointed out the path.

"This man Halyard," he said, "is an invalid. He lives at a cove called Black Harbor, and all his truck goes through to him over the company's road. We receive it here, and send a pack-mule through once a month. I've met him; he's a bad-tempered hypochondriac, a cynic at heart, and a man whose word is never doubted. If he says he has a great auk, you may be satisfied he has."

My heart was beating with excitement at the prospect; I looked out across the wooded headlands and tangled stretches of dune and hollow, trying to realize what it might mean to me, to Professor Farrago, to the world, if I should lead back to New York a live auk.

"He's a crank," said Lee; "frankly, I don't like him. If you find it unpleasant there, come back to us."

"Does Halyard live alone?" I asked.

"Yes—except for a professional trained nurse—poor thing!"

"A man?"

"No," said Lee, disgustedly.

Presently he gave me a peculiar glance; hesitated, and finally said: "Ask Halyard to tell you about his nurse and—the harbor-master. Good-bye—I'm due at the quarry. Come and stay with us whenever you care to; you will find a welcome at Port-of-Waves."

We shook hands and parted on the cliff, he turning back into the forest along the railway, I starting northward, pack slung, rifle over my shoulder. Once I met a group of quarrymen, faces burned brick-red, scarred hands swinging as they walked. And, as I passed them with a nod, turning, I saw that they also had turned to look after me, and I caught a word or two of their conversation, whirled back to me on the sea-wind.

They were speaking of the harbor-master.

III

Towards sunset I came out on a sheer granite cliff where the sea-birds were whirling and clamoring, and the great breakers dashed, rolling in double-thundered reverberations on the sun-dyed, crimson sands below the rock.

Across the half-moon of beach towered another cliff, and, behind this, I saw a column of smoke rising in the still air. It certainly came from Halyard's chimney, although the opposite cliff prevented me from seeing the house itself.

I rested a moment to refill my pipe, then resumed rifle and pack, and cautiously started to skirt the cliffs. I had descended half-way towards the beach, and was examining the cliff opposite, when something on the very top of the rock arrested my attention—a man darkly outlined against the sky. The next moment, however, I knew it could not be a man, for the object suddenly glided over the face of the cliff and slid down the sheer, smooth face like a lizard. Before I could get a square look at it, the thing crawled into the surf—or, at least, it seemed to—but the whole episode

218

occurred so suddenly, so unexpectedly, that I was not sure I had seen anything at all.

However, I was curious enough to climb the cliff on the land side and make my way towards the spot where I imagined I saw the man. Of course, there was nothing there—not a trace of a human being, I mean. Something *had* been there—a sea-otter, possibly—for the remains of a freshly killed fish lay on the rock, eaten to the back-bone and tail.

The next moment, below me, I saw the house, a freshly painted, trim, flimsy structure, modern, and very much out of harmony with the splendid savagery surrounding it. It struck a nasty, cheap note in the noble, gray monotony of headland and sea.

The descent was easy enough. I crossed the crescent beach, hard as pink marble, and found a little trodden path among the rocks, that led to the front porch of the house.

There were two people on the porch—I heard their voices before I saw them—and when I set my foot upon the wooden steps, I saw one of them, a woman, rise from her chair and step hastily towards me.

"Come back!" cried the other, a man with a smoothshaven, deeply lined face, and a pair of angry, blue eyes; and the woman stepped back quietly, acknowledging my lifted hat with a silent inclination.

The man, who was reclining in an invalid's rollingchair, clapped both large, pale hands to the wheels and pushed himself out along the porch. He had shawls pinned about him, an untidy, drab-colored hat on his head, and, when he looked down at me, he scowled.

"I know who you are," he said, in his acid voice; "you're one of the Zoological men from Bronx Park. You look like it, anyway."

"It is easy to recognize you from your reputation," I replied, irritated at his discourtesy.

"Really," he replied, with something between a sneer and a

laugh, "I'm obliged for your frankness. You're after my great auks, are you not?"

"Nothing else would have tempted me into this place," I replied, sincerely.

"Thank Heaven for that," he said. "Sit down a moment; you've interrupted us." Then, turning to the young woman, who wore the neat gown and tiny cap of a professional nurse, he bade her resume what she had been saying. She did so, with deprecating glance at me, which made the old man sneer again.

"It happened so suddenly," she said, in her low voice, "that I had no chance to get back. The boat was drifting in the cove; I sat in the stern, reading, both oars shipped, and the tiller swinging. Then I heard a scratching under the boat, but thought it might be sea-weed—and, next moment, came those soft thumpings, like the sound of a big fish rubbing its nose against a float."

Halyard clutched the wheels of his chair and stared at the girl in grim displeasure.

"Didn't you know enough to be frightened?" he demanded.

"No—not then," she said, coloring faintly; "but when, after a few moments, I looked up and saw the harbor-master running up and down the beach, I was horribly frightened."

"Really?" said Halyard, sarcastically; "it was about time." Then, turning to me, he rasped out: "And that young lady was obliged to row all the way to Port-of-Waves and call to Lee's quarrymen to take her boat in."

Completely mystified, I looked from Halyard to the girl, not in the least comprehending what all this meant.

"That will do," said Halyard, ungraciously, which curt phrase was apparently the usual dismissal for the nurse.

She rose, and I rose, and she passed me with an inclination, stepping noiselessly into the house.

"I want beef-tea!" bawled Halyard after her; then he gave me an unamiable glance.

"I was a well-bred man," he sneered; "I'm a Harvard graduate, too, but I live as I like, and I do what I like, and I say what I like."

"You certainly are not reticent," I said, disgusted.

"Why should I be?" he rasped; "I pay that young woman for my irritability; it's a bargain between us."

"In your domestic affairs," I said, "there is nothing that interests me. I came to see those auks."

"You probably believe them to be razor-billed auks," he said, contemptuously. "But they're not; they're great auks."

I suggested that he permit me to examine them, and he replied, indifferently, that they were in a pen in his backyard, and that I was free to step around the house when I cared to.

I laid my rifle and pack on the veranda, and hastened off with mixed emotions, among which hope no longer predominated. No man in his senses would keep two such precious prizes in a pen in his backyard, I argued, and I was perfectly prepared to find anything from a puffin to a penguin in that pen.

I shall never forget, as long as I live, my stupor of amazement when I came to the wire-covered enclosure. Not only were there two great auks in the pen, alive, breathing, squatting in bulky majesty on their sea-weed bed, but one of them was gravely contemplating two newly hatched chicks, all bill and feet, which nestled sedately at the edge of a puddle of salt-water, where some small fish were swimming.

For a while excitement blinded, nay, deafened me. I tried to realize that I was gazing upon the last individuals of an all but extinct race—the sole survivors of the gigantic auk, which, for thirty years, has been accounted an extinct creature.

I believe that I did not move muscle nor limb until the sun had gone down and the crowding darkness blurred my straining eyes and blotted the great, silent, bright-eyed birds from sight.

Even then I could not tear myself away from the enclosure; I listened to the strange, drowsy note of the male bird, the fainter responses of the female, the thin plaints of the chicks, huddling under her breast; I heard their flipperlike, embryotic wings beating sleepily as the birds stretched and yawned their beaks and clacked them, preparing for slumber.

"If you please," came a soft voice from the door, "Mr. Halyard awaits your company to dinner."

IV

I dined well—or, rather, I might have enjoyed my dinner if Mr. Halyard had been eliminated; and the feast consisted exclusively of a joint of beef, the pretty nurse, and myself. She was exceedingly attractive—with a disturbing fashion of lowering her head and raising her dark eyes when spoken to.

As for Halyard, he was unspeakable, bundled up in his snuffy shawls, and making uncouth noises over his gruel. But it is only just to say that his table was worth sitting down to and his wine was sound as a bell.

"Yah!" he snapped, "I'm sick of this cursed soup—and I'll trouble you to fill my glass—"

"It is dangerous for you to touch claret," said the pretty nurse.

"I might as well die at dinner as anywhere," he observed.

"Certainly," said I, cheerfully passing the decanter, but he did not appear overpleased with the attention.

"I can't smoke, either," he snarled, hitching the shawls around until he looked like Richard the Third.

However, he was good enough to shove a box of cigars at me, and I took one and stood up, as the pretty nurse slipped past and vanished into the little parlor beyond.

We sat there for a while without speaking. He picked irritably at the bread-crumbs on the cloth, never glancing in my direction; and I, tired from my long foot-tour, lay back in my chair, silently appreciating one of the best cigars I ever smoked.

"Well," he rasped out at length, "what do you think of my auks—and my veracity?"

I told him that both were unimpeachable.

"Didn't they call me a swindler down there at your museum?" he demanded.

I admitted that I had heard the term applied. Then I made a clean breast of the matter, telling him that it was I who had doubted; that my chief, Professor Farrago, had sent me against my will, and that I was ready and glad to admit that he, Mr. Halyard, was a benefactor of the human race.

"Bosh!" he said. "What good does a confounded wobbly, bandy-toed bird do to the human race?"

But he was pleased, nevertheless; and presently he asked me, not unamiably, to punish his claret again.

"I'm done for," he said; "good things to eat and drink are no good to me. Some day I'll get mad enough to have a fit, and then—"

He paused to yawn.

"Then," he continued, "that little nurse of mine will drink up my claret and go back to civilization, where people are polite."

Somehow or other, in spite of the fact that Halyard was an old pig, what he said touched me. There was certainly not much left in life for him—as he regarded life.

"I'm going to leave her this house," he said, arranging his shawls. "She doesn't know it. I'm going to leave her my money, too. She doesn't know that. Good Lord! What kind of a woman can she be to stand my bad temper for a few dollars a month!"

"I think," said I, "that it's partly because she's poor, partly because she's sorry for you."

He looked up with a ghastly smile.

"You think she really is sorry?"

Before I could answer he went on: "I'm no mawkish

sentimentalist, and I won't allow anybody to be sorry for me—do you hear?"

"Oh, I'm not sorry for you!" I said, hastily, and, for the first time since I had seen him, he laughed heartily, without a sneer.

We both seemed to feel better after that; I drank his wine and smoked his cigars, and he appeared to take a certain grim pleasure in watching me.

"There's no fool like a young fool," he observed, presently.

As I had no doubt he referred to me, I paid him no attention. After fidgeting with his shawls, he gave me an oblique scowl and asked me my age.

"Twenty-four," I replied.

"Sort of a tadpole, aren't you?" he said.

As I took no offence, he repeated the remark.

"Oh, come," said I, "there's no use in trying to irritate me. I see through you; a row acts like a cocktail on you—but you'll have to stick to gruel in my company."

"I call that impudence!" he rasped out, wrathfully.

"I don't care what you call it," I replied, undisturbed, "I am not going to be worried by you. Anyway," I ended, "it is my opinion that you could be very good company if you chose."

The proposition appeared to take his breath away—at least, he said nothing more; and I finished my cigar in peace and tossed the stump into a saucer.

"Now," said I, "what price do you set upon your birds, Mr. Halyard?"

"Ten thousand dollars," he snapped, with an evil smile.

"You will receive a certified check when the birds are delivered," I said, quietly.

"You don't mean to say you agree to that outrageous bargain—and I won't take a cent less, either—Good Lord!—haven't you any spirit left?" he cried, half rising from his pile of shawls.

His piteous eagerness for a dispute sent me into laughter

impossible to control, and he eyed me, mouth open, animosity rising visibly.

Then he seized the wheels of his invalid chair and trundled away, too mad to speak; and I strolled out into the parlor, still laughing.

The pretty nurse was there, sewing under a hanging lamp.

"If I am not indiscreet—" I began.

"Indiscretion is the better part of valor," said she, dropping her head but raising her eyes.

So I sat down with a frivolous smile peculiar to the appreciated.

"Doubtless," said I, "you are hemming a 'kerchief."

"Doubtless I am not," she said; "this is a night-cap for Mr. Halyard."

A mental vision of Halyard in a night-cap, very mad, nearly set me laughing again.

"Like the King of Yvetot, he wears his crown in bed," I said, flippantly.

"The King of Yvetot might have made that remark," she observed, re-threading her needle.

It is unpleasant to be reproved. How large and red and hot a man's ears feel.

To cool them, I strolled out to the porch; and, after a while, the pretty nurse came out, too, and sat down in a chair not far away. She probably regretted her lost opportunity to be flirted with.

"I have so little company—it is a great relief to see somebody from the world," she said. "If you can be agreeable, I wish you would."

The idea that she had come out to see me was so agreeable that I remained speechless until she said: "Do tell me what people are doing in New York."

So I seated myself on the steps and talked about the portion of the world inhabited by me, while she sat sewing in the dull light

225

that straggled out from the parlor windows.

She had a certain coquetry of her own, using the usual methods with an individuality that was certainly fetching. For instance, when she lost her needle—and, another time, when we both, on hands and knees, hunted for her thimble.

However, directions for these pastimes may be found in contemporary classics.

I was as entertaining as I could be—perhaps not quite as entertaining as a young man usually thinks he is. However, we got on very well together until I asked her tenderly who the harbor-master might be, whom they all discussed so mysteriously.

"I do not care to speak about it," she said, with a primness of which I had not suspected her capable.

Of course I could scarcely pursue the subject after that—and, indeed, I did not intend to—so I began to tell her how I fancied I had seen a man on the cliff that afternoon, and how the creature slid over the sheer rock like a snake.

To my amazement, she asked me to kindly discontinue the account of my adventures, in an icy tone, which left no room for protest.

"It was only a sea-otter," I tried to explain, thinking perhaps she did not care for snake stories.

But the explanation did not appear to interest her, and I was mortified to observe that my impression upon her was anything but pleasant.

"She doesn't seem to like me and my stories," thought I, "but she is too young, perhaps, to appreciate them."

So I forgave her—for she was even prettier than I had thought her at first—and I took my leave, saying that Mr. Halyard would doubtless direct me to my room.

Halyard was in his library, cleaning a revolver, when I entered.

"Your room is next to mine," he said; "pleasant dreams, and kindly refrain from snoring."

"May I venture an absurd hope that you will do the same!" I replied, politely.

That maddened him, so I hastily withdrew.

I had been asleep for at least two hours when a movement by my bedside and a light in my eyes awakened me. I sat bolt upright in bed, blinking at Halyard, who, clad in a dressing-gown and wearing a night-cap, had wheeled himself into my room with one hand, while with the other he solemnly waved a candle over my head.

"I'm so cursed lonely," he said—"come, there's a good fellow—talk to me in your own original, impudent way."

I objected strenuously, but he looked so worn and thin, so lonely and bad-tempered, so lovelessly grotesque, that I got out of bed and passed a spongeful of cold water over my head.

Then I returned to bed and propped the pillows up for a back-rest, ready to quarrel with him if it might bring some little pleasure into his morbid existence.

"No," he said, amiably, "I'm too worried to quarrel, but I'm much obliged for your kindly offer. I want to tell you something."

"What?" I asked, suspiciously.

"I want to ask you if you ever saw a man with gills like a fish?"

"Gills?" I repeated.

"Yes, gills! Did you?"

"No," I replied, angrily, "and neither did you."

"No, I never did," he said, in a curiously placid voice, "but there's a man with gills like a fish who lives in the ocean out there. Oh, you needn't look that way—nobody ever thinks of doubting my word, and I tell you that there's a man—or a thing that looks like a man—as big as you are, too—all slate-colored—with nasty red gills like a fish!—and I've a witness to prove what I say!"

"Who?" I asked, sarcastically.

"The witness? My nurse."

"Oh! She saw a slate-colored man with gills?"

"Yes, she did. So did Francis Lee, superintendent of the Mica Quarry Company at Port-of-Waves. So have a dozen men who work in the quarry. Oh, you needn't laugh, young man. It's an old story here, and anybody can tell you about the harbor-master."

"The harbor-master!" I exclaimed.

"Yes, that slate-colored thing with gills, that looks like a man—and—by Heaven! is a man—that's the harbormaster. Ask any quarryman at Port-of-Waves what it is that comes purring around their boats at the wharf and unties painters and changes the mooring of every cat-boat in the cove at night! Ask Francis Lee what it was he saw running and leaping up and down the shoal at sunset last Friday! Ask anybody along the coast what sort of a thing moves about the cliffs like a man and slides over them into the sea like an otter—"

"I saw it do that!" I burst out.

"Oh, did you? Well, what was it?"

Something kept me silent, although a dozen explanations flew to my lips.

After a pause, Halyard said: "You saw the harbor-master, that's what you saw!"

I looked at him without a word.

"Don't mistake me," he said, pettishly; "I don't think that the harbor-master is a spirit or a sprite or a hobgoblin, or any sort of damned rot. Neither do I believe it to be an optical illusion."

"What do you think it is?" I asked.

"I think it's a man—I think it's a branch of the human race—that's what I think. Let me tell you something: the deepest spot in the Atlantic Ocean is a trifle over five miles deep—and I suppose you know that this place lies only about a quarter of a mile off this headland. The British exploring vessel, *Gull*, Captain Marotte, discovered and sounded it, I believe. Anyway, it's there, and it's my belief that the profound depths are inhabited by the remnants of the last race of amphibious human beings!"

This was childish; I did not bother to reply.

"Believe it or not, as you will," he said, angrily; "one thing I know, and that is this: the harbor-master has taken to hanging around my cove, and he is attracted by my nurse! I won't have it! I'll blow his fishy gills out of his head if I ever get a shot at him! I don't care whether it's homicide or not—anyway, it's a new kind of murder and it attracts me!"

I gazed at him incredulously, but he was working himself into a passion, and I did not choose to say what I thought.

"Yes, this slate-colored thing with gills goes purring and grinning and spitting about after my nurse—when she walks, when she rows, when she sits on the beach! Gad! It drives me nearly frantic. I won't tolerate it, I tell you!"

"No," said I, "I wouldn't either." And I rolled over in bed convulsed with laughter.

The next moment I heard my door slam. I smothered my mirth and rose to close the window, for the landwind blew cold from the forest, and a drizzle was sweeping the carpet as far as my bed.

That luminous glare which sometimes lingers after the stars go out, threw a trembling, nebulous radiance over sand and cove. I heard the seething currents under the breakers' softened thunder—louder than I ever heard it. Then, as I closed my window, lingering for a last look at the crawling tide, I saw a man standing, ankle-deep, in the surf, all alone there in the night. But—was it a man? For the figure suddenly began running over the beach on all fours like a beetle, waving its limbs like feelers. Before I could throw open the window again it darted into the surf, and, when I leaned out into the chilling drizzle, I saw nothing save the flat ebb crawling on the coast—I heard nothing save the purring of bubbles on seething sands.

V

It took me a week to perfect my arrangements for transporting the great auks, by water, to Port-of-Waves, where a lumber schooner was to be sent from Petite Sainte Isole, chartered by me for a voyage to New York.

I had constructed a cage made of osiers, in which my auks were to squat until they arrived at Bronx Park. My telegrams to Professor Farrago were brief. One merely said "Victory!" Another explained that I wanted no assistance; and a third read: "Schooner chartered. Arrive New York July 1st. Send furniture-van to foot of Bluff Street."

My week as a guest of Mr. Halyard proved interesting. I wrangled with that invalid to his heart's content, I worked all day on my osier cage, I hunted the thimble in the moonlight with the pretty nurse. We sometimes found it.

As for the thing they called the harbor-master, I saw it a dozen times, but always either at night or so far away and so close to the sea that of course no trace of it remained when I reached the spot, rifle in hand. I had quite made up my mind that the so-called harbor-master was a demented darky—wandered from, Heaven knows where—perhaps shipwrecked and gone mad from his sufferings. Still, it was far from pleasant to know that the creature was strongly attracted by the pretty nurse.

She, however, persisted in regarding the harbor-master as a sea-creature; she earnestly affirmed that it had gills, like a fish's gills, that it had a soft, fleshy hole for a mouth, and its eyes were luminous and lidless and fixed.

"Besides," she said, with a shudder, "it's all slate color, like a porpoise, and it looks as wet as a sheet of india-rubber in a dissecting-room."

The day before I was to set sail with my auks in a catboat bound for Port-of-Waves, Halyard trundled up to me in his chair and announced his intention of going with me.

"Going where?" I asked.

"To Port-of-Waves and then to New York," he replied, tranquilly.

I was doubtful, and my lack of cordiality hurt his feelings.

"Oh, of course, if you need the sea-voyage—" I began.

"I don't; I need you," he said, savagely; "I need the stimulus of our daily quarrel. I never disagreed so pleasantly with anybody in my life; it agrees with me; I am a hundred per cent better than I was last week."

I was inclined to resent this, but something in the deep-lined face of the invalid softened me. Besides, I had taken a hearty liking to the old pig.

"I don't want any mawkish sentiment about it," he said, observing me closely; "I won't permit anybody to feel sorry for me—do you understand?"

"I'll trouble you to use a different tone in addressing me," I replied, hotly; "I'll feel sorry for you if I choose to!" And our usual quarrel proceeded, to his deep satisfaction.

By six o'clock next evening I had Halyard's luggage stowed away in the cat-boat, and the pretty nurse's effects corded down, with the newly hatched auk-chicks in a hatbox on top. She and I placed the osier cage aboard, securing it firmly, and then, throwing tablecloths over the auks' heads, we led those simple and dignified birds down the path and across the plank at the little wooden pier. Together we locked up the house, while Halyard stormed at us both and wheeled himself furiously up and down the beach below. At the last moment she forgot her thimble. But we found it, I forget where.

"Come on!" shouted Halyard, waving his shawls furiously; "what the devil are you about up there?"

He received our explanation with a sniff, and we trundled him aboard without further ceremony.

"Don't run me across the plank like a steamer trunk!" he shouted, as I shot him dexterously into the cock-pit. But the wind was dying away, and I had no time to dispute with him then.

The sun was setting above the pine-clad ridge as our sail flapped and partly filled, and I cast off, and began a long tack, east by south, to avoid the spouting rocks on our starboard bow.

The sea-birds rose in clouds as we swung across the shoal, the black surf-ducks scuttered out to sea, the gulls tossed their sun-tipped wings in the ocean, riding the rollers like bits of froth.

Already we were sailing slowly out across that great hole in the ocean, five miles deep, the most profound sounding ever taken in the Atlantic. The presence of great heights or great depths, seen or unseen, always impresses the human mind—perhaps oppresses it. We were very silent; the sunlight stain on cliff and beach deepened to crimson, then faded into sombre purple bloom that lingered long after the rose-tint died out in the zenith.

Our progress was slow; at times, although the sail filled with the rising land breeze, we scarcely seemed to move at all.

"Of course," said the pretty nurse, "we couldn't be aground in the deepest hole in the Atlantic."

"Scarcely," said Halyard, sarcastically, "unless we're grounded on a whale."

"What's that soft thumping?" I asked. "Have we run afoul of a barrel or log?"

It was almost too dark to see, but I leaned over the rail and swept the water with my hand.

Instantly something smooth glided under it, like the back of a great fish, and I jerked my hand back to the tiller. At the same moment the whole surface of the water seemed to begin to purr, with a sound like the breaking of froth in a champagne-glass.

"What's the matter with you?" asked Halyard, sharply.

"A fish came up under my hand," I said; "a porpoise or something—"

With a low cry, the pretty nurse clasped my arm in both her hands.

"Listen!" she whispered. "It's purring around the boat."

"What the devil's purring?" shouted Halyard. "I won't have anything purring around me!"

At that moment, to my amazement, I saw that the boat had stopped entirely, although the sail was full and the small pennant fluttered from the mast-head. Something, too, was tugging at the rudder, twisting and jerking it until the tiller strained and creaked in my hand. All at once it snapped; the tiller swung useless and the boat whirled around, heeling in the stiffening wind, and drove shoreward.

It was then that I, ducking to escape the boom, caught a glimpse of something ahead—something that a sudden wave seemed to toss on deck and leave there, wet and flapping—a man with round, fixed, fishy eyes, and soft, slaty skin.

But the horror of the thing were the two gills that swelled and relaxed spasmodically, emitting a rasping, purring sound—two gasping, blood-red gills, all fluted and scolloped and distended.

Frozen with amazement and repugnance, I stared at the creature; I felt the hair stirring on my head and the icy sweat on my forehead.

"It's the harbor-master!" screamed Halyard.

The harbor-master had gathered himself into a wet lump, squatting motionless in the bows under the mast; his lidless eyes were phosphorescent, like the eyes of living codfish. After a while I felt that either fright or disgust was going to strangle me where I sat, but it was only the arms of the pretty nurse clasped around me in a frenzy of terror.

There was not a fire-arm aboard that we could get at. Halyard's hand crept backward where a steel-shod boathook lay, and I also

233

made a clutch at it. The next moment I had it in my hand, and staggered forward, but the boat was already tumbling shoreward among the breakers, and the next I knew the harbor-master ran at me like a colossal rat, just as the boat rolled over and over through the surf, spilling freight and passengers among the sea-weedcovered rocks.

When I came to myself I was thrashing about kneedeep in a rocky pool, blinded by the water and half suffocated, while under my feet, like a stranded porpoise, the harbor-master made the water boil in his efforts to upset me. But his limbs seemed soft and boneless; he had no nails, no teeth, and he bounced and thumped and flapped and splashed like a fish, while I rained blows on him with the boat-hook that sounded like blows on a football. And all the while his gills were blowing out and frothing, and purring, and his lidless eyes looked into mine, until, nauseated and trembling, I dragged myself back to the beach, where already the pretty nurse alternately wrung her hands and her petticoats in ornamental despair.

Beyond the cove, Halyard was bobbing up and down, afloat in his invalid's chair, trying to steer shoreward. He was the maddest man I ever saw.

"Have you killed that rubber-headed thing yet?" he roared.

"I can't kill it," I shouted, breathlessly. "I might as well try to kill a football!"

"Can't you punch a hole in it?" he bawled. "If I can only get at him—"

His words were drowned in a thunderous splashing, a roar of great, broad flippers beating the sea, and I saw the gigantic forms of my two great auks, followed by their chicks, blundering past in a shower of spray, driving headlong out into the ocean.

"Oh, Lord!" I said. "I can't stand that," and, for the first time in my life, I fainted peacefully—and appropriately—at the feet of the pretty nurse.

❧

It is within the range of possibility that this story may be doubted. It doesn't matter; nothing can add to the despair of a man who has lost two great auks.

As for Halyard, nothing affects him—except his involuntary sea-bath, and that did him so much good that he writes me from the South that he's going on a walking-tour through Switzerland— if I'll join him. I might have joined him if he had not married the pretty nurse. I wonder whether— But, of course, this is no place for speculation.

In regard to the harbor-master, you may believe it or not, as you choose. But if you hear of any great auks being found, kindly throw a table-cloth over their heads and notify the authorities at the new Zoological Gardens in Bronx Park, New York. The reward is ten thousand dollars.

ANCIENT SORCERIES

By Algernon Blackwood

"Ancient Sorceries" is a story included in Algernon Blackwood's bestselling volume *John Silence—Physician Extraordinary* (1908). Lovecraft said of it that it is "perhaps the finest tale in the book" and that it "gives an almost hypnotically vivid account of an old French town where once the unholy Sabbath was kept by all the people in the form of cats" (*S* 67). It is possible that the notion of an *entire community* that undergoes metempsychosis fused with the notion of hybrid fish entities from such tales as "The Harbor-Master" and "Fishhead" to create the hybridized town of Innsmouth in "The Shadow over Innsmouth," as the latter two tales otherwise deal only with individual cases of hybridization.

Algernon Blackwood (1869–1951) produced an impressive array of weird and fantastic fiction over a long career, including *Jimbo: A Fantasy* (1909), *The Lost Valley and Other Stories* (1910), and *Shocks* (1935), all of which Lovecraft owned. Lovecraft considered Blackwood's "The Willows" (1907) the greatest single weird tale ever written. The novel *The Centaur* (1909) is Blackwood's spiritual autobiography.

here are, it would appear, certain wholly unremarkable persons, with none of the characteristics that invite adventure, who yet once or twice in the course of their smooth lives undergo an experience so strange that the world catches its breath—and looks the other way! And it was cases of this kind, perhaps, more than any other, that fell into the widespread net of John Silence, the psychic doctor, and, appealing to his deep humanity, to his patience, and to his great qualities of spiritual sympathy, led often to the revelation of problems of the strangest complexity, and of the profoundest possible human interest.

Matters that seemed almost too curious and fantastic for belief he loved to trace to their hidden sources. To unravel a tangle in the very soul of things—and to release a suffering human soul in the process—was with him a veritable passion. And the knots he untied were, indeed, after passing strange.

The world, of course, asks for some plausible basis to which it can attach credence—something it can, at least, pretend to explain. The adventurous type it can understand: such people carry about with them an adequate explanation of their exciting lives, and their characters obviously drive them into the circumstances which produce the adventures. It expects nothing else from them, and is satisfied. But dull, ordinary folk have no right to out-of-the-way experiences, and the world having been led to expect otherwise, is disappointed with them, not to say shocked. Its complacent judgment has been rudely disturbed.

"Such a thing happened to that man!" it cries—"a commonplace person like that! It is too absurd! There must be something wrong!"

Yet there could be no question that something did actually happen to little Arthur Vezin, something of the curious nature he described to Dr. Silence. Outwardly, or inwardly, it happened beyond a doubt, and in spite of the jeers of his few friends who heard the tale, and observed wisely that "such a thing might perhaps have come to Iszard, that crack-brained Iszard, or to that odd fish Minski, but it could never have happened to commonplace little Vezin, who was fore-ordained to live and die according to scale."

But, whatever his method of death was, Vezin certainly did not "live according to scale" so far as this particular event in his otherwise uneventful life was concerned; and to hear him recount it, and watch his pale delicate features change, and hear his voice grow softer and more hushed as he proceeded, was to know the conviction that his halting words perhaps failed sometimes to convey. He lived the thing over again each time he told it. His whole personality became muffled in the recital. It subdued him more than ever, so that the tale became a lengthy apology for an experience that he deprecated. He appeared to excuse himself and ask your pardon for having dared to take part in so fantastic an episode. For little Vezin was a timid, gentle, sensitive soul, rarely able to assert himself, tender to man and beast, and almost constitutionally unable to say No, or to claim many things that should rightly have been his. His whole scheme of life seemed utterly remote from anything more exciting than missing a train or losing an umbrella on an omnibus. And when this curious event came upon him he was already more years beyond forty than his friends suspected or he cared to admit.

John Silence, who heard him speak of his experience more

than once, said that he sometimes left out certain details and put in others; yet they were all obviously true. The whole scene was unforgettably cinematographed on to his mind. None of the details were imagined or invented. And when he told the story with them all complete, the effect was undeniable. His appealing brown eyes shone, and much of the charming personality, usually so carefully repressed, came forward and revealed itself. His modesty was always there, of course, but in the telling he forgot the present and allowed himself to appear almost vividly as he lived again in the past of his adventure.

He was on the way home when it happened, crossing northern France from some mountain trip or other where he buried himself solitary-wise every summer. He had nothing but an unregistered bag in the rack, and the train was jammed to suffocation, most of the passengers being unredeemed holiday English. He disliked them, not because they were his fellow-countrymen, but because they were noisy and obtrusive, obliterating with their big limbs and tweed clothing all the quieter tints of the day that brought him satisfaction and enabled him to melt into insignificance and forget that he was anybody. These English clashed about him like a brass band, making him feel vaguely that he ought to be more self-assertive and obstreperous, and that he did not claim insistently enough all kinds of things that he didn't want and that were really valueless, such as corner seats, windows up or down, and so forth.

So that he felt uncomfortable in the train, and wished the journey were over and he was back again living with his unmarried sister in Surbiton.

And when the train stopped for ten panting minutes at the little station in northern France, and he got out to stretch his legs on the platform, and saw to his dismay a further batch of the British Isles debouching from another train, it suddenly seemed impossible to him to continue the journey. Even his flabby soul revolted, and the idea of staying a night in the little town and going on next day by a slower, emptier train, flashed into his mind. The guard was already shouting *"en voiture"* and the corridor of his compartment was already packed when the thought came to him. And, for once, he acted with decision and rushed to snatch his bag.

Finding the corridor and steps impassible, he tapped at the window (for he had a corner seat) and begged the Frenchman who sat opposite to hand his luggage out to him, explaining in his wretched French that he intended to break the journey there. And this elderly Frenchman, he declared, gave him a look, half of warning, half of reproach, that to his dying day he could never forget; handed the bag through the window of the moving train; and at the same time poured into his ears a long sentence, spoken rapidly and low, of which he was able to comprehend only the last few words: *"à cause du sommeil et à cause des chats."*

In reply to Dr. Silence, whose singular psychic acuteness at once seized upon this Frenchman as a vital point in the adventure, Vezin admitted that the man had impressed him favourably from the beginning, though without being able to explain why. They had sat facing one another during the four hours of the journey, and though no conversation had passed between them—Vezin was timid about his stuttering French—he confessed that his eyes were being continually drawn to his face, almost, he felt, to rudeness, and that each, by a dozen nameless little politenesses and attentions, had evinced the desire to be kind. The men liked each other and their personalities did not clash, or would not have clashed had they chanced to come to terms of acquaintance. The Frenchman, indeed, seemed to have exercised a silent protective influence over the insignificant little Englishman, and without words or gestures betrayed that he wished him well and would gladly have been of service to him.

"And this sentence that he hurled at you after the bag?" asked

John Silence, smiling that peculiarly sympathetic smile that always melted the prejudices of his patient, "were you unable to follow it exactly?"

"It was so quick and low and vehement," explained Vezin, in his small voice, "that I missed practically the whole of it. I only caught the few words at the very end, because he spoke them so clearly, and his face was bent down out of the carriage window so near to mine."

"'À cause du sommeil et a cause des chats'?" repeated Dr. Silence, as though half speaking to himself.

"That's it exactly," said Vezin; "which, I take it, means something like 'because of sleep and because of the cats,' doesn't it?"

"Certainly, that's how I should translate it," the doctor observed shortly, evidently not wishing to interrupt more than necessary.

"And the rest of the sentence—all the first part I couldn't understand, I mean—was a warning not to do something—not to stop in the town, or at some particular place in the town, perhaps. That was the impression it made on me."

Then, of course, the train rushed off, and left Vezin standing on the platform alone and rather forlorn.

The little town climbed in straggling fashion up a sharp hill rising out of the plain at the back of the station, and was crowned by the twin towers of the ruined cathedral peeping over the summit. From the station itself it looked uninteresting and modern, but the fact was that the mediæval position lay out of sight just beyond the crest. And once he reached the top and entered the old streets, he stepped clean out of modern life into a bygone century. The noise and bustle of the crowded train seemed days away. The spirit of this silent hill-town, remote from tourists and motor-cars, dreaming its own quiet life under the autumn sun, rose up and cast its spell upon him. Long before he recognised this spell he acted under it. He walked softly, almost on tiptoe, down the winding narrow streets where the gables all but met over his head, and he entered the doorway of the solitary inn with a deprecating and modest demeanour that was in itself an apology for intruding upon the place and disturbing its dream.

At first, however, Vezin said, he noticed very little of all this. The attempt at analysis came much later. What struck him then was only the delightful contrast of the silence and peace after the dust and noisy rattle of the train. He felt soothed and stroked like a cat.

"Like a cat, you said?" interrupted John Silence, quickly catching him up.

"Yes. At the very start I felt that." He laughed apologetically. "I felt as though the warmth and the stillness and the comfort made me purr. It seemed to be the general mood of the whole place—then."

The inn, a rambling ancient house, the atmosphere of the old coaching days still about it, apparently did not welcome him too warmly. He felt he was only tolerated, he said. But it was cheap and comfortable, and the delicious cup of afternoon tea be ordered at once made him feel really very pleased with himself for leaving the train in this bold, original way. For to him it had seemed bold and original. He felt something of a dog. His room, too, soothed him with its dark panelling and low irregular ceiling, and the long sloping passage that led to it seemed the natural pathway to a real Chamber of Sleep—a little dim cubby hole out of the world where noise could not enter. It looked upon the courtyard at the back. It was all very charming, and made him think of himself as dressed in very soft velvet somehow, and the floors seemed padded, the walls provided with cushions. The sounds of the streets could not penetrate there. It was an atmosphere of absolute rest that surrounded him.

On engaging the two-franc room he had interviewed the only

person who seemed to be about that sleepy afternoon, an elderly waiter with Dundreary whiskers and a drowsy courtesy, who had ambled lazily towards him across the stone yard; but on coming downstairs again for a little promenade in the town before dinner he encountered the proprietress herself. She was a large woman whose hands, feet, and features seemed to swim towards him out of a sea of person. They emerged, so to speak. But she had great dark, vivacious eyes that counteracted the bulk of her body, and betrayed the fact that in reality she was both vigorous and alert. When he first caught sight of her she was knitting in a low chair against the sunlight of the wall, and something at once made him see her as a great tabby cat, dozing, yet awake, heavily sleepy, and yet at the same time prepared for instantaneous action. A great mouser on the watch occurred to him.

She took him in with a single comprehensive glance that was polite without being cordial. Her neck, he noticed, was extraordinarily supple in spite of its proportions, for it turned so easily to follow him, and the head it carried bowed so very flexibly.

"But when she looked at me, you know," said Vezin, with that little apologetic smile in his brown eyes, and that faintly deprecating gesture of the shoulders that was characteristic of him, "the odd notion came to me that really she had intended to make quite a different movement, and that with a single bound she could have leaped at me across the width of that stone yard and pounced upon me like some huge cat upon a mouse."

He laughed a little soft laugh, and Dr. Silence made a note in his book without interrupting, while Vezin proceeded in a tone as though he feared he had already told too much and more than we could believe.

"Very soft, yet very active she was, for all her size and mass, and I felt she knew what I was doing even after I had passed and was behind her back. She spoke to me, and her voice was smooth and running. She asked if I had my luggage, and was comfortable in my room, and then added that dinner was at seven o'clock, and that they were very early people in this little country town. Clearly, she intended to convey that late hours were not encouraged."

Evidently, she contrived by voice and manner to give him the impression that here he would be "managed," that everything would be arranged and planned for him, and that he had nothing to do but fall into the groove and obey. No decided action or sharp personal effort would be looked for from him. It was the very reverse of the train. He walked quietly out into the street feeling soothed and peaceful. He realised that he was in a milieu that suited him and stroked him the right way. It was so much easier to be obedient. He began to purr again, and to feel that all the town purred with him.

About the streets of that little town he meandered gently, falling deeper and deeper into the spirit of repose that characterised it. With no special aim he wandered up and down, and to and fro. The September sunshine fell slantingly over the roofs. Down winding alleyways, fringed with tumbling gables and open casements, he caught fairylike glimpses of the great plain below, and of the meadows and yellow copses lying like a dream-map in the haze. The spell of the past held very potently here, he felt.

The streets were full of picturesquely garbed men and women, all busy enough, going their respective ways; but no one took any notice of him or turned to stare at his obviously English appearance. He was even able to forget that with his tourist appearance he was a false note in a charming picture, and he melted more and more into the scene, feeling delightfully insignificant and unimportant and unself-conscious. It was like becoming part of a softly-coloured dream which he did not even realise to be a dream.

On the eastern side the hill fell away more sharply, and the plain below ran off rather suddenly into a sea of gathering shadows in which the little patches of woodland looked, like islands and the stubble fields like deep water. Here he strolled along the old ramparts of ancient fortifications that once had been formidable, but now were only vision-like with their charming mingling of broken grey walls and wayward vine and ivy. From the broad coping on which he sat for a moment, level with the rounded tops of clipped plane trees, he saw the esplanade far below lying in shadow. Here and there a yellow sunbeam crept in and lay upon the fallen yellow leaves, and from the height he looked down and saw that the townsfolk were walking to and fro in the cool of the evening. He could just hear the sound of their slow footfalls, and the murmur of their voices floated up to him through the gaps between the trees. The figures looked like shadows as he caught glimpses of their quiet movements far below.

He sat there for some time pondering, bathed in the waves of murmurs and half-lost echoes that rose to his ears, muffled by the leaves of the plane trees. The whole town, and the little hill out of which it grew as naturally as an ancient wood, seemed to him like a being lying there half asleep on the plain and crooning to itself as it dozed.

And, presently, as he sat lazily melting into its dream, a sound of horns and strings and wood instruments rose to his ears, and the town band began to play at the far end of the crowded terrace below to the accompaniment of a very soft, deep-throated drum. Vezin was very sensitive to music, knew about it intelligently, and had even ventured, unknown to his friends, upon the composition of quiet melodies with low-running chords which he played to himself with the soft pedal when no one was about. And this music floating up through the trees from an invisible and doubtless very picturesque band of the townspeople wholly charmed him. He recognised nothing that they played, and it sounded as though they were simply improvising without a conductor. No definitely marked time ran through the pieces, which ended and began oddly after the fashion of wind through an Æolian harp. It was part of the place and scene, just as the dying sunlight and faintly-breathing wind were part of the scene and hour, and the mellow notes of old-fashioned plaintive horns, pierced here and there by the sharper strings, all half smothered by the continuous booming of the deep drum, touched his soul with a curiously potent spell that was almost too engrossing to be quite pleasant.

There was a certain queer tense of bewitchment in it all. The music seemed to him oddly unartificial. It made him think of trees swept by the wind, of night breezes singing among wires and chimney-stacks, or in the rigging of invisible ships; or—and the simile leaped up in his thoughts with a sudden sharpness of suggestion—a chorus of animals, of wild creatures, somewhere in desolate places of the world, crying and singing as animals will, to the moon. He could fancy he heard the wailing, half-human cries of cats upon the tiles at night, rising and falling with weird intervals of sound, and this music, muffled by distance and the trees, made him think of a queer company of these creatures on some roof far away in the sky, uttering their solemn music to one another and the moon in chorus.

It was, he felt at the time, a singular image to occur to him, yet it expressed his sensation pictorially better than anything else. The instruments played such impossibly odd intervals, and the crescendos and diminuendos were so very suggestive of cat-land on the tiles at night, rising swiftly, dropping without warning to deep notes again, and all in such strange confusion of discords and accords. But, at the same time a plaintive sweetness resulted on the whole, and the discords of these half-broken instruments were so singular that they did not distress his musical soul like fiddles out of tune.

He listened a long time, wholly surrendering himself as his character was, and then strolled homewards in the dusk as the air grew chilly.

"There was nothing to alarm?" put in Dr. Silence briefly. "Absolutely nothing," said Vezin; "but you know it was all so fantastical and charming that my imagination was profoundly impressed. Perhaps, too," he continued, gently explanatory, "it was this stirring of my imagination that caused other impressions; for, as I walked back, the spell of the place began to steal over me in a dozen ways, though all intelligible ways. But there were other things I could not account for in the least, even then."

"Incidents, you mean?"

"Hardly incidents, I think. A lot of vivid sensations crowded themselves upon my mind and I could trace them to no causes. It was just after sunset and the tumbled old buildings traced magical outlines against an opalescent sky of gold and red. The dusk was running down the twisted streets. All round the hill the plain pressed in like a dim sea, its level rising with the darkness. The spell of this kind of scene, you know, can be very moving, and it was so that night. Yet I felt that what came to me had nothing directly to do with the mystery and wonder of the scene."

"Not merely the subtle transformations of the spirit that come with beauty," put in the doctor, noticing his hesitation.

"Exactly," Vezin went on, duly encouraged and no longer so fearful of our smiles at his expense. "The impressions came from somewhere else. For instance, down the busy main street where men and women were bustling home from work, shopping at stalls and barrows, idly gossiping in groups, and all the rest of it, I saw that I aroused no interest and that no one turned to stare at me as a foreigner and stranger. I was utterly ignored, and my presence among them excited no special interest or attention.

"And then, quite suddenly, it dawned upon me with conviction that all the time this indifference and inattention were merely feigned. Everybody as a matter of fact was watching me closely. Every movement I made was known and observed. Ignoring me was all a pretence—an elaborate pretence."

He paused a moment and looked at us to see if we were smiling, and then continued, reassured—

"It is useless to ask me how I noticed this, because I simply cannot explain it. But the discovery gave me something of a shock. Before I got back to the inn, however, another curious thing rose up strongly in my mind and forced my recognition of it as true. And this, too, I may as well say at once, was equally inexplicable to me. I mean I can only give you the fact, as fact it was to me."

The little man left his chair and stood on the mat before the fire. His diffidence lessened from now onwards, as he lost himself again in the magic of the old adventure. His eyes shone a little already as he talked.

"Well," he went on, his soft voice rising somewhat with his excitement, "I was in a shop when it came to me first—though the idea must have been at work for a long time subconsciously to appear in so complete a form all at once. I was buying socks, I think," he laughed, "and struggling with my dreadful French, when it struck me that the woman in the shop did not care two pins whether I bought anything or not. She was indifferent whether she made a sale or did not make a sale. She was only pretending to sell.

"This sounds a very small and fanciful incident to build upon what follows. But really it was not small. I mean it was the spark that lit the line of powder and ran along to the big blaze in my mind.

"For the whole town, I suddenly realised, was something other than I so far saw it. The real activities and interests of the people were elsewhere and otherwise than appeared. Their true lives lay somewhere out of sight behind the scenes. Their busy-ness was but the outward semblance that masked their actual purposes. They bought and sold, and ate and drank, and walked about the streets, yet all the while the main stream of their existence lay somewhere beyond my ken, underground, in secret places. In the shops and at the stalls they did not care whether I purchased their articles or not; at the inn, they were indifferent to my staying or going; their life lay remote from my own, springing from hidden, mysterious sources, coursing out of sight, unknown. It was all a great elaborate pretence, assumed possibly for my benefit, or possibly for purposes of their own. But the main current of their energies ran elsewhere. I almost felt as an unwelcome foreign substance might be expected to feel when it has found its way into the human system and the whole body organises itself to eject it or to absorb it. The town was doing this very thing to me.

"This bizarre notion presented itself forcibly to my mind as I walked home to the inn, and I began busily to wonder wherein the true life of this town could lie and what were the actual interests and activities of its hidden life.

"And, now that my eyes were partly opened, I noticed other things too that puzzled me, first of which, I think, was the extraordinary silence of the whole place. Positively, the town was muffled. Although the streets were paved with cobbles the people moved about silently, softly, with padded feet, like cats. Nothing made noise. All was hushed, subdued, muted. The very voices were quiet, low-pitched like purring. Nothing clamorous, vehement or emphatic seemed able to live in the drowsy atmosphere of soft dreaming that soothed this little hill-town into its sleep. It was like the woman at the inn—an outward repose screening intense inner activity and purpose.

"Yet there was no sign of lethargy or sluggishness anywhere about it. The people were active and alert. Only a magical and uncanny softness lay over them all like a spell."

Vezin passed his hand across his eyes for a moment as though the memory had become very vivid. His voice had run off into a whisper so that we heard the last part with difficulty. He was telling a true thing obviously, yet something that he both liked and hated telling.

"I went back to the inn," he continued presently in a louder voice, "and dined. I felt a new strange world about me. My old world of reality receded. Here, whether I liked it or no, was something new and incomprehensible. I regretted having left the train so impulsively. An adventure was upon me, and I loathed adventures as foreign to my nature. Moreover, this was the beginning apparently of an adventure somewhere deep within me, in a region I could not check or measure, and a feeling of alarm mingled itself with my wonder—alarm for the stability of what I had for forty years recognised as my 'personality.'

"I went upstairs to bed, my mind teeming with thoughts that were unusual to me, and of rather a haunting description. By way of relief I kept thinking of that nice, prosaic noisy train and all those wholesome, blustering passengers. I almost wished I were with them again. But my dreams took me elsewhere. I dreamed of cats, and softmoving creatures, and the silence of life in a dim muffled world beyond the senses."

II

Vezin stayed on from day to day, indefinitely, much longer than he had intended. He felt in a kind of dazed, somnolent condition. He did nothing in particular, but the place fascinated him and he could not decide to leave. Decisions were always very difficult for him and he sometimes wondered how he had ever brought himself to the point of leaving the train. It seemed as though some one else must have arranged it for him, and once or twice his thoughts ran to the swarthy Frenchman who had sat opposite. If only he could have understood that long sentence ending so strangely with "*à cause du sommeil et à cause des chats.*" He wondered what it all meant.

Meanwhile the hushed softness of the town held him prisoner

and he sought in his muddling, gentle way to find out where the mystery lay, and what it was all about. But his limited French and his constitutional hatred of active investigation made it hard for him to buttonhole anybody and ask questions. He was content to observe, and watch, and remain negative.

The weather held on calm and hazy, and this just suited him. He wandered about the town till he knew every street and alley. The people suffered him to come and go without let or hindrance, though it became clearer to him every day that he was never free himself from observation. The town watched him as a cat watches a mouse. And he got no nearer to finding out what they were all so busy with or where the main stream of their activities lay. This remained hidden. The people were as soft and mysterious as cats.

But that he was continually under observation became more evident from day to day.

For instance, when he strolled to the end of the town and entered a little green public garden beneath the ramparts and seated himself upon one of the empty benches in the sun, he was quite alone at first. Not another seat was occupied; the little park was empty, the paths deserted. Yet, within ten minutes of his coming, there must have been fully twenty persons scattered about him, some strolling aimlessly along the gravel walks, staring at the flowers, and others seated on the wooden benches enjoying the sun like himself. None of them appeared to take any notice of him; yet he understood quite well they had all come there to watch. They kept him under close observation. In the street they had seemed busy enough, hurrying upon various errands; yet these were suddenly all forgotten and they had nothing to do but loll and laze in the sun, their duties unremembered. Five minutes after he left, the garden was again deserted, the seats vacant. But in the crowded street it was the same thing again; he was never alone. He was ever in their thoughts.

By degrees, too, he began to see how it was he was so cleverly watched, yet without the appearance of it. The people did nothing *directly*. They behaved *obliquely*. He laughed in his mind as the thought thus clothed itself in words, but the phrase exactly described it. They looked at him from angles which naturally should have led their sight in another direction altogether. Their movements were oblique, too, so far as these concerned himself. The straight, direct thing was not their way evidently. They did nothing obviously. If he entered a shop to buy, the woman walked instantly away and busied herself with something at the farther end of the counter, though answering at once when he spoke, showing that she knew he was there and that this was only her way of attending to him. It was the fashion of the cat she followed. Even in the dining-room of the inn, the be-whiskered and courteous waiter, lithe and silent in all his movements, never seemed able to come straight to his table for an order or a dish. He came by zigzags, indirectly, vaguely, so that he appeared to be going to another table altogether, and only turned suddenly at the last moment, and was there beside him.

Vezin smiled curiously to himself as he described how he began to realize these things. Other tourists there were none in the hostel, but he recalled the figures of one or two old men, inhabitants, who took their *déjeuner* and dinner there, and remembered how fantastically they entered the room in similar fashion. First, they paused in the doorway, peering about the room, and then, after a temporary inspection, they came in, as it were, sideways, keeping close to the walls so that he wondered which table they were making for, and at the last minute making almost a little quick run to their particular seats. And again he thought of the ways and methods of cats.

Other small incidents, too, impressed him as all part of this queer, soft town with its muffled, indirect life, for the way some of the people appeared and disappeared with extraordinary swiftness puzzled him exceedingly. It may have been all perfectly natural, he knew, yet he could not make it out how the alleys swallowed them up and shot them forth in a second of time when there were no visible doorways or openings near enough to explain the phenomenon. Once he followed two elderly women who, he felt, had been particularly examining him from across the street—quite near the inn this was—and saw them turn the corner a few feet only in front of him. Yet when he sharply followed on their heels he saw nothing but an utterly deserted alley stretching in front of him with no sign of a living thing. And the only opening through which they could have escaped was a porch some fifty yards away, which not the swiftest human runner could have reached in time.

And in just such sudden fashion people appeared, when he never expected them. Once when he heard a great noise of fighting going on behind a low wall, and hurried up to see what was going on, what should he see but a group of girls and women engaged in vociferous conversation which instantly hushed itself to the normal whispering note of the town when his head appeared over the wall. And even then none of them turned to look at him directly, but slunk off with the most unaccountable rapidity into doors and sheds across the yard. And their voices, he thought, had sounded so like, so strangely like, the angry snarling of fighting animals, almost of cats.

The whole spirit of the town, however, continued to evade him as something elusive, protean, screened from the outer world, and at the same time intensely, genuinely vital; and, since he now formed part of his life, this concealment puzzled and irritated him; more—it began rather to frighten him.

Out of the mists that slowly gathered about his ordinary surface thoughts, there rose again the idea that the inhabitants were waiting for him to declare himself, to take an attitude, to do this, or to do that; and that when he had done so they in their turn would at length make some direct response, accepting or rejecting him. Yet the vital matter concerning which his decision was awaited came no nearer to him.

Once or twice he purposely followed little processions or groups of the citizens in order to find out, if possible, on what purpose they were bent; but they always discovered him in time and dwindled away, each individual going his or her own way. It was always the same: he never could learn what their main interest was. The cathedral was ever empty, the old church of St. Martin, at the other end of the town, deserted. They shopped because they had to, and not because they wished to. The booths stood neglected, the stalls unvisited, the little cafés desolate. Yet the streets were always full, the townsfolk ever on the bustle.

"Can it be," he thought to himself, yet with a deprecating laugh that he should have dared to think anything so odd, "can it be that these people are people of the twilight, that they live only at night their real life, and come out honestly only with the dusk? That during the day they make a sham though brave pretence, and after the sun is down their true life begins? Have they the souls of nightthings, and is the whole blessed town in the hands of the cats?"

The fancy somehow electrified him with little shocks of shrinking and dismay. Yet, though he affected to laugh, he knew that he was beginning to feel more than uneasy, and that strange forces were tugging with a thousand invisible cords at the very centre of his being. Something utterly remote from his ordinary life, something that had not waked for years, began faintly to stir in his soul, sending feelers abroad into his brain and heart, shaping queer thoughts and penetrating even into certain of his minor actions. Something exceedingly vital to himself, to his soul, hung in the balance.

And, always when he returned to the inn about the hour of sunset, he saw the figures of the townsfolk stealing through the dusk from their shop doors, moving sentrywise to and fro at the corners of the streets, yet always vanishing silently like shadows at his near approach. And as the inn invariably closed its doors at ten o'clock he had never yet found the opportunity he rather half-heartedly sought to see for himself what account the town could give of itself at night.

"—*à cause du sommeil et à cause des chats*"—the words now rang in his ears more and more often, though still as yet without any definite meaning.

Moreover, something made him sleep like the dead.

III

It was, I think, on the fifth day—though in this detail his story sometimes varied—that he made a definite discovery which increased his alarm and brought him up to a rather sharp climax. Before that he had already noticed that a change was going forward and certain subtle transformations being brought about in his character which modified several of his minor habits. And he had affected to ignore them. Here, however, was something he could no longer ignore; and it startled him.

At the best of times he was never very positive, always negative rather, compliant and acquiescent; yet, when necessity arose he was capable of reasonably vigorous action and could take a strongish decision. The discovery he now made that brought him up with such a sharp turn was that this power had positively dwindled to nothing. He found it impossible to make up his mind. For, on this fifth day, he realised that he had stayed long enough in the town and that for reasons he could only vaguely define to himself it was wiser *and safer* that he should leave.

And he found that he could not leave!

This is difficult to describe in words, and it was more by gesture and the expression of his face that he conveyed to Dr. Silence the state of impotence he had reached. All this spying and watching, he said, had as it were spun a net about his feet so that he was trapped and powerless to escape; he felt like a fly that had blundered into the intricacies of a great web; he was caught, imprisoned, and could not get away. It was a distressing sensation. A numbness had crept over his will till it had become almost incapable of decision. The mere thought of vigorous action—action towards escape—began to terrify him. All the currents of his life had turned inwards upon himself, striving to bring to the surface something that lay buried almost beyond reach, determined to force his recognition of something he had long forgotten—forgotten years upon years, centuries almost ago. It seemed as though a window deep within his being would presently open and reveal an entirely new world, yet somehow a world that was not unfamiliar. Beyond that, again, he fancied a great curtain hung; and when that too rolled up he would see still farther into this region and at last understand something of the secret life of these extraordinary people.

"Is this why they wait and watch?" he asked himself with rather a shaking heart, "for the time when I shall join them—or refuse to join them? Does the decision rest with me after all, and not with them?"

And it was at this point that the sinister character of the adventure first really declared itself, and he became genuinely alarmed. The stability of his rather fluid little personality was at stake, he felt, and something in his heart turned coward.

Why, otherwise should he have suddenly taken to walking stealthily, silently, making as little sound as possible, for ever looking behind him? Why else should he have moved almost on tiptoe about the passages of the practically deserted inn, and when he was abroad have found himself deliberately taking advantage of what cover presented itself? And why, if he was not afraid, should the wisdom of staying indoors after sundown have suddenly occurred to him as eminently desirable? Why, indeed?

And, when John Silence gently pressed him for an explanation of these things, he admitted apologetically that he had none to give.

"It was simply that I feared something might happen to me unless I kept a sharp look-out. I felt afraid. It was instinctive," was all he could say. "I got the impression that the whole town was after me—wanted me for something; and that if it got me I should lose myself, or at least the Self I knew, in some unfamiliar state of consciousness. But I am not a psychologist, you know," he added meekly, "and I cannot define it better than that."

It was while lounging in the courtyard half an hour before the evening meal that Vezin made this discovery, and he at once went upstairs to his quiet room at the end of the winding passage to think it over alone. In the yard it was empty enough, true, but there was always the possibility that the big woman whom he dreaded would come out of some door, with her pretence of knitting, to sit and watch him. This had happened several times, and he could not endure the sight of her. He still remembered his original fancy, bizarre though it was, that she would spring upon him the moment his back was turned and land with one single crushing leap upon his neck. Of course it was nonsense, but then it haunted him, and once an idea begins to do that it ceases to be nonsense. It has clothed itself in reality.

He went upstairs accordingly. It was dusk, and the oil lamps had not yet been lit in the passages. He stumbled over the uneven surface of the ancient flooring, passing the dim outlines of doors along the corridor—doors that he had never once seen opened— rooms that seemed never occupied. He moved, as his habit now was, stealthily and on tiptoe.

Half-way down the last passage to his own chamber there was a sharp turn, and it was just here, while groping round the walls with outstretched hands, that his fingers touched something that was not wall—something that moved. It was soft and warm in texture, indescribably fragrant, and about the height of his shoulder; and he immediately thought of a furry, sweet-smelling kitten. The next minute he knew it was something quite different.

Instead of investigating, however,—his nerves must have been too overwrought for that, he said,—he shrank back as closely as possible against the wall on the other side. The thing, whatever it was, slipped past him with a sound of rustling and, retreating with light footsteps down the passage behind him, was gone. A breath of warm, scented air was wafted to his nostrils.

Vezin caught his breath for an instant and paused, stockstill, half leaning against the wall—and then almost ran down the remaining distance and entered his room with a rush, locking the door hurriedly behind him. Yet it was not fear that made him run: it was excitement, pleasurable excitement. His nerves were tingling, and a delicious glow made itself felt all over his body. In a flash it came to him that this was just what he had felt twenty-five years ago as a boy when he was in love for the first time. Warm currents of life ran all over him and mounted to his brain in a whirl of soft delight. His mood was suddenly become tender, melting, loving.

The room was quite dark, and he collapsed upon the sofa by the window, wondering what had happened to him and what it all meant. But the only thing he understood clearly in that instant was that something in him had swiftly, magically changed: he no longer wished to leave, or to argue with himself about leaving. The encounter in the passage-way had changed all that. The strange perfume of it still hung about him, bemusing his heart and mind. For he knew that it was a girl who had passed him, a girl's face that his fingers had brushed in the darkness, and he felt in some extraordinary way as though he had been actually kissed by her, kissed full upon the lips.

Trembling, he sat upon the sofa by the window and struggled to collect his thoughts. He was utterly unable to understand how the mere passing of a girl in the darkness of a narrow passage-way could communicate so electric a thrill to his whole being that he still shook with the sweetness of it. Yet, there it was! And he found it as useless to deny as to attempt analysis. Some ancient fire had entered his veins, and now ran coursing through his blood; and that he was forty-five instead of twenty did not matter one little jot. Out of all the inner turmoil and confusion emerged the one salient fact that the mere atmosphere, the merest casual touch, of this girl, unseen, unknown in the darkness, had been sufficient to stir dormant fires in the centre of his heart, and rouse his whole being from a state of feeble sluggishness to one of tearing and tumultuous excitement.

After a time, however, the number of Vezin's years began to assert their cumulative power; he grew calmer, and when a knock came at length upon his door and he heard the waiter's voice suggesting that dinner was nearly over, he pulled himself together and slowly made his way downstairs into the dining-room.

Every one looked up as he entered, for he was very late, but he took his customary seat in the far corner and began to eat. The trepidation was still in his nerves, but the fact that he had passed through the courtyard and hall without catching sight of a petticoat served to calm him a little. He ate so fast that he had almost caught up with the current stage of the table d'hôte, when a slight commotion in the room drew his attention.

His chair was so placed that the door and the greater portion of the long *salle à manger* were behind him, yet it was not necessary to turn round to know that the same person he had passed in the dark passage had now come into the room. He felt the presence, long before he heard or saw any one. Then he became aware that the old men, the only other guests, were rising one by one in their places, and exchanging greetings with some one who passed among them from table to table. And when at length he turned with his heart beating furiously to ascertain for himself, he saw

260

the form of a young girl, lithe and slim, moving down the centre of the room and making straight for his own table in the corner. She moved wonderfully, with sinuous grace, like a young panther, and her approach filled him with such delicious bewilderment that he was utterly unable to tell at first what her face was like, or discover what it was about the whole presentment of the creature that filled him anew with trepidation and delight.

"*Ah, Mámselle est de retour!*" he heard the old waiter murmur at his side, and he was just able to take in that she was the daughter of the proprietress, when she was upon him, and he heard her voice. She was addressing him. Something of red lips he saw and laughing white teeth, and stray wisps of fine dark hair about the temples; but all the rest was a dream in which his own emotion rose like a thick cloud before his eyes and prevented his seeing accurately, or knowing exactly what he did. He was aware that she greeted him with a charming little bow; that her beautiful large eyes looked searchingly into his own; that the perfume he had noticed in the dark passage again assailed his nostrils, and that she was bending a little towards him and leaning with one hand on the table at this side. She was quite close to him—that was the chief thing he knew—explaining that she had been asking after the comfort of her mother's guests, and was now introducing herself to the latest arrival—himself.

"*M'sieur* has already been here a few days," he heard the waiter say; and then her own voice, sweet as singing, replied—

"Ah, but *M'sieur* is not going to leave us just yet, I hope. My mother is too old to look after the comfort of our guests properly, but now I am here I will remedy all that." She laughed deliciously. "*M'sieur* shall be well looked after."

Vezin, struggling with his emotion and desire to be polite, half rose to acknowledge the pretty speech, and to stammer some sort of reply, but as he did so his hand by chance touched her own that was resting upon the table, and a shock that was for all the world

ANCIENT SORCERIES

like a shock of electricity, passed from her skin into his body. His soul wavered and shook deep within him. He caught her eyes fixed upon his own with a look of most curious intentness, and the next moment he knew that he had sat down wordless again on his chair, that the girl was already half-way across the room, and that he was trying to eat his salad with a dessertspoon and a knife.

Longing for her return, and yet dreading it, he gulped down the remainder of his dinner, and then went at once to his bedroom to be alone with his thoughts. This time the passages were lighted, and he suffered no exciting contretemps; yet the winding corridor was dim with shadows, and the last portion, from the bend of the walls onwards, seemed longer than he had ever known it. It ran downhill like the pathway on a mountain side, and as he tiptoed softly down it he felt that by rights it ought to have led him clean out of the house into the heart of a great forest. The world was singing with him. Strange fancies filled his brain, and once in the room, with the door securely locked, he did not light the candles, but sat by the open window thinking long, long thoughts that came unbidden in troops to his mind.

IV

This part of the story he told to Dr. Silence, without special coaxing, it is true, yet with much stammering embarrassment. He could not in the last understand, he said, how the girl had managed to affect him so profoundly, and even before he had set eyes upon her. For her mere proximity in the darkness had been sufficient to set him on fire. He knew nothing of enchantments, and for years had been a stranger to anything approaching tender relations with any member of the opposite sex, for he was encased in shyness, and realised his overwhelming defects only too well. Yet this bewitching young creature came to him deliberately.

ALGERNON BLACKWOOD

Her manner was unmistakable, and she sought him out on every possible occasion. Chaste and sweet she was undoubtedly, yet frankly inviting; and she won him utterly with the first glance of her shining eyes, even if she had not already done so in the dark merely by the magic of her invisible presence.

"You felt she was altogether wholesome and good!" queried the doctor. "You had no reaction of any sort—for instance, of alarm?"

Vezin looked up sharply with one of his inimitable little apologetic smiles. It was some time before he replied. The mere memory of the adventure had suffused his shy face with blushes, and his brown eyes sought the floor again before he answered.

"I don't think I can quite say that," he explained presently. "I acknowledged certain qualms, sitting up in my room afterwards. A conviction grew upon me that there was something about her— how shall I express it?—well, something unholy. It is not impurity in any sense, physical or mental, that I mean, but something quite indefinable that gave me a vague sensation of the creeps. She drew me, and at the same time repelled me, more than—than—"

He hesitated, blushing furiously, and unable to finish the sentence.

"Nothing like it has ever come to me before or since," he concluded, with lame confusion. "I suppose it was, as you suggested just now, something of an enchantment. At any rate, it was strong enough to make me feel that I would stay in that awful little haunted town for years if only I could see her every day, hear her voice, watch her wonderful movements, and sometimes, perhaps, touch her hand."

"Can you explain to me what you felt was the source of her power?" John Silence asked, looking purposely anywhere but at the narrator.

"I am surprised that *you* should ask me such a question," answered Vezin, with the nearest approach to dignity he could

263

manage. "I think no man can describe to another convincingly wherein lies the magic of the woman who ensnares him. I certainly cannot. I can only say this slip of a girl bewitched me, and the mere knowledge that she was living and sleeping in the same house filled me with an extraordinary sense of delight.

"But there's one thing I can tell you," he went on earnestly, his eyes aglow, "namely, that she seemed to sum up and synthesise in herself all the strange hidden forces that operated so mysteriously in the town and its inhabitants. She had the silken movements of the panther, going smoothly, silently to and fro, and the same indirect, oblique methods as the townsfolk, screening, like them, secret purposes of her own—purposes that I was sure had me for their objective. She kept me, to my terror and delight, ceaselessly under observation, yet so carelessly, so consummately, that another man less sensitive, if I may say so"—he made a deprecating gesture—"or less prepared by what had gone before, would never have noticed it at all. She was always still, always reposeful, yet she seemed to be everywhere at once, so that I never could escape from her. I was continually meeting the stare and laughter of her great eyes, in the corners of the rooms, in the passages, calmly looking at me through the windows, or in the busiest parts of the public streets."

Their intimacy, it seems, grew very rapidly after this first encounter which had so violently disturbed the little man's equilibrium. He was naturally very prim, and prim folk live mostly in so small a world that anything violently unusual may shake them clean out of it, and they therefore instinctively distrust originality. But Vezin began to forget his primness after awhile. The girl was always modestly behaved, and as her mother's representative she naturally had to do with the guests in the hotel. It was not out of the way that a spirit of camaraderie should spring up. Besides, she was young, she was charmingly pretty, she was French, and—she obviously liked him.

At the same time, there was something indescribable—a certain indefinable atmosphere of other places, other times—that made him try hard to remain on his guard, and sometimes made him catch his breath with a sudden start. It was all rather like a delirious dream, half delight, half dread, he confided in a whisper to Dr. Silence; and more than once he hardly knew quite what he was doing or saying, as though he were driven forward by impulses he scarcely recognised as his own.

And though the thought of leaving presented itself again and again to his mind, it was each time with insistence, so that he stayed on from day to day, becoming more and more a part of the sleepy life of this dreamy mediæval town, losing more and more of his recognisable personality. Soon, he felt, the Curtain within would roll up with an awful rush, and he would find himself suddenly admitted into the secret purposes of the hidden life that lay behind it all. Only, by that time, he would have become transformed into an entirely different being.

And, meanwhile, he noticed various little signs of the intention to make his stay attractive to him: flowers in his bedroom, a more comfortable arm-chair in the corner, and even special little extra dishes on his private table in the dining-room. Conversations, too, with "*Mademoiselle* Ilsé" became more and more frequent and pleasant, and although they seldom travelled beyond the weather, or the details of the town, the girl, he noticed, was never in a hurry to bring them to an end, and often contrived to interject little odd sentences that he never properly understood, yet felt to be significant.

And it was these stray remarks, full of a meaning that evaded him, that pointed to some hidden purpose of her own and made him feel uneasy. They all had to do, he felt sure, with reasons for his staying on in the town indefinitely.

"And has *M'sieur* not even yet come to a decision?" she said softly in his ear, sitting beside him in the sunny yard before *déjeuner*, the acquaintance having progressed with significant rapidity. "Because, if it's so difficult, we must all try together to help him!"

The question startled him, following upon his own thoughts. It was spoken with a pretty laugh, and a stray bit of hair across one eye, as she turned and peered at him half-roguishly. Possibly he did not quite understand the French of it, for her near presence always confused his small knowledge of the language distressingly. Yet the words, and her manner, and something else that lay behind it all in her mind, frightened him. It gave such point to his feeling that the town was waiting for him to make his mind up on some important matter.

At the same time, her voice, and the fact that she was there so close beside him in her soft dark dress, thrilled him inexpressibly.

"It is true I find it difficult to leave," he stammered, losing his way deliciously in the depths of her eyes, "and especially now that *Mademoiselle* Ilsé has come."

He was surprised at the success of his sentence, and quite delighted with the little gallantry of it. But at the same time he could have bitten his tongue off for having said it.

"Then after all you like our little town, or you would not be pleased to stay on," she said, ignoring the compliment.

"I am enchanted with it, and enchanted with you," he cried, feeling that his tongue was somehow slipping beyond the control of his brain. And he was on the verge of saying all manner of other things of the wildest description, when the girl sprang lightly up from her chair beside him, and made to go.

"It is *soupe à l'oignon* to-day!" she cried, laughing back at him through the sunlight, "and I must go and see about it. Otherwise, you know, *M'sieur* will not enjoy his dinner, and then, perhaps, he will leave us!"

He watched her cross the courtyard, moving with all the grace and lightness of the feline race, and her simple black dress clothed her, he thought, exactly like the fur of the same supple species. She turned once to laugh at him from the porch with the glass door, and then stopped a moment to speak to her mother, who sat knitting as usual in her corner seat just inside the hall-way.

But how was it, then, that the moment his eye fell upon this ungainly woman, the pair of them appeared suddenly as other than they were? Whence came that transforming dignity and sense of power that enveloped them both as by magic? What was it about that massive woman that made her appear instantly regal, and set her on a throne in some dark and dreadful scenery, wielding a sceptre over the red glare of some tempestuous orgy? And why did this slender stripling of a girl, graceful as a willow, lithe as a young leopard, assume suddenly an air of sinister majesty, and move with flame and smoke about her head, and the darkness of night beneath her feet?

Vezin caught his breath and sat there transfixed. Then, almost simultaneously with its appearance, the queer notion vanished again, and the sunlight of day caught them both, and he heard her laughing to her mother about the *soupe à l'oignon*, and saw her glancing back at him over her dear little shoulder with a smile that made him think of a dew-kissed rose bending lightly before summer airs.

And, indeed, the onion soup was particularly excellent that day, because he saw another cover laid at his small table, and, with fluttering heart, heard the waiter murmur by way of explanation that "*Mamselle* Ilsé would honour *M'sieur* to-day at *déjeuner*, as her custom sometimes is with her mother's guests."

So actually she sat by him all through that delirious meal, talking quietly to him in easy French, seeing that he was well looked after, mixing the salad-dressing, and even helping him with her own hand. And, later in the afternoon, while he was smoking in the courtyard, longing for a sight of her as soon as her duties were done, she came again to his side, and when he rose to meet her, she stood facing him a moment, full of a perplexing sweet shyness before she spoke—

"My mother thinks you ought to know more of the beauties of our little town, and I think so too! Would *M'sieur* like me to be his guide, perhaps? I can show him everything, for our family has lived here for many generations."

She had him by the hand, indeed, before he could find a single word to express his pleasure, and led him, all unresisting, out into the street, yet in such a way that it seemed perfectly natural she should do so, and without the faintest suggestion of boldness or immodesty. Her face glowed with the pleasure and interest of it, and with her short dress and tumbled hair she looked every bit the charming child of seventeen that she was, innocent and playful, proud of her native town, and alive beyond her years to the sense of its ancient beauty.

So they went over the town together, and she showed him what she considered its chief interest: the tumbledown old house where her forebears had lived; the sombre, aristocratic-looking mansion where her mother's family dwelt for centuries, and the ancient marketplace where several hundred years before the witches had been burnt by the score. She kept up a lively running stream of talk about it all, of which he understood not a fiftieth part as he trudged along by her side, cursing his forty-five years and feeling all the yearnings of his early manhood revive and jeer at him. And, as she talked, England and Surbiton seemed very far away indeed, almost in another age of the world's history. Her voice touched something immeasurably old in him, something that slept deep. It lulled the surface parts of his consciousness to sleep, allowing what was far more ancient to awaken. Like the town, with its elaborate pretence of modern active life, the upper layers of his being became dulled, soothed, muffled, and what lay underneath began to stir in its sleep. That big Curtain swayed a little to and fro. Presently it might lift altogether....

He began to understand a little better at last. The mood of the town was reproducing itself in him. In proportion as his ordinary external self became muffled, that inner secret life, that was far more real and vital, asserted itself. And this girl was surely the high-priestess of it all, the chief instrument of its accomplishment. New thoughts, with new interpretations, flooded his mind as she walked beside him through the winding streets, while the picturesque old gabled town, softly coloured in the sunset, had never appeared to him so wholly wonderful and seductive.

And only one curious incident came to disturb and puzzle him, slight in itself, but utterly inexplicable, bringing white terror into the child's face and a scream to her laughing lips. He had merely pointed to a column of blue smoke that rose from the burning autumn leaves and made a picture against the red roofs, and had then run to the wall and called her to his side to watch the flames shooting here and there through the heap of rubbish. Yet, at the sight of it, as though taken by surprise, her face had altered dreadfully, and she had turned and run like the wind, calling out wild sentences to him as she ran, of which he had not understood a single word, except that the fire apparently frightened her, and she wanted to get quickly away from it, and to get him away too.

Yet five minutes later she was as calm and happy again as though nothing had happened to alarm or waken troubled thoughts in her, and they had both forgotten the incident.

They were leaning over the ruined ramparts together listening to the weird music of the band as he had heard it the first day of his arrival. It moved him again profoundly as it had done before, and somehow he managed to find his tongue and his best French. The girl leaned across the stones close beside him. No one was about. Driven by some remorseless engine within he began to stammer something—he hardly knew what—of his strange admiration for her. Almost at the first word she sprang lightly off the wall and came up smiling in front of him, just touching his knees as he sat there. She was hatless as usual, and the sun caught her hair and one side of her cheek and throat.

"Oh, I'm *so* glad!" she cried, clapping her little hands softly in his face, "so very glad, because that means that if you like me you must also like what I do, and what I belong to."

Already he regretted bitterly having lost control of himself. Something in the phrasing of her sentence chilled him. He knew the fear of embarking upon an unknown and dangerous sea.

"You will take part in our real life, I mean," she added softly, with an indescribable coaxing of manner, as though she noticed his shrinking. "You will come back to us."

Already this slip of a child seemed to dominate him; he felt her power coming over him more and more; something emanated from her that stole over his senses and made him aware that her personality, for all its simple grace, held forces that were stately, imposing, august. He saw her again moving through smoke and flame amid broken and tempestuous scenery, alarmingly strong, her terrible mother by her side. Dimly this shone through her smile and appearance of charming innocence.

"You will, I know," she repeated, holding him with her eyes.

They were quite alone up there on the ramparts, and the sensation that she was overmastering him stirred a wild sensuousness in his blood. The mingled abandon and reserve in her attracted him furiously, and all of him that was man rose up and resisted the creeping influence, at the same time acclaiming it with the full delight of his forgotten youth. An irresistible desire came to him to question her, to summon what still remained to him of his own little personality in an effort to retain the right to his normal self.

The girl had grown quiet again, and was now leaning on the broad wall close beside him, gazing out across the darkening plain, her elbows on the coping, motionless as a figure carved in stone. He took his courage in both hands.

"Tell me, Ilsé," he said, unconsciously imitating her own purring softness of voice, yet aware that he was utterly in earnest, "what is the meaning of this town, and what is this real life you speak of? And why is it that the people watch me from morning to night? Tell me what it all means? And, tell me," he added more quickly with passion in his voice, "what you really are—yourself?"

She turned her head and looked at him through halfclosed eyelids, her growing inner excitement betraying itself by the faint colour that ran like a shadow across her face.

"It seems to me,"—he faltered oddly under her gaze—"that I have some right to know—"

Suddenly she opened her eyes to the full. "You love me, then?" she asked softly.

"I swear," he cried impetuously, moved as by the force of a rising tide, "I never felt before—I have never known any other girl who—"

"Then you *have* the right to know," she calmly interrupted his confused confession, "for love shares all secrets."

She paused, and a thrill like fire ran swiftly through him. Her words lifted him off the earth, and he felt a radiant happiness, followed almost the same instant in horrible contrast by the thought of death. He became aware that she had turned her eyes upon his own and was speaking again.

"The real life I speak of," she whispered, "is the old, old life within, the life of long ago, the life to which you, too, once belonged, and to which you still belong."

A faint wave of memory troubled the deeps of his soul as her low voice sank into him. What she was saying he knew instinctively to be true, even though he could not as yet understand its full purport. His present life seemed slipping from him as he listened, merging his personality in one that was far older and greater. It was this loss of his present self that brought to him the thought of death.

"You came here," she went on, "with the purpose of seeking it, and the people felt your presence and are waiting to know what you decide, whether you will leave them without having found it, or whether—"

Her eyes remained fixed upon his own, but her face began to change, growing larger and darker with an expression of age.

"It is their thoughts constantly playing about your soul that makes you feel they watch you. They do not watch you with their eyes. The purposes of their inner life are calling to you, seeking to claim you. You were all part of the same life long, long ago, and now they want you back again among them."

Vezin's timid heart sank with dread as he listened; but the girl's eyes held him with a net of joy so that he had no wish to escape. She fascinated him, as it were, clean out of his normal self.

"Alone, however, the people could never have caught and held you," she resumed. "The motive force was not strong enough; it has faded through all these years. But I"—she paused a moment and looked at him with complete confidence in her splendid eyes—"I possess the spell to conquer you and hold you: the spell of old love. I can win you back again and make you live the old life with me, for the force of the ancient tie between us, if I choose to use it, is irresistible. And I do choose to use it. I still want you. And you, dear soul of my dim past"—she pressed closer to him so that her breath passed across his eyes, and her voice positively sang—"I mean to have you, for you love me and are utterly at my mercy."

Vezin heard, and yet did not hear; understood, yet did not understand. He had passed into a condition of exaltation. The world was beneath his feet, made of music and flowers, and he was flying somewhere far above it through the sunshine of pure delight. He was breathless and giddy with the wonder of her words. They intoxicated him. And, still, the terror of it all, the dreadful thought of death, pressed ever behind her sentences. For flames shot through her voice out of black smoke and licked at his soul.

And they communicated with one another, it seemed to him, by a process of swift telepathy, for his French could never have compassed all he said to her. Yet she understood perfectly, and what she said to him was like the recital of verses long since known. And the mingled pain and sweetness of it as he listened were almost more than his little soul could hold.

"Yet I came here wholly by chance—" he heard himself saying.

"No," she cried with passion, "you came here because I called to you. I have called to you for years, and you came with the whole force of the past behind you. You had to come, for I own you, and I claim you."

She rose again and moved closer, looking at him with a certain insolence in the face the insolence of power.

The sun had set behind the towers of the old cathedral and the darkness rose up from the plain and enveloped them. The music of the band had ceased. The leaves of the plane trees hung motionless, but the chill of the autumn evening rose about them and made Vezin shiver. There was no sound but the sound of their voices and the occasional soft rustle of the girl's dress. He could hear the blood rushing in his ears. He scarcely realised where he was or what he was doing. Some terrible magic of the imagination drew him deeply down into the tombs of his own being, telling him in no unfaltering voice that her words shadowed forth the truth. And this simple little French maid, speaking beside him with so strange authority, he saw curiously alter into quite another being. As he stared into her eyes, the picture in his mind grew and lived, dressing itself vividly to his inner vision with a degree of reality he was compelled to acknowledge. As once before, he saw her tall and stately, moving through wild and broken scenery of forests and mountain caverns, the glare of flames behind her head and clouds of shifting smoke about her feet. Dark leaves

273

encircled her hair, flying loosely in the wind, and her limbs shone through the merest rags of clothing. Others were about her too, and ardent eyes on all sides cast delirious glances upon her, but her own eyes were always for One only, one whom she held by the hand. For she was leading the dance in some tempestuous orgy to the music of chanting voices, and the dance she led circled about a great and awful Figure on a throne, brooding over the scene through lurid vapours, while innumerable other wild faces and forms crowded furiously about her in the dance. But the one she held by the hand he knew to be himself, and the monstrous shape upon the throne he knew to be her mother.

The vision rose within him, rushing to him down the long years of buried time, crying aloud to him with the voice of memory reawakened.... And then the scene faded away and he saw the clear circle of the girl's eyes gazing steadfastly into his own, and she became once more the pretty little daughter of the innkeeper, and he found his voice again.

"And you," he whispered tremblingly—"you child of visions and enchantment, how is it that you so bewitch me that I loved you even before I saw?"

She drew herself up beside him with an air of rare dignity.

"The call of the Past," she said; "and besides," she added proudly, "in the real life I am a princess—"

"A princess!" he cried.

"—and my mother is a queen!"

At this, little Vezin utterly lost his head. Delight tore at his heart and swept him into sheer ecstasy. To hear that sweet singing voice, and to see those adorable little lips utter such things, upset his balance beyond all hope of control. He took her in his arms and covered her unresisting face with kisses.

But even while he did so, and while the hot passion swept him, he felt that she was soft and loathsome, and that her answering kisses stained his very soul.... And when, presently, she

274

had freed herself and vanished into the darkness, he stood there, leaning against the wall in a state of collapse, creeping with horror from the touch of her yielding body, and inwardly raging at the weakness that he already dimly realised must prove his undoing.

And from the shadows of the old buildings into which she disappeared there rose in the stillness of the night a singular, long-drawn cry, which at first he took for laughter, but which later he was sure he recognised as the almost human wailing of a cat.

V

For a long time Vezin leant there against the wall, alone with his surging thoughts and emotions. He understood at length that he had done the one thing necessary to call down upon him the whole force of this ancient Past. For in those passionate kisses he had acknowledged the tie of olden days, and had revived it. And the memory of that soft impalpable caress in the darkness of the inn corridor came back to him with a shudder. The girl had first mastered him, and then led him to the one act that was necessary for her purpose. He had been waylaid, after the lapse of centuries—caught, and conquered.

Dimly he realised this, and sought to make plans for his escape. But, for the moment at any rate, he was powerless to manage his thoughts or will, for the sweet, fantastic madness of the whole adventure mounted to his brain like a spell, and he gloried in the feeling that he was utterly enchanted and moving in a world so much larger and wilder than the one he had ever been accustomed to.

The moon, pale and enormous, was just rising over the sea-like plain, when at last he rose to go. Her slanting rays drew all the houses into new perspective, so that their roofs, already glistening with dew, seemed to stretch much higher into the sky than usual, and their gables and quaint old towers lay far away in its purple reaches.

The cathedral appeared unreal in a silver mist. He moved softly, keeping to the shadows; but the streets were all deserted and very silent; the doors were closed, the shutters fastened. Not a soul was astir. The hush of night lay over everything; it was like a town of the dead, a churchyard with gigantic and grotesque tombstones.

Wondering where all the busy life of the day had so utterly disappeared to, he made his way to a back door that entered the inn by means of the stables, thinking thus to reach his room unobserved. He reached the courtyard safely and crossed it by keeping close to the shadow of tile wall. He sidled down it, mincing along on tiptoe, just as the old man did when they entered the *salle à manger*. He was horrified to find himself doing this instinctively. A strange impulse came to him, catching him somehow in the centre of his body—an impulse to drop upon all fours and run swiftly and silently. He glanced upwards and the idea came to him to leap up upon his window-sill overhead instead of going round by the stairs. This occurred to him as the easiest, and most natural way. It was like the beginning of some horrible transformation of himself into something else. He was fearfully strung up.

The moon was higher now, and the shadows very dark along the side of the street where he moved. He kept among the deepest of them, and reached the porch with the glass doors.

But here there was light; the inmates, unfortunately, were still about. Hoping to slip across the hall unobserved and reach the stairs, he opened the door carefully and stole in. Then he saw that the hall was not empty. A large dark thing lay against the wall on his left. At first he thought it must be household articles. Then it moved, and he thought it was an immense cat, distorted in some way by the play of light and shadow. Then it rose straight up before him and he saw that it was the proprietress.

What she had been doing in this position he could only venture a dreadful guess, but the moment she stood up and faced him he was aware of some terrible dignity clothing her about that instantly recalled the girl's strange saying that she was a queen. Huge and sinister she stood there under the little oil lamp; alone with him in the empty hall. Awe stirred in his heart, and the roots of some ancient fear. He felt that he must bow to her and make some kind of obeisance. The impulse was fierce and irresistible, as of long habit. He glanced quickly about him. There was no one there. Then he deliberately inclined his head towards her. He bowed.

"*Enfin! M'sieur s'est done décidé. C'est bien alors. J'en suis contente.*"

Her words came to him sonorously as through a great open space.

Then the great figure came suddenly across the flagged hall at him and seized his trembling hands. Some overpowering force moved with her and caught him.

"*On pourrait faire un p'tit tour ensemble, n'est-ce pas? Nous y allons cette nuit et il faut s'exercer un peu d'avance pour cela. Ilsé, Ilsé, viens donc ici. Viens vite!*"

And she whirled him round in the opening steps of some dance that seemed oddly and horribly familiar. They made no sound on the stones, this strangely assorted couple. It was all soft and stealthy. And presently, when the air seemed to thicken like smoke, and a red glare as of flame shot through it, he was aware that some one else had joined them and that his hand the mother had released was now tightly held by the daughter. Ilsé had come in answer to the call, and he saw her with leaves of vervain twined in her dark hair, clothed in tattered vestiges of some curious garment, beautiful as the night, and horribly, odiously, loathsomely seductive.

"To the Sabbath! to the Sabbath!" they cried. "On to the Witches' Sabbath!"

Up and down that narrow hall they danced, the women on each side of him, to the wildest measure he had ever imagined, yet which he dimly, dreadfully remembered, till the lamp on the wall flickered and went out, and they were left in total darkness. And the devil woke in his heart with a thousand vile suggestions and made him afraid.

Suddenly they released his hands and he heard the voice of the mother cry that it was time, and they must go. Which way they went he did not pause to see. He only realised that he was free, and he blundered through the darkness till he found the stairs and then tore up them to his room as though all hell was at his heels.

He flung himself on the sofa, with his face in his hands, and groaned. Swiftly reviewing a dozen ways of immediate escape, all equally impossible, he finally decided that the only thing to do for the moment was to sit quiet and wait. He must see what was going to happen. At least in the privacy of his own bedroom he would be fairly safe. The door was locked. He crossed over and softly opened the window which gave upon the courtyard and also permitted a partial view of the hall through the glass doors.

As he did so the hum and murmur of a great activity reached his ears from the streets beyond—the sound of footsteps and voices muffled by distance. He leaned out cautiously and listened. The moonlight was clear and strong now, but his own window was in shadow, the silver disc being still behind the house. It came to him irresistibly that the inhabitants of the town, who a little while before had all been invisible behind closed doors, were now issuing forth, busy upon some secret and unholy errand. He listened intently.

At first everything about him was silent, but soon he became aware of movements going on in the house itself. Rustlings and

278

cheepings came to him across that still moonlit yard. A concourse of living beings sent the hum of their activity into the night. Things were on the move everywhere. A biting, pungent odour rose through the air, coming he knew not whence. Presently his eyes became glued to the windows of the opposite wall where the moonshine fell in a soft blaze. The roof overhead, and behind him, was reflected clearly in the panes of glass, and he saw the outlines of dark bodies moving with long footsteps over the tiles and along the coping. They passed swiftly and silently, shaped like immense cats, in an endless procession across the pictured glass, and then appeared to leap down to a lower level where he lost sight of them. He just caught the soft thudding of their leaps. Sometimes their shadows fell upon the white wall opposite, and then he could not make out whether they were the shadows of human beings or of cats. They seemed to change swiftly from one to the other. The transformation looked horribly real, for they leaped like human beings, yet changed swiftly in the air immediately afterwards, and dropped like animals.

The yard, too, beneath him, was now alive with the creeping movements of dark forms all stealthily drawing towards the porch with the glass doors. They kept so closely to the wall that he could not determine their actual shape, but when he saw that they passed on to the great congregation that was gathering in the hall, he understood that these were the creatures whose leaping shadows he had first seen reflected in the windowpanes opposite. They were coming from all parts of the town, reaching the appointed meetingplace across the roofs and tiles, and springing from level to level till they came to the yard.

Then a new sound caught his ear, and he saw that the windows all about him were being softly opened, and that to each window came a face. A moment later figures began dropping hurriedly down into the yard. And these figures, as they lowered themselves down from the windows, were human, he saw; but once safely in the yard they fell upon all fours and changed in the swiftest possible second into—cats—huge, silent cats. They ran in streams to join the main body in the hall beyond.

So, after all, the rooms in the house had not been empty and unoccupied.

Moreover, what he saw no longer filled him with amazement. For he remembered it all. It was familiar. It had all happened before just so, hundreds of times, and he himself had taken part in it and known the wild madness of it all. The outline of the old building changed, the yard grew larger, and he seemed to be staring down upon it from a much greater height through smoky vapours. And, as he looked, half remembering, the old pains of long ago, fierce and sweet, furiously assailed him, and the blood stirred horribly as he heard the Call of the Dance again in his heart and tasted the ancient magic of Ilsé whirling by his side.

Suddenly he started back. A great lithe cat had leaped softly up from the shadows below on to the sill close to his face, and was staring fixedly at him with the eyes of a human. "Come," it seemed to say, "come with us to the Dance! Change as of old! Transform yourself swiftly and come!" Only too well he understood the creature's soundless call.

It was gone again in a flash with scarcely a sound of its padded feet on the stones, and then others dropped by the score down the side of the house, past his very eyes, all changing as they fell and darting away rapidly, softly, towards the gathering point. And again he felt the dreadful desire to do likewise; to murmur the old incantation, and then drop upon hands and knees and run swiftly for the great flying leap into the air. Oh, how the passion of it rose within him like a flood, twisting his very entrails, sending his heart's desire flaming forth into the night for the old, old Dance of the Sorcerers at the Witches' Sabbath! The whirl of the stars was about him; once more he met the magic of the moon. The power of the wind, rushing from precipice and forest, leaping from cliff to cliff across the valleys, tore him away.... He heard the cries of the dancers and their wild laughter, and with this savage girl in his embrace he danced furiously about the dim Throne where sat the Figure with the sceptre of majesty....

Then, suddenly, all became hushed and still, and the fever died down a little in his heart. The calm moonlight flooded a courtyard empty and deserted. They had started. The procession was off into the sky. And he was left behind—alone.

Vezin tiptoed softly across the room and unlocked the door. The murmur from the streets, growing momentarily as he advanced, met his ears. He made his way with the utmost caution down the corridor. At the head of the stairs he paused and listened. Below him, the hall where they had gathered was dark and still, but through opened doors and windows on the far side of the building came the sound of a great throng moving farther and farther into the distance.

He made his way down the creaking wooden stairs, dreading yet longing to meet some straggler who should point the way, but finding no one; across the dark hall, so lately thronged with living, moving things, and out through the opened front doors into the street. He could not believe that he was really left behind, really forgotten, that he had been purposely permitted to escape. It perplexed him.

Nervously he peered about him, and up and down the street; then, seeing nothing, advanced slowly down the pavement.

The whole town, as he went, showed itself empty and deserted, as though a great wind had blown everything alive out of it. The doors and windows of the houses stood open to the night; nothing stirred; moonlight and silence lay over all. The night lay about him like a cloak. The air, soft and cool, caressed his cheek like the touch of a great furry paw. He gained confidence and began to walk quickly, though still keeping to the shadowed side. Nowhere could he discover the faintest sign of the great unholy exodus he knew had just taken place. The moon sailed high over all in a sky cloudless, and serene.

Hardly realising where he was going, he crossed the open market-place and so came to the ramparts, whence he knew a pathway descended to the high road and along which he could make good his escape to one of the other little towns that lay to the northward, and so to the railway.

But first he paused and gazed out over the scene at his feet where the great plain lay like a silver map of some dream country. The still beauty of it entered his heart, increasing his sense of bewilderment and unreality. No air stirred, the leaves of the plane trees stood motionless, the near details were defined with the sharpness of day against dark shadows, and in the distance the fields and woods melted away into haze and shimmering mistiness.

But the breath caught in his throat and he stood stock-still as though transfixed when his gaze passed from the horizon and fell upon the near prospect in the depth of the valley at his feet. The whole lower slopes of the hill, that lay hid from the brightness of the moon, were aglow, and through the glare he saw countless moving forms, shifting thick and fast between the openings of the trees; while overhead, like leaves driven by the wind, he discerned flying shapes that hovered darkly one moment against the sky and then settled down with cries and weird singing through the branches into the region that was aflame.

Spellbound, he stood and stared for a time that he could not measure. And then, moved by one of the terrible impulses that seemed to control the whole adventure, he climbed swiftly upon the top of the broad coping, and balanced a moment where the valley gaped at his feet.

But in that very instant, as he stood hovering, a sudden movement among the shadows of the houses caught his eye, and he turned to see the outline of a large animal dart swiftly across the open space behind him, and land with a flying leap upon the top of the wall a little lower down. It ran like the wind to his feet and then rose up beside him upon the ramparts. A shiver seemed to run through the moonlight, and his sight trembled for a second. His heart pulsed fearfully. Ilsé stood beside him, peering into his face.

Some dark substance, he saw, stained the girl's face and skin, shining in the moonlight as she stretched her hands toward him; she was dressed in wretched tattered garments that yet became her mightily; rue and vervain twined about her temples; her eyes glittered with unholy light. He only just controlled the wild impulse to take her in his arms and leap with her from their giddy perch into the valley below.

"See!" she cried, pointing with an arm on which the rags fluttered in the rising wind toward the forest aglow in the distance. "See where they await us! The woods are alive! Already the Great Ones are there, and the dance will soon begin! The salve is here! Anoint yourself and come!"

Though a moment before the sky was clear and cloudless, yet even while she spoke the face of the moon grew dark and the wind began to toss in the crests of the plane trees at his feet. Stray gusts brought the sounds of hoarse singing and crying from the lower slopes of the hill, and the pungent odour he had already noticed about the courtyard of the inn rose about him in the air.

"Transform, transform!" she cried again, her voice rising like a song. "Rub well your skin before you fly. Come! Come with me to the Sabbath, to the madness of its furious delight, to the sweet abandonment of its evil worship! See! the Great Ones are there, and the terrible Sacraments prepared. The Throne is occupied. Anoint and come! Anoint and come!"

She grew to the height of a tree beside him, leaping upon the wall with flaming eyes and hair strewn upon the night. He too began to change swiftly. Her hands touched the skin of his face and neck, streaking him with the burning salve that sent the old magic into his blood with the power before which fades all that is good.

A wild roar came up to his ears from the heart of the wood, and the girl, when she heard it, leaped upon the wall in the frenzy of her wicked joy.

"Satan is there!" she screamed, rushing upon him and striving to draw him with her to the edge of the wall. "Satan has come. The Sacraments call us! Come, with your dear apostate soul, and we will worship and dance till the moon dies and the world is forgotten!"

Just saving himself from the dreadful plunge, Vezin struggled to release himself from her grasp, while the passion tore at his reins and all but mastered him. He shrieked aloud, not knowing what he said, and then he shrieked again. It was the old impulses, the old awful habits instinctively finding voice; for though it seemed to him that he merely shrieked nonsense, the words he uttered really had meaning in them, and were intelligible. It was the ancient call. And it was heard below. It was answered.

The wind whistled at the skirts of his coat as the air round him darkened with many flying forms crowding upwards out of the valley. The crying of hoarse voices smote upon his ears, coming closer. Strokes of wind buffeted him, tearing him this way and that along the crumbling top of the stone wall; and Ilsé clung to him with her long shining arms, smooth and bare, holding him fast about the neck. But not Ilsé alone, for a dozen of them surrounded him, dropping out of the air. The pungent odour of the anointed bodies stifled him, exciting him to the old madness of the Sabbath, the dance of the witches and sorcerers doing honour to the personified Evil of the world.

"Anoint and away! Anoint and away!" they cried in wild chorus about him. "To the Dance that never dies! To the sweet and fearful fantasy of evil!"

Another moment and he would have yielded and gone, for his will turned soft and the flood of passionate memory all but overwhelmed him, when—so can a small thing alter the whole course of an adventure—he caught his foot upon a loose stone in the edge of the wall, and then fell with a sudden crash on to the ground below. But he fell towards the houses, in the open space of dust and cobblestones, and fortunately not into the gaping depth of the valley on the farther side.

And they, too, came in a tumbling heap about him, like flies upon a piece of food, but as they fell he was released for a moment from the power of their touch, and in that brief instant of freedom there flashed into his mind the sudden intuition that saved him. Before he could regain his feet he saw them scrabbling awkwardly back upon the wall, as though bat-like they could only fly by dropping from a height, and had no hold upon him in the open. Then, seeing them perched there in a row like cats upon a roof, all dark and singularly shapeless, their eyes like lamps, the sudden memory came back to him of Ilsé's terror at the sight of fire.

Quick as a flash he found his matches and lit the dead leaves that lay under the wall.

Dry and withered, they caught fire at once, and the wind carried the flame in a long line down the length of the wall, licking upwards as it ran; and with shrieks and wailings, the crowded row of forms upon the top melted away into the air on the other side, and were gone with a great rush and whirring of their bodies down into the heart of the haunted valley, leaving Vezin breathless and shaken in the middle of the deserted ground.

"Ilsé!" he called feebly; "Ilsé!" for his heart ached to think that she was really gone to the great Dance without him, and that he had lost the opportunity of its fearful joy. Yet at the same time his relief was so great, and he was so dazed and troubled in mind with the whole thing, that he hardly knew what he was saying, and only cried aloud in the fierce storm of his emotion....

The fire under the wall ran its course, and the moonlight came out again, soft and clear, from its temporary eclipse. With one last shuddering look at the ruined ramparts, and a feeling of horrid wonder for the haunted valley beyond, where the shapes still crowded and flew, he turned his face towards the town and slowly made his way in the direction of the hotel.

And as he went, a great wailing of cries, and a sound of howling, followed him from the gleaming forest below, growing fainter and fainter with the bursts of wind as he disappeared between the houses.

VI

"It may seem rather abrupt to you, this sudden tame ending," said Arthur Vezin, glancing with flushed face and timid eyes at Dr. Silence sitting there with his notebook, "but the fact is—er—from that moment my memory seems to have failed rather. I have no distinct recollection of how I got home or what precisely I did.

"It appears I never went back to the inn at all. I only dimly recollect racing down a long white road in the moonlight, past woods and villages, still and deserted, and then the dawn came up, and I saw the towers of a biggish town and so came to a station.

"But, long before that, I remember pausing somewhere on the road and looking back to where the hill-town of my adventure stood up in the moonlight, and thinking how exactly like a great monstrous cat it lay there upon the plain, its huge front paws lying down the two main streets, and the twin and broken towers of the cathedral marking its torn ears against the sky. That picture stays in my mind with the utmost vividness to this day.

"Another thing remains in my mind from that escape—namely, the sudden sharp reminder that I had not paid my bill, and the decision I made, standing there on the dusty highroad, that the small baggage I had left behind would more than settle for my indebtedness.

"For the rest, I can only tell you that I got coffee and bread at a café on the outskirts of this town I had come to, and soon after found my way to the station and caught a train later in the day. That same evening I reached London."

"And how long altogether," asked John Silence quietly, "do you think you stayed in the town of the adventure?"

Vezin looked up sheepishly.

"I was coming to that," he resumed, with apologetic wrigglings of his body. "In London I found that I was a whole week out in my reckoning of time. I had stayed over a week in the town, and it ought to have been September 15th,—instead of which it was only September 10th!"

"So that, in reality, you had only stayed a night or two in the inn?" queried the doctor.

Vezin hesitated before replying. He shuffled upon the mat.

"I must have gained time somewhere," he said at length— "somewhere or somehow. I certainly had a week to my credit. I can't explain it. I can only give you the fact."

"And this happened to you last year, since when you have never been back to the place?"

"Last autumn, yes," murmured Vezin; "and I have never dared to go back. I think I never want to."

"And, tell me," asked Dr. Silence at length, when he saw that the little man had evidently come to the end of his words and had nothing more to say, "had you ever read up the subject of the old witchcraft practices during the Middle Ages, or been at all interested in the subject?"

"Never!" declared Vezin emphatically. "I had never given a thought to such matters so far as I know—"

"Or to the question of reincarnation, perhaps?"

"Never—before my adventure; but I have since," he replied significantly.

There was, however, something still on the man's mind that he wished to relieve himself of by confession, yet could with difficulty bring himself to mention; and it was only after the sympathetic tactfulness of the doctor had provided numerous openings that he at length availed himself of one of them, and stammered that he would like to show him the marks he still had on his neck where, he said, the girl had touched him with her anointed hands.

He took off his collar after infinite fumbling hesitation, and lowered his shirt a little for the doctor to see. And there, on the surface of the skin, lay a faint reddish line across the shoulder and extending a little way down the back towards the spine. It certainly indicated exactly the position an arm might have taken in the act of embracing. And on the other side of the neck, slightly higher up, was a similar mark, though not quite so clearly defined.

"That was where she held me that night on the ramparts," he whispered, a strange light coming and going in his eyes.

It was some weeks later when I again found occasion to consult John Silence concerning another extraordinary case that had come under my notice, and we fell to discussing Vezin's story. Since hearing it, the doctor had made investigations on his own account, and one of his secretaries had discovered that Vezin's ancestors had actually lived for generations in the very town where the adventure came to him. Two of them, both women, had been tried and convicted as witches, and had been burned alive at the stake. Moreover, it had not been difficult to prove that the very inn where Vezin stayed was built about 1700 upon the spot where the funeral pyres stood and the executions took place. The town was a sort of headquarters for all the sorcerers and witches of the entire region, and after conviction they were burnt there literally by scores.

"It seems strange," continued the doctor, "that Vezin should have remained ignorant of all this; but, on the other hand, it was not the kind of history that successive generations would have been anxious to keep alive, or to repeat to their children. Therefore I am inclined to think he still knows nothing about it.

"The whole adventure seems to have been a very vivid revival of the memories of an earlier life, caused by coming directly into contact with the living forces still intense enough to hang about the place, and, by a most singular chance too, with the very souls who had taken part with him in the events of that particular life. For the mother and daughter who impressed him so strangely must have been leading actors, with himself, in the scenes and practices of witchcraft which at that period dominated the imaginations of the whole country.

"One has only to read the histories of the times to know that these witches claimed the power of transforming themselves into various animals, both for the purposes of disguise and also to convey themselves swiftly to the scenes of their imaginary orgies. Lycanthropy, or the power to change themselves into wolves, was everywhere believed in, and the ability to transform themselves into cats by rubbing their bodies with a special salve of ointment provided by Satan himself, found equal credence. The witchcraft trials abound in evidences of such universal beliefs."

Dr. Silence quoted chapter and verse from many writers on the subject, and showed how every detail of Vezin's adventure had a basis in the practices of those dark days.

"But that the entire affair took place subjectively in the man's own consciousness, I have no doubt," he went on, in reply to my questions; "for my secretary who has been to the town to investigate, discovered his signature in the visitors' book, and proved by it that he had arrived on September 8th, and left suddenly without paying his bill. He left two days later, and they still were in possession of his dirty brown bag and some tourist clothes. I paid a few francs in settlement of his debt, and have sent his luggage on to him. The daughter was absent from home, but the proprietress, a large woman very much as he described her, told my secretary that he had seemed a very strange, absent-minded kind of gentleman, and after his disappearance she had feared for a long time that he had met with a violent end in the neighbouring forest where he used to roam about alone.

"I should like to have obtained a personal interview with the daughter so as to ascertain how much was subjective and how much actually took place with her as Vezin told it. For her dread of fire and the sight of burning must, of course, have been the intuitive memory of her former painful death at the stake, and have thus explained why he fancied more than once that he saw her through smoke and flame."

"And that mark on his skin, for instance?" I inquired.

"Merely the marks produced by hysterical brooding," he replied, "like the stigmata of the *religieuses*, and the bruises which appear on the bodies of hypnotised subjects who have been told to expect them. This is very common and easily explained. Only it seems curious that these marks should have remained so long in Vezin's case. Usually they disappear quickly."

"Obviously he is still thinking about it all, brooding, and living it all over again," I ventured.

"Probably. And this makes me fear that the end of his trouble is not yet. We shall hear of him again. It is a case, alas! I can do little to alleviate."

Dr. Silence spoke gravely and with sadness in his voice.

"And what do you make of the Frenchman in the train?" I asked further—"the man who warned him against the place, *à cause du sommeil et à cause des chats*? Surely a very singular incident?"

"A very singular incident indeed," he made answer slowly, "and one I can only explain on the basis of a highly improbable coincidence—"

"Namely?"

"That the man was one who had himself stayed in the town and undergone there a similar experience. I should like to find this man and ask him. But the crystal is useless here, for I have no slightest clue to go upon, and I can only conclude that some singular psychic affinity, some force still active in his being out of the same past life, drew him thus to the personality of Vezin, and enabled him to fear what might happen to him, and thus to warn him as he did.

"Yes," he presently continued, half talking to himself, "I suspect in this case that Vezin was swept into the vortex of forces arising out of the intense activities of a past life, and that he lived over again a scene in which he had often played a leading part centuries before. For strong actions set up forces that are so slow to exhaust themselves, they may be said in a sense never to die. In this case they were not vital enough to render the illusion complete, so that the little man found himself caught in a very distressing confusion of the present and the past; yet he was sufficiently sensitive to recognise that it was true, and to fight against the degradation of returning, even in memory, to a former and lower state of development.

"Ah yes!" he continued, crossing the floor to gaze at the darkening sky, and seemingly quite oblivious of my presence, "subliminal up-rushes of memory like this can be exceedingly painful, and sometimes exceedingly dangerous. I only trust that this gentle soul may soon escape from this obsession of a passionate and tempestuous past. But I doubt it, I doubt it."

His voice was hushed with sadness as he spoke, and when he turned back into the room again there was an expression of profound yearning upon his face, the yearning of a soul whose desire to help is sometimes greater than his power.

CASSIUS

By Henry S. Whitehead

Lovecraft came in touch with pulp writer Henry S. Whitehead (1882–1932) in the summer of 1931, when he visited Whitehead at his home in Dunedin, Florida. It appears that at this time Lovecraft suggested to Whitehead that he write up an unused story plot from Lovecraft's commonplace book: "Man has miniature shapeless Siamese twin—exhib. in circus—twin surgically detached—disappears—does hideous things with malign life of its own" (entry 133). Whitehead wrote up the plot as "Cassius" (*Strange Tales*, November 1931). Lovecraft later admitted, however, that his own development of the plot would have been very different and would have taken one of two forms: "One would have had the monster escape as Whitehead had it—but would have had it much more terrible and much less human. I would have had it grow in size, and frighten people much more terribly than 'Cassius' did. Indeed, I would have tried to convey the implication that some 'Outside' force of daemon had taken possession of the brainless, twisted body—impelling it to strange acts of *apparently deliberate but plainly nonhuman motivation*" (*SL* 5.33; the rest of the letter states in detail the other form the plot would have taken). Lovecraft's plot-germ was inspired by a strange anthropoid excrescence found in a man at a freak show that Lovecraft visited in New York in 1925.

Whitehead was a prolific contributor to *Weird Tales, Strange Tales*, and other pulps during his short literary career. August

Derleth published two collections of his tales with Arkham House, *Jumbee and Other Uncanny Tales* (1944) and *West India Lights* (1946). Whitehead and Lovecraft collaborated on the tale "The Trap" (*Strange Tales*, March 1932), published under Whitehead's name only.]

My houseman, Stephen Penn, who presided over the staff of my residence in St. Thomas, was not, strictly speaking, a native of that city. Penn came from the neighboring island of St. Jan. It is one of the ancient West Indian names, although there remain in the islands nowadays no Caucasians to bear that honorable cognomen.

Stephen's travels, however, had not been limited to the crossing from St. Jan—which, incidentally, is the authentic scene of R. L. Stevenson's *Treasure Island*—which lies little more than a rowboat's journey away from the capital of the Virgin Islands. Stephen had been "down the Islands," which means that he had been actually as far from home as Trinidad, or perhaps, British Guiana, down through the great sweep of former mountaintops, submerged by some vast, cataclysmic, prehistoric inundation and named the Bow of Ulysses by some fanciful, antique geographer. That odyssey of humble Stephen Penn had taken place because of his love for ships. He had had various jobs afloat and his exact knowledge of the houseman's art had been learned under various man-driving ship's stewards.

During this preliminary training for his life's work, Stephen had made many acquaintances. One of these, an upstanding, slim, parchment-colored Negro of thirty or so, was Brutus Hellman. Brutus, like Stephen, had settled down in St. Thomas as a houseman. It was, in fact, Stephen who had talked him into leaving his native British Antigua, to try his luck in our American

Virgin Islands. Stephen had secured for him his first job in St. Thomas, in the household of a naval officer.

For this friend of his youthful days, Stephen continued to feel a certain sense of responsibility; because, when Brutus happened to be abruptly thrown out of employment by the sudden illness and removal by the Naval Department of his employer in the middle of the winter season in St. Thomas, Stephen came to me and requested that his friend Brutus be allowed to come to me "on board-wages" until he was able to secure another place.

I acquiesced. I knew Brutus as a first-rate houseman. I was glad to give him a hand, to oblige the always agreeable and highly efficient Stephen, and, indeed, to have so skillful a servant added to my little staff in my bachelor quarters. I arranged for something more substantial than the remuneration asked for, and Brutus Hellman added his skilled services to those of the admirable Stephen. I was very well served that season and never had any occasion to regret what both men alluded to as my "very great kindness!"

It was not long after Brutus Hellman had moved his simple belongings into one of the servants'-quarters cabins in my stone-paved yard, that I had another opportunity to do something for him. It was Stephen once more who presented his friend's case to me. Brutus, it appeared, had need of a minor operation, and, Negro-like, the two of them, talking the matter over between themselves, had decided to ask me, their present patron, to arrange it.

I did so, with my friend, Dr. Pelletier, Chief Surgeon, in charge of our Naval Station Hospital and regarded in Naval circles as the best man in the Medical Corps. I had not inquired about the nature of Brutus' affliction. Stephen had stressed the minor aspect of the required surgery, and that was all I mentioned to Dr. Pelletier.

It is quite possible that if Dr. Pelletier had not been going to
Porto Rico on Thursday of that week, this narrative, the record
of one of the most curious experiences I have ever had, would
never have been set down. If Pelletier, his mind set on sailing at
eleven, had not merely walked out of his operating-room as soon
as he had finished with Brutus a little after eight that Thursday
morning, left the dressing of the slight wound upon Brutus' groin
to be performed by his assistants, then that incredible affair which
I can only describe as the persecution of the unfortunate Brutus
Hellman would never have taken place.

It was on Wednesday, about two P.M., that I telephoned to Dr.
Pelletier to ask him to perform an operation on Brutus.

"Send him over to the hospital this afternoon," Pelletier had
answered, "And I'll look him over about five and operate the first
thing in the moming—if there is any need for an operation! I'm
leaving for San Juan at eleven, for a week."

I thanked him and went upstairs to my siesta, after giving
Stephen the message to Brutus, who started off for the hospital
about an hour later. He remained in the hospital until the following
Sunday afternoon. He was entirely recovered from the operation,
he reported. It had been a very slight affair, really, merely the
removal of some kind of growth. He thanked me for my part in
it when he came to announce dinner while I was reading on the
gallery.

It was on the Saturday morning, the day before Brutus got
back, that I discovered something very curious in an obscure
corner of my house-yard, just around the corner of the wall of the
three small cabins which occupy its north side. These cabins were
tenantless except for the one at the east end of the row. That one
was Brutus Hellman's. Stephen Penn, like my cook, washer, and
scullery-maid, lived somewhere in the town.

I had been looking over the yard, which was paved with old-
fashioned flagging. I found it an excellent condition, weeded,

freshly swept, and clean. The three stone servants' cubicles had been recently whitewashed and glistened like cake icing in the morning sun. I looked over this portion of my domain with approval, for I like things shipshape. I glanced into the two narrow air spaces between the little, two-room houses. There were no cobwebs visible. Then I took a look around the east corner of Brutus Hellman's little house where there was a narrow passageway between the house and the high wall of antique Dutch brick, and there, well in towards the north wall, I saw on the ground what I first took to be a discarded toy which some child had thrown there, probably, it occurred to me, over the wall at the back of the stone cabins.

It looked like a doll's house, which, if it had been thrown there, had happened to land right-side-up. It looked more or less like one of the quaint old-fashioned beehives one still sees occasionally in the conservative Lesser Antilles. But it could hardly be a beehive. It was far too small.

My curiosity mildly aroused, I stepped into the alleyway and looked down at the odd little thing. Seen from where I stopped it rewarded scrutiny. For it was, although, made in a somewhat bungling way, a reproduction of an African village hut, thatched, circular, conical. The thatching, I suspected, had formerly been most of the business-end of a small house-broom of fine twigs tied together around the end of a stick. The little house's upright "logs" were a heterogenous medley of little round sticks among which I recognized three dilapidated lead pencils and the broken-off handle of a tooth-brush. These details will serve to indicate its size and to justify my original conclusion that the thing was a rather cleverly made child's toy. How such a thing had got into my yard unless over the wall, was an unimportant little mystery. The little hut, from the ground up to its thatched peak, stood about seven inches in height. Its diameter was, perhaps, eight or nine inches.

My first reaction was to pick it up, look at it more closely, and then throw it into the wire cage in another corner of the yard where Stephen burned up waste paper and scraps at frequent intervals. The thing was plainly a discarded toy, and had no business cluttering up my spotless yard. Then I suddenly remembered the washer's pick'ny, a small, silent, very black child of six or seven, who sometimes played quietly in the yard while his stout mother toiled over the washtub set up on a backless chair near the kitchen door where she could keep up a continous stream of chatter with my cook.

I stayed my hand accordingly. Quite likely this little thatched hut was a valued item of that pick'ny's possessions. Thinking pleasantly to surprise little Aesculapius, or whatever the child's name might be, I took from my pocket a fifty-bit piece—value ten cents—intending to place the coin inside the little house, through its rounded, low entranceway.

Stooping down, I shoved the coin through the doorway, and, as I did so, something suddenly scuttered about inside the hut, and pinched viciously at the ends of my thumb and forefinger.

I was, naturally, startled. I snatched my fingers away, and stood hastily erect. A mouse, perhaps even a rat, inside there! I glanced at my fingers. There was no mark on them. The skin was not broken. The rodent's vicious little sharp teeth had fortunately missed their grip as he snapped at me, intruding on his sacred privacy. Wondering a little, I stepped out of the alleyway and into the sunny, open yard, somewhat upset at this Lilliputian contretemps, and resolved upon telling Stephen to see to it that there was no ugly rodent there when next little Aesculapius should retrieve his plaything.

But when I arrived at the gallery steps my friend Colonel Lorriquer's car was just drawing up before the house, and, in hastening to greet welcome early-moming callers and later in accepting Mrs. Lorriquer's invitation to dinner and contract at their house that evening, the little hut and its unpleasant inhabitant were driven wholly out of my mind.

I did not think of it again until several days later, on the night when my premises had become the theater for one of the most inexplicable, terrifying and uncanny happenings I have ever experienced.

My gallery is a very pleasant place to sit evenings, except in that spring period during which the West Indian candle-moths hatch in their myriads and, for several successive days, make it impossible to sit outdoors in any lighted, unscreened place.

It was much too early for the candle-moths, however, at the time I am speaking of, and on the evening of that Sunday upon which Brutus Hellman returned from the hospital, a party of four persons including myself, occupied the gallery.

The other man was Arthur Carswell, over from Hayti on a short visit. The two ladies were Mrs. Spencer, Colonel Lorriquer's widowed daughter, and her friend, Mrs. Squire. We had dined an hour previously at the Grand Hotel as guests of Carswell, and, having taken our coffee at my house, were remaining outdoors on the gallery "for a breath of air" on a rather warm and sultry February evening. We were sitting, quietly talking in a rather desultory manner, all of us unspokenly reluctant to move inside the house for a projected evening at contract.

It was, as I recall the hour, about nine o'clock, the night warm, as I have said, and very still. Above, in a cloudless sky of luminous indigo, the tropical stars glowed enormous. The intoxicating sweet odors of white jessamine and tuberoses made the still air redolent. No sound, except an occasional rather languid remark from one of ourselves, broke the exquisite, balmy stillness.

Then, all at once, without any warning and with an abruptness which caused Carswell and me to stand up, the exquisite perfection of the night was rudely shattered by an appalling, sustained scream of sheer mortal terror.

That scream inaugurated what seems to me, as I look back upon the next few days, to be one of the most unnerving, devastating, and generally horrible periods I can recall in a lifetime not devoid of adventure. I formulated at that time, and still retain, mentally, a phrase descriptive of it. It was "the Reign of Terror."

Carswell and I, following the direction of the scream, rushed down the outer gallery steps and back through the yard towards the negro-cabins. As I have mentioned, only one of these was occupied, Brutus Hellman's. As we rounded the corner of the house a faint light—it was Brutus' oil lamp—appeared in the form of a wide vertical strip at the entrance of the occupied cabin. To that we ran as to a beacon, and pushed into the room.

The lamp, newly lighted, and smoking, its glass chimney set on askew as though in great haste, dimly illuminated a strange scene. Doubled up and sitting on the side of his bed, the bedclothes near the bed's foot lumped together where he had flung them, cowered Brutus. His face was a dull, ashen gray in the smoky light, his back was bent, his hands clasped tightly about his shin. And, from between those clenched hands, a steady stream of blood stained the white sheet which hung over the bed's edge and spread below into a small pool on the cabin room's stone-paved floor.

Brutus, groaning dismally, rocked back and forth, clutching his leg. The lamp smoked steadily, defiling the close air, while, incongruously, through the now open doorway poured streams and great pulsing breaths of nightblooming tropical flowers, mingling strangely with the hot acrid odor of the smoking lampwick.

Carswell went directly to the lamp, straightened the chimney, turned down the flame. The lamp ceased its ugly reek and the air of the cabin cleared as Carswell, turning away from the lamp, threw wide the shutters of the large window which, like most West Indian Negroes, Brutus had closed against the "night air" when he retired.

I gave my attention directly to the man, and by the time the air had cleared somewhat I had him over on his back in a reclining position, and with a great strip torn from one of his bedsheets, was binding up the ugly, deep little wound in the lower muscle of his leg just at the outside of the shinbone. I pulled the improvised bandage tight, and the flow of blood ceased, and Brutus, his mind probably somewhat relieved by this timely aid, put an end to his moaning, and turned his ashy face up to mine.

"Did you see it, sar?" he inquired, biting back the trembling of his mouth.

I paid practically no attention to this remark. Indeed, I barely heard it. I was, you see, very busily engaged in staunching the flow of blood. Brutus had already lost a considerable quantity, and my rough bandaging was directed entirely to the end of stopping this. Instead of replying to Brutus' question I turned to Carswell, who had finished with the lamp and the window, and now stood by, ready to lend a hand in his efficient way.

"Run up to the bathroom, will you, Carswell, and bring me a couple of rolls of bandage, from the medicine closet, and a bottle of mercurochrome." Carswell disappeared on this errand and I sat, holding my hands tightly around Brutus' leg, just above the bandage. Then, he repeated his question, and this time I paid attention to what he was saying.

"See what, Brutus?" I inquired, and looked at him, almost for the first time—into his eyes, I mean. Hitherto I had been looking at my bandaging.

I saw a stark terror in those eyes.

"It," said Brutus; "de T'ing, sar."

I sat on the side of the bed and looked at him. I was, naturally, puzzled.

"What thing, Brutus?" I asked, very quietly, almost soothingly. Such terror possessed my second houseman that, I considered, he must, for the time being, be treated like a frightened child.

"De T'ing what attack me, sar," explained Brutus.

"What was it like?" I countered. "Do you mean it is still here—in your room?"

At that Brutus very nearly collapsed. His eyes rolled up and their irises nearly disappeared; he shuddered as though with a violent chill, from head to foot. I let go his leg. The blood would be no longer flowing, I felt sure, under that tight bandaging of mine. I turned back the bedclothes, rolled poor Brutus under them, tucked him in. I took his limp hands and rubbed them smartly. At this instant Carswell came in through the still open doorway, his hands full of first-aid material. This he laid without a word on the bed beside me, and stood, looking at Brutus, slightly shaking his head. I turned to him.

"And would you mind bringing some brandy, old man? He's rather down and out, I'm afraid—trembling from head to foot."

"It's the reaction, of course," remarked Carswell quietly. "I have the brandy here." The efficient fellow drew a small flask from his jacket pocket, uncorked it, and poured out a dose in the small silver cup which covered the patent stopper.

I raised Brutus' head from the pillow, his teeth audibly chattering as I did so, and just as I was getting the brandy between his lips, there came a slight scuttering sound from under the bed, and something, a small, dark, sinister-looking animal of about the size of a mongoose, dashed on all fours across the open space between the bed's corner and the still open doorway and disappeared into the night outside. Without a word Carswell ran after it, turning sharply to the left and running past the open window. I dropped the empty brandy cup, lowered Brutus' head hastily to its pillow, and dashed out of the cabin. Carswell was at the end of the cabins, his flashlight stabbing the narrow alleyway, where I had found the miniature African hut. I ran up to him.

"It went up here," said Carswell laconically.

I stood beside him in silence, my hand on his shoulder. He

303

brightened every nook and cranny of the narrow alleyway with his light. There was nothing, nothing alive, to be seen. The Thing had had, of course, ample time to turn some hidden corner behind the cabins, to bury itself out of sight in some accustomed hiding-place, even to climb over the high, rough-surfaced back wall. Carswell brought his flashlight to rest finally on the little hut-like thing which still stood in the alleyway.

"What's that?" he inquired. "Looks like some child's toy."

"That's what I supposed when I discovered it," I answered. "I imagine it belongs to the washer's pickaninny."

We stepped into the alleyway. It was not quite wide enough for us to walk abreast. Carswell followed me in. I turned over the little hut with my foot. There was nothing under it. I daresay the possibility of this as a cache for the Thing had occurred to Carswell and me simultaneously. The Thing, mongoose, or whatever it was, had got clean away. We returned to the cabin and found Brutus recovering from his ague-like trembling fit. His eyes were calmer now. The reassurance of our presence, the bandaging, had had their effect. Brutus proceeded to thank us for what we had done for him.

Helped by Carswell, I gingerly removed my rough bandage. The blood about that ugly bite—for a bite it certainly was, with unmistakable tooth-marks around its badly torn edges—was clotted now. The flow had ceased. We poured mercurochrome over and through the wound, disinfecting it, and then I placed two entire rolls of three-inch bandage about Brutus' wounded ankle. Then, with various encouragements and reassurances, we left him, the lamp still burning at his request, and went back to the ladies.

Our contract game was, somehow, a jumpy one, the ladies having been considerably upset by the scare down there in the yard, and we concluded it early, Carswell driving Mrs. Spencer home and I walking down the hill with Mrs. Squire to the Grand

Hotel where she was spending that winter.

It was still several minutes short of midnight when I returned, after a slow walk up the hill, to my house. I had been thinking of the incident all the way up the hill. I determined to look in upon Brutus Hellman before retiring, but first I went up to my bedroom and loaded a small automatic pistol, and this I carried with me when I went down to the cabins in the yard. Brutus' light was still going, and he was awake, for he responded instantly to my tap on his door.

I went in and talked with the man for a few minutes. I left him the gun, which he placed carefully under his pillow. At the door I turned and addressed him:

"How do you suppose the thing—whatever it was that attacked you, Brutus—could have got in, with everything closed up tight?"

Brutus replied that he had been thinking of this himself and had come to the conclusion that "de T'ing" had concealed itself in the cabin before he had retired and closed the window and door. He expressed himself as uneasy with the window open, as Carswell and I had left it.

"But, man, you should have the fresh air while you sleep. You don't want your place closed up like a field-laborer's, do you?" said I, rallyingly. Brutus grinned.

"No, sar," said he, slowly, "ain't dat I be afeared of de Jumbee! I daresay it born in de blood, sar. I is close up everyfing by instinct! Besides, sar, now dat de T'ing attackin' me, p'raps bes' to have the window close up tightly. Den de T'ing cyant possibly mek an entrance 'pon me!"

I assured Brutus that the most agile mongoose could hardly clamber up that smooth, whitewashed wall outside and come in that window. Brutus smiled, but shook his head nevertheless.

"'Tain't a mongoose, nor a rat, neither, sar," he remarked, as he settled himself for rest under the bed-clothes.

"What do you think it is, then?" I inquired.

"Only de good Gawd know, sar," replied Brutus cryptically.

I was perhaps half-way across the house-yard on my way to turn in when my ears were assailed by precisely one of those suppressed combinations of squeals and grunts which John Masefield describes as presaging an animal tragedy under the hedge of an English countryside on a moonlit summer night. Something—a brief, ruthless combat for food or blood, between two small ground animals—was going on somewhere in the vicinity. I paused, listened, my senses the more readily attuned to this bitter duel because of what had happened in Brutus' cabin. As I paused, the squeals of the fighting animals abruptly ceased. One combatant, apparently, had given up the ghost! A grunting noise persisted for a few instants, however, and it made me shudder involuntarily. These sounds were low, essentially bestial, commonplace. Yet there was in them something so savage, albeit on the small scale of our everyday West Indian fauna, as to give me pause. I could feel the beginning of a cold shudder run down my spine under my white drill jacket!

I turned about, almost reluctantly, drawn somehow, in spite of myself, to the scene of combat. The grunts had ceased now, and to my ears, in the quiet of that perfect night of soft airs and moonlight, there came the even more horrible little sound of the tearing of flesh! It was gruesome, quite horrible, well-nigh unbearable. I paused again, a little shaken, it must be confessed, my nerves a trifle unstrung. I was facing in the direction of the ripping sounds now. Then there was silence—complete, tranquil, absolute!

Then I stepped towards the scene of this small conflict, my flashlight sweeping that corner of the yard nearest the small alleyway.

It picked up the victim almost at once, and I thought—I

could not be quite sure—that I saw at the very edge of the circle of illumination, the scrambling flight of the victor. The victim was commonplace. It was the body, still slightly palpitating, of a large, well-nourished rat. The dead rat lay well out in the yard, its freshly drawn vital fluid staining a wide smear on the flagstone which supported it—a ghastly-looking affair. I looked down at it curiously. It had, indeed, been a ruthless attack to which this lowly creature had succumbed. Its throat was torn out, it was disembowelled, riven terrifically. I stepped back to Brutus' cabin, went in, and picked up from a pile of them on his bureau a copy of one of our small-sheet local newspapers. With this, nodding smilingly at Brutus, I proceeded once more to the scene of carnage. I had an idea. I laid the paper down, kicked the body of the rat upon it with my foot, and, picking up the paper, carried the dead rat into Brutus' cabin. I turned up his lamp and carried it over to the bedside.

"Do you suppose this was your animal, Brutus?" I asked. "If so, you seem to be pretty well avenged!"

Brutus grinned and looked closely at the riven animal. Then:

"No, sar," he said, slowly, "'twas no rat whut attacked me, sar. See de t'roat, please, sar. Him ahl tore out, mos' effectively! No, sar. But—I surmise—from de appearance of dis t'roat, de mouf which maim me on de laig was de same mouf whut completely ruin dis rat!"

And, indeed, judging from the appearance of the rat Brutus' judgment might well be sound.

I wrapped the paper about it, said good night once more to Hellman, carried it out with me, threw it into the metal waste-basket in which the house-trash is burned every morning, and went to bed.

At three minutes past four the next morning I was snatched out of my comfortable bed and a deep sleep by the rattle of successive shots from the wicked little automatic I had left with Brutus. I jumped into my bathrobe, thrust my feet into my slippers, and was downstairs on the run, almost before the remnants of sleep were out of my eyes and brain. I ran out through the kitchen, as the nearest way, and was inside Brutus' cabin before the empty pistol, still clutched in his hand and pointed towards the open window, had ceased smoking. My first words were:

"Did you get It, Brutus?" I was thinking of the thing in terms of "It."

"Yes, sar," returned Brutus, lowering his pistol. "I t'ink I scotch him, sar. Be please to look on de window-sill. P'raps some blood in evidence, sar."

I did so, and found that Brutus' marksmanship was better than I had anticipated when I entrusted him with the gun. To be sure, he had fired off all seven bullets, and, apparently, scored only one hit. A small, single drop of fresh blood lay on the white-painted wooden window-sill. No other trace of the attacker was in evidence. My flashlight revealed no marks, and the smooth, freshly-whitewashed wall outside was unscathed. Unless the Thing had wings— Something suddenly touched me on the forehead, something light and delicate. I reached up, grasping. My hand closed around something like a string. I turned the flashlight up and there hung a thin strand of liana stem. I pulled it. It was firmly fastened somewhere up above there. I stepped outside, with one of Brutus' chairs, placed this against the outer wall under the window and, standing on it, raked the eaves with the flashlight. The upper end of the liana stem was looped about a small projection in the gutter, just above the window.

The Thing, apparently, knew enough to resort to this mechanical method for its second attack that night.

Inside, Brutus, somewhat excited over his exploit, found a certain difficulty in describing just what it was that had drawn his aim.

"It hav de appearance of a frog, sar," he vouchsafed. "I is

wide awake when de T'ing land himse'f 'pon de sill, an' I have opportunity for takin' an excellent aim, sar." That was the best I could get out of Brutus. I tried to visualize a "Thing" which looked like a frog, being able to master one of our big, ferocious rats and tear out its inner parts and go off with them, not to mention liana stems with loopknots in them to swing from a roof to an open window, and which could make a wound like the one above Brutus Hellman's ankle. It was rather too much for me. But—the Reign of Terror had begun, and no mistake!

Running over this summary in my mind as I stood and listened to Brutus telling about his marksmanship, it occurred to me, in a somewhat fantastic light, I must admit—the idea of calling in "science" to our aid, forming the fantastic element— that the Thing had left a clue which might well be unmistakable; something which, suitably managed, might easily clear up the mounting mystery.

I went back to the house, broached my medicine closet, and returned to the cabin with a pair of glass microscopic slides. Between these I made a smear of the still fresh and fluid blood on the window-sill, and went back to my room, intending to send the smear later in the morning to Dr. Pelletier's laboratory-man at the Municipal Hospital.

I left the slides there myself, requesting Dr. Brownell to make me an analysis of the specimen with a view to determining its place in the gamut of West Indian fauna, and that afternoon, shortly after the siesta hour, I received a telephone call from the young physician. Dr. Brownell had a certain whimsical cast apparent in his voice which was new to me. He spoke, I thought, rather banteringly.

"Where did you get your specimen, Mr. Canevin?" he inquired. "I understood you to say it was the blood of some kind of lower animal."

"Yes," said I, "that was what I understood, Dr. Brownell. Is there something peculiar about it?"

"Well—" said Dr. Brownell slowly, and somewhat banteringly, "yes—and no. The only queer thing about it is that it's—human blood, probably a Negro's."

I managed to thank him, even to say that I did not want the specimen returned, in answer to his query, and we rang off.

The plot, it seemed to me, was, in the language of the tradition of strange occurrences, thickening! This, then, must be Brutus' blood. Brutus' statement, that he had shot at and struck the marauder at his open window, must be imagination—Negro talk! But, even allowing that it was Brutus' blood—there was, certainly, no one else about to supply that drop of fresh fluid which I had so carefully scraped up on my two glass slides—how had he got blood, from his wounded lower leg, presumably, on that high window-sill? To what end would the man lie to me on such a subject? Besides, certainly he had shot at something—the pistol was smoking when I got to his room. And then—the liana stem? How was that to be accounted for?

Dr. Brownell's report made the whole thing more complicated than it had been before. Science, which I had so cheerfully invoked, had only served to make this mystery deeper and more inexplicable.

Handicapped by nothing more than a slight limp, Brutus Hellman was up and attending to his duties about the house the next day. In response to my careful questioning, he had repeated the story of his shooting in all particulars just as he had recounted that incident to me in the gray hours of the early morning. He had even added a particular which fitted in with the liana stem as the means of ingress. The Thing, he said, had appeared to swing down onto the window-sill from above, as he, awake for the time being between cat-naps, had first seen it and reached for the pistol underneath his pillow and then opened fire.

Nothing happened throughout the day; nor, indeed, during the Reign of Terror as I have called it, did anything untoward occur throughout, except at night. That evening, shortly after eight o'clock, Brutus retired, and Stephen Penn, who had accompanied him to his cabin, reported to me that, in accordance with my suggestion, the two of them had made an exhaustive search for any concealed "Thing" which might have secreted itself about Brutus' premises. They had found nothing, and Brutus, his window open, but provided with a tight-fitting screen which had been installed during the day, had fallen asleep before Stephen left. Penn had carefully closed the cabin door behind him, making sure that it was properly latched.

The attack that night—I had been sleeping "with one eye open"—did not come until two o'clock in the morning. This time Brutus had no opportunity to use the gun, and so I was not awakened until it was all over. It was, indeed, Brutus calling me softly from the yard at a quarter past two that brought me to my feet and to the window.

"Yes," said I, "what is it, Brutus?"

"You axed me to inform you, sar, of anything," explained Brutus from the yard.

"Right! What happened? Wait, Brutus, I'll come down," and I hurriedly stepped into bathrobe and slippers.

Brutus was waiting for me at the kitchen door, a hand to his left cheek, holding a hankerchief rolled into a ball. Even in the moonlight I could see that this makeshift dressing was bright red. Brutus, it appeared, had suffered another attack of some kind. I took him into the house and upstairs, and dressed the three wounds in his left cheek in my bathroom. He had been awakened without warning, fifteen minutes before, with a sudden hurt, had straightened up in bed, but not before two more stabs, directly through the cheek, had been delivered. He had only just seen the Thing scrambling down over the foot of the bed, as he came

311

awake under the impetus of these stabs, and, after a hasty search for the attacker, had wisely devoted himself to staunching his bleeding face. Then, trembling in every limb, he had stepped out into the yard and come under my window to call me.

The three holes through the man's cheek were of equal size and similar appearance, obviously inflicted by some stabbing implement of about the diameter of a quarter-inch. The first stab, Brutus thought, had been the one highest up, and this one had not only penetrated into the mouth like the others, but had severely scratched the gum of the upper jaw just above his eye-tooth.

I talked to him as I dressed these three wounds. "So the Thing must have been concealed inside your room, you think, Brutus?"

"Undoubtedly, sar," returned Brutus. "There was no possible way for it to crawl in 'pon me—de door shut tight, de window-screen undisturb', sar."

The poor fellow was trembling from head to foot with shock and fear, and I accompanied him back to his cabin. He had not lighted his lamp. It was only by the light of the moon that he had seen his assailant disappear over the foot of the bed. He had seized the handkerchief and run out into the yard in his pajamas.

I lit the lamp, determining to have electricity put into the cabin the next day, and, with Brutus' assistance, looked carefully over the room. Nothing, apparently, was hidden anywhere; there was only a little space to search through; Brutus had few belongings; the cabin furniture was adequate but scanty. There were no superfluities, no place, in other words, in which the Thing could hide itself.

Whatever had attacked Brutus was indeed going about its work with vicious cunning and determination.

Brutus turned in, and after sitting beside him for a while, I left the lamp turned down, closed the door, and took my departure.

Brutus did not turn up in the morning, and Stephen Penn, returning from an investigatory visit to the cabin, came to me on the gallery about nine o'clock with a face as gray as ashes. He had found Brutus unconscious, the bed soaked in blood, and, along the great pectoral muscle where the right arm joins the body, a long and deep gash from which the unfortunate fellow had, apparently, lost literally quarts of blood. I telephoned for a doctor and hurried to the cabin.

Brutus was conscious upon my arrival, but so weakened from loss of blood as to be quite unable to speak. On the floor, beside the bed, apparently where it had fallen, lay a medium-sized pocket knife, its largest blade open, soaked in blood. Apparently this had been the instrument with which he had been wounded.

The doctor, soon after his arrival, declared a blood-transfusion to be necessary, and this operation was performed at eleven o'clock in the cabin, Stephen contributing a portion of the blood, a young Negro from the town, paid for his service, the rest. After that, and the administration of a nourishing hot drink, Brutus was able to tell us what had happened.

Against his own expectations, he had fallen asleep immediately after my departure, and curiously, had been awakened not by any attack upon him, but by the booming of a rata drum from somewhere up in the hills back of the town where some of the Negroes were, doubtless, "making magic," a common enough occurrence in any of the *vodu*-ridden West India islands. But this, according to Brutus, was no ordinary awakening.

No—for, on the floor, beside his bed, *dancing to the distant drumbeats*, he had seen—It!

That Brutus had possessed some idea of the identity or character of his assailant, I had, previous to this occurrence of his most serious wound, strongly suspected. I had gathered this impression from half a dozen little things, such as his fervid denial that the creature which had bitten him was either a rat or a mongoose; his "Gawd know" when I had asked him what the Thing was like.

Now I understood, clearly, of course, that Brutus knew what kind of creature had concealed itself in his room. I even elicited the fact, discovered by him, just how I am quite unaware, that the Thing had hidden under a loose floor board beneath his bed and so escaped detection on the several previous searches.

But to find out from Brutus—the only person who knew—that, indeed, was quite another affair. There can be, I surmise, no human being as consistently and completely shut-mouthed as a West Indian Negro, once such a person has definitely made up his mind to silence on a given subject! And on this subject, Brutus had, it appeared, quite definitely made up his mind. No questions, no cajolery, no urging even with tears, on the part of his lifelong friend Stephen Penn—could elicit from him the slightest remark bearing on the description or identity of the Thing. I myself used every argument which logic and common-sense presented to my Caucasian mind. I urged his subsequent safety upon Brutus, my earnest desire to protect him, the logical necessity of co-operating, in the stubborn fellow's own obvious interest, with us who had his welfare at heart. Stephen, as I have said, even wept! But all these efforts on our parts were of no avail. Brutus Hellman resolutely refused to add a single word to what he had already said. He had awakened to the muted booming of the distant drum. He had seen the Thing dancing beside his bed. He had, it appeared, fainted from this shock, whatever the precise nature of that shock may have been, and knew nothing more until he came slowly to a vastly weakened consciousness between Stephen Penn's visit to him late in the morning, and mine which followed it almost at once.

There was one fortunate circumstance. The deep and wide cut which had, apparently, been inflicted upon him with his own pocket-knife—and had been lying, open, by mere chance, on a small tabouret beside his bed—had been delivered lengthwise of the pectoral muscle, not across the muscle. Otherwise the fellow's right arm would have been seriously crippled for life. The major damage he had suffered in this last and most serious attack had been the loss of blood, and this, through my employment of one donor of blood and Stephen Penn's devotion in giving him the remainder, had been virtually repaired.

However, whether he spoke or kept silent, it was plain to me that I had a very definite duty towards Brutus Hellman. I could not, if anything were to be done to prevent it, have him attacked in this way while in my service and living on my premises.

The electricity went in that afternoon, with a pullswitch placed near the hand of whoever slept in the bed, and, later in the day, Stephen Penn brought up on a donkey cart from his town lodging-place, his own bedstead, which he set up in Brutus' room, and his bureau containing the major portion of his belongings, which he placed in the newly-swept and garnished cabin next door. If the Thing repeated its attack that night, it would have Stephen, as well as Brutus, to deal with.

One contribution to our knowledge Stephen made, even before he had actually moved into my yard. This was the instrument with which Brutus had been stabbed through the cheek. He found it cached in the floor-space underneath that loose board where the Thing had hidden itself. He brought it to me, covered with dried blood. It was a rough, small-scale reproduction of an African "assegai," or stabbing-spear. It was made out of an ordinary butcher's hardwood meat-skewer, its head a splinter of pointed glass such as might be picked up anywhere about the town. The head—and this was what caused the resemblance to an "assegai"—was very exactly and neatly bound on to the cleft end of the skewer, with fishline. On the whole, and considered as a piece of work, the "assegai" was a highly creditable job.

It was on the morning of this last-recorded attack on Brutus Hellman during the period between my visit to him and the arrival of the doctor with the man for the blood-transfusion, that I sat down, at my desk, in an attempt to figure out some conclusion from the facts already known.

I had progressed somewhat with my theoretical investigation at that time. When later, after Brutus could talk, he mentioned the circumstance of the Thing's dancing there on his cabin floor, to the notes of a drum, in the pouring moonlight which came through his screened window and gave its illumination to the little room, I came to some sort of indeterminate decision. I will recount the steps—they are very brief—which led up to this.

The facts, as I noted them down on paper that day, pointed to a pair of alternatives. Either Brutus Hellman was demented and had invented his "attacks," having inflicted them upon himself for some inscrutable reason; or—the Thing was possessed of qualities not common among the lower animals! I set the two groups of facts side by side, and compared them.

Carswell and I had actually seen the Thing as it ran out of the cabin that first night. Something, presumably the same Thing, had torn a large rat to pieces. The same Thing had bitten savagely Brutus' lower leg. Brutus' description of it was that it looked "like a frog." Those four facts seemed to indicate one of the lower animals, though its genus and the motive for its attacks were unknown!

On the other hand, there was a divergent set of facts. The Thing had used mechanical means, a liana stem with a looped knot in it, to get into Brutus' cabin through the window. It had used some stabbing instrument, later found, and proving to be a manufactured affair. Again, later, it had used Brutus' knife in its final attack. All these facts pointed to some such animal as a small monkey. This theory was strengthened by the shape of the bites on Brutus' leg and on the rat's throat.

That it was not a monkey, however, there was excellent evidence. The Thing looked like a frog. A frog is a very different-looking creature from any known kind of monkey. There were, so far as I knew, no monkeys at the time on the island of St. Thomas.

I added to these sets of facts two other matters: The blood alleged to be drawn from the Thing had, on analysis, turned out to be human blood. The single circumstance pointed very strongly to the insanity theory. On the other hand, Brutus could hardly have placed the fresh blood which I had myself scraped up on my slides, on the windowsill where I found it. Still, he might have done so, if his "insanity" were such as to allow for an elaborately "planted" hoax or something of the kind. He could have placed the drop of blood there, drawn from his own body by means of a pin-prick, before he fired the seven cartridges that night. It was possible. But, knowing Brutus, it was so improbable as to be quite absurd.

The final circumstance was the little "African" hut. That, somehow, seemed to fit in with the "assegai." The two naturally went together.

It was a jumble, a puzzle. The more I contrasted and compared these clues, the more impossible the situation became.

Well, there was one door open, at least. I decided to go through that door and see where it led me. I sent for Stephen. It was several hours after the blood-transfusion. I had to get some of Brutus' blood for my experiment, but it must be blood drawn previous to the transfusion. Stephen came to see what I wanted.

"Stephen," said I, "I want you to secure from Hellman's soiled things one of those very bloody sheets which you changed on his bed today, and bring it here."

Stephen goggled at me, but went at once on this extraordinary errand. He brought me the sheet. On one of its corners, there was an especially heavy mass of clotted blood. From the underside of this I managed to secure a fresh enough smear on a pair of glass slides, and with these I stepped into my car and ran down to the hospital and asked for Dr. Brownell.

I gave him the slides and asked him to make for me an analysis for the purpose of comparing this blood with the specimen I had given him two days before. My only worry was whether or not they had kept a record of the former analysis, it being a private job and not part of the hospital routine. They had recorded it, however, and Dr. Brownell obligingly made the test for me then and there. Half an hour after he had stepped into the laboratory he came back to me.

"Here are the records," he said. "The two specimens are unquestionably from the same person, presumably a Negro. They are virtually identical."

The blood alleged to be the Thing's, then, was merely Brutus' blood. The strong presumption was, therefore, that Brutus had lost his mind.

Into this necessary conclusion, I attempted to fit the remaining facts. Unfortunately for the sake of any solution, they did not fit! Brutus might, for some insane reason, have inflicted the three sets of wounds upon himself. But Brutus had not made the "African" hut, which had turned up before he was back from the hospital. He had not, presumably, fastened that liana stem outside his window. He had not, certainly, slain that rat, nor could he have "invented" the creature which both Carswell and I had seen, however vaguely, running out of his cabin that night of the first attack.

At the end of all my cogitations, I knew absolutely nothing, except what my own senses had conveyed to me; and these discordant facts I have already set down in their order and sequence, precisely and accurately, as they occurred.

To these I now add the additional fact that upon the night following the last recorded attack on Brutus Hellman nothing whatever happened. Neither he nor Stephen Penn, sleeping side by side in their two beds in the cabin room, was in any way disturbed.

I wished, fervently, that Dr. Pelletier were at hand. I needed someone like him to talk to. Carswell would not answer, somehow. No one would answer. I needed Pelletier, with his incisive mind, his scientific training, his vast knowledge of the West Indies, his open-mindedness to facts wherever these and their contemplation might lead the investigator. I needed Pelletier very badly indeed!

And Pelletier was still over in Porto Rico.

Only one further circumstance, and that, apparently, an irrelevant one, can be added to the facts already narrated—those incongruous facts which did not appear to have any reasonable connection with one another and seemed to be mystifyingly contradictory. The circumstance was related to me by Stephen Penn, and it was nothing more or less than the record of a word, a proper name. This, Stephen alleged, Brutus had repeated, over and over, as, under the effects of the two degrees of temperature which he was carrying as the result of his shock and of the blood-transfusion, he had tossed about restlessly during a portion of the night. That name was, in a sense, a singularly appropriate one for Brutus to utter, even though one would hardly suspect the fellow of having any acquaintance with Roman history, or, indeed, with the works of William Shakespeare!

The name was—Cassius!

I figured that anyone bearing the Christian name, Brutus, must, in the course of a lifetime, have got wind of the original Brutus' side-partner. The two names naturally go together, of course, like Damon and Pythias, David and Jonathan! However, I said nothing about this to Brutus.

I was on the concrete wharf beside the Naval Administration Building long before the Grebe arrived from San Juan on the Thursday morning a week after Brutus Hellman's operation.

I wanted to get Pelletier's ear at the earliest possible moment. Nearby, in the waiting line against the wall of the Navy building, Stephen Penn at the wheel, stood my car. I had telephoned

Pelletier's man that he need not meet the doctor. I was going to do that myself, to get what facts, whatever explanation Pelletier might have to offer as I drove him through the town and up the precipitous roadways of Denmark Hill to his house at its summit.

My bulky, hard-boiled, genial naval surgeon friend, of the keen, analytical brain and the skillful hands which so often skirted the very edges of death in his operating-room, was unable, however, to accompany me at once upon his arrival. I had to wait more than twenty minutes for him, while others, who had prior claims upon him, interviewed him. At last he broke away from the important ones and heaved his unwieldy bulk into the back seat of my car beside me. Among those who had waylaid him, I recognized Doctors Roots and Maguire, both naval surgeons.

I had not finished my account of the persecution to which Brutus Hellman had been subjected by the time we arrived at the doctor's hilltop abode. I told Stephen to wait for me and finished the story inside the house while Pelletier's houseman was unpacking his traveling valises. Pelletier heard me through in virtual silence, only occasionally interrupting with a pertinent question. When I had finished he lay back in his chair, his eyes closed.

He said nothing for several minutes. Then, his eyes still shut, he raised and slightly waved his big, awkwardlooking hand, that hand of such uncanny skill when it held a knife, and began to speak, very slowly and reflectively:

"Dr. Roots mentioned a peculiar circumstance on the wharf."

"Yes?" said I.

"Yes," said Dr. Pelletier. He shifted his ungainly bulk in his big chair, opened his eyes and looked at me. Then, very deliberately:

"Roots reported the disappearance of the thing—it was a parasitic growth—that I removed from your houseman's side a week ago. When they had dressed the fellow and sent him back to the ward Roots intended to look the thing over in the laboratory.

It was quite unusual. I'll come to that in a minute. But when he turned to pick it up, it was gone; had quite disappeared. The nurse, Miss Charles, and he looked all over for it, made a very thorough search. That was one of the things he came down for this morning—to report that to me." Once again Pelletier paused, looked at me searchingly, as though studying me carefully. Then he said:

"I understand you to say that the Thing, as you call it, is still at large?"

The incredible possible implication of this statement of the disappearance of the "growth" removed from Hellman's body and the doctor's question, stunned me for an instant. Could he possibly mean to imply—? I stared at him, blankly, for an instant.

"Yes," said I, "it is still at large, and poor Hellman is barricaded in his cabin. As I have told you, I have dressed those bites and gashes myself. He absolutely refuses to go to the hospital again. He lies there, muttering to himself, ash-gray with fear."

"Hm," vouchsafed Dr. Pelletier. "How big would you say the Thing is, Canevin, judging from your glimpse of it and the marks it leaves?"

"About the size, say, of a rat," I answered, "and black. We had that one sight of it, that first night. Carswell and I both saw it scuttering out of Hellman's cabin right under our feet when this horrible business first started."

Dr. Pelletier nodded, slowly. Then he made another remark, apparently irrelevant:

"I had breakfast this morning on board the Grebe. Could you give me lunch?" He looked at his watch.

"Of course," I returned. "Are you thinking of—"

"Let's get going," said Dr. Pelletier, heaving himself to his feet.

We started at once, the doctor calling out to his servants that he would not be back for one o'clock "breakfast," and Stephen Penn who had driven us up the hill drove us down again. Arrived at my house we proceeded straight to Hellman's cabin. Dr. Pelletier talked soothingly to the poor fellow while examining those ugly wounds. On several he placed fresh dressings from his professional black bag. When he had finished he drew me outside.

"You did well, Canevin," he remarked, reflectively, "in not calling in anybody, dressing those wounds yourself! What people don't know, er—won't hurt 'em!"

He paused after a few steps away from the cabin.

"Show me," he commanded, "which way the Thing ran, that first night."

I indicated the direction, and we walked along the line of it, Pelletier forging ahead, his black bag in his big hand. We reached the corner of the cabin in a few steps, and Pelletier glanced up the alleyway between the cabin's side and the high yard-wall. The little toy house, looking somewhat dilapidated now, still stood where it had been, since I first discovered it. Pelletier did not enter the alleyway. He looked in at the queer little miniature hut.

"Hm," he remarked, his forehead puckered into a thick frowning wrinkle. Then, turning abruptly to me:

"I suppose it must have occurred to you that the Thing lived in that," said he, challengingly.

"Yes—naturally; after it went for my fingers—whatever that creature may have been. Three or four times I've gone in there with a flashlight after one of the attacks on Brutus Hellman; picked it up, even, and looked inside—"

"And the Thing is never there," finished Dr. Pelletier, nodding sagaciously.

"Never," I corroborated.

"Come on up to the gallery," said the doctor, "and I'll tell you what I think."

We proceeded to the gallery at once and Dr. Pelletier, laying down his black bag, caused a lounge-chair to groan and creak beneath his recumbent weight while I went into the house to command the usual West Indian preliminary to a meal.

A few minutes later Dr. Pelletier told me what he thought, according to his promise. His opening remark was in the form of a question; about the very last question anyone in his senses would have regarded as pertinent to the subject in hand.

"Do you know anything about twins, Canevin?" he inquired.

"Twins?" said I. "Twins!" I was greatly puzzled. I had not been expecting any remarks about twins.

"Well," said I, as Dr. Pelletier stared at me gravely, "only what everybody knows about them, I imagine. What about them?"

"There are two types of twins, Canevin—and I don't mean the difference arising out of being separate or attached-at-birth, the 'Siamese' or ordinary types. I mean something far more basic than that accidental division into categories; more fundamental—deeper than that kind of distinction. The two kinds of twins I have reference to are called in biological terminology 'monozygotic' and 'dizygotic,' respectively; those which originate, that is, from one cell, or from two."

"The distinction," I threw in, "which Johannes Lange makes in his study of criminal determinism, his book, *Crime and Destiny*. The one-cell-originated twins, he contends, have identical motives and personalities. If one is a thief, the other has to be! He sets out to prove—and that pompus ass, Haldane, who wrote the foreword, believes it, too—that there is no free will; that man's moral course is predetermined, inescapable—a kind of scientific Calvinism."

"Precisely, just that," said Dr. Pelletier. "Anyhow, you understand that distinction." I looked at him, still somewhat puzzled.

"Yes," said I, "but still, I don't see its application to this nasty business of Brutus Hellman."

"I was leading up to telling you," said Dr. Pelletier, in his matter-of-fact, forthright fashion of speech; "to telling you,

Canevin, that the Thing is undoubtedly the parasitic 'Siamese-twin' that I cut away from Brutus Hellman last Thursday morning, and which disappeared out of the operating-room. Also, from the evidence, I'd be inclined to think it is of the 'dizygotic' type. That would not occur, in the case of 'attached' twins, more than once in ten million times!"

He paused at this and looked at me. For my part, after that amazing, that utterly incredible statement, so calmly made, so dispassionately uttered, I could do nothing but sit limply in my chair and gaze woodenly at my guest. I was so astounded that I was incapable of uttering a word. But I did not have to say anything. Dr. Pelletier was speaking again, developing his thesis.

"Put together the known facts, Canevin. It is the scientific method, the only satisfactory method, when you are confronted with a situation like this one. You can do so quite easily, almost at random, here. To begin with, you never found the Thing in that little thatched hut after one of its attacks—did you?"

"No," I managed to murmur, out of a strangely dry mouth. Pelletier's theory held me stultified by its unexpectedness, its utter, weird strangeness. The name, "Cassius," smote my brain. That identical blood—

"If the Thing had been, say, a rat," he continued, "as you supposed when it went for your fingers, it would have gone straight from its attacks on Brutus Hellman to its diggings—the refuge-instinct; 'holing-up.' But it didn't. You investigated several times and it wasn't inside the little house, although it ran towards it, as you believed, after seeing it start that way the first night; although the creature that went for your hand was there, inside, *before it suspected pursuit*. You see? That gives us a lead, a clue. The Thing possesses a much higher level of intelligence than that of a mere rodent. Do you grasp that significant point, Canevin? The Thing, anticipating pursuit, avoided capture by instinctively outguessing the pursuer. It went towards its diggings but deferred

324

entrance until the pursuer had investigated and gone away. Do you get it?" I nodded, not desiring to interrupt. I was following Pelletier's thesis eagerly now. He resumed:

"Next—consider those wounds, those bites, on Brutus Hellman. They were never made by any small, grounddwelling animal, a rodent, like a rat or a mongoose. No; those teeth-marks are those of—well, say, a marmoset or any very small monkey; or, Canevin, *of an unbelievably small human being!*"

Pelletier and I sat and looked at each other. I think that, after an appreciable interval, I was able to nod my head in his direction. Pelletier continued:

"The next point we come to—before going on to something a great deal deeper, Canevin—is the color of the Thing. You saw it. It was only a momentary glimpse, as you say, but you secured enough of an impression to seem pretty positive on that question of its color. Didn't you?"

"Yes," said I, slowly. "It was as black as a derby hat, Pelletier."

"There you have one point definitely settled, then." The doctor was speaking with a judicial note in his voice, the scientist in full stride now. "The well-established ethnic rule, the biological certainty in cases of miscegenation between Causacians or quasi-Caucasians and the Negro or negroid types is that the offspring is never darker than the darker of the two parents. The 'black-baby' tradition, as a 'throw-back' being produced by mulatto or nearly Caucasian parents is a bugaboo, Canevin, sheer bosh! It doesn't happen that way. It cannot happen. It is a biological impossibility, my dear man. Although widely believed, that idea falls into the same category as the ostrich burying its head in the sand and thinking it is concealed! It falls in with the Amazon myth! The 'Amazons' were merely long-haired Scythians, those 'women-warriors' of antiquity. Why, damn it, Canevin, it's like believing in the Centaur to swallow a thing like that."

The doctor had become quite excited over his expression

325

of biological orthodoxy. He glared at me, or appeared to, and lighted a fresh cigarette. Then, considering for a moment, while he inhaled a few preliminary puffs, he resumed:

"You see what that proves, don't you, Canevin?" he inquired, somewhat more calmly now.

"It seems to show," I answered, "since Brutus is very 'clear-colored,' as the Negroes would say, that one of his parents was a black; the other very considerably lighter, perhaps even a pure Caucasian."

"Right, so far," acquiesced the doctor. "And the other inference, in the case of twins—what?"

"That the twins were 'dizygotic,' even though attached," said I, slowly, as the conclusion came clear in my mind after Pelletier's preparatory speech. "Otherwise, of course, if they were the other kind, the mono-cellular or 'monozygotic,' they would have the same coloration, derived from either the dark or the light-skinned parent."

"Precisely," exclaimed Dr. Pelletier. "Now—"

"You mentioned certain other facts," I interrupted, "'more deep-seated,' I think you said. What—"

"I was just coming to those, Canevin. There are, actually, two such considerations which occur to me. First—why did the Thing degenerate, undoubtedly after birth, of course, if there were no pre-natal process of degeneration? They would have been nearly of a size, anyway, when born, I'd suppose. Why did 'It' shrink up into a withered, apparently lifeless little homunculus, while its fellow twin, Brutus Hellman, attained to a normal manhood? There are some pretty deep matters involved in those queries, Canevin. It was comatose, shrunken, virtually dead while attached."

"Let's see if we can't make a guess at them," I threw in.

"What would you say?" countered Dr. Pelletier.

I nodded, and sat silently for several minutes trying to put what was in my mind together in some coherent form so as to express it adequately. Then:

"A couple of possibilities occur to me," I began. "One or both of them might account for the divergence. First, the failure of one or more of the ductless glands, very early in the Thing's life after birth. It's the pituitary gland, isn't it, that regulates the physical growth of an infant—that makes him grow normally. If that fails before it has done its full work, about the end of the child's second year, you get a midget. If, on the other hand, it keeps on too long—does not dry up as it should, and cease functioning, its normal task finished—the result is a giant; the child simply goes on growing, bigger and bigger! Am I right, so far? And, I suppose, the cutting process released it from its coma."

"Score one!" said Dr. Pelletier, wagging his head at me. "Go on—what else? There are many cases, of course, of blood-letting ending a coma."

"The second guess is that Brutus had the stronger constitution, and outstripped the other one. It doesn't sound especially scientific, but that sort of thing does happen as I understand it. Beyond those two possible explanations I shouldn't care to risk any more guesses."

"I think both those causes have been operative in this case," said Dr. Pelletier, reflectively. "And, having performed that operation, you see, I think I might add a third, Canevin. It is purely conjectural. I'll admit that frankly, but one outstanding circumstance supports it. I'll come back to that shortly. In short, Canevin, I imagine—my instinct tells me—that almost from the beginning, quite unconsciously, of course, and in the automatic processes of outstripping his twin in physical growth, *Brutus absorbed the other's share of nutriments.*

"I can figure that out, in fact, from several possible angles. The early nursing, for instance! The mother—she was, undoubtedly, the black parent—proud of her 'clear' child, would favor it, nurse it first. There is, besides, always some more or less obscure interplay, some balanced adjustment, between physically attached twins. In this case, God knows how, that invariable 'balance' became disadjusted; the adjustment became unbalanced, if you prefer it that way. The mother, too, from whose side the dark twin probably derived its constitution, may very well have been a small, weakly woman. The fair-skinned other parent was probably robust, physically. But, whatever the underlying causes, we know that Brutus grew up to be normal and fully mature, and I know, from that operation, that the Thing I cut away from him was his twin brother, degenerated into an apparently lifeless homunculus, a mere appendage of Brutus, something which, *apparently, had quite lost nearly everything of its basic humanity*; even most of its appearance, Canevin—a Thing to be removed surgically, like a wen."

"It is a terrible idea," said I, slowly, and after an interval. "But, it seems to be the only way to explain, er—the facts! Now tell me, if you please, what is that 'outstanding circumstance' you mentioned which corroborates this, er—theory of yours."

"It is the Thing's *motive*, Canevin," said Dr Pelletier, very gravely, "allowing, of course, that we are right—that I am right— in assuming for lack of a better hypothesis that what I cut away from Hellman had life in it; that it 'escaped'; that it is now—well, trying to get at a thing like that, under the circumstances, I'd be inclined to say, we touch bottom!"

"Good God—the *motive!*" I almost whispered. "Why, it's horrible, Pelletier; it's positively uncanny. The Thing becomes, quite definitely, a horror. The motive—in that Thing! You're right, old man. Psychologically speaking, it 'touches bottom,' as you say."

"And humanly speaking," added Dr. Pelletier, in a very quiet voice.

Stephen came out and announced breakfast. It was one o'clock. We went in and ate rather silently. As Stephen was serving the dessert Dr. Pelletier spoke to him:

"Was Hellman's father a white man, do you happen to know, Stephen?"

"De man was an engineer on board an English trading vessel, sar."

"What about his mother?" probed the doctor.

"Her a resident of Antigua, sar," replied Stephen promptly, "and is yet alive. I am acquainted with her. Hellman ahlways send her some portion of his earnings, sar, very regularly. At de time Hellman born, her a 'ooman which do washing for ships' crews, an' make an excellent living. Nowadays, de poor soul liddle more than a piteous invalid, sar. Her ahlways a small liddle 'ooman, not too strong."

"I take it she is a dark woman?" remarked the doctor, smiling at Stephen.

Stephen, who is a medium brown young man, a "Zambo," as they say in the English Islands like St. Kitts and Montserrat and Antigua, grinned broadly at this, displaying a set of magnificent, glistening teeth.

"Sar," he replied, "Hellman's mother de precisely identical hue of dis fella," and Stephen touched with his index finger the neat black bow-tie which set off the snowy whiteness of his immaculate drill houseman's jacket.

Pelletier and I exchanged glances as we smiled at Stephen's little joke. On the gallery immediately after lunch, over coffee, we came back to that bizarre topic which Dr. Pelletier had called the "motive." Considered quite apart from the weird aspect of attributing a motive to a quasi-human creature of the size of a rat, the matter was clear enough. The Thing had relentlessly attacked Brutus Hellman again and again, with an implacable fiendishness; its brutal, single-minded efforts being limited in their disastrous effects only by its diminutive size and native deficiency of strength. Even so, it had succeeded in driving a full-grown man, its victim, into a condition not very far removed from imbecility.

What obscure processes had gone on piling up cumulatively to a fixed purpose of pure destruction in that primitive, degenerated organ that served the Thing for a brain! What dreadful weeks and months and years of semiconscious brooding, of existence endured parasitically as an appendage upon the instinctively loathed body of the normal brother! What savage hatred had burned itself into that minute, distorted personality! What incalculable instincts, deep buried in the backgrounds of the black heredity through the mother, had come into play—as evidenced by the Thing's construction of the typical African hut as its habitation—once it had come, after the separation, into active consciousness, the new-born, freshly-realized freedom to exercise and release all that acrid, seething hatred upon him who had usurped its powers of self-expression, its very life itself! What manifold thwarted instincts had, by the processes of substitution, crystallized themselves into one overwhelming, driving desire—the consuming instinct for revenge!

I shuddered as all this clarified itself in my mind, as I formed, vaguely, some kind of mental image of that personality. Dr. Pelletier was speaking again. I forced my engrossed mind to listen to him. He seemed very grave and determined, I noticed....

"We must put an end to all this, Canevin," he was saying. "Yes, we must put an end to it."

Ever since that first Sunday evening when the attacks began, as I look back over that hectic period, it seems to me that I had had in mind primarily the idea of capture and destruction of what had crystallized in my mind as "The Thing." Now a new and totally bizarre idea came in to cause some mental conflict with the destruction element in that vague plan. This was the almost inescapable conviction that the Thing had been originally—whatever it might be properly named now—a human being. As such, knowing well, as I did, the habits of the blacks of our Lesser Antilles, it had, unquestionably, been received into the church by the initial process of baptism. That indescribable creature which had been an appendage on Brutus Hellman's body, had been, was now, according to the teaching of the church, a Christian. The idea popped into my mind along with various other sidelights on the situation, stimulated into being by the discussion with Dr. Pelletier which I have just recorded.

The idea itself was distressing enough, to one who, like myself, have always kept up the teachings of my own childhood, who has never found it necessary, in these days of mental unrest, to doubt, still less to abandon, his religion. One of the concomitants of this idea was that the destruction of the Thing after its problematical capture, would be an awkward affair upon my conscience, for, however far departed the Thing had got from its original status as "A child of God—an Inheritor of the Kingdom of Heaven," it must retain, in some obscure fashion, its human, indeed it Christian, standing. There are those doubtless who might well regard this scruple of mine as quite utterly ridiculous, who would lay all the stress on the plain necessity of stopping the Thing's destructive malignancy without reference to any such apparently far-fetched and artificial considerations. Nevertheless this aspect of our immediate problem, Pelletier's gravely enunciated dictum: "We must put an end to all this," weighed heavily on my burdened mind. It must be remembered that I had put in a dreadful week over the affair.

I mention this "scruple" of mine because it throws up into relief, in a sense, those events which followed very shortly after Dr. Pelletier had summed up what necessarily lay before us, in that phrase of his.

We sat on the gallery and cogitated ways and means, and it was in the midst of this discussion that the scruple alluded to occurred to me. I did not mention it to Pelletier. I mentally conceded, of course, the necessity of capture. The subsequent disposal of the Thing could wait on that.

We had pretty well decided, on the evidence, that the Thing had been lying low during the day in the little hutlike arrangement which it appeared to have built for itself. Its attacks so far had occurred only at night. If we were correct, the capture would be a comparatively simple affair. There was, as part of the equipment in my house, a small bait net, of the circular closing-in-from-the-bottom kind, used occasionally when I took guests on a deep-sea fishing excursion out to Congo or Levango Bays. This I unearthed, and looked over. It was intact, recently mended, without any holes in the tightly meshed netting designed to capture and retain small fish to be used later as live bait.

Armed with this, our simple plan readily in mind, we proceeded together to the alleyway about half-past two that afternoon, or, to be more precise, we were just at that moment starting down the gallery steps leading into my yard, when our ears were assailed by a succession of piercing, childish screams from the vicinity of the house's rear.

I rushed down the steps, four at a time, the more unwieldy Pelletier following me as closely as his propulsive apparatus would allow. I was in time to see, when I reached the corner of the house, nearly everything that was happening, almost from its beginning. It was a scene which, reproduced in a drawing accurately limned, would appear wholly comic. Little Aesculapius, the washer's small, black child, his eyes popping nearly from his head, his diminutive black legs twinkling under his single flying garment, his voice uttering blood-curdling yowls of pure terror, raced diagonally across the yard in the direction of his mother's washtub near the kitchen door, the very embodiment of crude, ungovernable fright, a veritable caricature, a figure of fun.

And behind him, coming on implacably, for all the world like a misshapen black frog, bounded the Thing, in hot pursuit, Its red tongue lolling out of Its gash of a mouth, Its diminutive blubbery lips drawn back in a wide snarl through which a murderous row of teeth flashed viciously in the pouring afternoon sunlight. Little Aesculapius was making good the promise of his relatively long, thin legs, fright driving him. He outdistanced the Thing hopelessly, yet It forged ahead in a rolling, leaping series of bounds, using hands and arms, frog-like, as well as Its strange, withered, yet strangely powerful bandied legs.

The sight, grotesque as it would have been to anyone unfamiliar with the Thing's history and identity, positively sickened me. My impulse was to cover my face with my hands, in the realization of its underlying horror. I could feel a faint nausea creeping over me, beginning to dim my senses. My washer-woman's screams had added to the confusion within a second or two after those of the child had begun, and now, as I hesitated in my course towards the scene of confusion, those of the cook and scullery-maid were added to the cacophonous din in my back yard. Little Aesculapius, his garment stiff against the breeze of his own progress, disappeared around the rear-most corner of the house to comparative safety through the open kitchen door. He had, as I learned sometime afterwards, been playing about the yard and had happened upon the little hut in its obscure and seldom-visited alleyway. He had stooped, and picked it up. "The Thing"—the child used that precise term to describe It—lay, curled up, asleep within. It had leaped to Its splayed feet with a snarl of rage, and gone straight for the little Negro's foot.

Thereafter the primitive instinct for self-preservation and Aesculapius' excellent footwork had solved his problem. He reached the kitchen door, around the corner and out of our sight, plunged within, and took immediate refuge atop the shelf of a kitchen cabinet well out of reach of that malignant, unheard-of demon like a big black frog which was pursuing him and which, doubtless, would haunt his dreams for the rest of his existence. So much for little Aesculapius, who thus happily passes out of the affair.

My halting was, of course, only momentary. I paused, as I have mentioned, but for so brief a period as not to allow Dr. Pelletier to catch up with me. I ran, then, with the net open in my hands, diagonally across the straight course being pursued by the Thing. My mind was made up to intercept It, entangle It in the meshes. This should not be difficult considering its smallness and the comparative shortness of Its arms and legs; and, having rendered It helpless, to face the ultimate problem of Its later disposal.

But this plan of mine was abruptly interfered with. Precisely as the flying body of the pursued pick'ny disappeared around the corner of the house, my cook's cat, a ratter with a neighborhood reputation and now, although for the moment I failed to realize it, quite clearly an instrument of that Providence responsible for my "scruple," came upon the scene with violence, precision, and that uncanny accuracy which actuates the feline in all its physical manifestations.

This avatar, which, according to a long-established custom, had been sunning itself demurely on the edge of the rain-water piping which ran along the low eaves of the three yard cabins, aroused by the discordant yells of the child and the three women in four distinct keys, had arisen, taken a brief, preliminary stretch, and condescended to turn its head towards the scene below....

The momentum of the cat's leap arrested instantaneously the Thing's course of pursuit, bore it, sprawled out and flattened, to the ground, and twenty sharp powerful retractile claws sank simultaneously into the prone little body.

The Thing never moved again. A more merciful snuffing out would be difficult to imagine.

It was a matter of no difficulty to drive Junius, the cat, away from his kill. I am on terms of pleasant intimacy with Junius. He allowed me to take the now limp and flaccid little body away from him quite without protest, and sat down where he was, licking his paws and readjusting his rumpled fur.

And thus, unexpectedly, without intervention on our part, Pelletier and I saw brought to its sudden end, the tragical dénouement of what seems to me to be one of the most outlandish and most distressing affairs which could ever have been evolved out of the mad mentality of Satan, who dwells in his own place to distress the children of men.

And that night, under a flagstone in the alleyway, quite near where the Thing's strange habitation had been taken up, I buried the mangled leathery little body of that unspeakably grotesque homunculus which had once been the twin brother of my houseman, Brutus Hellman. In consideration of my own scruple which I have mentioned, and because, in all probability, this handful of strange material which I lowered gently into its last resting-place had once been a Christian, I repeated the Prayer of Committal from the Book of Common Prayer. It may have been—doubtless was, in one sense—a grotesque act on my part. But I cherish the conviction that I did what was right.

THE SPIDER

By Hanns Heinz Ewers
Translated by Walter F. Kohn

Lovecraft mentioned Hanns Heinz Ewers's "The Spider" ("Die Spinne") in the revised version of "Supernatural Horror in Literature," stating somewhat vaguely that it and other works by Ewers "contain distinctive qualities which raise them to a classic level" (*S* 39). We can identify precisely when Lovecraft read the story: it was included, along with his own "The Music of Erich Zann," in Dashiell Hammett's anthology *Creeps by Night* (1931). The story, which tells of a man fascinated by a spiderlike woman whom he sees through a window, bears remarkable affinities with Lovecraft's "The Haunter of the Dark" (1935), especially in the use of a diary at the end of the narrative.

Ewers (1871–1943) was the author of numerous volumes of weird tales as well as several novels, including *Die Zauberlehrling* (1910; Eng. tr. as *The Sorcerer's Apprentice*, 1927) and *Alraune* (1911; Eng. tr. 1929). "Die Spinne" first appeared in the volume *Die Spinne* (1913). It appeared in an English translation in the *International* (December 1915); this translation was reprinted in *Creeps by Night* and is presented below.

When Richard Bracquemont, medical student, decided to move into Room No. 7 of the little Hotel Stevens at 6 Rue Alfred Stevens, three people had already hanged themselves from the window-sash of the room on three successive Fridays.

The first was a Swiss traveling salesman. His body was not discovered until Saturday evening; but the physician established the fact that death must have come between five and six o'clock on Friday afternoon. The body hung suspended from a strong book which had been driven into the window-sash, and which ordinarily served for hanging clothes. The window was closed, and the dead man had used the curtain cord as a rope. Since the window was rather low, his legs dragged on the ground almost to his knees. The suicide must consequently have exercised considerable will power in carrying out his intention. It was further established that he was married and the father of four children; that he unquestionably had an adequate and steady income; and that he was of a cheerful disposition, and well contented in life. Neither a will nor anything in writing that might give a clue to the cause of the suicide was found; nor had he ever intimated leanings toward suicide to any of his friends or acquaintances.

The second case was not very different. The actor Karl Krause, who was employed at the nearby Cirqué Medrano as a lightning bicycle artiste, engaged Room No. 7 two days after the first suicide. When he failed to appear at the performance the following Friday evening, the manager of the theater sent an usher to the little hotel. The usher found the actor hanged from the window-sash in the unlocked room, in identically the same circumstances that had attended the suicide of the Swiss traveling salesman. This second suicide seemed no less puzzling than the first: the actor was popular, drew a very large salary, was only twenty-five years old, and seemed to enjoy life to the utmost. Again, nothing was left in writing, nor were there any other clues that might help solve the mystery. The actor was survived only by an aged mother, to whom he used to send three hundred marks for her support promptly on the first of each month.

For Madame Dubonnet, who owned the cheap little hotel, and whose clientele was made up almost exclusively of the actors of the nearby vaudevilles of Montmartre, this second suicide had very distressing consequences. Already several of her guests had moved out, and other regular customers had failed to come back. She appealed to the Commissioner of the IXth Ward, whom she knew well, and he promised to do everything in his power to help her. So he not only pushed his investigation of reasons for the suicides with considerable zeal, but he also placed at her disposal a police officer who took up his residence in the mysterious room.

It was the policeman Charles-Maria Chaumié who had volunteered his services in solving the mystery. An old "Marousin" who had been a marine infantryman for eleven years, this sergeant had guarded many a lonely post in Tonkin and Annam single-handed, and had greeted many an uninvited deputation of river pirates, sneaking like cats through the jungle darkness, with a refreshing shot from his rifle. Consequently he felt himself well heeled to meet the "ghosts" of which the Rue Stevens gossiped. He moved into the room on Sunday evening and went contentedly to sleep after doing high justice to the food and drink Madame Dubonnet set before him.

Every morning and evening Chaumié paid a brief visit to the police station to make his reports. During the first few days his reports confined themselves to the statement that he had not noticed even the slightest thing out of the ordinary. On Wednesday evening, however, he announced that he believed he had found a clue. When pressed for details he begged to be allowed to say nothing for the present: he said he was not certain that the thing he thought he had discovered necessarily had any bearing on the two suicides. And he was afraid of being ridiculed in case it should all turn out to be a mistake. On Thursday evening he seemed to be even more uncertain, although somewhat graver; but again he had nothing to report. On Friday morning he seemed quite excited: half seriously and half in jest he ventured the statement that the window of the room certainly had a remarkable power of attraction. Nevertheless he still clung to the theory that that fact had nothing whatever to do with the suicides, and that he would only be laughed at if he told more. That evening he failed to come to the police station: they found him hanged from the hook on the window-sash.

Even in this case the circumstances, down to the minutest detail, were again the same as they had been in the other cases: the legs dragged on the floor, and the curtain cord had been used as a rope. The window was closed, and the door had not been locked; death had evidently come at about six o'clock in the afternoon. The dead man's mouth was wide open and his tongue hung out.

As a consequence of this third suicide in Room No. 7, all the guests left the Hotel Stevens that same day, with the exception of the German high school teacher in Room No. 16, who took advantage of this opportunity to have his rent reduced one-third. It was small consolation for Madame Dubonnet to have Mary Garden, the famous star of the Opera Comique, drive by in her Renault a few days later and stop to buy the red curtain cord for a price she beat down to two hundred francs. Of course she had two reasons for buying it: in the first place, it would bring luck; and in the second—well, it would get into the newspapers.

If these things had happened in summer, say in July or August, Madame Dubonnet might have got three times as much for her curtain cord; at that time of the year the newspapers would certainly have filled their columns with the case for weeks. But at an uneasy time of the year, with elections, disorders in the Balkans, a bank failure in New York, a visit of the English King and Queen—well, where could the newspapers find room for a mere murder case? The result was that the affair in the Rue Alfred Stevens got less attention than it deserved, and such notices of it as appeared in the newspapers were concise and brief, and confined themselves practically to repetitions of the police reports, without exaggerations.

These reports furnished the only basis for what little knowledge of the affair the medical student Richard Bracquemont had. He knew nothing of one other little detail that seemed so inconsequential that neither the Commissioner nor any of the other witnesses had mentioned it to the reporters. Only afterwards, after the adventure the medical student had in the room, was this detail remembered. It was this: when the police took the body of Sergeant Charles-Maria Chaumié down from the window-sash, a large black spider crawled out of the mouth of the dead man. The porter flicked it away with his finger, crying: "Ugh! Another such ugly beast!" In the course of the subsequent autopsy—that is, the one held later for Bracquemont—the porter told that when they had taken down the corpse of the Swiss traveling salesman, a similar spider had been seen crawling on his shoulder— But of this Richard Bracquemont knew nothing.

He did not take up his lodging in the room until two weeks after the last suicide, on a Sunday. What he experienced there he entered very conscientiously in a diary.

☙

THE DIARY OF RICHARD BRACQUEMONT,
MEDICAL STUDENT

Monday, February 28. I moved in here last night. I unpacked my two suitcases, put a few things in order, and went to bed. I slept superbly: the clock was just striking nine when a knock at the door awakened me. It was the landlady, who brought me my breakfast herself. She is evidently quite solicitous about me, judging from the eggs, the ham, and the splendid coffee she brought me. I washed and dressed, and then watched the porter make up my room. I smoked my pipe while he worked.

So, here I am. I know right well that this business is dangerous, but I know too that my fortune is made if I solve the mystery. And if Paris was once worth a mass—one could hardly buy it that cheaply nowadays—it might be worth risking my little life for it. Here is my chance, and I intend to make the most of it.

At that there were plenty of others who saw this chance. No less than twenty-seven people tried, some through the police, some through the landlady, to get the room. Three of them were women. So there were enough rivals—probably all poor devils like myself.

But I got it! Why? Oh, I was probably the only one who could offer a "solution" to the police. A neat solution! Of course it was a bluff.

These entries are of course intended for the police, too. And it amuses me considerably to tell these gentlemen right at the outset that it was all a trick on my part. If the Commissioner is sensible he will say, "Hm! Just because I knew he was tricking us, I had all the more confidence in him!" As far as that is concerned, I don't care what he says afterward: now I'm here. And it seems to me a good omen to have begun my work by bluffing the police so thoroughly.

Of course I first made my application to Madame Dubonnet,

but she sent me to the police station. I lounged about the station every day for a week, only to be told that my application "was being given consideration" and to be asked always to come again next day. Most of my rivals had long since thrown up the sponge; they probably found some better way to spend their time than waiting for hour after hour in the musty police court. But it seems the Commissioner was by this time quite irritated by my perseverance. Finally he told me point blank that my coming back would be quite useless. He was very grateful to me as well as to all the other volunteers for our good intentions, but the police could not use the assistance of "dilettante laymen." Unless I had some carefully worked out plan of procedure …

So I told him that I had exactly that kind of a plan. Of course I had no such thing and couldn't have explained a word of it. But I told him that I could tell him about my plan—which was good, although dangerous, and which might possibly come to the same conclusion as the investigation of the police sergeant—only in case he promised me on his word of honor that he was ready to carry it out. He thanked me for it, but regretted that he had no time for such things. But I saw that I was getting the upper hand when he asked me whether I couldn't at least give him some intimation of what I planned doing.

And I gave it to him. I told him the most glorious nonsense, of which I myself hadn't had the least notion even a second beforehand. I don't know even now how I came by this unusual inspiration so opportunely. I told him that among all the hours of the week there was one that had a secret and strange significance. That was the hour in which Christ left His grave to go down to hell: the sixth hour of the afternoon of the last day of the Jewish week. And he might take into consideration, I went on, that it was exactly in this hour, between five and six o'clock on Friday afternoon, in which all three of the suicides had been committed. For the present I could not tell him more, but I might refer him to the Book of Revelations according to St. John.

The Commissioner put on a wise expression, as if he had understood it all, thanked me, and asked me to come back in the evening. I came back to his office promptly at the appointed time; I saw a copy of the New Testament lying in front of him on the table. In the meantime I had done just what he had: I had read the Book of Revelations through and—had not understood a word of it. Perhaps the Commissioner was more intelligent than I was; at least he told me that he understood what I was driving at in spite of my very vague hints. And that he was ready to grant my request and to aid me in every possible way.

I must admit that he has actually been of very considerable assistance. He has made arrangements with the landlady under which I am to enjoy all the comforts and facilities of the hotel free of charge. He has given me an exceptionally fine revolver and a police pipe. The policemen on duty have orders to go through the little Rue Alfred Stevens as often as possible, and to come up to the room at a given signal. But the main thing is his installation of a desk telephone that connects directly with the police station. Since the station is only four minutes' walk from the hotel, I am thus enabled to have all the help I want immediately. With all this, I can't understand what there is to be afraid of....

Tuesday, March 1. Nothing has happened, neither yesterday nor today. Madame Dubonnet brought me a new curtain cord from another room—Heaven knows she has enough of them vacant. For that matter, she seems to take every possible opportunity to come to my room; every time she comes she brings me something. I have again had all the details of the suicides told me, but have discovered nothing new. As far as the causes of the suicides were concerned, she had her own opinions. As for the actor, she thought he had had an unhappy love affair; when he had been her guest the year before, he had been visited frequently by a young woman who had not come at all this year.

She admittedly couldn't quite make out why the Swiss gentleman had decided to commit suicide, but of course one couldn't know everything. But there was no doubt that the police sergeant had committed suicide only to spite her.

I must confess these explanations of Madame Dubonnet's are rather inadequate. But I let her gabble on; at least she helps break up my boredom.

Thursday, March 3. Still nothing. The Commissioner rings me up several times a day and I tell him that everything is going splendidly. Evidently this information doesn't quite satisfy him. I have taken out my medical books and begun to work. In this way I am at least getting something out of my voluntary confinement.

Friday, March 4, 2 P.M. I had an excellent luncheon. Madame Dubonnet brought a half bottle of champagne along with it. It was the kind of dinner you get before your execution. She already regards me as being three-fourths dead. Before she left me she wept and begged me to go with her. Apparently she is afraid I might also hang myself "just to spite her."

I have examined the new curtain cord in considerable detail. So I am to hang myself with that? Well, I can't say that I feel much like doing it. The cord is raw and hard, and it would make a good slipknot only with difficulty—one would have to be pretty powerfully determined to emulate the example of the other three suicides in order to make a success of the job. But now I'm sitting at the table, the telephone at my left, the revolver at my right. I certainly have no fear—but I am curious.

6 P.M. Nothing happened—I almost write it with regret. The crucial hour came and went, and was just like all the others. Frankly I can't deny that sometimes I felt a certain urge to go to the window—oh, yes, but for other reasons! The Commissioner called me up at least ten times between five and six. He was just as impatient as I was. But Madame Dubonnet is satisfied: someone has lived for a week in No. 7 without hanging himself. Miraculous!

Monday, March 7. I am now convinced that I shall discover nothing ; and I am inclined to think that the suicides of my predecessors were a matter of pure coincidence. I have asked the Commissioner to go over all the evidence in all three cases again, for I am convinced that eventually a solution of the mystery will be found. But as far as I am concerned, I intend to stay here as long as possible. I probably will not conquer Paris, but in the meantime I'm living here free and am already gaining considerably in health and weight. On top of it all I'm studying a great deal, and I notice I am rushing through in great style. And of course there is another reason that keeps me here.

Wednesday, March 9. I've progressed another step. Clarimonde—

Oh, but I haven't said a word about Clarimonde yet. Well, she is—my third reason for staying here. And it would have been for her sake that I would gladly have gone to the window in that fateful hour—but certainly not to hang myself. Clarimonde— but why do I call her that? I haven't the least idea as to what her name might be; but it seems to me as if I simply *must* call her Clarimonde. And I'd like to bet that some day I'll find out that that is really her name.

I already noticed Clarimonde the first few days I was here. She lives on the other side of this very narrow street, and her window is directly opposite mine. She sits there back of her curtains. And let me also say that she noticed me before I was aware of her, and that she visibly manifested an interest in me. No wonder—every one on the street knows that I am here, and knows why, too. Madame Dubonnet saw to that.

I am in no way the kind of person who falls in love. My relations with women have always been very slight. When one comes to Paris from Verdun to study medicine and hardly has enough money to have a decent meal once every three days, one has other things besides love to worry about. I haven't much experience, and I probably began this affair pretty stupidly.

Anyhow, it's quite satisfactory as it stands.

At first it never occurred to me to establish communications with my strange neighbor. I simply decided that since I was here to make observations, and that I probably had nothing real to investigate anyhow, I might as well observe my neighbor while I was at it. After all, one can't pore over one's books all day long. So I have come to the conclusion that, judging from appearances, Clarimonde lives all alone in her little apartment. She has three windows, but she sits only at the one directly opposite mine. She sits there and spins, spins at a little old-fashioned distaff. I once saw such a distaff at my grandmother's, but even my grandmother never used it. It was merely an heirloom left her by some great-aunt or other. I didn't know that they were still in use. For that matter, Clarimonde's distaff is a very tiny, fine thing, white, and apparently made of ivory. The threads she spins must be infinitely fine. She sits behind her curtains all day long and works incessantly, stopping only when it gets dark. Of course it gets dark very early these foggy days. In this narrow street the loveliest twilight comes about five o'clock. I have never seen a light in her room.

How does she look?—Well, I really don't know. She wears her black hair in wavy curls, and is rather pale. Her nose is small and narrow, and her nostrils quiver. Her lips are pale, too, and it seems as if her little teeth might be pointed, like those of a beast of prey. Her eyelids throw long shadows; but when she opens them her large, dark eyes are full of light. Yet I seem to sense rather than know all this. It is difficult to identify anything clearly back of those curtains.

One thing further: she always wears a black, closely buttoned dress, with large purple dots. And she always wears long black gloves, probably to protect her hands while working. It looks strange to see her narrow black fingers quickly taking and drawing the threads, seemingly almost through each other—really almost like the wriggling of an insect's legs.

Our relations with each other? Oh, they are really quite superficial. And yet it seems as if they were truly much deeper. It began by her looking over to my window, and my looking over to hers. She noticed me, and I her. And then I evidently must have pleased her, because one day when I looked at her she smiled. And of course I did, too. That went on for several days, and we smiled at each other more and more. Then I decided almost every hour that I would greet her; I don't know exactly what it is that keeps me from carrying out my decision.

I have finally done it, this afternoon. And Clarimonde returned the greeting. Of course the greeting was ever so slight, but nevertheless I distinctly saw her nod.

Thursday, March 10. Last night I sat up late over my books. I can't truthfully say that I studied a great deal: I spent my time building air castles and dreaming about Clarimonde. I slept very lightly, but very late into the morning.

When I stepped up to the window, Clarimonde was sitting at hers. I greeted her and she nodded. She smiled, and looked at me for a long time.

I wanted to work, but couldn't seem to find the necessary peace of mind. I sat at the window and stared at her. Then I suddenly noticed that she, too, folded her hands in her lap. I pulled at the cord of the white curtain and—practically at the same instant— she did the same. We both smiled and looked at one another.

I believe we must have sat like that for an hour. Then she began spinning again.

Saturday, March 12. These days pass swiftly. I eat and drink, and sit down to work. I light my pipe and bend over my books. But I don't read a word. Of course I always make the attempt, but I know beforehand that it won't do any good. Then I go to the window. I greet Clarimonde, and she returns my greeting. We smile and gaze at one another—for hours.

Yesterday afternoon at six I felt a little uneasy. Darkness settled very early, and I felt a certain nameless fear. I sat at my desk and waited. I felt an almost unconquerable urge to go to the window—certainly not to hang myself, but to look at Clarimonde. I jumped up and stood back of the curtain. It seemed as if I had never seen her so clearly, although it was already quite dark. She was spinning, but her eyes looked across at me. I felt a strange comfort and a very subtle fear.

The telephone rang. I was furious at the silly old Commissioner for interrupting my dreams with his stupid questions.

This morning he came to visit me, along with Madame Dubonnet. She seems to be satisfied enough with my activities: she takes sufficient consolation from the fact that I have managed to live in Room No. 7 for two whole weeks. But the Commissioner wants results besides. I confided to him that I had made some secret observations, and that I was tracking down a very strange clue. The old fool believed all I told him. In any event I can still stay here for weeks—and that's all I care about. Not on account of Madame Dubonnet's cooking and cellar—God, how soon one becomes indifferent to that when one always has enough to eat!—only because of the window, which she hates and fears, and which I love so dearly: this window that reveals Clarimonde to me.

When I light the lamp I no longer see her. I have strained my eyes trying to see whether she goes out, but I have never seen her set foot on the street. I have a comfortable easy chair and a green lampshade whose glow warmly suffuses me. The Commissioner has sent me a large package of tobacco. I have never smoked such good tobacco. And yet I cannot do any work. I read two or three pages, and when I have finished I realize that I haven't understood a word of their contents. My eyes grasp the significance of the letters, but my brain refuses to supply the connotations. Queer! Just as if my brain bore the legend: "No Admittance." Just as if it refused to admit any thought other than the one: Clarimonde …

Finally I push my books aside, lean far back in my chair, and dream.

Sunday, March 13. This morning I witnessed a little tragedy. I was walking up and down in the corridor while the porter made up my room. In front of the little court window there is a spider web hanging, with a fat garden spider sitting in the middle of it. Madame Dubonnet refuses to let it be swept away: spiders bring luck, and Heaven knows she has had enough bad luck in her house. Presently I saw another much smaller male spider cautiously running around the edge of the web. Tentatively he ventured down one of the precarious threads toward the middle; but the moment the female moved, he hastily withdrew. He ran around to another end of the web and tried again to approach her. Finally the powerful female spider in the center of the web seemed to look upon his suit with favor, and stopped moving. The male spider pulled at one of the threads of the web—first lightly, then so vigorously that the whole web quivered. But the object of his attention remained immovable. Then he approached her very quickly, but carefully. The female spider received him quietly and let him embrace her delicately while she retained the utmost passivity. Motionless the two of them hung for several minutes in the center of the large web.

Then I saw how the male spider slowly freed himself, one leg after another. It seemed as if he wanted to retreat quietly, leaving his companion alone in her dream of love. Suddenly he let her go entirely and ran out of the web as fast as he could. But at the same instant the female seemed to awaken to a wild rush of activity, and she chased rapidly after him. The weak male spider let himself down by a thread, but the female followed immediately. Both of them fell to the window-sill; and, gathering all his energies, the male spider tried to run away. But it was too late. The female spider seized him in her powerful grip, carried him back up into the net, and set him down squarely in the middle of it. And this same place that had just been a bed for passionate desire now became the scene of something quite different. The lover kicked in vain, stretched his weak legs out again and again, and tried to disentangle himself from this wild embrace. But the female would not let him go. In a few minutes she had spun him in so completely that he could not move a single member. Then she thrust her sharp pincers into his body and sucked out the young blood of her lover in deep draughts. I even saw how she finally let go of the pitiful, unrecognizable little lump—legs, skin and threads—and threw it contemptuously out of the net.

So that's what love is like among these creatures! Well, I can be glad I'm not a young spider.

Monday, March 14. I no longer so much as glance at my books. Only at the window do I pass all my days. And I keep on sitting there even after it gets dark. Then she is no longer there; but I close my eyes and see her anyhow....

Well, this diary has become quite different than I thought it would be. It tells about Madame Dubonnet and the Commissioner, about spiders and about Clarimonde. But not a word about the discovery I had hoped to make.—Well, is it my fault?

Tuesday, March 15. Clarimonde and I have discovered a strange new game, and we play it all day long. I greet her, and immediately she returns the greeting. Then I drum with my fingers on my windowpane. She has hardly had time to see it before she begins drumming on hers. I wink at her, and she winks at me. I move my lips as if I were talking to her and she follows suit. Then I brush the hair back from my temples, and immediately her hand is at the side of her forehead. Truly child's play. And we both laugh at it. That is, she really doesn't laugh: it's only a quiet, passive smile she has, just as I suppose mine must be.

For that matter all this isn't nearly as senseless as it must seem. It isn't imitation at all: I think we would both tire of that very quickly. There must be a certain telepathy or thought transference involved in it. For Clarimonde repeats my motions in the smallest conceivable fraction of a second. She hardly has time to see what I am doing before she does the same thing. Sometimes it even seems to me that her action is simultaneous with mine. That is what entices me: always doing something new and unpremeditated. And it's astounding to see her doing the same thing at the same time. Sometimes I try to catch her. I make a great many motions in quick succession, and then repeat them again; and then I do them a third time. Finally I repeat them for the fourth time, but change their order, introduce some new motion, or leave out one of the old ones. It's like children playing Follow the Leader. It's really remarkable that Clarimonde never makes a single mistake, although I sometimes change the motions so rapidly that she hardly has time to memorize each one.

That is how I spend my days. But I never feel for a second that I'm squandering my time on something nonsensical. On the contrary, it seems as if nothing I had ever done were more important.

Wednesday, March 16. Isn't it queer that I have never thought seriously about putting my relations with Clarimonde on a more sensible basis than that of these hour-consuming games? I thought about it last night. I could simply take my hat and coat and go down two flights of stairs, five steps across the street, and then up two other flights of stairs. On her door there is a little coat-of-arms engraved with her name: "Clarimonde ..." Clarimonde what? I don't know what; but the name Clarimonde is certainly there. Then I could knock, and then ...

That far I can imagine everything perfectly, down to the last move I might make. But for the life of me I can't picture what would happen after that. The door would open—I can conceive that. But I would remain standing in front of it and looking into her room, into a darkness—a darkness so utter that not a solitary thing could be distinguished in it. She would not come—nothing would come; as a matter of fact, there would be nothing there. Only the black impenetrable darkness.

Sometimes it seems as if there could be no other Clarimonde than the one I play with at my window. I can't picture what this woman would look like if she wore a hat, or even some dress other than her black one with the large purple dots; I can't even conceive her without her gloves. If I could see her on the street, or even in some restaurant, eating, drinking, talking—well, I really have to laugh: the thing seems so utterly inconceivable.

Sometimes I ask myself whether I love her. I can't answer that question entirely, because I have never been in love. But if the feeling I bear toward Clarimonde is really—well, love— then love is certainly very, very different than I saw it among my acquaintances or learned about it in novels.

It is becoming quite difficult to define my emotions. In fact, it is becoming difficult even to think about anything at all that has no bearing on Clarimonde—or rather, on our game. For there is truly no denying it: it's really the game that preoccupies me— nothing else. And that's the thing I understand least of all.

Clarimonde—well, yes, I feel attracted to her. But mingled with the attraction there is another feeling—almost like a sense of fear. Fear? No, it isn't fear either: it is more of a temerity, a certain inarticulate alarm or apprehension before something I cannot define. And it is just this apprehension that has some strange compulsion, something curiously passionate that keeps me at a distance from her and at the same time draws me constantly nearer to her. It is as if I were going around her in a wide circle, came a little nearer at one place, withdrew again, went on, approached her again at another point and again retreated rapidly. Until finally—of that I am absolutely certain—I *must* go to her.

Clarimonde is sitting at her window and spinning. Threads— long, thin, infinitely fine threads. She seems to be making some fabric—I don't know just what it is to be. And I can't understand how she can make the network without tangling or tearing the delicate fabric. There are wonderful patterns in her work—patterns full of fabulous monsters and curious grotesques.

For that matter—but what am I writing? The fact of the matter is that I can't even see what it is she is spinning: the threads are much too fine. And yet I can't help feeling that her work must be exactly as I see it—when I close my eyes. Exactly. A huge network peopled with many creatures—fabulous monsters, and curious grotesques ...

Thursday, March 17. I find myself in a strange state of agitation. I no longer talk to any one; I hardly even say good morning to Madame Dubonnet or the porter. I hardly take time to eat; I only want to sit at the window and play with her. It's an exacting game. Truly it is.

And I have a premonition that to-morrow something must happen.

Friday, March 18. Yes, yes. Something must happen to-day ... I tell myself—oh, yes, I talk aloud, just to hear my own voice—that it is just for that that I am here. But the worst of it is that I am afraid. And this fear that what has happened to my predecessors in this room may also happen to me is curiously mingled with my other fear—the fear of Clarimonde. I can hardly keep them apart.

I am afraid. I would like to scream.

6 P.M. Let me put down a few words quickly, and then get into my hat and coat.

By the time five o'clock came, my strength was gone. Oh, I know now for certain that it must have something to do with this sixth hour of the next to the last day of the week.... Now I can no longer laugh at the fraud with which I duped the Commissioner. I sat on my chair and stayed there only by exerting my will power to the utmost. But this thing drew me, almost pulled me to the window. I had to play with Clarimonde—and then again there rose that terrible fear of the window. I saw them hanging there—the Swiss traveling salesman, a large fellow with a thick neck and a gray stubble beard. And the lanky acrobat and the stocky, powerful police sergeant. I saw all three of them, one after another and then all three together, hanging from the same hook with open mouths and with tongues lolling far out. And then I saw myself among them.

Oh, this fear! I felt I was as much afraid of the windowsash and the terrible hook as I was of Clarimonde. May she forgive me for it, but that's the truth: in my ignominious fear I always confused her image with that of the three who hung there, dragging their legs heavily on the floor. But the truth is that I never felt for an instant any desire or inclination to hang myself: I wasn't even afraid I would do it. No—I was afraid only of the window itself—and of Clarimonde—and of something terrible, something uncertain and unpredictable that was now to come. I had the pathetic irresistible longing to get up and go to the window. And I *had* to do it....

Then the telephone rang. I grabbed the receiver and before I could hear a word I myself cried into the mouthpiece: "Come! Come at once!"

It was just as if my unearthly yell had instantly chased all the shadows into the farthest cracks of the floor. I became composed immediately. I wiped the sweat from my forehead and drank a glass of water. Then I considered what I ought to tell the Commissioner when he came. Finally I went to the window, greeted Clarimonde, and smiled.

And Clarimonde greeted me and smiled.

Five minutes later the Commissioner was here. I told him that I had finally struck the root of the whole affair; if he would only refrain from questioning me to-day, I would certainly be able to make some remarkable disclosures in the very near future. The queer part of it was that while I was lying to him I was at the same time fully convinced in my own mind that I was telling the truth.

And I still feel that that is the truth—against my better judgment.

He probably noticed the unusual condition of my temper, especially when I apologized for screaming into the telephone and tried to explain—and failed to find any plausible reason for my agitation. He suggested very amiably that I need not take undue consideration of him: he was always at my service—that was his duty. He would rather make a dozen useless trips over here than to let me wait for him once when I really needed him. Then he invited me to go out with him to-night, suggesting that that might help distract me—it wasn't a good thing to be alone all the time. I have accepted his invitation, although I think it will be difficult to go out: I don't like to leave this room.

Saturday, March 19. We went to the Gaieté Rochechouart, to the Cigale, and to the Lune Rousse. The Commissioner was right: it was a good thing for me to go out and breathe another atmosphere. At first I felt rather uncomfortable, as if I were doing something wrong, as if I were a deserter, running away from our flag. But by and by that feeling died; we drank a good deal, laughed, and joked.

When I went to the window this morning, I seemed to read a reproach in Clarimonde's look. But perhaps I only imagined it: how could she know that I had gone out last night? For that matter, it seemed to last for only a moment; then she smiled again.

We played all day long.

Sunday, March 20. To-day I can only repeat: we played all day long.

Monday, March 21. We played all day long.

Tuesday, March 22. Yes, and to-day we did the same. Nothing, absolutely nothing else. Sometimes I ask myself why we do it. What is it all for? Or, what do I really want, to what can it all lead? But I never answer my own question. For it's certain that I want, nothing other than just this. Come what may, that which is coming is exactly what I long for. We have been talking to one another these last few days, of course not with any spoken word. Sometimes we moved our lips, at other times we only looked at one another. But we understood each other perfectly.

I was right: Clarimonde reproached me for running away last Friday. But I begged her forgiveness and told her I realized that it had been very unwise and horrid of me. She forgave me and I promised her never again to leave the window. And we kissed each other, pressing our lips against the panes for a long, long time.

Wednesday, March 23. I know now that I love her. It must be love—I feel it tingling in every fiber of my being. It may be that with other people love is different. But is there any one among a thousand millions who has a head, an ear, a hand that is like any one else's? Every one is different, so it is quite conceivable that our love is unlike that of other people. I know that my love is very singular. But does that make it any less beautiful? I am almost happy in this love.

If only there would not be this fear! Sometimes it falls asleep. Then I forget it. But only for a few minutes. Then it wakes up again and will not let me go. It seems to me like a poor little mouse fighting against a huge and beautiful snake, trying to free itself from its overpowering embrace. Just wait, you poor foolish little fear, soon our love will devour you!

Thursday. March 24. I have made a discovery: I don't play with Clarimonde—*she plays with me.*

It happened like this.

Last night, as usual, I thought about our game. I wrote down five intricate movements with which I wanted to surprise her to-day. I gave every motion a number. I practiced them so as to be able to execute them as quickly as possible, first in order, and then backwards. Then only the even numbers and then the odd, and then only the first and last parts of each of the five motions. It was very laborious, but it gave me great satisfaction because it brought me nearer to Clarimonde, even though I could not see her. I practiced in this way for hours, and finally they went like clock-work.

This morning I went to the window. We greeted each other, and the game began. Forward, backward—it was incredible to see how quickly she understood me, and how instantaneously she repeated all the things I did.

Then there was a knock at my door. It was the porter, bringing me my boots. I took them; but when I was going back to the window my glance fell on the sheet of paper on which I had recorded the order of the movements. *And I saw that I had not executed a single one of these movements.*

I almost reeled. I grabbed the back of the easy chair and let myself down into it. I couldn't believe it. I read the sheet again and again. But it was true: of all the motions I had made at the window, not a single one was mine.

And again I was aware of a door opening somewhere far away—her door. I was standing before it and looking in … nothing, nothing—only an empty darkness. Then I knew that if I went out, I would be saved; and I realized that now I *could* go. Nevertheless I did not go. That was because I was distinctly aware of one feeling: that I held the secret of the mystery. Held it tightly in both hands.—Paris—I was going to conquer Paris!

For a moment Paris was stronger than Clarimonde. Oh, I've dropped all thought of it now. Now I am aware only of my love, and in the midst of it this quiet, passionate fear.

But in that instant I felt suddenly strong. I read through the details of my first movement once more and impressed it firmly in my memory. Then I went back to the window.

And I took exact notice of what I did: *not a single motion I executed was among those I had set out to do.*

Then I decided to run my index finger along my nose. But instead I kissed the window-pane. I wanted to drum on the window-sill, but ran my hand through my hair instead. So it was true: Clarimonde did not imitate the things I did: on the contrary, I repeated the things she indicated. And I did it so quickly, with such lightning rapidity, that I followed her motions in the same second, so that even now it seems as if I were the one who exerted the will power to do these things.

So it is I—I who was so proud of the fact that I had determined her mode of thought—I was the one who was being so completely influenced. Only, her influence is so soft, so gentle that it seems as if nothing on earth could be so soothing.

I made other experiments. I put both my hands in my pockets and resolved firmly not to move them; then I looked across at her. I noticed how she lifted her hand and smiled, and gently chided me with her index finger. I refused to budge. I felt my right hand wanting to take itself out of my pocket, but I dug my fingers deep into the pocket lining. Then slowly, after several minutes, my fingers relaxed, my hand came out of the pocket, and I lifted my arm. And I chided her with my index finger and smiled. It seemed as if it were really not I that was doing all this, but some stranger whom I watched from a distance. No, no—that wasn't the way of it. I, I was the one who did it—and some stranger was watching me. It was the stranger—that other me—who was so strong, who wanted to solve this mystery with some great discovery. But that was no longer I.

I—oh, what do I care about the discovery? I am only here to do her bidding, the bidding of my Clarimonde, whom I love with such tender fear.

Friday, March 25. I have cut the telephone wire. I can no longer stand being perpetually bothered by the silly old Commissioner, least of all when the fateful hour is at hand....

God, why am I writing all this? Not a word of it is true. It seems as if some one else were guiding my pen.

But I do—I do want to set down here what actually happens. It is costing me a tremendous effort. But I want to do it. If only for the last time to do—what I really want to do.

I cut the telephone wire … oh …

Because I had to … There, I finally got it out! Because I had to, I had to!

We stood at the window this morning and played. Our game has changed a little since yesterday. She goes through some motions and I defend myself as long as possible. Until finally I have to surrender, powerless to do anything but her bidding. And I can scarcely tell what a wonderful sense of exaltation and joy it gives me to be conquered by her will, to make this surrender.

We played. And then suddenly she got up and went back into her room. It was so dark that I couldn't see her; she seemed to disappear into the darkness. But she came back very shortly, carrying in her hands a desk telephone just like mine. Smiling, she set it down on the windowsill, took a knife, cut the wire, and carried it back again.

I defended myself for about a quarter of an hour. My fear was greater than ever, but that made my slow surrender all the more delectable. And I finally brought my telephone to the window, cut the wire, and set it back on the table.

That is how it happened.

I am sitting at the table. I have had my tea, and the porter has just taken the dishes out. I asked him what time it was—it seems my watch isn't keeping time. It's five fifteen … five fifteen … I know that if I look up now Clarimonde will be doing something or other. Doing something or other that I will have to do too.

I look up anyhow. She is standing there and smiling. Well … if I could only tear my eyes away from her…! now she is going to the curtain. She is taking the cord off—it is red, just like the one on my window. She is tying a knot—a slipknot. She is hanging the cord up on the hook in the window-sash.

She is sitting down and smiling.

… No, this is no longer a thing one can call fear, this thing I am experiencing. It is a maddening, choking terror—but nevertheless I wouldn't trade it for anything in the world. It is a compulsion of an unheard of nature and power, yet so subtly sensual in its inescapable ferocity.

Of course I could rush up to the window and do exactly what she wants me to do. But I am waiting, struggling, and defending myself. I feel this uncanny thing getting stronger every minute …

So, here I am, still sitting here. I ran quickly to the window and did the thing she wanted me to do: I took the curtain cord, tied a slipknot in it, and hung it from the hook …

And now I am not going to look up any more. I am going to stay here and look only at this sheet of paper. For I know now what she would do if I looked up again—now in the sixth hour of the next to the last day of the week. If I see her, I shall have to do her bidding … I shall have to …

I shall refuse to look at her.

But I am suddenly laughing—loudly. No, I'm not laughing—it is something laughing within me. I know why, too: it's because of this "I will not …"

I don't want to, and yet I know certainly that I must. I must look at her … must, must do it … and then—the rest.

I am only waiting to stretch out the torment. Yes, that is it,… For these breathless sufferings are my most rapturous transports. I am writing … quickly, quickly, so that I can remain sitting here longer in order to stretch out these seconds of torture, which carry the ecstasy of love into infinity.… More … longer …

Again this fear, again! I know that I shall look at her, that I shall get up, that I shall hang myself. *But it isn't that that I fear.* Oh, no—that is sweet, that is beautiful.

But there is something else … something else associated with it—*something that will happen afterward.* I don't know what it will be—but it is coming, it is certainly coming, certainly … certainly. For the joy of my torments is so infinitely great—oh, I feel it is so great that something terrible must follow it.

Only I must not think....

Let me write something, anything, no matter what. Only quickly, without thinking ...

My name—Richard Bracquemont, Richard Bracquemont, Richard—oh, I can't go any farther—Richard Bracquemont—Richard Bracquemont—now—now—I must look at her ... Richard Bracquemont—I must—no—no, more—more ... Richard ... Richard Bracque—

ↄ

The Commissioner of the IXth Ward, after failing repeatedly to get a reply to his telephone calls, came to the Hotel Stevens at five minutes after six. In Room No. 7 he found the body of the student Richard Bracquemont hanging from the window-sash, in exactly the same position as that of his three predecessors.

Only his face had a different expression; it was distorted in a horrible fear, and his eyes, wide open, seemed to be pushing themselves out of their sockets. His lips were drawn apart, but his powerful teeth were firmly and desperately clenched.

And glued between them, bitten and crushed to pieces, there was a large black spider, with curious purple dots.

On the table lay the medical student's diary. The Commissioner read it and went immediately to the house across the street. There he discovered that the second apartment had been vacant and unoccupied for months and months.

BLIND MAN'S BUFF

By H. Russell Wakefield

Lovecraft was impressed enough with the short stories of H. Russell Wakefield (1888–1965)—particularly those colleced in *They Return at Evening* (1928) and *Others Who Returned* (1929)—to cite them in the revised version of "Supernatural Horror in Literature." Among those he mentions is "Blind Man's Buff," included in the latter collection. His reasons for noting it may only indicate his enjoyment of this potent brief tale, but it may also point to an influence on his work: the maze into which the narrator stumbles reminds us of the similar invisible maze used to such powerful effect in the collaboration with Kenneth Sterling, "In the Walls of Eryx" (1936). (The idea of using a maze, however, is Sterling's, although the development of the device may be Lovecraft's.)

Wakefield went on to publish more collections of horror tales, including two published by Arkham House, *The Clock Strikes Twelve* (1946) and *Strayers from Sheol* (1961). Other stories of Wakefield's cited by Lovecraft are "The Red Lodge," "He Cometh and He Passeth By …," "And He Shall Sing," "The Cairn," "Look Up There!," and "The Seventeenth Hole at Duncaster."

ell, thank heavens that yokel seemed to know the place," said Mr. Cort to himself. "'First to the right, second to the left, black gates.' I hope the oaf in Wendover who sent me six miles out of my way will freeze to death. It's not often like this in England—cold as the penny in a dead man's eye."

He'd barely reach the place before dusk. He let the car out over the rasping, frozen roads. "'First to the right'"—must be this—second to the left, must be this—and there were the black gates. He got out, swung them open, and drove cautiously up a narrow, twisting drive, his headlights peering suspiciously round the bends. Those hedges wanted clipping, he thought, and this lane would have to be remetalled—full of holes. Nasty drive up on a bad night; would cost some money, though.

The car began to climb steeply and swing to the right, and presently the high hedges ended abruptly, and Mr. Cort pulled up in front of Lorn Manor. He got out of the car, rubbed his hands, stamped his feet, and looked about him.

Lorn Manor was embedded half-way up a Chiltern spur and, as the agent had observed, "commanded extensive vistas." The place looked its age, Mr. Cort decided, or rather ages, for the double Georgian brick chimneys warred with the Queen Anne left front. He could just make out the date, 1703, at the base of the nearest chimney. All that wing must have been added later.

"Big place, marvellous bargain at seven thousand, can't understand it. How those windows with their little curved eyebrows seem to frown down on one!" And then he turned and examined the "vistas." The trees were tinted exquisitely to an uncertain glory as the great red sinking sun flashed its rays on their crystal mantle. The vale of Aylesbury was drowsing beneath a slowly deepening shroud of mist. Above it, the hills, their crests rounded and shaded by silver and rose coppices, seemed to have set in them great smoky eyes of flame where the last rays burned in them.

"It is like some dream world," thought Mr. Cort. "It is curious how, wherever the sun strikes, it seems to make an eye, and each one fixed on me; those hills, even those windows. But, judging from that mist, I shall have a slow journey home; I'd better have a quick look inside though I have already taken a prejudice against the place—I hardly know why. Too lonely and isolated, perhaps."

And then the eyes blinked and closed, and it was dark. He took a key from his pocket and went up three steps and thrust it into the key-hole of the massive oak door. The next moment he looked forward into absolute blackness, and the door swung to and closed behind him. This, of course, must be the "palatial panelled hall" which the agent described. He must strike a match and find the light-switch. He fumbled in his pockets without success, and then he went through them again. He thought for a moment, "I must have left them on the seat in the car," he decided; "I'll go and fetch them. The door must be just behind me here."

He turned and groped his way back, and then drew himself up sharply, for it had seemed that something had slipped past him, and then he put out his hands—to touch the back of a chair, brocaded, he judged. He moved to the left of it and walked into a wall, changed his direction, went back past the chair, and found the wall again. He went back to the chair, sat down, and went through his pockets again, more thoroughly and carefully this time. Well, there was nothing to get fussed about; he was bound to find the door sooner or later. Now, let him think. When he came in he had gone straight forward, three yards perhaps; but he couldn't have gone straight back, because he'd stumbled into this chair. The door must be a little to the left or the right of it. He'd try each in turn. He turned to the left first, and found himself going down a little narrow passage; he could feel its sides when he stretched out his hands. Well, then, he'd try the right. He did so, and walked into a wall. He groped his way along it, and again it seemed as if something slipped past him. "I wonder if there's a bat in here?" he asked himself, and then found himself back at the chair.

How Rachel would laugh if she could see him now; surely he had a stray match somewhere. He took off his overcoat and ran his hands round the seam of every pocket, and then he did the same to the coat and waistcoat of his suit. And then he put them on again. Well, he'd try again. He'd follow the wall along. He did so, and found himself in a little narrow passage. Suddenly he shot out his right hand, for he had the impression that something had brushed his face very lightly.

"I'm beginning to get a little bored with that bat, and with this blasted room generally," he said to himself. "I could imagine a more nervous person than myself getting a little fussed and panicky; but that's the one thing not to do." Ah, here was that chair again. "Now, I'll try the wall the other side." Well, that seemed to go on for ever, so he retraced his steps till he found the chair, and sat down again. He whistled a little snatch resignedly. What an echo! The little tune had been flung back at him so fiercely, almost menacingly. Menacingly: that was just the feeble, panicky word a nervous person would use. Well, he'd go to the left again this time.

As he got up, a quick spurt of cold air fanned his face. "Is anyone there?" he said. He had purposely not raised his voice—there was no need to shout. Of course, no one answered. Who could there have been to answer since the caretaker was away? Now let him think it out. When he came in he must have gone straight forward and then swerved slightly on the way back; therefore—no, he was getting confused.

At that moment he heard the whistle of a train, and felt reassured. The line from Wendover to Aylesbury ran half-left from the front door, so it should be about there—he pointed with his finger, got up, groped his way forward, and found himself in a little narrow passage. Well, he must turn back and go to the right this time. He did so, and something seemed to slip just past him, and then he scratched his finger slightly on the brocade of the chair. "Talk about a maze," he thought to himself; "it's nothing to this." And then he said to himself, under his breath: "Curse this vile, godforsaken place!"

A silly, panicky thing to do he realised—almost as bad as shouting aloud. Well, it was obviously no use trying to find the door, he *couldn't* find it—*couldn't*. He'd sit in the chair till the light came. He sat down.

How very silent it was; his hands began searching in his pockets once more. Except for that sort of whispering sound over on the left somewhere—except for that, it was absolutely silent—except for that. What could it be? The caretaker was away. He turned his head slightly and listened intently. It was almost as if there were several people whispering together. One got curious sounds in old houses.

How absurd it was! The chair couldn't be more than three or four yards from the door. There was no doubt about that. It must be slightly to one side or the other. He'd try the left once more. He got up, and something lightly brushed his face. "Is anyone there?" he said, and this time he knew he had shouted. "Who touched me? Who's whispering? Where's the door?"

What a nervous fool he was to shout like that; yet someone outside might have heard him. He went groping forward again, and touched a wall. He followed along it, touching it with his finger-tips, and there was an opening.

The door, the door, it must be! And he found himself going down a little narrow passage. He turned and ran back. And then he remembered! He had put a match-booklet in his note-case! What a fool to have forgotten it, and made such an exhibition of himself. Yes, there it was; but his hands were trembling, and the booklet slipped through his fingers. He fell to his knees, and began searching about on the floor. "It must be just here, it can't be far"—and then something icy-cold and damp was pressed against his forehead. He flung himself forward to seize it, but there was nothing there. And then he leapt to his feet, and with tears streaming down his face, cried: "Who is there? Save me! Save me!" And then he began to run round and round, his arms outstretched. At last he stumbled against something, the chair— and something touched him as it slipped past. And then he ran screaming round the room; and suddenly his screams slashed back at him, for he was in a little narrow passage.

"Now, Mr. Runt," said the coroner, "you say you heard screaming coming from the direction of the Manor. Why didn't you go to find out what was the matter?"

"None of us chaps goes to Manor after sundown," said Mr. Runt.

"Oh, I know there's some absurd superstition about the house; but you haven't answered the question. There were screams, obviously coming from someone who wanted help. Why didn't you go to see what was the matter, instead of running away?"

"None of us chaps goes to Manor after sundown," said Mr. Runt.

"Don't fence with the question. Let me remind you that the doctor said Mr. Cort must have had a seizure of some kind, but that had help been quickly forthcoming, his life might have been saved. Do you mean to tell me that, even if you had known this, you would still have acted in so cowardly a way?"

Mr. Runt fixed his eyes on the ground and fingered his cap.

"None of us chaps goes to Manor after sundown," he repeated.

About the Editor

S. T. Joshi is the author of *The Weird Tale* (1990), *H. P. Lovecraft: The Decline of the West* (1990), and *Unutterable Horror: A History of Supernatural Fiction* (2012). He has prepared corrected editions of H. P. Lovecraft's work for Arkham House and annotated editions of Lovecraft's stories for Penguin Classics. He has also prepared editions of Lovecraft's collected essays and poetry. His exhaustive biography, *H. P. Lovecraft: A Life* (1996), was expanded as *I Am Providence: The Life and Times of H. P. Lovecraft* (2010). He is the editor of the anthologies *American Supernatural Tales* (Penguin, 2007), *Black Wings I–II–III* (PS Publishing, 2010, 2012, 2013), *A Mountain Walked: Great Tales of the Cthulhu Mythos* (Centipede Press, 2014), *The Madness of Cthulhu* (Titan Books, 2014–15), and *Searchers After Horror: New Tales of the Weird and Fantastic* (Fedogan & Bremer, 2014). He is the editor of the *Lovecraft Annual* (Hippocampus Press), the *Weird Fiction Review* (Centipede Press), and the *American Rationalist* (Center for Inquiry). His Lovecraftian novel *The Assaults of Chaos* appeared in 2013.

CPSIA information can be obtained
at www.ICGtesting.com
Printed in the USA
LVOW03s2149190118
563269LV00002B/257/P